TOWER HAMLETS PUBLIC LIBRARY

C001828618

✔ KU-521-611

NOBODY'S GIRL

id**e**a

Library Learning Information

To renew this item call:

0333 370 4700
(Local rate call)

or visit
www.ideastore.co.uk

TOWER HAMLETS
Created and managed by Tower Hamlets Council

Also by Sarra Manning

Guitar Girl
Pretty Things
Diary of a Crush: French Kiss
Diary of a Crush: Kiss and Make Up
Diary of a Crush: Sealed With a Kiss
Let's Get Lost
Fashionistas: Laura
Fashionistas: Hadley
Fashionistas: Irina
Fashionistas: Candy

TOWER HAMLE
IDEA STORES

DON: PRICE £5.99

16/8/2016

LOCN. ISB CLASS JF

ACC. No. C0018286166

Sarra Manning
NOBODY'S
GIRL

*Hodder
Children's
Books*

A division of Hachette Children's Books

Text copyright © 2010 Sarra Manning

First published in Great Britain in 2010
by Hodder Children's Books

The right of Sarra Manning to be identified as the Author of
the Work has been asserted by her in accordance with the
Copyright, Designs and Patents Act 1988.

2

All rights reserved. Apart from any use permitted under UK copyright law,
this publication may only be reproduced, stored or transmitted, in any
form, or by any means with prior permission in writing from the
publishers or in the case of reprographic production in accordance with
the terms of licences issued by the Copyright Licensing Agency and may
not be otherwise circulated in any form of binding or cover other than
that in which it is published and without a similar condition being
imposed on the subsequent purchaser.

All characters in this publication are fictitious and any resemblance to real
persons, living or dead, is purely coincidental.

A Catalogue record for this book is available from the British Library

ISBN-13: 978 0 340 88373 0

Typeset in Bembo by Avon DataSet Ltd,
Bidford on Avon, Warwickshire

Printed and bound in Great Britain by
CPI Bookmarque Ltd, Croydon, Surrey

The paper and board used in this paperback by Hodder Children's Books
are natural recyclable products made from wood grown in sustainable
forests. The manufacturing processes conform to the environmental
regulations of the country of origin.

Hodder Children's Books
a division of Hachette Children's Books
338 Euston Road,
London NW1 3BH
An Hachette UK company
www.hachette.co.uk

PROLOGUE

I went a little bit stark-raving bonkers. That's the only explanation that makes any sense.

Usually, I'm not the kind of girl who does crazy, stupid or irresponsible things. I look both ways before I cross the road. I drink two litres of water and eat at least five portions of fruit and vegetables every day. I aim for eight hours' sleep a night. Respect my elders. Don't talk back. Mind my Ps and Qs. Floss twice daily.

Let's face it, no one can be as boring and perfect as me and not lose it just once. But I couldn't lose it in a safe, controlled environment. No, I had to lose it at a train station in Malaga.

I stood there looking at the destination board and hoped that the Spanish for airport would be easy to translate like *aeroporte* or *la aeroporta* or something like that.

Then it occurred to me that I was in Europe. And Europe was this hulking great land mass made up of all these different countries and theoretically you should be able to get from one to the other by train. They probably wouldn't even make you hop off the train and walk across the border. I was sure that I'd seen a film once where some customs guy with epaulettes and a peaked cap had got on the train and simply looked at everyone's passports.

So if I was in Spain, then France was next to Spain. And

I could probably get a train to Paris. Paris! Where my dad lived. As soon as I'd thought that, I couldn't unthink it. In fact, I didn't want to unthink it because right then it seemed like the best idea I'd ever had.

Really, there was no contest. Five weeks stuck at home doing Mum-approved activities specifically chosen so I wouldn't come into contact with any teenage boys, get knocked up and ruin my life forever. Or head to Paris where I could sit in cafés on the Left Bank drinking *café noir* and eating flaky croissants while I bonded with the dad I'd never met because, according to my mum, he'd skipped town the moment the pregnancy test came back positive. Besides, my French teacher, Monsieur Bradley, always said that the only way to learn a language was to go to a country and soak it in. So, a little unscheduled sojourn to Paris was going to be good for my grades too.

My mind was made up. I grabbed hold of my suitcase and wended it through the heaving crowds of holidaymakers towards the ticket office and my destiny.

I just never realized my destiny would have a really thick Spanish accent.

Chapter One

But first we have to rewind to the moment four months before I met with my destiny and came out of Wilson's to find Ayesha waiting outside. Technically she wasn't outside but a couple of doors down because no one under the age of seventy-five would want to be seen outside Wilson's.

Because I am the most boring teenager in the world, I have the world's most boring Saturday job. Wilson's is a smart double-fronted shop on the High Street that has been there since 1907. It's where clothes go to die but once they get inside its dark, funky-smelling interior, they decided to linger for a few more years. Mr Wilson, grandson of the original proprietor, didn't seem to notice that there were hardly any customers for his poly-blend floral shirtwaisters, shiny plastic macs and granny panties, or maybe he just didn't care.

Needless to say, it was a total Mum-approved Saturday job. There was zero chance of meeting any snackable boys while I wrote out cards to stick on the mannequins in the window that said cheery things like 'Perfect for Mothers' Day' and 'Lovely in Lilac'. Mr Wilson was all right – mostly I kept his tea levels topped up and he stayed in the back doing wordsearch puzzles. He came into the shop as I was marking down some ancient American-tan tights that had probably disintegrated in their packets, at 1.03 precisely, and told me I could take my lunch, just like he did every Saturday.

Clutching three pound coins for Mr Wilson's coronation chicken sandwich, KitKat 'and get yourself something nice with the change', I finally got to open the door and had hardly managed to get a good few lungfuls of fresh air when I heard someone shout, 'Bea! Over here!'

Ayesha was standing outside the Cancer Research shop in a teeny, tiny little tunic, black leggings and a pair of outsized shades even though the day was overcast and grey.

I slowly walked towards her, painfully conscious of my knee-length navy-blue dress because I was forbidden from wearing trousers in the shop or anything that was even vaguely fashionable. I hoped my prim little dress was verging on sexy secretary but from the way Ayesha gave me a quick up and down, then visibly gulped, it was verging on frump.

'Let's do lunch,' she said brightly as if it wasn't the first time she'd spoken to me in six months, three weeks and five days. 'God, I can't believe you still work there. There's a well nasty red suit in the window. Looks like it's made from boiled wool.'

Ayesha had already linked her arm through mine and looked surprised when she took a step and I stayed exactly where I was.

'Actually I'm having lunch with Ruth,' I muttered, my face twisting into an apologetic grimace, though I didn't have anything to be sorry about. With perfect timing, I saw Ruth crossing the road, her scarf ends fluttering in the breeze and a ferocious scowl on her face when she saw who I was with.

'What's she doing here?' she demanded as she drew closer so she could step right into Ayesha's personal space and force her to take two hasty steps backwards. 'Have your new friends dumped you because they realize you're a two-faced cow?'

People think Ruth is really quiet because of the whole headscarf/being a Plymouth Brethren thing, but they couldn't be more wrong. If Ruth and Ayesha were going to throw down, then I didn't fancy Ayesha's chances. I hoped it wasn't going to come to that, but there was some really hardcore glaring going on.

'Me and Bea are doing lunch,' Ayesha informed Ruth icily. 'And just because I don't hang out with you any more, doesn't mean I'm two-faced. It means that I've . . . evolved,' she finished with smug satisfaction, like Ruth and I were still playing with Barbies. 'Come on, Bea. We'll go to Planet Organic.'

'We're going to McDonald's,' Ruth bit out, upgrading her glare a few notches up the thunderous scale before she turned to me. 'You promised. You know I've been dreaming of a Big Mac all bloody week.'

'I did promise,' I said to Ayesha with a half-hearted shrug, because hey, rock, hard place, my name's Bea. 'Sorry, Ayesha, but I don't know why you're even speaking to me, let alone asking me to have lu—'

'Fine! Whatever!' Ayesha snapped. 'We'll go to McDonald's then.'

That wasn't what I'd meant at all. But even though Ruth clicked her teeth and her eyes flashed, nothing was going to come between her and a Big Mac, even if it meant she had to eat it in the company of Ayesha, who still had her arm in mine and was practically dragging me along.

As lunches go, it was pretty horrific. Ruth and Ayesha snapped and snarled at each other like two pitbulls straining at their studded body harnesses.

Ruth's parents don't let her eat anything fried or sugary because apparently being a Plymouth Brethren means not being allowed to have any kind of fun, so she kept shooting furtive glances over her shoulder as she ordered her Big Mac with extra-large fries and Coke and saw every one of the faces that Ayesha was pulling behind her back.

I thought Ayesha would just have a black coffee to show how totally sophisticated she was these days but she got exactly the same as Ruth. 'I'm so lucky I can eat what I want and never put on any weight,' she drawled with a pointed look at Ruth's size 16 hips.

I ordered a chicken salad. 'Have fries,' Ruth demanded. 'I'm going to look like a gigantic pig if I eat all this and you're having lettuce.'

'Ayesha's having fries.'

'She doesn't count; she's an unwelcome hanger-on. Mind you, she must be used to that if she's hanging out with Ruby Davies.'

'Excuse me! Standing right here, headscarf girl,' Ayesha snapped. 'And I'm part of Ruby's inner circle. Not that it's your business.'

'If you were part of the inner circle, then you wouldn't have to go round telling people you were part of the inner circle.'

People were turning to look. The boy behind the counter had to ask me to repeat my order three times.

'Could you maybe not be so aggro with each other?' I suggested as we threaded our way through the restaurant to the one empty table, which was heaped with empty trays and Happy Meal detritus. 'We used to get on.'

Ayesha and Ruth stood and watched as I put my salad on the chair and quickly cleared the table. Then they sat down.

'We didn't all get on,' Ayesha said, carefully squeezing ketchup on to her fries. 'We ended up together because we weren't weird enough or geeky enough or popular enough to belong to any of the other groups in our year. I mean, yeah, we used to be mates, Bea, but you're really immature.'

'I am not,' I said, sneaking a fry off Ruth's tray, though she slapped my hand to try and stop me.

'Hey! Go and order your own,' she said through a mouthful of burger.

'But I'm having chips tonight,' I said. '*Pommes frites.*' It's a little nervous tic I have that I translate random words and phrases into French. Don't ask me why.

'See?' Ayesha remarked triumphantly. 'You've been doing that ever since I've known you. You're emotionally stunted or something.'

5

'That doesn't prove anything,' I protested. 'Just that I like saying stuff in French.'

'OK, what you doing tonight, then?' Ayesha asked with raised eyebrows.

I wished desperately that I was doing something exciting or that I had the ability to lie without stuttering and blinking rapidly. 'Well, I'm babysitting,' I admitted. 'But the grandmas can't cope with the twins when they're throwing a wobbly and Mum doesn't like to—'

'Think that you might leave the house and talk to actual real live boys because you might end up having sex with them five minutes later,' Ayesha finished for me. 'And anyway who would you go out with? Ruth probably has Bible study, Polly will be polishing her tack and Lydia will be hanging out with her Polish friends who don't go to our school. So you'll be staying in and making up silly stories in your head about boys you've never even spoken to because you're not a normal seventeen-year-old.'

'That's not fair,' I said dully, pushing my salad away because suddenly I wasn't very hungry.

'You've turned into such a bitch,' Ruth said, patting my hand. 'And I can't help it if I was born into some freaky religious sect.'

'I'm not being a bitch, I'm just telling it like it is.'

I wondered again, for the eleventy millionth time if Ayesha and I would still be friends if she hadn't suddenly got pretty last summer and moved up the social ladder.

I'd never had a boyfriend so I didn't know what being dumped by one would be like. But I imagined it was something like the way Ayesha had treated me when she decided that I wasn't good enough to be her friend any more. We'd sat next to each other every day all the way through primary school and secondary school. Then one day, she was sitting in the back row with Ruby Davies, going to lunch with Ruby, walking home from school with Ruby. When she was with me, she'd pick fights and holes in everything I said and did and wore. She stopped calling me, stopped emailing me, blocked me on Google Chat, but it was only after I heard that she'd got off with Jack that we finally had it out.

I knew that I had no real claim on Jack, he was just a beautiful boy that I had an outsize crush on; but Ayesha knew how I felt about him. She knew how red I got when I saw him across the road and would always nudge me to make sure I'd seen him sauntering along the Broadway, his gold hair glinting in the sun. Knew how I lived off the memory of him serving me in Burger King for weeks.

In fact, Ayesha had totally enabled my crush on Jack. Before she'd got cool, we'd spend hours inventing these long, detailed fantasies about me going out with Jack and her going out with his friend, Col. And when I say detailed, I mean we would describe our outfits and what we'd order from the menu when they took us to Pizza Express on a double date and what it felt like to hold their hands as we walked up to Ally Pally to see the stars.

So when I heard that Ayesha had been seen with her tongue down Jack's throat and his hand up her skirt, it hit me hard. It took a long time to confront Ayesha about it –

because I don't do confrontations and she was avoiding me even more than usual. When I finally did find her after staking out the cloakroom, she'd stood there with her arms folded and a bored look on her face as I read her the riot act. Actually the riot act had consisted of me whimpering, 'How could you? With Jack? Why would you do that when you know how I felt about him?'

Ayesha didn't say anything until I'd got so swept up in my 'How could yous?' that I started to cry. Then she'd given me this look that wasn't so much unkind as pitying. 'You're so wet, you're practically dripping,' she'd said coolly. 'You make up all this stupid shit and because you have no life, you actually start believing it's true. Well, it's not and Jack was never your boyfriend and he was a crap snog anyway.'

'Why would you say that to me?' I'd implored her. 'Why are you being like this? You're meant to be my best friend.'

'For fuck's sake, Bea, when are you going to get it into your thick head that I'm not your friend any more?' Ayesha had all but howled. 'You act like a twelve-year-old; a really boring twelve-year-old with the same boring hair you had when you were twelve – and I can't stand it!'

It had been the single worst moment of my life to date. The pain just ripped right through me so it was all I could do to catch my breath. Ayesha and I had been friends since nursery school and the fourteen years we'd spent with our lives entwined meant nothing to her. Wasn't worth fighting for, wasn't worth saving, because I'd stopped being her friend and had turned into an embarrassment.

At least I hadn't made even more of a fool of myself by

begging Ayesha to rethink my role in her life. I'd just walked out of the cloakroom without a word and we hadn't exchanged so much as a friendly glance since. But now here I was with Ayesha in Maccy D's when I should have just told her to take a hike as soon I saw her outside Wilson's. Maybe even thrown in a few swears.

'I don't make up silly stories,' I informed Ayesha haughtily. 'It's called having a rich inner life.'

'It's the only life you've got,' Ayesha said mockingly. 'Christ! Get angry with me! Call me out for being a heinous bitch but don't just sit there with your lip wobbling, Bea.'

It took every ounce of strength I possessed to will my mouth to stay still. 'We've already established that you don't like me so why did you suddenly think it was a good idea to meet for lunch?'

Ayesha shrugged one of her elegant, careless shrugs that was designed to make her long black hair ripple under the fluorescent lights and her breasts gave this amazing shimmy that made the harried dad at the next table turn to stare. 'I do like you,' she insisted. 'But you drive me mad. You're so . . . so . . . what's the word?'

I waited with anticipation to hear this wondrous word that summed up everything that was wrong with me.

'Passive,' Ruth piped up. 'You just go with the flow, even if the flow isn't the direction you want to go in.'

Ayesha nodded and it was funny (funny peculiar, not funny ha ha) that the two of them could only get on when they were putting me down.

I stood up and looked at a spot somewhere above their heads. 'I have to go now,' I said in a voice that I hoped resonated with quiet dignity. 'I have to get Mr Wilson a sandwich and maybe down some bottles of cider before I get back to work. Would that be age-appropriate enough for you?'

'You've can't even do a snappy putdown,' Ayesha sighed. 'Look, I'll see you Monday, unless you're free tomorrow. There's this club that starts at three in Camden.'

'I can't,' I muttered. 'I'm going to Pilates with my grandma.'

There was nothing either of them could say that would make me feel any worse. Because I didn't have a life, I was boring. Everything about me was boring. I even had the world's most boring bra size, 34B. But the thing was that I didn't want to do what other girls my age did, which was get drunk, get off with boys and get in trouble with their parents. I mean, what was the point? All you ended up with was a hangover, lovebites and no allowance.

Feeling weighed down by the halo above my head, which was practically glowing with goodness, I tried to walk out of Maccy D's with my head up.

Later that night, as I ignored the whimpers coming from the baby monitor (Alfie always grouses himself to sleep) and forced myself to eat my steak really rare like a proper French person, Ayesha's words echoed around my head.

I was at home on a Saturday night because I had nothing

else to do and even if the offers had come flying in and there were a steady stream of boys wanting to mark my dance card, my mum would never let me leave the house. Not without a chastity belt and a 9.30 p.m. curfew.

I had to face facts; I sucked at being a teenager.

Having to confront my extreme suckitude and how I was so very made of fail put a damper on the rest of the weekend. On Sundays I go to Pilates with Grandma Minor, then we go to Grandma Major's house for Sunday lunch, like we always do. She's Grandma Minor's mum. Before James and the twins arrived, we were a very girly clan.

'You come from a family of strong women,' Grandma Major always says, because she drove an ambulance during the Second World War and Grandma Minor was a student activist in the Sixties and marched to ban the bomb. And Mum still managed to get a degree with me in tow so I guess she qualifies. I'm still waiting for my strong-woman gene to kick in.

'It's not like you to have such a gloomy expression on your face,' Grandma Minor said as I morosely peeled potatoes like the good girl I was. 'What's the matter?'

'Nothing,' I said, because how could I tell her that I wasn't meant to be helping with lunch but doing cool Sunday afternoon things like going round Camden Market or looking for vintage dresses at jumble sales or watching subtitled foreign films at independent cinemas or drinking black coffee and reading dog-eared Penguin paperbacks in small cafés that sold home-made cakes, and generally hanging out with arty, interesting people with really good hair and eclectic outfits who would never waste their Sundays topping and tailing Brussels sprouts, which I moved on to once I finished the potatoes.

'Oh, darling, don't be a sulky teenager,' Grandma Minor drawled, sharing an amused glance with Grandma Major, who was directing the proceedings from her spot at the kitchen table. 'It's so predictable. We expect more from you.'

'I'm not!' I protested. 'I just feel like, I don't know, I'm not living up to my full potential.'

'Plenty of time for that,' Grandma Major decreed. 'You should enjoy being young while you can. No responsibility, no pressure, no expectations.'

She had to be kidding me. I slanted my gaze through the serving hatch to the living room where Mum was playing with the twins and probably thinking up new ways to load me up with responsibility, pressure and expectations. She'd already told the grandmas that she was going to have an interview with my headmistress about my Oxbridge entry. Though she didn't need to bother as it was going to be a very short interview.

'Hey, I get my fair share of pressure,' I said feelingly, but they both laughed.

Then Grandma Major got down her copy of *The Art of French Cooking* and asked me if I felt up to tackling a chocolate mousse, or *pot au chocolat*, and as diversions went that one was a winner.

Chapter Two

I pinched the last *pot au chocolat* for my lunch the next day. Polly, Ruth, Lydia and I always sat in the same spot on the grass verge by the tennis courts when it was warm enough to sit outside. It was a good patch – you could see everything and everyone.

In teen films, they always do this long pan of the lunchroom or the cafeteria or whatever and there's some all-knowing voiceover giving the viewer a rundown on the different cliques. But it wasn't like that at our school. Yeah, there were different social clusters. Like, the emo-girls who drew MCR logos on their arms with biros, and the really bright top-streamers that spent their lunch-hour bent over their coursework, and even the little coterie of Year 13 girls who were all dating boys from the art college and wore little ballet dresses from American Apparel and coloured tights. But mostly if you weren't with Ruby Davies, then you weren't anyone. Ruby was all that anyone at our school talked about, even the Year 13s, because Ruby and her cohorts partied hard, stole each other's boyfriends and had intrigues. I was always amazed they weren't the subject of daily posts on perezhilton.com.

Meanwhile, I sat in social Siberia eating my *baguette avec Brie*, well, actually it was French bread with Dairylea, and let the conversation drift over me. The four of us only ever talked about our homework, the lesson we'd just been in, the class we were about to go to and what we'd watched on TV the night before. When those topics had been exhausted, Ruth went on and on about how completely rubbish it was to be a Plymouth Brethren, Polly banged on about Dancer, her pony, and Lydia never said anything. Ever. My job was to stop us lapsing into silence by asking inane questions, like, 'What was Miss Demetriou wearing?' and 'Would you say you're more Blair than Serena?'

Polly would not stop talking about someone who happened to be riding a horse in some bonnet drama on BBC1 and how they'd had all the wrong tack, when I saw Ayesha detach herself from the cool kids and start walking towards us.

'Your new old best friend is coming over,' Ruth hissed and though I really didn't want a repeat of Ayesha telling me how crap my life was, it was still a welcome diversion from adventures in period riding gear. I put down my sandwich as Ayesha reached us and nodded her head in the direction of where she'd just come.

'Ruby says you can eat your lunch with us,' she said casually.

As my mouth dropped open so wide that my chin scraped the ground, Ruth was already standing up.

'Not you,' Ayesha said in her best 'like, duh' voice. 'Just Bea.'

Four pairs of eyes stared at me without blinking, which was odd. Usually people put me in the corner and forget about me.

'I can't,' I said, because what else could I say? 'I'm having lunch with my friends.'

'Are you mad?' Polly breathed. 'Don't worry about us. Go over there and get us some dirt. I heard that Emma got off with Chloe's boyfriend on Friday night.'

'Hello! Standing right here,' Ayesha sniffed, but I could tell from the glint in her eyes that she loved being part of a group that was all anyone else could talk about. 'Nothing's going on with Emma and Chloe. We're all friends and everything's cool.'

I looked over at Ruby. She caught my eye for a split second, then glanced away.

'I'm not sure,' I said. 'Why would Ruby want me to eat my lunch over there? She doesn't know me.'

'Yeah, she does,' Ayesha insisted breezily as she picked up my bottle of water and my lunch box. 'You're my friend and that's good enough for Ruby. Really, why does everyone think she's so scary? She's nice.'

'Go on,' Lydia urged, and Lydia never said anything when more than two people were present, and Ruth and Polly looked like they might start crying if I didn't go over and earwig for any small crumbs of gossip.

'OK,' I sighed as if I didn't care one way or another and it was no big deal. But it was a huge deal and my knees were shaking, my hands were sweating and when I looked down I could see that my chest had gone blotchy. I could never freak out prettily like girls in French films who bit their pouty bottom lips and made their eyes go all wide and liquid. I also wished desperately that I was dressed like a girl in a French film and not wearing black capris and a little pin-tucked blouse, which was meant to channel Audrey Hepburn, but simply looked mumsy as usual because I didn't have any panache.

We'd got to the shaded spot under the oak tree in the centre of the lawn, where Ruby's posse always sat. It seemed like Ayesha wasn't going to make any introductions, because she'd gone to sit next to Ruby and was whispering in her ear, so I found an empty patch of grass on the outskirts of the group and willed my knees to bend.

At least I sank gracefully to the ground, the Pilates was obviously paying off. There was no way I was going to tear at my French bread or eat my *pot au chocolat* in front of Ruby, whose thighs were the same size as my upper arms, so I took baby sips of my water and sat there with a frozen grimace on my face that was meant to be a self-contained smile. It was odd because they knew nothing about me and I knew everything about them. Like the time that Ruby had forced Chloe to shoplift a pair of earrings from TopShop. Or that Emma had had an argument with her boyfriend last winter and thrown him out of her house in his underwear. Or that Ruby had persuaded the same boyfriend to dump Emma, then she'd got tired of him after a week and he'd started seeing Emma again.

But maybe that stuff had been unsubstantiated gossip because no one was saying anything remotely interesting. They were talking about some girl called Shauna, who didn't go to our school, who'd worn a particularly vile outfit last Saturday night and I was just marvelling at how Ruby's reputation was more fiercesome than the actual reality, when she suddenly looked straight at me with a feline smile.

'So, Bea, who's your daddy, then?' she purred.

I spilt water down my blouse and Ruby's smile became even more cat-like. It struck me that she wasn't really that pretty. Ayesha had got so beautiful last summer that she didn't even resemble the girl with train-track braces and acne that I used to know and Chloe was probably the most beautiful girl I'd ever seen in real life – she looked like a Forties pin-up in skinny jeans.

But Ruby? It was more like she managed to hypnotize people into believing she was gorgeous because when it came to charisma, Ruby had it by the bucket-load. She was thin, painfully but naturally thin, and she always wore clothes that were slightly too big for her. In fact, everything seemed like it was slightly too big for her; her pale-blue eyes, the downward gash of her mouth on her angular face. The rest of her girls had super-shiny, super-straight hair but Ruby's was really fine, and neither straight nor curly so it always looked stringy, but she worked that waif thing like her life depended on it. She was half a head shorter than me, about thirty pounds lighter and she absolutely terrified me.

'Pardon?' I bleated.

'Your step-papa,' Ruby clarified and I almost breathed out because at least Ayesha hadn't been gabbing about French exchange students who'd buggered off back to

17

Paris five days after Mum's period should have arrived. 'He's well fit.'

'Oh, James? Yeah, he plays football twice a week,' I muttered and I knew that wasn't what Ruby meant but James's alleged fitness wasn't something I wanted to talk about.

'He's unbelievably foxy,' Ruby continued dreamily. 'Seriously, if he was my stepdad I'd always find excuses to wander around in just a towel that might accidentally slip down a few crucial inches.'

It was really hard not to squinch up my face in horror and let out the loudest 'Ew!' ever heard. 'James isn't that good-looking and he burps a lot,' I squeaked.

'Men do that,' Ruby informed me kindly. 'They're animals really. Wild, untamed beasts. So, what car does he drive?'

I really wished that I'd stayed with Ruth and the others. 'I don't know,' I lied, because I knew very well that it was a BMW hybrid and Mum had nearly choked on her tea when he'd bought it because she was still used to being a poor single parent. 'It's blue.'

'And your mum's really pretty.' Ruby paused to stare at me intently like she was checking and confirming that the prettiness hadn't been passed down. 'So, what are you doing this weekend?'

The punchline was coming soon, I was certain of it. 'I'm not sure.'

'We're all going to see this band, then there's this club after. Loads of boys from Christ's College will be there,'

Ruby added and my heart skipped a couple of beats because Jack went to Christ's College and now he no longer worked in Burger King I never saw him. 'Not that we bother with the Christ's College lads any more. They're so callow. You should come.'

Ayesha managed an encouraging smile. 'Yeah, you really should. You could sleep over at my place after.'

I was pretty sure that if I let myself get sucked in to Ruby's gravitational pull, no good would come of it. Like, if I eagerly agreed to go clubbing with her on Saturday night, I'd turn up at the appointed time and place and everyone else would be a no-show. Worse, they'd probably hide around the corner and laugh themselves stupid as they saw me check my watch and my phone as the minutes ticked away and my shoulders slumped lower and lower.

'I'm probably doing something on Saturday night,' I said vaguely, like my Saturday night plans didn't involve babysitting and having another bash at choux pastry.

'Do it some other time,' Ruby demanded, shucking off her usual disaffected air so she could sit up straight and pin me in place with her eyes. 'I never realized just how cool you are. You're so chilled. Do you meditate?'

It was some powerful mojo that Ruby was giving me. I didn't trust her, not one little bit, but it was hard to resist the imploring look on her face and it was even harder to resist the hope that some of Ruby's magic dust might get sprinkled on me. 'I do Pilates,' I offered.

'That's why you're so toned,' Ruby cooed. 'God, we've been going to the same school all this time and I don't know anything about you. You have hidden depths, I can tell.'

'I really don't.' I held out my arms to show that I wasn't packing any secrets and gave Ruby my rueful, retarded smile that always felt like an attack of Bell's palsy. 'What you see is all there is.'

'I don't believe you,' Ruby said, shaking her head. 'I'm never wrong about these things. Let's swap digits.'

Half in a daze, I rattled off my mobile number – and it wasn't just Ruby tapping it into her iPhone, but everyone was pulling out their iPhones (I had my Mum's old Nokia that she gave me when she upgraded last year) and taking down my number.

'You should totally come out with us on Saturday night,' Emma murmured, as she rang my phone so I'd have her number stored. 'We always have a laugh and there'll be tons of foxy boys there. You seeing someone?'

I shook my head dumbly.

'Oh, well, we'll soon change that,' Ayesha said brightly. She stood up, leaving her lunch debris on the ground because when you were too cool for school, you were definitely too cool to walk ten steps to the rubbish bin. 'Come on, I'll walk you to your next class.'

Ruby treated me to a smile so brilliant it should have had its own display case in Tiffany's window. 'So I'd better be seeing you on Saturday night, or you'll be in a world of trouble.'

Chapter Three

If I did have hidden depths like Ruby insisted then they were buried so deep it would need a professional excavation team to dig them out, I thought unhappily as I walked to the childminder's after school to pick up the twins. It wasn't something I particularly enjoyed. Manhandling the double pushchair along the streets at the same time that the upper classes got out of the boys' school was a daily lesson in abject humiliation. Every day one of them would shout: 'So you haven't got your figure back, then?' That was without the disapproving looks from total strangers who thought that Alfie and Ben had popped out of my underage vay-jay-jay.

When I got home, I played with Ben and Alfie for half an hour. Playing with them mostly involved monkey impressions and doing an exaggerated booty shake to Pussycat Dolls. After playtime was over, I shoved them in their playpen so they wouldn't stick their fingers in any plug sockets and made a start on dinner.

It sounds like I'm an indentured servant instead of the first born, but I don't mind. My stepdad James gives me a whopping fifty quid to pick up the twins and cook dinner because Mum can just about make toast with supervision. It was ironic that my French language skills sucked when my French cuisine was coming along nicely. I had a *boeuf bourguignon* marinating in the fridge that I'd started the night before and was having another bash at mastering the art of choux pastry (because the other ace thing about cooking the evening meal is always making a pudding) when Mum arrived home from work.

I could hear frenzied squeals from the playpen before she walked into the kitchen.

'Hello, you,' she murmured, ruffling my hair. 'Did you have a good day?'

Mum perched on one of the stalls and went into this long, complicated story about Lisa, her arch nemesis at the office. Mum's a book editor for a company that publishes a lot of books about cats for middle-aged women that like looking at pictures of cats and reading about cats and collecting stuff about cats.

'And in the end I said to her I have better things to do than stand here debating whether the bloody cat is a tabby or a tortoiseshell,' Mum finished with a sniff, her eyes dancing wickedly and, even in the fading afternoon light, she looked so beautiful. My face was just a faint echo of hers, her delicate nose and chin blunted by the time they got to me, my eyes not so blue, my hair drained of all the auburn tones, my body shorter and sturdier and just something less, especially the ninety-five per cent of me that was covered in freckles. It was no wonder that people asked if we were sisters, then their eyes would linger on Mum like she'd drained every last drop of goodness out of the gene pool and left me with the dregs.

They also asked if we were sisters because Mum looks

good for her age. Really good – like she's still in her late twenties, instead of thirty-four. It was weird to think that Mum was the same age I am now when she had me. Thirty-four is old enough to be a proper grown-up with a mortgage and a pension plan and an unhealthy passion for Cath Kidston but it's really young to be the mother of a seventeen-year-old. Not that she ever lets something like that get in the way of her Mumly duties such as making sure she knows what I'm doing during every second that I'm not with her.

'So I phoned Barb,' she said casually, eyes lowered as she blew on her tea. 'Not to check up on you, but I wanted to ask her about this toddlers' group and she said you were late to pick up the twins.' She gave me her patented laser-beam look, even though her voice was so neutral, it was beige. 'Where were you?'

'I had to talk to Monsieur Bradley after school. About my French homework and how much it sucked. But he did say that my accent was *très formidable*.'

'French,' she muttered darkly. 'Maybe it's time to jack it in. You'll still be doing four A levels, that's enough to get you into Oxbridge.'

Except I wasn't going to Oxbridge. I didn't have the book smarts or the street smarts or any other kind of smarts. 'I'm not going to Oxbridge, Mum. You talked to Mrs Chambers about this and she said if I maintained my grades and didn't do anything dumb on my A-level exams, I'd *probably* get a place at somewhere that wasn't Oxbridge.'

'But a lot could happen between now and next June. You're probably just a late bloomer and dropping French would take some of the pressure off.' Mum had this note of finality in her voice like it was all done and dusted. Move it along. Nothing to see here. 'Besides, this French thing isn't going to magically make your dad turn up on the doorstep, y'know.' She always flinches when she says the D-word – it makes her think of her first love and my absentee father, Pierre, the dashing foreign exchange student who went back to Paris and never contacted her again.

'I know that,' I said evenly. 'But if he did . . .'

'He's not going to, Bea. Not ever.'

'But if he did, he'd be thrilled that I was *parlez vous*ing like a native. And anyway, I like French. I like everything that's French. I can't help it. I'm half French.'

'All I'm saying is that maybe you could use the extra effort in your other subjects. You might be able to get your history mark up to an A.'

'Mum, please . . .' We never fought. Getting a really whiny top note to my voice was about as far as it went. 'I really, really don't want to give up French.'

Mum sighed. I didn't know if it was in defeat or because she'd been lumbered with a daughter who wasn't smart enough to be all that she could be and harness her unlimited potential. 'So, what else happened today?'

I skipped the thrilling tale of how I got my usual B- for psychology and started telling her about being summoned to eat lunch with Ruby. I'd already told her about my lunch with Ayesha and she hadn't been too happy about that. Now her brows knitted further and further together until it seemed like Botox would be the only thing to unknit them.

'So, don't you think it's weird that Ayesha's being all friendly and stuff like nothing ever happened and now Ruby's getting in on the act?' I asked. 'Did I suddenly become cool and no one bothered to tell me?'

'Of course you're cool and I already told you, I wouldn't even give her the time of day,' Mum snapped. 'She treated you like dirt and a couple of lunches isn't going to change that.' One of the good things about having a young mum is that she doesn't have to cast her mind too far back in order to empathize about my teenage woes.

'Yeah, I know but I do miss her. Or I miss having a best friend.'

'You have friends! Polly and Lydia and the little religious one that always wears a headscarf . . .'

'Ruth – and she can't help it if her family are Plymouth Brethren. And we hang out at school but we're not best friends. Not like Ayesha was.'

'You should stay away from her, Bea,' Mum said warningly, jumping down from the stool so she could stand with her hands on her hips, which she just loved to do. 'She'd be a bad influence on you. I saw Mrs Singh in Tesco's and Ayesha's driving her insane. She even found cigarettes and condoms in her bag.'

It was on the tip of my tongue to stick up for Ayesha and say that at least she was having safe sex, but then I realized that one of the boys she'd probably had safe sex with was

Jack. *My* Jack. Each realization was worse than the last, until I saw Mum giving my school bag a suspicious look.

That stuff I said about how having a young mum was cool? I take it all back. She's still a mum and has a copy of the mum handbook that says searching through your child's personal property isn't wrong and should actually be carried out on a regular basis.

'I know Ayesha isn't the same person any more,' I said, surprised by the throb in my voice, because I thought I was over it but just talking about Ayesha made it hurt all over again. 'And she can't be a bad influence on me because I'm too sensible for that. Hey, it's me! The most boring, sensible teenager in the world.'

'Oh, don't start all that again. You're not boring or sensible. I just did a wicked job raising you,' Mum teased, and I guess she'd decided not to frisk me for condoms or cigarettes or rocks of crack. 'I just don't want you making the same mistakes I did when I was your age . . .'

I was saved by the sound of a key in the lock and then James appeared in the kitchen doorway. 'Leave poor Bea alone,' he said to Mum as he dropped a kiss on the top of her head.

'I'm not doing anything to Bea,' Mum pouted. 'We're just having our daily dose of girl talk. No boys allowed.'

James looked down at Mum with a mixture of exasperation and tenderness. That was why I liked him so much and didn't have any of the stepchild angst that I was supposed to have and why we were using James's copy of *The Dummy's Guide to Being A Step-Parent* as a doorstop because we really didn't need it. James loved my mum and made her happy so he was cool with me. And the lovely, shiny Apple Mac with a DVD superdrive that he bought me before they told me the twins were on their way had sealed the deal.

Right now he was pulling something out of his man-purse, which Mum and I mocked on a daily basis. 'Gossip Girl in French,' he said, passing me a couple of DVDs. 'Got one of the lads at work to illegally download it off the interwebs for you.'

I squeezed James' arm because we didn't do the huggy thing and hurried to the stairs just as Ben let out an unearthly wail, which probably meant that Alfie had him in a headlock. But they weren't on my watch any more and I could probably get a couple of episodes of Gossip Girl in while the twins were being fed and watered. I hadn't mentioned the invitation for Saturday night because there was no way in hell Mum would let me go and it was probably just a mean-girl stitch up. The best thing to do was just forget about it.

It turned out that it was impossible to forget about Saturday because Ruby, Ayesha and even Chloe and Emma mentioned it every time I saw them at school. 'Don't forget about Saturday night,' they kept saying. 'It's going to be awesome.'

By Thursday, when I still hadn't committed one way or another because I was too much of a coward to tell Ruby that my mother would never let me out to play, they started texting me. Actually, it was less texting and more text stalking.

As I sat in the kitchen after school with Mum and Grandma Minor, my phone wouldn't stop buzzing and vibrating.

'You're very popular today,' Grandma Minor said as I opened the latest message from Ayesha: U COMING SAT NITE OR WOT?

'Oh, some girls from school want to know if I can go out on Saturday night,' I murmured vaguely. Mum's eyebrows signalled that vague didn't please her in the slightest. 'You remember Ayesha? Well, her and some of her friends.'

'Well, it's nice that she's reaching out to you again,' Grandma said, as she rooted through our biscuit tin – we always saved the custard creams for her. 'Probably seen the error of her ways.'

'Do you think I should go out with her and her friends on Saturday night, then?' I asked doubtfully. 'Ayesha said I could sleep over.'

'No, you can't,' Mum said quickly. 'You're babysitting, remember?'

I didn't remember because she hadn't asked. She'd just assumed.

If I'd been a normal teenager that would have been my cue to throw a hissy fit of epic proportions and scream that I was going out and she couldn't stop me because she couldn't work the deadlock on the front door and I was seventeen and anyway she wasn't the boss of me. Ayesha

28

screamed at her mum on the phone on a daily basis so I'd been picking up tips. But I wasn't a normal teenager and anyway, Grandma Minor got there first.

'I'll babysit,' she offered serenely. 'Do Bea good to get out of the house.'

'She goes out of the house . . .'

'Well, she goes to and from school and the childminder and she goes to Pilates and to her Saturday job after providing you with a timeline of her movements.' Gran made it sound like I was under house arrest until I was eighteen. It wasn't *that* bad.

Mum folded her arms and smiled thinly. It didn't reach her eyes, which were looking very squinty. 'Fine, go out on Saturday but you're not sleeping over—'

'Of course she is,' Gran interrupted. 'Give me Ayesha's address and I'll pick you up and take you straight to Pilates. You'd better run upstairs and get your mat.'

The moment they heard my foot on the first stair, there were raised voices. Something about backseat parenting from Mum and then Gran shouted about poachers turned gamekeepers. I wasn't sure what that meant but Mum seemed to and she didn't like it one little bit.

I skulked in my room until the yelling stopped, then poked my head around the door. 'Have you finished rowing?'

'We're not rowing,' Gran snapped. 'We're just having a healthy exchange of opinions.'

Mum was furiously polishing glasses when I ventured down but Gran was all smiles because she'd won the argument. She always did, unless she was arguing with Grandma Major, who wielded her seniority like a weapon. 'Bea's a good girl with a sensible head on her shoulders,' she announced. 'She won't get into any trouble.'

Chapter Four

'Just down it in one,' Chloe ordered as she handed me a mug filled to the brim with a lot of vodka and not very much Diet Coke. 'Honestly, there's no point in even going to the club if we're not all absolutely hammered first.'

I wasn't a stranger to alcohol. I'd been allowed the occasional glass of wine with dinner, so it was more like alcohol and I were casual acquaintances, but as I gingerly put the glass to my lips I was almost asphyxiated by the stench of pure, grainy alcoholness that assaulted my nostrils and made my eyes roll back. One sniff and I already felt absolutely hammered. Emma and Chloe were watching carefully so I took a sip and pretended that I was savouring the rich bouquet and not having all my taste buds suddenly stripped from my mouth. 'Hmmm.' They were still watching, like they expected me to wimp out. 'Is Ruby smoking in the garden? I'm going to cadge a fag off her.'

I had no intention of cadging anything off Ruby, but the moment I stepped out of the back door of Ruby's ginormous Shaker-style kitchen I upended my mug into the herbaceous border.

'Bea?'

Apart from a few tealights, the patio was pretty dark so I hoped Ruby and Ayesha hadn't seen me. I still gave a nervous start before I padded over to the wrought-iron chairs where they were sitting with Ruby's mum, star of stage, screen and numerous interviews in the local paper. If I was a famous actress, I'd have had better things to do on a Saturday night than hang out with a gang of teenagers who were hell bent on getting drunk.

Ruby's mum, Michelle, didn't seem to mind though. She sipped from a huge glass of white wine and smiled brilliantly at me. We went way back actually – I always manned the refreshments table at PTA meetings – and all mothers loved me. I was the poster child for what their own daughters could be, rather than what they actually were.

'You having fun, Bea?' she asked kindly. 'Hope Ruby's not leading you astray.'

'Piss off, Ma,' Ruby said without any heat. 'Bea's way too mature to be led astray by the likes of little old me.'

'And how's your mum? I saw her in Marks the other day. She got her figure back pretty quickly after the twins. Who's her personal trainer?'

'She doesn't have one,' I said. 'She does yoga on the Wii Fit though.' I heard Ruby snort because chatting to her mum about my mum was not the cool thing to do. Neither was tugging down Ruby's loaned dress so I didn't flash my gusset but I did it anyway.

Ruby had been horrified when I turned up in the outfit I'd spent two hours putting together.

'No one wears dresses over jeans any more,' she'd exclaimed sharply. 'And not dresses like that! It's from

32

Primark. I've seen a million other girls wearing that dress. And bootcut jeans? Oh. My. God. No.'

Ruby had started wearing high-waisted, wide-legged jeans when everyone else was just figuring out skinnies so I'd submitted without a murmur when she pulled a handful of purple stretchy material from a drawer and told me to put it on.

It did absolutely nothing for my complexion and I was pretty sure that you could see the outline of my pants through it but I didn't dare tell Ruby that as she'd probably have made me take them off. As it was, when we piled into Michelle's honking great, environmentally unfriendly people carrier, she attacked me with the contents of her make-up bag.

There'd been one agonizing moment when her mum took a speed bump too fast and I thought Ruby was going to gouge my eye out with her mascara wand. She got Ayesha to backcomb my hair, though it was too straight for it to hold, while she held my chin in an uncompromising grip as she dusted powder on my face.

'You'll do,' she sighed as her mum pulled up outside a club on Chalk Farm Road, which was just across the road from Camden Market. 'Just subtract one year from your date of birth if they ask you.'

No one did. The doorman was too busy trying to look down the front of Chloe's top to pay much attention to me bringing up the rear.

'Bar,' Ruby decided as soon as we'd dumped our coats and bags. 'Bea, be an angel and get us a bottle of wine, will you? Chloe, go and get us a table, Ayesha, come with me to the loo.'

Emma pouted. 'What about me?'

'You can help Bea with the drinks,' Ruby sniffed. 'Jeesh, do I have to think of everything?'

Emma and I fought our way to the bar. There was a huge crowd of hot, sweaty people five deep, but Emma grabbed my hand and wormed her way through until we were pressed against the sticky counter. 'Don't worry about Rubes. She's a bit stressed that she might see her ex tonight. Bad break-up,' she added obliquely.

I nodded like I'd had my fair share of bad break-ups. 'Poor Ruby.'

'So you got your eye on anyone?' Emma shouted over an eardrum-perforating squeal of feedback as a band took to the tiny little stage next to the bar.

'Not really.' I didn't know Emma that well. She was tiny and blonde; like a little pixie, which automatically made me feel like a great, hulking brute of a girl, even though she seemed really friendly. 'I liked this guy last summer but nothing happened and it turned out that he liked someone else anyway.'

Someone like Ayesha . . .

'Plenty more foxy boys to be had,' Emma said, rolling her eyes as I failed to attract the attention of any of the bar staff. She hitched herself on to the little ledge that was at ankle level and then stuck out her chest. Within two seconds, the boys behind the bar were descending on us.

Emma didn't say a word or offer to go halves as I parted with twelve of my hard-earned pounds for a bottle of white wine. But then again, Ruby had supplied us with pizza and copious amounts of vodka and maybe Emma had chipped in for that.

Ruby, Ayesha and Chloe were sitting around a small table at the back of the club deep in conversation. Ruby looked up as we approached and her glance flickered over me for an instant then darted away; her face absolutely expressionless like it had done a week ago, before she'd decided I had hidden depths. I could feel my stomach plummeting all the way down to my little sequinned ballet flats, which hadn't met with Ruby's approval either.

But I must have imagined it because she looked again and then she smiled at me. 'Thanks for getting the wine, Bea. You're a star. I actually wanted red but I guess I can force this down. Really, Emma, you know I only like red wine.'

Emma murmured sorry and hovered by the table as Ruby pulled me down between her and Ayesha. She started pointing out boys to me. 'He can't kiss for shit. Retaking all the A levels that he failed. Gay. Should be gay. Can't get it up. Smells like wet dog . . .'

I giggled because it was more boys than I'd ever spoken to and Ruby had the inside track on all of them. She waved energetically at someone on the other side of the room and I took a moment to marvel at the fact that I was sitting next to Ruby Davies. Close enough to smell the heavy musk of her perfume and the freshmint gum, vodka and cigarettes when she opened her mouth to talk to me and she was acting like I was her new best friend.

'Don't worry, I'll introduce you to some much nicer specimens of boykind when we get to the party. I know what you quiet types are like when you get some alcohol in you. Drink up.'

I took an enthusiastic gulp of my wine, which I'd diluted with some water from the bottle I had in my bag. I knew that Ruby was just trying to bring me out of myself, but I didn't want to be brought too out of myself. And I definitely didn't want to go back to Ayesha's even a little bit tipsy because her mum would be on the phone to mine at 7 a.m. sharp on Sunday morning.

'Shall we go and see the band?' I asked Ruby and Ayesha, as the feedback stopped and something that almost resembled a melody could be heard. I hadn't been to a gig for ages. James and I had gone to one day of the Reading Festival the summer before and Mum had taken me to see Arcade Fire at Ally Pally but I'd never seen an unknown band in a little club where you could get right down the front.

'God, no!' Ruby gasped like I'd suggested kicking some puppies.

'Yeah, they suck anyway,' Ayesha added. 'Every band that ever plays here sucks. We've got a table, we can see all the boys, so just chillax, will you?'

'Drink your wine,' Ruby demanded, watching with narrowed eyes as I took a little sip. Her eyes travelled downwards to where my 34Bs were straining against the low neckline of her dress. 'You know what? You're actually pretty hot, Bea.'

I *was* hot. As in starting to lightly perspire hot. I blew at my fringe, which was sticking to my forehead and tried to laugh it off. 'Yeah, well, I don't think they have any air conditioning in here.'

Ruby and Ayesha both rolled their eyes. 'Dude, learn to take a sodding compliment,' Ayesha snapped, digging me in the ribs and smiling to take the sting out of her words. 'We are so going to hook you up after the gig.'

Her words filled me with dread, as if we were going to go to a dentist who wanted to yank out all my teeth without an anaesthetic, then rub something abrasive against my bleeding gums.

'You've hooked up before, right?' Ayesha whispered in my ear and I was really grateful that she hadn't just blurted it out so Ruby could hear. 'Sometime in the last year? God, Bea, you're seventeen, you have to have had at least one rubbish snog in your life.'

I shook my head. 'It's no big deal,' I hissed.

'It is a big deal,' Ayesha hissed back. 'Your first kiss, Bea. My little girl's going to get all growed up.'

Ayesha was right. It *was* a big deal. But when you got to the advanced age of seventeen without ever locking lips, that first kiss had to be special. In fact, it had to be spectacular with a side order of swooning. The only element I was foggy on, even though I'd spent hours honing the details, is who my kissee would be. Well, he'd be French and high of cheekbone and tousled of hair but apart from that I couldn't really picture him in my head, though the fireworks were really clear as my first kiss was going to happen on Bastille Day on the Pont Neuf bridge in Paris.

The band had finished and more boys were appearing. Sweaty boys who'd been pogoing in a big writhing mass and were now damp and glowing as they came to pay court to Ruby, like she was a sun that everyone else revolved around. Even the sweaty boys' girlfriends didn't give her any trouble but smiled and waved when Ruby caught their eye.

As the next band came on, Ruby stood up before any of the boys around us could converge on the stage.

'This place blows,' she said. 'We're leaving.'

I thought that it was up for discussion and I was about to open my mouth and ask if we could stay a bit because a girl had just stepped up to the mic with a dramatic bob and an adorable short red dress – how I wished that I looked, if I didn't look like me – but Ayesha flashed me a warning look and mimed keeping my lips zipped shut.

We all piled out onto the street. No one had introduced me to any of the sweaty boys and their girlfriends, who ignored me when I tried to smile at them. Ruby, Ayesha, Chloe and Emma went marching up the street and I found myself at the back of the clump of unknown people.

We'd walked all the way up the big hill towards Hampstead, until Ruby came to a halt outside a late night convenience store.

'Bea!' she shouted and peered through the sweaty boys,

who obligingly parted. 'There you are! We need to buy some booze.'

Ruby tucked her arm in mine and led me into the brightly lit shop. 'You'll have no problem getting served the way your boobs are popping out of my dress. Don't think anyone's going to be looking at your face.'

Aghast, I hauled up the sagging neckline as Ruby hefted up two six-packs of lager. 'Be a love and get these, will you,' she said, dumped them on the counter and walked out. I counted out another ten hard-earned pounds and staggered out of the shop to be fallen on with excited cries by the others.

We started walking again, winding down narrow roads and stopping every now and again to listen closely for the sounds of music and merriment, as no one actually seemed to know where the party we were going to was being held. I was a little ticked off that no one had given me any money for the lager that I totally wasn't going to be drinking, but if I asked for some, then everyone would think I was tight.

I fretted a little bit longer until I remembered that Ruby was rich and Ayesha's dad did something in the City and was loaded and people who have a lot of money just automatically assume that everyone else has too. Like, when Mum first started seeing James – who owns his own software company – and she wasn't sure if it was serious, she insisted on splitting the dinner bill and would get angry because he always took her to these really expensive restaurants. Even though she'd married James and what was his was now ours, Mum insisted I should be financially aware and wouldn't give me an allowance unless I worked for it. She even made me bank the money that the grandmas and James slipped me, unless I could squirrel it away and spend it on books and DVDs before she found out about it.

I almost walked into the back of one of the sweaty boys when we suddenly stopped outside a big, sprawling house with all the lights on, music blaring out and several waifish girls sitting on the steps outside the open front door. It seemed as if we'd arrived at our destination.

Still making adjustments to the neckline of the dress and marvelling at the idea that, for once, my breasts seemed too big, I trooped after the others. I didn't care what Ruby thought, my first priority was to find a bathroom with a lock on it and change back into what I'd been wearing before, even if it was from Primark.

Ruby was exchanging air kisses with a wasted girl who asked her if anyone had been throwing up in the flowerbeds, obviously our hostess, and I sneaked up the stairs to join the queue for the loo. It was a big posh house full of posh strangers who went to very posh schools. The girl in front of me even had a Chanel bag and she didn't look like the type of person who'd bought it off a stall at Holloway market.

When I finally made it into the bathroom, there was a smell of vomit, which was almost preferable to the cloying stench of really synthetic perfume that someone had sprayed to get rid of pukey odour. Ruby's dress was tighter

40

than a bandage and it took some major wiggling to extricate myself. As I stood there in my rainbow-patterned pants and matching bra someone banged on the door.

It was all I could do not to squeal in alarm. I hauled on my lovely, comfy jeans and fashion-backwards, black lace Primark dress. Then I wet my fingers and carefully wiped them under my sooty eyes, which looked more racoon than anything else, and decided that I didn't scream teen hooker so loudly any more.

'Jesus! What the hell are you doing in there?' The banging on the door increased in volume and frequency. I quickly stuffed Ruby's dress into my overnight bag, took a deep, centring breath and pulled the bolt back on the door to be confronted by a sulky-faced girl who was coiled around Jack . . . My Jack.

Except he wasn't really my Jack and never had been, apart from those few fleeting moments months ago when I'd ordered two Happy Meals and a small cheeseburger and fries and had declined his kind offer to supersize. And the time before that when he'd trod on my foot in the post office and apologized, not just profusely, but prettily too. He was still pretty. He always reminded me of this John Betjeman poem we'd done in English about a girl called Joan who '*was furnished and burnished by the Aldershot sun*'. That was how Jack looked to me; like he was always bathed in sunlight, with his golden hair and his golden skin and his sleepy blue eyes.

Now he looked at me without interest or even a glimmer of recognition, but over my shoulder into the

41

empty bathroom. 'Shall we?' he said to the waifish girl like he was asking her to waltz with him on some highly polished dancefloor while an orchestra played in the background and girls in sherbet-coloured taffeta dresses sipped champagne.

'Get out of my way then,' she barked at me, before she stuck her tongue in Jack's ear.

I sidled past them and wondered if that sinking feeling in my chest way my heart breaking a little bit, just in time to hear another two waif-like posh girls say, 'Urgh! That girl's wearing a Primark dress. Amy should have had someone on the door to keep out the chavs.'

I wasn't a chav. And anyway chav was just a word posh people used when they meant working class. And there was nothing wrong with being working class. Or buying clothes from competitively priced high street chains unless you were a mean, nasty girl with rich parents and an overinflated sense of your own importance. I bit down on the rising wave of self-pity as I sat down on the stairs and started rummaging in my bag for my phone so I could call James. Even if he and Mum were in the middle of dinner, I knew he'd come and rescue me from the horrible public school girls and their sweaty boys. And if Mum wouldn't stop saying 'I told you so,' then that was my own particular cross to bear.

My fingers were poised above the key pad when Ruby plopped down next to me. 'I've been looking for you everywhere,' she whined, like the lack of Bea by her side was a very bad thing. 'You changed.'

'Yeah, see, it was really nice of you to lend me your dress but it was a little too figure-hugging.'

'That was the whole point,' Ruby sighed. She straightened her shoulders. 'Oh well, it's too late to do anything about it now. Now, I really tried to find you a good snog, but it was very short notice . . .'

I followed her gaze to the foot of the stairs where a giggling Chloe and Emma were dragging a tall boy behind them. His face fell all the way down to the floor when Chloe pointed at me.

'I don't think he's that into me,' I said quickly, but Ruby already had her hand wedged under my arm as she hauled me to my feet and started up the stairs.

'Don't talk rubbish. He's gagging for you,' she said, marching me up another flight of stairs. 'Amy said you could use her room. But don't get anything sticky on her duvet cover.'

'Ewww, that's disgusting!'

Ruby took advantage of my shock to push me through the door. I turned round, only to have the boy almost tackle me to the ground as he was pushed inside too. The door slammed behind us as I was trying to free my tangled limbs, and I almost had my fingers around the door handle when I heard the sound of a key being turned.

'Don't do anything we wouldn't do,' someone cackled and I had no choice but to turn around and so I could tell the boy that I was sure he was a really nice person but I wasn't going to do anything with him and I had a rape alarm in my bag (Grandma Major had bought it from an ad at the back of *Saga* magazine) and I knew how to use it.

'Not a word!' he ordered, before I could even open my mouth. 'You're absolutely not my type.'

I should have felt relieved. Instead I felt crushed. Again. There was only so much crushing a girl could take in one night.

'You don't know anything about me!' I burst out hotly.

'Any friend of Ruby Davies is a sworn enemy of mine,' he said.

'She's not my friend. Well, not exactly. She's a friend of someone who used to be my friend but might be my friend again . . . it's complicated.' Giving him an anxious look, I decided that it was probably safe to sit on the bed without him trying to ravish my unwilling flesh.

Not that he looked the ravishing type. The ravishing would have required far too much effort on his part, because he wasn't one of the sweaty boys. He was sweat-free, his standard-issue skinny jeans and baggy jumper neatly pressed and on him, rather than being worn by him, as if they were fancy dress. He was tall and raw-boned and had a glossy cowlick of dark-brown hair that he kept pushing back so it wouldn't fall into his eyes. He had nice eyes at least.

'So you're just an innocent victim in all this?' he asked disbelievingly.

'I was just about to call my stepdad and ask him to rescue me from this sucky party,' I sniffed, because he was really arrogant to think that I couldn't wait to jump his bones.

The boy sighed and didn't look that convinced, but he sat down on the bed too – a respectable metre between us. 'You're really not my type,' he repeated, like I hadn't got the message the first time he'd said it. 'I'm Harry.' He held out his hand. 'I'm a closet homosexual.'

'I'm Bea,' I said, shaking his hand and later I'd be really proud of the way I didn't miss a beat. 'I'm a closet romantic.'

Harry paused for a moment as if he wasn't sure whether I was taking the piss, and I suppose I was just a little, but then he shook his head and chuckled. 'I think this might be the start of a beautiful friendship.'

'Why are you in the closet?' I asked, tucking my legs up under me. 'Why don't you just come out?'

'My dad's a Tory councillor and he's already threatened to make me join the army for failing my A levels.'

'Really? My uncle's gay. I made cupcakes for the reception when he had a civil partnership thingy with his boyfriend, and he said both my grandmas were super supportive when he came out. Apparently, they'd known forever.' I could never find a happy medium between being tongue-tied and not being able to shut up. Not ever.

Harry didn't seem to mind though. 'Do you think they'd adopt me? Everything will be different if, *when*, I get to university,' he muttered morosely, like he was trying to convince himself rather than me.

'God, I hope so!' It came out with a hell of a lot of fervour.

Harry looked at me with a lot less suspicion, then took a packet of cards out of the back pocket of his jeans. 'Don't suppose you play gin rummy?'

He supposed wrong. 'Actually I do. And whist, canasta and bridge, though I'm not very good at bridge.'

Harry started shuffling the cards. 'So, why are you in the closet? Are your pro-gay grannies anti-romance?'

I won the first two games but as I got more impassioned my concentration disappeared. 'I don't want to kiss strange boys in strange bedrooms,' I ranted. 'I want romance. I want to be crazy about a boy and have him be crazy about me too so even if we did end up making a mistake, he wouldn't abandon me at a moment's notice. But romance seems to be as unfashionable as wearing Primark dresses.'

'I like your dress,' Harry insisted, producing a set of aces and totally kicking my arse. 'It looks vintage, rather than Primark. I'm gay, I know these things.'

It was a pity that Harry was gay because I think he was the first person I'd ever met who really got me. Or maybe it was good that he was gay and there was no possibility of falling in love with him because he didn't fit the bill for my romantic hero; he was far too ruddy-faced. And he was beating me at gin rummy.

We played a couple more hands and talked about stuff that I never normally got to talk about, books I'd read, films I'd seen, songs that I loved. It was unremarkable stuff but I didn't get to babble on about it usually before the eye rolling and the, 'God, do you like anything that isn't French or set in France?' started.

I was just trying to persuade Harry to let me teach him canasta when we heard a thump on the door. 'Are you two done in there?'

It sounded like Chloe or Emma; they were pretty interchangeable.

'Go away!' Harry shouted. 'We'll be out when we're good and ready.'

'I could give you a lovebite if you like,' I offered, though I wasn't sure of the technical details. 'Just so we don't blow our cover.'

'We do look very unkissed,' Harry agreed, reaching over to run his thumb over my lips and smear my lipgloss so to the casual observer it would look as if I'd seen some action. 'Y'know, it was a pleasure not getting off with you.'

'Right back at you.' I scrambled off the bed and tried to shake the creases out of my dress. 'Maybe we could do this again sometime?'

'If you're going to become a regular fixture at these parties, then I think you can count on it,' Harry said, walking to the door and banging on it. 'Unless you meet the answer to all of your romantic dreams.'

'I don't think he lives in north London.'

We could hear giggling and, finally, the sound of a key and the door slowly swung open to reveal Chloe and Emma standing there with mobile phones poised. Harry put his arm round me and we dutifully posed for a picture, one of those blurry, wide-eyed, weirdly angled snaps that people put on their MySpace pages.

'Well, thanks for the snog then, Bea,' Harry murmured,

kissing me on the cheek and he was facing away from Chloe and Emma so they didn't see the massive wink he gave me. 'See you around.'

He sauntered down the hall and I was left with two expectant not-really-friends. 'So, how was it?'

'It was great. We really seemed to hit it off,' I said. Not a word of it was a lie.

'You were meant to be snogging him not picking out china patterns,' Chloe scoffed. 'Anyway, Ruby wants to see you so she can hear all the gory details.'

I didn't get why Ruby couldn't come and find me herself instead of sending someone else to request an audience, but I meekly followed them down the stairs and into a huge kitchen where Ruby sat holding court. She looked up and a smile crept over her face. It wasn't a particularly nice smile but I put that down to the rather harsh fluorescent lighting. She beckoned me with one crooked finger. 'Come here. I want to know everything,' she demanded loudly.

'Nothing much to tell,' I hedged because there were ten people in the kitchen and I only knew four of them.

'What happened?'

'What usually happens when you lock two consenting teenagers in a room together,' I said and I could tell from the tightening of Ruby's jaw that that wasn't good enough. 'The duvet got seriously rumpled.'

Ruby wasn't to know that any rumpling occurred from sitting cross-legged on the bed with our shoes on but her eyes lit up. 'How far did you go? Snog or a romp?'

'What's the diff?'

'A snog's a snog and a romp's a romp,' Emma butted in.

'I'm surprised that you did anything with Harry,' Ruby purred. 'He gives off a really gay vibe.'

'I don't think so,' I said and that got me another black look. 'He wasn't particularly gay when we were on the bed together.'

Usually I found it difficult to lie, but Ruby was my toughest challenge yet. The really dumb thing was that over the last five minutes my mind had swung back to not trusting her again, but even so I wanted her to like me. Mrs Wilson, our guidance counsellor, had been wrong when she said that nothing was more harmful than crystal meth; peer pressure was much, much worse.

'Thanks for setting me up, Ruby,' I said, clutching my hands behind my back so I wouldn't start twisting them nervously.

'Are you taking the piss?'

'No! No. I appreciate you looking out for me and, like, hooking me up.'

There was a teeny, tiny moment when I thought Ruby might get all riled up again but, hallelujah, a sweet smile (much nicer than the earlier version) slowly crept on to her face. 'Bea, you are so fucking precious,' she clucked. 'Do you want to hook up with Harry next weekend or shall we find you someone shiny and new?'

I pretended to ponder the question for a bit and tried to tamp down the half-giddy, half-terrified feeling because I was officially hanging with the gang. In with the in-crowd, too cool for sch . . . you get the picture. 'Harry will do for now,' I decided like I was just using him for practice until someone better came along.

Chapter Five

Not many people seemed happy about my new social circle. In fact, I wasn't certain that I was happy about it either.

I made sure that I hung with Lydia, Polly and Ruth for at least one break each day and alternate lunchtimes because there's nothing more lame than dumping your old friends for new friends. I knew exactly how that felt and it wasn't much fun. But they still gave me a hard time because I was doing a lousy job at talking them up to Ruby & Co. so they'd suddenly welcome them with open arms.

Ruby had other ideas. 'I don't know why you hang out with that bunch of social nonentities,' was just one of the nicer things she'd said about Ruth, Lydia and Polly. That was when she wasn't telling me that I needed 'to sex up the outfits, Bea, for God's sake'. Occasionally I'd wonder what I was doing when Ruby told me I was never to set foot in Primark again or interrogating me about how far I'd gone with Harry.

But every time I seriously considered slinking back to Ruth, Lydia and Polly with my tail between my legs, Ruby would smile at me, tuck her arm into mine and say something that would make me like her all over again. 'Anyone ever tell you that you look like a young Audrey Hepburn?' being a personal favourite. And Chloe, Emma and Ayesha were always really nice to me. I think it was because they saw me as an impartial third party, or maybe too chicken to ever talk smack, but they told me all sorts of things that I could have done without knowing.

I knew that Chloe had got off with Emma's boyfriend three times. Emma was having text sex with a boy that Ayesha had been pursuing. Ayesha had kissed the boy who'd broken Ruby's heart and was living in fear that Ruby might find out, and there seemed to be a hundred other combinations of the four of them snogging, getting off with and generally doing the dirty on each other with various boys that they'd either dated, were dating, or were thinking about dating. It was quite hard to keep track of it all really. I was tempted to draw a little flowchart and I was also eternally grateful that I had Harry. He always turned up during a Saturday evening, like he had some kind of electronic device that beeped at the precise moment that Ruby was surveying a party for likely candidates to be locked in a bedroom with me. I knew she was just looking out for me, but I was always relieved to see Harry shouldering his way through the crowd.

'You all right, Bea?' he'd ask, then before I could reply, he'd grab my hand and say, 'Let's go somewhere quiet so I can take advantage of you,' while Ruby would snort in disbelief because she still insisted that Harry was conflicted about his sexuality.

So, when I added up all the different factors involved in being friends with Ruby (and Ayesha and Chloe and Emma, because they came as a set), I decided that I

52

was ahead on points. I was getting out more, meeting new people and doing teenagery stuff. In fact, I was pretty happy.

My mum, though, was totally not happy. She was like the definition of not happy. I think the grandmas and James had ganged up on her and told her that it was time to cut the apron strings because she didn't say anything but there was a lot of frowning and unnecessary clanking of china when she was loading the dishwasher. 'Oh, you're going out *again*?' she'd say when I got home from Wilson's on a Saturday and started getting ready to go out.

We still had our daily me and Mum time but she never said anything funny about cats and book covers any more. She was just constantly on my case about my grades suffering because I was out all the time. And when I'd point out that one night every week wasn't all the time, she'd get really narked. I missed my cool mum.

So I was all ready for more sighing and muttering when she knocked on my bedroom door as I was getting ready to go out one Saturday evening a few weeks after I'd starting hanging with Ayesha and Ruby.

'Come in,' I called out, but my mind was on other things like trying to get a perfect sweeping line of black liquid eyeliner, so I was surprised when I looked beyond my smeared eyelid in the mirror to see Mum perch nervously on the edge of my bed.

'You know, if you put a little bit of powder on your eyelid before you start, it doesn't smudge so much,' she said. 'And don't scrunch up your eyes. Here, let me do it.'

This was the kind of motherly advice I could get behind. I gladly relinquished my eyeliner so she could get to work.

'I can get my right eyelid done, but my left eyelid seems to be more crinkly,' I complained, as Mum rested one hand on my forehead to keep me still and drew a steady line.

'I feel the same way about my left eyelid,' Mum said, smiling as she made some minor adjustments, then stepped back. 'I think that's OK. You wanted the Amy Winehouse look, right?'

I was just about to scream in horror when she started laughing and I let out a huge sigh of relief. 'Very funny, Mum,' I said, as I picked up my mascara and ran the brush against my lashes from side to side like she'd shown me.

'You're getting so grown up,' she murmured, sitting down again. 'Don't you think that dress is a little short?'

My new poppy-sprigged dress came to a very decorous three centimetres above my knees. 'I'm wearing black opaque tights with it.'

'And your ballet flats?'

'No, my red Converses.'

I could see Mum smile to herself because Converses and poppy-sprigged dresses were not bringing sexy back or bringing sexy anywhere in my general vicinity.

'So, I was thinking that we need to make an appointment at the doctor's,' she said casually.

'Why, do the twins need more shots?'

'Well, no. I think it's time you went on the pill, before you get into trouble.'

'What?! God, no!' I whirled round to face her. 'I absolutely do not need to go on the pill.'

'I know you really believe that, but it's very easy to get swept up in the heat of the moment. Then you have to deal with the consequences of that moment for the rest of your life.' Mum wouldn't look at me – the flesh and blood consequences of what she had to deal with for the rest of her life – she just kept fingering the edge of my duvet. 'You have been talking about someone called Harry a lot.'

'I maybe mentioned him once or twice,' I protested as I pulled on my tights. 'He's just a friend who's a boy. Not a boyfriend.' I could have told her that Harry was gay but it was his secret, not mine to blurt out just to get Mum off my back.

'I'll be absolutely furious if you *are* having sex. Beyond furious.' Mum paused, then shrugged. 'But if you are having sex behind my back, despite everything I've told you – well, it's better to be safe than sorry.'

'I am safe! I'm not doing anything with anyone that means I need to go on the pill, unless you can get pregnant from just looking at boys.' You'd think it wouldn't be possible to put Converses on aggressively but I managed it. There was a lot of yanking on the laces. 'I think if that was the case, then there might have been something on the news about that scientific breakthrough.'

It was the most narked I'd ever got with Mum and she didn't like it one bit. She narrowed her eyes but she was too busy huffing to say anything at first. Unfortunately that didn't last very long. 'This is why I don't like you being friends with people who are obviously such a bad influence on you,' she informed me snottily. 'You'd never have spoken to me like that a couple of months ago.'

'Look, I'm sorry, I didn't mean to snap, but I am not doing anything that would mean I need to go on the pill. I promise.' I snatched up the little beaded evening bag that Grandma Major had let me borrow on an indefinite loan and stuffed lipstick, mascara and mobile phone into it. 'I'm going now. I'll see you tomorrow morning.'

'We haven't finished talking,' Mum insisted, on her feet in an instant so she was hot on my heels as I raced down the stairs.

'Mum! Why can't you have a little faith in me? I know what I'm doing and what I'm not doing.'

'You're seventeen! You don't even know how to put on liquid eyeliner properly!'

Sometimes it was pointless trying to reason with Mum. And it was also annoying how she could worm her way under my skin and always know what to say to cause maximum pissed-offness. I made this weird frustrated noise that was half scream, half growl as I wrestled with the latch on the front door.

'I thought James was going to give you a lift,' Mum said, calm now because she'd totally got the last word in.

I opened the door to discover it was raining. Not just the usual April shower but a torrential downpour that would soak through the soles of my Converses. However, I couldn't let that get in the way of my first good storming out. Except, bloody hell, she'd raised me too well to storm out without saying goodbye first. 'I'm OK to walk,' I insisted, bracing myself for the inevitable deluge. 'I'll see you tomorrow.'

'OK, but we're taking a raincheck on this discussion, excuse the pun,' Mum grinned. 'See you tomorrow, kiddo. Behave yourself. No drinking, no smoking, no kissing, no fornicating . . .'

She was still listing all the things I wasn't meant to be doing as I squelched down the garden path.

Ruby complimented me on my outfit for the first time ever, which should have made me ecstatically happy, but my hair was hanging round my face in rats' tails and when I borrowed her hairdryer, it went all staticky.

'You look like you stuck your finger in the plug socket,' Ruby sniffed when I was finally ready to leave her house and pile into a parental people carrier to be driven to Camden. 'And you've made us late.'

Ruby always made us late. She'd always decide to have another glass of wine, or have to go into a huddle with Ayesha because she knew that if she made us late, then she could make an entrance. Apparently arriving anywhere on time was more uncool than bootcut jeans and Primark dresses.

'Well, fine,' I said peevishly. 'I'd have gone out with sopping wet hair and got pneumonia if I'd known you were in such a tearing hurry.'

It was the first time that I'd ever talked back but Mum's latest scheme to protect my uterus from encroaching sperm had put me in a foul mood.

We were standing in Ruby's hall, though it was too grand to be a hall – it was more of a foyer or a vestibule – and I took a nervous step back as Ruby gaped at me. Then this strange look flitted across her face and for one moment I thought she might cry, before she smiled tremulously.

'Sorry,' she mumbled, eyes downcast. 'I know I can be a bitch but you never call me on it. You should.'

'You're not being a bitch,' I said quickly because she wasn't. Not really. 'I *was* being a bitch. I had a row with my mum before I left and it's made me all out of sorts.'

'I mean it, Bea. If I have an attack of the Paris Hiltons, God forbid, then you have to let me know 'cause, well, I really like you and I don't want my little Miss Diva act to drive you away,' Ruby said, still with her head hanging low, like if she looked me in the eye then she'd lose her nerve.

I wanted to tell her that it was an honour to be plucked from obscurity and catapulted straight into the inner circle, but it would have sounded extremely lame. So I just took the hand she was holding out and we ran to the car, both of us shrieking and jostling as we fought to get in the car before we got soaked.

Ruby hardly left my side all evening as we sat in a pub in Hampstead. I could see Chloe and Emma casting bitter looks in my direction, which was ridiculous. They weren't being ousted – Ruby simply appreciated how good I was at nodding.

'You're so easy to talk to, Bea,' Ruby breathed, when she came to the end of her heartfelt rant about how she wasn't really the hard-nosed dictator of the upper school that people thought she was – she just had a really strong personality. She squeezed my arm. 'I can just be myself with you. I can't tell you what a relief it is.'

I *was* a good listener. You kind of had to be when you never had anything interesting to say, so I just blushed and contemplated my soggy Converses. When I looked up again, Ruby clapped her hands.

'I've just had the most wicked idea,' she exclaimed. 'What are you doing for the summer holidays?'

'Well, I don't know,' I said. 'We usually go to Cornwall for a couple of weeks in August, but James said something about going to Tuscany.'

Ruby squinched up her face like she'd just downed a pot of yoghurt that was way past its sell-by date. 'You can't go on holiday with your family,' she said, sounding appalled. 'They'll totally cramp your style. No! You should come to Spain with us.'

Ayesha had been talking to one of the floppy-haired, sweaty boys who still all looked the same to me, but she paused their conversation so she could nudge my arm. 'You totally should. We're going to have so much fun.'

Even Chloe and Emma were enthusiastically agreeing, the dirty looks of half an hour ago forgotten. Again, I had this nagging voice in my head that insisted it was all just a really elaborate wind-up and the moment I agreed, they'd all laugh and tell me they'd only been joking.

'Well, it's really sweet of you, but my mum's more likely to let me become a stripper than go on holiday on my own.'

'Oh Bea, don't be so defeatist,' Ruby exclaimed sharply. 'You're nearly eighteen . . .'

'Not for ages and ages. Not for another ten months.'

'God! Tell her you want to go on holiday with us and there's nothing she can do about it. End of,' Ruby snapped, and that might be how it worked in her house but it sure as hell wasn't how it worked in mine.

'Or you could at least ask her,' Ayesha suggested, because she had a mother who liked to get on her case too. Not without good reason from what her mum told my mum. 'Tell her you're done with the babysitting, cooking and bringing home perfect marks unless she lets you go on holiday with us.'

'I get a lot of Bs,' I said very weakly because I wasn't even sure if I wanted to go on holiday with them. Saturday nights were all right. But a week of Saturday nights?

'Jesus, Bea! It's a fortnight out of your entire life,' Ruby said. Correction. Two weeks of Saturday nights. 'And you'll be going to uni this time next year. Tell her it's a dry run.'

'Well, I guess there's no harm in asking,' I prevaricated, as both Ayesha and Ruby linked arms with me, like we were going to get up at that very second so they could march me home and force me to ask permission in front of them.

'My godmother has this amazing apartment overlooking the beach in Malaga,' Ruby said and the four of them started talking about picnics on the beach and this little train that wended its way up hills dotted with lemon groves and a café that served fish that had been caught half an hour before – and it did sound lovely. Way better than last year when we'd gone camping and it had rained the entire time.

I could see Harry fighting his way through the crowd to get to me as Chloe insisted that she was going to have a holiday romance with a cabana boy. 'I think his name will be Pedro and he's totally gonna teach me how to salsa,' she was saying when Harry finally reached our table, lifted my hand and kissed it.

'Fancy a snog, sweetcakes?' he asked and I willingly let him pull me to my feet because I didn't want to hear any more about bloody Spain.

Chapter Six

I was still conflicted on the subject of Spain as I heaped roast potatoes on my plate the next day. When I'd switched my phone on after Pilates that morning, I'd had two text messages apiece from Ruby, Ayesha, Chloe and Emma demanding to know if I'd asked my mum yet.

It seemed that they really, genuinely liked me for me. I still didn't know why but it filled me with enough of the warm fuzzies that I waited until Mum's second helping of apple pie, so I knew she'd be all sugared up and in a really good mood, before I blurted out, 'So, can I go on holiday to Spain with Ruby and the others this summer? They're going for a fortnight, but, like, a week would be cool and it's Ruby's godmother's apartment so I'd only have to pay for my flight and I've got loads of money in the bank. So, can I? Like, go?'

In my head it had sounded far more reasonable. Rational even. But it came hurtling out of my mouth in unwieldly clumps like the congealing custard in my pudding bowl. Both grandmas were looking at me, James put down his spoon, even the twins were staring wide-eyed and not hurling bits of food across the table.

Only Mum kept her eyes on her coffee cup. 'Really, Bea, don't be ridiculous,' she said lightly. 'Let you go to Spain on your own? As if!'

'I wouldn't be on my own—'

'As good as.' She carefully stirred her coffee, her movements slow and purposeful like she was making them for the very first time. 'Maybe next year. If you do really, really well in your A levels.'

I wasn't disappointed. Not exactly, 'cause I still wasn't sure whether I wanted to go, so I shrugged. 'OK, can't blame a girl for trying, can you?'

Mum shot me an approving smile because if there was a contest for the most perfect child in the world, I'd take gold every time.

James frowned. 'I went to Greece with my mates when I was sixteen,' he pointed out, and spread his hands wide. 'See, I'm still in one piece.'

'And the summer I was seventeen, I spent a wonderful month on the Isle of Wight,' piped up Grandma Minor. 'There was a rock festival. Jimi Hendrix played.'

Mum rolled her eyes so hard that, for a second, her pupils completely disappeared. 'That was then, this is now.'

'Just what exactly do you think Bea's going to get up to?' Grandma Major enquired, deftly removing Alfie's spoon before he could brain Ben with it. 'When I was seventeen, I was driving an ambulance during the day and dancing with American GIs all through the night.'

'It's not Bea I'm worried about,' Mum said. 'It's her new friends whom I know nothing about, apart from what Ayesha's mum tells me, which is nothing good. Then there's the boys she's likely to meet with their date-rape drugs and their STIs. And I'd just like to remind you all that when I was seventeen I was already pregnant with Bea, and I'd like to make sure that history doesn't repeat itself, thank you very much.'

That was that. There were sympathetic looks but everyone shut up because Mum had two burning spots on her cheeks, which meant she was one more piece of unsolicited advice away from totally losing it.

I thought Ruby was going to cry when I told her that she'd have to go to Malaga without me. Actual, genuine tears.

'She thinks that the minute she lets me out of her sight, I'm going to get pregnant,' I admitted grudgingly, the next day at lunch.

'Well, go on the pill then!' Chloe snorted. 'It's really easy not to get pregnant.'

'It's not just the getting pregnant,' I mumbled, my face flushing as the four of them looked at me as if I was a circus freak. 'It's getting date raped, or alcohol poisoning, or a gazillion other things she's convinced are going to happen the minute I step off the plane.'

'You wouldn't do anything like that,' Ruby insisted fiercely. 'You're far too square. Like, no offence.'

'None taken,' I said miserably, because I was square. I was so square, I could change my name to rhombus. 'You know, it means a lot that you want me to come but it's not going to happen. When my mum makes her mind up about something . . .' I let my voice trail off before I could share any of the similar incidents, like when she wouldn't let me have a MySpace, or a pair of winter shorts to be worn *over* woolly tights, or a pony. Yes, even a pony. Because apparently disgusting boys hung out in riding stables and would have been driven to unspeakable acts of lust at the sight of me in a pair of jodhpurs. I knew Mum was just being protective, but if she wasn't so cool about non-boy stuff like staying up late and letting me borrow her clothes, life would be very grim.

'You should, like, totally divorce her,' Emma muttered darkly. 'On the grounds of irreconcilable differences. That's what my mum told the judge when she kicked my step-dad to the kerb.'

'More like emotional cruelty,' Ayesha said. 'I don't know why you take so much crap from her. I don't let my mum tell me shit any more.'

'Let's just drop it,' I begged, picking up my bag because this was my day to have lunch with Lydia, Ruth and Polly. 'And I'm not going to get huffy if you want to talk about your holiday. I'm excited for you really.' I expected to hear the halo above my head ping, but all I heard was Ruby scrunch up her crisp packet.

'There's no holiday,' she said flatly. 'If you can't go, then we're not going.'

'That's ridiculous! Honestly, I really don't mind,' I said, but I was secretly thrilled to hear Ruby say that. I was in. I was golden. 'You're being so silly. Go to Spain but come back and tell me all about it so I can live vicariously through you until I'm eighteen.'

Ruby grinned but it didn't look like her heart was really

in it. 'If you think that being eighteen is going to give your mum an attitude makeover, then you're very mistaken,' she insisted, looking up at me from under her lashes. 'Where are you going?'

'I promised I'd have lunch with the others,' I said, nodding my head in the direction of my other posse (I was a two-posse girl, who'd have thunk it?) who were waiting by the tennis courts. 'I'll see you later.'

And that was that. Spain was nothing more than an idle daydream about lemon groves and adding *paella* to my repertoire of recipes. Really, I wasn't that bothered about going. I could wait another year.

No one mentioned Spain at all for the next few days, but on Thursday evening as I was struggling to understand a French book for ages ten and up, there was a ring on the doorbell.

Nothing unusual about that; our doorbell rang all the time. I heard Mum open the door then her voice calling up the stairs. 'Bea! Can I borrow you for a second?' I could hear this shrill top note of panic in her voice as I stuck my head out over the banisters and nearly toppled headfirst over them. Standing in our hall was Ruby looking at the twins' double buggy like she'd never seen one before and her mum, Michelle, staring at the picture on the wall. It was a framed poster of *Lost In Translation*, the film Mum and James had gone to see on their first date. I thought it was romantic and no reason for Michelle to be gazing at it with this tiny, amused smile.

'Bea,' Mum said weakly as I appeared at the top of the stairs. 'Look who's here!'

She sounded really flustered, as she pushed her hair back from her face. It wasn't often that we had a genuine famous person in our hall and Michelle was wearing an elegant black dress while Mum's *I ♥ geeks* T-shirt ('borrowed' from me) was clinging to her damply because she'd just bathed the twins.

'Hello, sweetie,' Michelle cooed, gathering me up for a hug and some air-kissing when I reached the bottom of the stairs. 'Hope you don't mind us dropping in unannounced.'

Over Michelle's shoulder I could see both Mum and Ruby pulling faces. 'No, it's OK. Nice to see you.'

'She's such a credit to you, Alison,' Michelle said, turning to Mum. 'Bea's always so polite when she comes round. Not like a certain person I could mention.'

Ruby rolled her eyes again. 'I am polite,' she protested. 'Just you're never there to see it. You have a lovely home; it's very cosy. See?' she added to Michelle. 'I can do polite.'

Mum ushered them into the living room, which was covered in the twins' paraphernalia, where James was playing on the Xbox. He turned it off pretty quick when he saw we had company and after introductions muttered something about making tea.

Michelle sat down, Gucci handbag on her lap, and smiled at Mum, who was perched nervously on the edge of an armchair like she was at a job interview. 'Are those adorable little twins in bed? Pity. I must say, Alison, you got your figure back very quickly.'

'Well, it's more like I don't have time to eat.' Mum folded her arms. 'So, what brings you—'

'I practically had to stop eating once I had Ruby,' Michelle continued as if Mum hadn't even spoken. 'And Bea has a lovely figure too. You can't beat good genes. Oh, what a fantastic photo,' she added, as her gaze rested on the picture of the five of us on the beach at Whitstable, which sat on the mantelpiece. 'You're such a good-looking family.'

Mum smiled weakly and I know just how she felt because it was pretty much what I felt when Ruby was on a charm offensive. I looked over at Ruby, who was still standing by the door. She grinned and gave me a wink. 'So, Bea, can I see your room?'

I looked over at Mum, who was listening to Michelle now complimenting her on her taste in soft furnishings, and she nodded absently.

'Don't worry,' Ruby said as she followed me up the stairs. 'Everything is going to be OK. Operation Lemon Grove is under control.'

'She's not going to let me go,' I said, because it would take more than serious sucking up from a BAFTA-nominated actress to sway Mum. I opened my bedroom door and waved a hand. 'Sorry about the mess.'

'Holy shit,' Ruby gasped, stepping past me, into my bedroom. 'Oh my God, I fucking love it. I'm moving in. Seriously.'

My room was my very favourite place in the world, after Paris, because I hadn't been to Paris yet. When they'd bought the house, James and Mum had given me free rein to have my room any way I wanted. What I'd wanted was a replica of Amélie's bedroom and that was what I'd got.

The walls were painted a deep, rich red and Mum and I had spent hours with little tubs of gold paint carefully picking out a tangly, tendrilly stencil that she'd made. I had an old-fashioned iron bedstead, two patchwork quilts made by the grandmas, two rugs covered in a Japanese cherry blossom pattern on the wooden floor that James had bought me when he went to New York, and on the wall I'd stuck the nineteen-thirties' French travel posters I'd bought on eBay. Ruby walked over to my shelves and looked at my collection of Paris snowstorms and the little china ornaments I collected from charity shops. The room wasn't finished; it was still a work in progress but I liked that. It was the kind of room I could just keep adding to and it never looked cluttered – but like a place where you wanted to stay for hours and keep finding new things to amuse you. Like the old dress form Grandma Major had given me where I tried out my Saturday night outfits before I put them on. Ruby fingered the hem of a dress and turned to me with a smile.

'This is the most amazing room I've ever seen,' she said and there were two things different about her. It was the first time I'd ever seen her take genuine pleasure over something and smile so she was all teeth and gums, rather than the slight upward quirk of her lips, which was how she usually smiled. The second thing was the way Ruby was looking at me like I might actually have some cool in me after all. I know Ruby thought I was a good listener and she must have got a kick out of my wide-eyed deference but she didn't think I was cool.

'Your room's amazing too,' I said, trying not to sound so pleased as Ruby pored over my little knick-knacks.

'I'm too messy to really do the minimalist thing,' Ruby said ruefully, pulling a face as she thought about her own bedroom, which was completely white and had a red neon sign that spelt out her name over her massive white bed, which was covered in a canopy of floaty white drapes. 'But this . . . this is really something. I think you've been holding out on me, Bea. Remember what I said about you having hidden depths. I bet when we get to Malaga, I'm going to see them.'

'About this whole going to Malaga thing? What did you mean when you said you had it under control?'

Ruby shrugged her skinny shoulders. 'Michelle's working her magic as we speak. She's a trained actress. Failure isn't an option.'

'But how—'

'Patience, grasshopper. So, like, have you actually been to Paris?'

Ruby sat on my bed as I showed her my Paris scrapbooks and the vintage dresses the grandmas had given me, which I couldn't get into because they must have been teeny, tiny size double zeros when they were younger. It was the nicest time I'd had with Ruby, away from the others, when she stopped putting on a show and just *was*. It was like I was getting the essence of Ruby and it lasted until we heard James call me from downstairs.

Then Ruby straightened her spine, tossed back her hair and this time when she smiled, it didn't reach her eyes. 'Right, here we go,' she murmured under her breath.

I could hear Mum and Michelle talking as I opened the living-room door. Or Michelle was talking and Mum was trying to get a word in edgeways.

'It's not that,' she was trying to say. 'But five teenage girls on their own . . .'

'Oh, but Claudia's promised to drop in,' Michelle assured her. 'She's my very best friend from drama school and Ruby's godmother. It's her apartment . . .'

'But would she be sleeping there? Every night?' Mum was perched uncomfortably right on the very edge of the sofa, James rubbing her hand as Michelle sat back in the armchair like it was her house and not the other way round.

'Well, she has an acting job in Barcelona, but she'd be there for the weekend and it's a very family-orientated complex. Claudia says she'll make sure the housekeeper looks in on them, and Iban and Linda who live next door – lovely couple, he's an architect and she does something with textiles – they have two small children so they're not going to take kindly to five teenagers banging in and out at all hours.'

Mum wasn't wavering. Not exactly, but she was twitching for sure. 'Yes, but—'

'Alison, if it's a question of money . . .' Michelle said delicately. 'I'd love to pay for Bea's flight.'

Michelle was as good as Ruby had said she was, Mum was backed into a corner and there was nothing she could do. 'Of course it's not. We can pay for Bea's flight.' Her shoulders slumped. 'Well, guess you're going to Malaga, kiddo.'

'I am?' I ventured nervously, even though Ruby gave me a vicious jab in the ribs to make me shut up. 'Are you sure?'

Mum painted on a smile that was as fake as Michelle's acrylic tips. 'Of course I'm sure. It will be good for you to have a bit of independence before you go to university.' She looked at James, who pulled a 'don't ask me' face because this wasn't his battle. 'But there will be provisos. Conditions. And I see a lot of grade improving in your immediate future if you want to get on that plane.'

'Sure, yeah!' I nodded fervently. I'd get my French grade up even if it meant having to listen to French podcasts in my sleep, because suddenly I wanted to go to Malaga with Ruby more than I'd ever wanted anything in my life. Except going to Paris and meeting my dad. I still had no intention of going on the pill but I'd argue that point at a later date without Ruby present.

Chapter Seven

It would have been cool to say that the next two months sped by and then I was headed for sunny Spain with a carefree heart and a recipe for *paella* that I'd painstakingly copied out of a Spanish cookbook in Waterstone's.

But the weeks seemed to drag along, weighted down by revision and exams and a relentless campaign waged by my mother to ensure that she'd work each one of my last nerves before I cleared Passport Control. She'd given up on forcing me to ingest huge quantities of contraceptives, but we'd had the sex talk every single day of those two months, with a special focus on STIs that would need a stay in hospital, an IV drip, make me completely infertile and cover my girl parts in suppurating sores.

Mum also went bikini shopping with me. Though I don't know why she billed it as bikini shopping as there was no way she was letting me out in public in a two-piece bathing suit that left my midriff bare. There were bikinis with perfectly respectable bottoms, shorts if you will, but the way she carried on in the middle of New Look, anyone would have thought I was packing a Playboy centrefold body under my hoodie and jeans that would inflame men with lust as soon as they looked at me. In the end we got two one-piece suits, though Mum wasn't happy that one of them had a halter neck and I sneaked to Dorothy Perkins when she went to look in Baby Gap and bought a tankini.

Even when I was predicted three As and a B in French for my As levels (I think Monsieur Bradley felt sorry for me) Mum still wasn't happy. And when Mum wasn't happy, then no one else was allowed to be happy.

So I was relieved when the twenty-fifth of July rolled around and I was getting up at dawn o'clock to go to the airport. The excitement of going on holiday had been completely overshadowed by the sheer giddy delight of getting shot of my mother.

'I am trusting you not to have sex under any circumstances but I hope you remembered to pack those condoms I bought you,' she said as she drove me to Stansted. 'Because I'm pretty sure that Spain is a Catholic country and you won't be able to get the morning-after pill.'

'I'm not going to need the morning-after pill,' I protested but my heart wasn't in it. I just didn't have the energy to go down that well-trodden path again so I just shut my eyes and pretended I was asleep.

I didn't pretend to wake up until we arrived. 'Right, well, I guess I'll see you in a couple of weeks,' I said enthusiastically as I hauled my case out of the boot. I leant over to give Mum a kiss but she grabbed my case and started wheeling it in towards the airport's revolving doors.

'Of course, I'm going to see you off,' she called over her shoulder. 'What kind of mother do you think I am?'

It wasn't until we got to Passport Control, where there were several uniformed officials who'd have had a problem if she'd tried to follow me through the gate, that Mum had to leave.

She pulled me over to one side. 'I have to go now, but are you sure you'll be all right?'

'I'll be fine.' I sighed for like the fifteenth time.

Mum smiled and brushed my fringe back from my face. 'If you're not having a good time, then you can come back early. Just give us a call. Oh, don't forget to charge up your phone. You did pack the adaptor James gave you . . .'

'Mum, please.' I tried to keep the exasperation out of my mouth so I wouldn't be the clichéd sulky teenager even if she was being the clichéd overprotective mum. 'Just go.'

She grinned suddenly. 'I'm embarrassing you in front of your friends, aren't I? God, I've turned into my mother.'

'Grandma Minor is way cooler than you,' I said right on cue and now I smiled and squeezed her back just as tightly when she hugged me. There might even have been some tears pricking my eyelids as I walked back to where the others were standing impatiently, but I blinked them away.

'Your mother has a huge stick up her arse,' Ruby informed me coolly. 'No offence.'

I was so excited about going to Spain *and* getting away from my mum that I think I really annoyed the others. It was only the second time I'd gone abroad and even the stewardess taking us through the safety demonstration had me bouncing in my seat. 'Stop acting like a spaz,' Chloe hissed from across the aisle. And then the four of them did this synchronized eye roll, which stopped me mid-bounce.

Once the plane landed it was a confusing scramble to get our luggage, find Ruby who'd wandered off, then queue up at the taxi rank.

There was a lot of shoving and pushing but I ended up in a car with Emma, who seemed really put out about it. 'Did you see the way Ayesha elbowed me out of the way?' she whined, but she recovered enough to show me some pornographic text messages she'd got from a guy that Ayesha had got off with the last three Saturdays in a row.

I tuned out Emma's voice and stared out of the window as we sped through the streets of Malaga's Old Town. I'd been expecting rows of high-rise apartment blocks and burger bars like the time Mum and I had gone on a package holiday to Corfu but Malaga was so much prettier than that. I looked up at brightly coloured flowers trailing over wrought-iron balconies, two wizened old ladies dressed in black hobbling down the street, and a totally cute boy on a little moped. It wasn't Paris, but I was already a little bit in love with Malaga.

Our taxi pulled up outside a sweet old apartment block to find Ruby already waiting with Chloe and Ayesha. 'You'll have to pay our taxi as well, Bea,' she said. 'None of us had time to get any euros.'

I had lots of euros on me. Mum had let me take some of my savings out of the bank, but she'd also given me a hundred quid in traveller's cheques. Both grandmas had slipped me holiday money and James had given me all the euros that he'd never got round to swapping back to pounds. It was such a massive wad of notes that I hadn't even been able to get them all in my purse. So, yes, I had euros but a please would have been great.

I was fuming a little bit as I followed them up three flights of stairs to our apartment, which was on the top floor. When Ruby finally managed to get the big, carved oak door open, after much swearing and a few false starts, we piled through the door and ran for the bedrooms, Ruby leading the way.

'I'm in here,' she shouted as she opened the door of a huge airy room. 'You lot can have the other room.'

There was a double bed and a single bed in the smaller room, which were already occupied by Ayesha, Chloe and Emma so I traipsed back into Ruby's room. She was lying on the bed with her eyes closed. I thought she was asleep until she sat up and fixed me with a look that made me want to back out slowly. 'What are you doing here?'

It felt like she wasn't talking about my sudden appearance in the room but me being there, in Spain, with them. 'Um, I'll have to sleep in here 'cause, like, there's not enough . . .'

Ruby propped herself up on one elbow. 'There's one bed in here and I'm not sharing it with you.'

'But Chloe and Emma are sharing the double bed in the other room,' I pointed out quietly. 'So I have to bunk in here with you.'

'Are you, like, some kind of lesbian?' Ruby demanded. A smile of smug satisfaction appeared on her face as I flushed deep red.

'No! And Chloe and Emma aren't gay either but they're—'

'They've known each other for years so it doesn't count,' Ruby mused. 'But really, what do we know about you, apart from the fact that you might be a great fat dyke?'

'I'm not,' I protested incredulously because I could hardly believe what I was hearing or the venom in Ruby's voice. 'Not that there's anything wrong with being gay, but I'm not, and I don't have anywhere—'

'You can have the bloody sofa!' Ruby snapped, pointing an imperious finger in the direction of the living room. 'Now get out!'

I was furious. Not furious enough to flounce out of Ruby's room with an angry toss of my head, but definitely furious enough to close the door with a resounding bang.

The lounge was huge but the sofa was an angular piece of furniture made of slippery white leather and there didn't seem to be any spare pillows or sheets. I sat there vibrating with the sheer unfairness of it all until the view from the big patio windows gradually worked its magic on me. I got up and opened the windows so I could step out onto a little balcony and stare at the haphazard streets below that seemed to twist in on themselves. When I stood on tiptoe I could see over the rooftops to a glittering sliver of silvery blue that shimmered in the brilliant sunlight – the sea! Just like that, I began to feel my spirits lift because I was in Spain and Ruby's sleep deprivation couldn't last forever.

It was still present though when Ruby stormed out of her room and announced that we were going out because she was starving, and we had five minutes to pack our beach gear.

It felt like Ruby's bad mood had claws and fangs, so we all dutifully and quietly trailed after her as she stomped down the street.

'That café looks nice,' Ayesha ventured as we came to a pretty market square and a café that had tables arranged under big, white umbrellas so we'd be shielded from the sun. 'I'm dying for a Diet Coke.'

Ruby glared at the assembled diners, her face scrunched up in a ferocious frown. 'No,' she said. 'I just can't deal with Spanish people right now.'

'But all you have to say is "*Cinco Diet Cokes, per favore*",' Chloe gritted. 'It's not that difficult. That woman is eating the most fantastic-looking sandwich. Let's just sit down.'

Chloe was way braver than me. She tilted her chin defiantly and wouldn't look at Ruby but started striding towards an empty table.

'Get back here, beeyatch!' Ruby barked. It was exactly the same tone that Grandma Major's horrible friend Margery used when she was calling one of her equally horrible pug dogs to order. It had the same effect on Chloe. Her spine stiffened before she turned round and come to heel.

'It was just an idea,' she groused.

'Since when did you start having them?' Ruby asked sweetly. 'We'll find a supermarket and buy some Diet Coke and crisps, then we can go to the beach and sunbathe. Isn't that a much better idea?'

After a quick stop for provisions (which meant I had to peel off yet more euros) and trundling down many streets, we turned a corner and there was the beach. It was as blue and golden as it should be, although it was hard to know for sure because every inch of it was covered in scantily clad people. We settled on a small patch of sand – the only empty spot we could find. I spread out my towel and wriggled out of my sundress so my polka dot tankini could get its first public airing and started slathering on factor gazillion sunblock so my freckles wouldn't multiply.

Ruby was finally smiling because there was acres of bronzed boy flesh as far as the eye could see. A group of lads a little distance off had all stopped playing frisbee as we trooped across the sand. Now they resumed their game, but their frisbee kept landing nearer and nearer to where we were setting up our base camp.

I could see Ruby surreptitiously eyeing them from behind her Dior sunglasses as she stripped down to a tiny black string bikini and with a triumphant look slipped off the top. 'Everyone sunbathes topless on the Continent,' she said smugly, though Emma was already eagerly whipping off her bikini top too because this was one area where she had Ruby beat. In fact, she had all of us beat. She had the most perfect breasts I'd ever seen and no, that didn't make me a lesbian.

Chloe took one look at Emma's boobs that managed to be both pert and buxom at the same time and swallowed nervously. 'If I had breasts like you, then yeah, I'd totally go topless.' She was talking to Emma but Ruby smiled serenely and nodded her head in tacit acknowledgement as Ayesha sighed heavily then untied the halter neck of her bikini but kept her elbows clamped over her breasts as she lay down.

I settled on my tummy and rested my head on my arms as I felt the sun beat down on my back. I even let myself breathe out because I could hear the gentle lap of the waves as they tickled the sand and the sounds of children playing, and smell the salt tang of the sea that didn't smell anything like English sea. I was on the beach, on holiday and I had two weeks to work on my tan and maybe even have a little romance if there were any cute boys in Malaga who weren't dripping with hair gel and obsessed with ogling girls and playing frisbee. Maybe I'd find a waiter, who was actually a sculptor, but needed to wait tables to afford clay and stuff and he'd ask me to pose for him and—

'Oh my God! What the hell are you wearing?' Ruby's sharp enquiry completely ruined my daydream. 'Bea! You look fugging stupid in that thing. What is it? A bikini for a nun?'

'It's a tankini,' I said, and I took advantage of my position to indulge in a hidden bit of eye rolling because if Ruby didn't get over her sleep deprivation soon it was going to be a terrible holiday.

'It's like something my gran would wear,' Chloe giggled. 'At least it's not a one-piece.'

I was going to have to give in to peer pressure and buy

some bikinis in the next couple of days, because my Mum-sanctioned swimsuits just wouldn't pass muster.

'Take your top off, Bea,' Ruby demanded. 'Then it won't look so bad.'

I lifted my head. 'No way.' I didn't care what Ruby and the others thought of me, I was not going topless and if that made me uptight, then yes, I was the most uptight girl in uptight town.

'Do it, Bea,' Ruby growled and it was her most scary 'don't mess with me' voice, but I'd much rather face Ruby's wrath than get my girls out.

'It's like Chloe said, my boobs aren't up to much,' I mumbled, though I didn't think they were really that bad. Still, I wouldn't have minded going up to a 34C. 'Anyway, you four are so hot that no one is paying any attention to what I'm wearing.'

I thought that was a pretty skilful way to get Ruby off my case. I put my head back down just in time to hear Emma whisper, 'My God, you were right, Bea's a total lez.'

'Shut up,' Ayesha snapped. 'Some of us are trying to relax.'

At least Ayesha had stuck up for me, or got everyone to shut up so we could sunbathe in peace. Actually I wasn't so much sunbathing as sulking and wishing that I'd stood up to my mum on the swimsuit issue.

There was blissful silence for at least ten minutes until I heard Emma and Ruby giggling. The giggling got louder and louder until I heard Emma say, 'It does looks exactly like orange peel. Imagine having cellulite at her age.'

'Who's got cellulite?' Chloe asked, sitting up with her bikini top clutched to her boobs. 'Is it that fat old woman over there?'

'Little bit closer to home,' Ruby drawled. 'At your three o'clock.'

It took Chloe a little while to get it because she really sucked at maths but out of the corner of my eye I saw her scan my bottom and legs. 'Riiiight. Yeah. See what you mean. Gross.'

All of sudden I didn't feel like a carefree girl on holiday soaking up the sun – I felt like a beached whale. I wanted to sit up but I was worried that my tummy would ripple and they'd all start teasing me about that too so I just lay there and pretended to doze.

'She's just so fleshy,' Emma was saying. 'And solid. Like she plays hockey all the time with her lesbian mates. She must be what? Like, a size 16.'

I was a size 10. Or a size 12 if I was buying jeans in TopShop, and Chloe was pretty much the same size as me. In five minutes, Ruby had managed to undo seventeen years of Mum trumpeting that it was more important to be the right size for you than the right size for other people.

'Don't be so mean,' Ruby cooed. 'Bea can't help it if she's kinda fat. You know when I lent her my purple American Apparel tube dress, she completely stretched it out.'

I couldn't stand it a second longer. 'If it's bothering you so much, Ruby, then I'll pay for the dress. In fact, your share of the taxi fare and what I've just forked out buying food should cover it,' I snapped. Like, really snapped in a way I'd never, ever done before. I was almost shaking from the ferocity of my snapping because when you don't normally do confrontation, it takes a lot out of you.

'Jeez, Bea, there's no need to be like that,' Ruby said sounding all reproachful, like I'd hurt *her* feelings. 'We're not going to have a great holiday if you're going to be so touchy about everything. I mean, seriously . . .' She trailed off into a meaningful silence, which I was meant to fill with an abject apology. It was going to be a long wait.

Ruby gave a hiss of what had to be sheer outrage and flopped down on her towel, and for the rest of the afternoon the silence was as golden as the sand that we lay on.

Chapter Eight

Ruby had got over herself by the time we got back to the apartment. She was all smiles as I managed to turn on the oven and heat up the frozen pizza we'd got at the supermarket on the way back.

'You're such a star, Bea,' she said, watching me approvingly as I chopped up tomatoes for a salad. 'I'm sorry about before. Not enough sleep and too much sun. You were right to call me on it.'

'I didn't call you on it,' I reminded her, but I wasn't snapping any more. There was something about Ruby's smile that made me more wary than when she was tight-lipped and squinty-eyed. At least I had some idea of where I was when Ruby was glaring.

'You gave me the silent treatment and I have to say, Bea, you give great glower. I thought you were going to smack me,' Ruby giggled.

'Hardly . . .' I glanced over at Ruby where she was curled up on one of the kitchen chairs – she was one of those girls who could never sit on a chair properly – and her smile seemed genuine, no bitchiness, no bite. 'Might have pulled your hair a little bit.'

Ruby got up from the chair and wandered over to the counter where I was chopping. 'Maybe we should have a little pizza buffet and everyone can grab something to eat while they're getting ready.'

There were already plans to visit a bar that Ruby had been to last year, which positively welcomed underaged drinkers with open arms, then on to a club where girls got in free. I was trying to kickstart the fizz of excitement I got on a Saturday night in London when we were going out, but mostly I just wanted to fall onto the sofa and sleep right through till next morning.

Instead, I hung out in the kitchen and waited and waited for the others to finish in the bathroom. I couldn't even change because the lounge and the kitchen were completely open plan and after today's comments about my alleged cellulite, no way was I stripping down to my undies in full view. Every time I thought they were finished, Ayesha would mutter something about the light in the bathroom being better for false eyelash application. It was getting on for ten o'clock and I still had grains of sand chafing in all sorts of unmentionable places.

Finally the four of them trooped out of the bathroom; the three hours they'd taken getting ready had really been worth it. I expected them to power walk across the lounge with a wind machine lifting their hair. They were wearing teeny, tiny shorts, except for Chloe who was wearing a teeny, tiny skirt, and teeny, tiny vests, the kind of vests my mother, and even the grandmas, wouldn't let me wear as they said I'd get a chill on my kidneys. They'd completed their micro-sized ensembles with teetering heels that were going to make the cobbled streets outside hard to negotiate, but the overall effect was pretty mesmerizing.

Like Girls Aloud's little sisters had formed their own group.

'Bathroom's all yours,' Emma said kindly. 'Don't take too long, we want to be out of here by eleven.'

It was currently 10.43 and I was totally rethinking my outfit, which had been a sweet little floral print dress. I'd have looked like I was on my way to a garden party.

I was already on my feet and racing to the bathroom because seventeen minutes, give or take, to shower, dry my hair, come up with a new outfit and try to apply liquid eyeliner wasn't very long. Especially as I lost a minute tripping over my open suitcase and had to pick myself up off the floor as the four of them tried to stifle their giggles.

'There's no need to break a leg,' Ruby said, helping me up. 'I'll wait for you if everyone else wants to go on ahead. You can even use my Clarins body cream.'

I managed to do everything, minus hot water, in twenty-three minutes. That included three possible outfit tries until I eventually decided on my own version of the teeny, tiny garment; a denim mini-skirt which came to mid-thigh and a vest which covered my kidneys. I couldn't do heels so I wore my flip-flops but they were Marc Jacobs flip-flops that James had bought me in New York. Somewhere between hastily slapping on tinted moisturizer and applying lip gloss, I even felt that tiny fizz of Saturday night excitement and when I opened the bathroom door, my hands were shaking, but in a good way.

'OK, I'm ready to go,' I announced, striking a little pose until I realized I was talking to an empty room. Chloe, Emma and Ayesha had already left, so I knocked on Ruby's closed door. 'Ruby! Sorry I took so long – I had a major wardrobe malfunction.'

There was no reply and when I pressed my ear to the door, I couldn't hear anything but a car horn tooting in the street below. Inwardly steeling myself, I opened the door but Ruby was nowhere to be seen.

I checked the other bedroom, I checked the balcony and, God help me, I even checked behind the sofa in case Ruby was playing a trick on me, but I was the only one left in the apartment. Then I dug out my phone for the inevitable text message explaining that they couldn't wait any longer because the lure of cheap jugs of sangria was too strong to ignore, but there was just a message from Mum (well, three messages actually) asking if I'd got there safely.

I texted her back, then sent a mass text to my four absent friends: WHAT HAPPENED TO YOU GUYS? WHERE SHALL I MEET YOU?

After ten minutes and no replies, that Saturday night fizz had been replaced by irritation. And annoyance and overwhelming feelings of being really, really pissed off because how hard was it to wait an extra ten minutes for me to finish getting ready? It wasn't hard at all, even less hard than texting me back to tell me where the hell they were.

I didn't want to spend the entire two weeks getting mad and then trying to pretend that I wasn't mad, but it took me a good five minutes and two glasses of water before I was calm enough to call Ayesha – there was no way I was speaking to Ruby when I felt this scratchy.

Ayesha's phone went straight to voicemail and I was just about to leave a frantic, fractious message, when I glanced up and saw the massive whiteboard that took up a huge expanse of one of the kitchen walls. I think the idea was to scribble down recipes and reminders, but Ruby had gone one better. Scrawled in her messy writing were the words: '*Hey Bea, it looked like you needed an early night. Don't wait up. See ya, wouldn't want to be ya!!!*'

There was no way to put a positive spin on this even though I liked to think I was always a glass–half–full kind of girl. They didn't want me coming out with them, they didn't care about my feelings and I was starting to wonder why the hell they'd asked me to come on holiday with them.

I contemplated phoning my mum for all of five seconds, but she'd be all 'I *knew* this would happen . . .' So, instead I curled up on the slippery white leather sofa and I cried.

Halfway through my crying jag, I got up to take my make–up off because I was getting streaks of mascara on the leather, but once that was done, I carried on crying because I was stuck here with *them* for another thirteen sleeps and they hated me because they thought I was boring and dull, and actually I *was* boring and dull and no matter how much I tried to dress it up in being half French and yearning for *la vie Parisienne*, I was the Queen of Dullsville. In fact, I was too dull to be the queen of anything. It all went round and round in my head until eventually I cried myself into the deep sleep of the hopeless.

The front door crashing back on its hinges woke me a

few hours later. I heard some muffled giggles and the clinking of bottles and counted more than four people shuffling across the living room to get to Ruby's room, but I forced myself go back to sleep.

But even sleep was not my friend and I was woken up again by the shrieking and laughing coming from Ruby's room and the sound of footsteps padding across the living room. I half opened my eyes to see two shadowy shapes advancing towards me and I steeled myself for something really bad to happen like a glass of water being thrown over me, but the two figures got as far as the sofa, then collapsed on it, with no consideration for the fact that it was already occupied.

I lay there for a second with a dead weight on my leg, not really sure how to react until it became obvious that my two nocturnal visitors were locked together in . . . well, what seemed like mortal combat.

Then I heard a grunt and a giggle. A really annoying giggle, which always made me grit my teeth on a Saturday night because once Emma got drunk she giggled and giggled at such a high pitch that it was like someone running their nails down a blackboard.

Then there were other sounds, sounds that will be etched into my memory if I live to be a hundred and twenty. Horrible slurping sounds that became *squelching* sounds and then the Emma beast started writhing and with each writhe, they banged against me and cut off the blood circulation to my lower limbs so I had no choice but to sit up. 'What *are* you doing?'

There was no answer, just a bitten-off groan. I simultaneously groped for the switch on the lamp next to me and kicked out my legs with every ounce of strength I possessed. Guess I was stronger than I thought because the two-headed beast slid onto the floor at the same time that my finger tripped the switch.

I think all three of us screamed as I finally saw Emma and the boy she was with. Or rather I saw his naked arse and more of Emma than I ever wanted to see. I clapped my hands over my eyes. 'What are you doing?' I shrieked again though it was the most rhetorical question in the history of rhetorical questions.

'What . . .? Can't you . . .! Get out!' Emma finally spluttered and even though she was the one who had a perfectly good bed in the other room, I hurled myself off the couch and ran to the bathroom so I could splash cold water on my face, and scrub my brain with bleach and wipe the memories of the last ten minutes out of my head. Because, urgh! *Squelching* sounds. If Mum had wanted to keep me on the straight and narrow, all she'd had to do was play me a recording of squelching sounds and I'd have happily signed a legally binding document promising that I was never going to have sex ever, ever. Seriously.

But that wasn't on my mind right then as I burst through the bathroom door to see Ayesha perched on the side of the tub smoking a cigarette as another boy knelt over the toilet and regurgitated the contents of his stomach. Ayesha gave me a glassy-eyed stare as I came to a sudden halt in the doorway.

'Oh, hi, Bea,' she said casually. 'Won't be long.'

The puking boy raised his head momentarily so I got a good look at the long line of drool hanging out of his mouth, before he moaned and started retching again.

'My God, this is totally, bloody unbelievable,' I hissed. I didn't know what to do with my hands, which were flailing wildly as if they were acting completely independently of my brain.

Ayesha waved the hand that wasn't clutching a cigarette. 'Yeah, sorry about ducking out like that,' she murmured, not sounding sorry at all. 'It was Ruby's idea and I don't want to get into a fight with her about it. You didn't miss much. This is Kieran, by the way.'

'It's Joshua,' the boy said, lifting his head again.

'Whatever,' Ayesha said, shrugging.

'Emma's just been shagging some guy on the sofa,' I ground out. 'The sofa I was sleeping on.'

'Yeah, but you were asleep and she couldn't do that in her bed when we were in the room,' Ayesha pointed out in a slurred voice as she stared at me. 'You look weird.'

'No, this is what I look like when I'm furious.' I really wanted to unleash that fury but I didn't even know where to start. 'This is no way to treat people . . . to treat me . . .'

'For God's sake, Bea, I've got a really nice buzz going on. Why are you doing your best to ruin it?' Ayesha asked plaintively. 'Just kick Emma off the sofa and go back to sleep. I can't deal with this. I'm looking after Kieran.'

'It's Joshua,' the boy and I said in unison before he threw

up again. I'd never seen anyone be that sick. The smell in the bathroom was really pungent and I knew if I stayed there much longer, I'd be pushing Joshua to one side so I could throw up too.

'We're talking about this in the morning, *later* in the morning,' I warned Ayesha, but she just raised her eyebrows and pursed her lips. It reminded me of last summer when I'd had all those one-sided conversations with her as I begged her to let me know what I'd done wrong. She'd given me exactly the same face then.

I slumped back on the sofa (after I'd given it a vigorous wipe down with a wet cloth) and tried to get to sleep. I was still trying an hour later when the four boys finally trooped out. I pretended I was deep in dreamland as I heard one of the boys ask who was on the sofa and Ruby drawl, 'An albatross around our necks, that's who.'

Chapter Nine

Sleep definitely wasn't an option after that. I tossed and turned and seethed and simmered until the sun was high in the sky and it was eight o'clock. There were no signs of life from the two bedrooms as I tiptoed into the bathroom and, after pouring an entire bottle of bleach down the loo, I very quietly showered and dressed. Part of me longed to make a racket and wake the four of them up. But my sensible side won, because there was no point in having a confrontation until I'd worked out what I wanted to say and got my head straight. Even though they really deserved to be woken up loudly and rudely.

I quietly opened the front door and sped down the stairs, until I was stepping out into a glorious, bright white day. It lifted my spirits a little as I scrabbled for my sunglasses and set off down the hill to find somewhere to have breakfast. I found myself back at the square we'd come to yesterday and even though Ruby was snoring her head off, I got a little kick out of defying her edict from the day before and settling myself at a table outside.

The town was sleepily coming to life. There were a few holidaymakers ambling slowly through the square on their way to the beach, but mostly it was people walking briskly to work; the waiters still laying table settings, a laundry van unloading piles of snowy-white linens and the owner of the café coming out to water the banks of scarlet geraniums that sectioned off her tables.

She took a liking to me, or else she totally appreciated my pathetic attempt to speak Spanish, which consisted of '*Hola!*', '*Si*' and '*Bien*'. After I'd had toast and apricot jam and a glass of orange juice, she personally delivered a plate of *churros*, a stack of still warm finger biscuits with a cup of melted chocolate to dip them in. Then she pinched my cheek and told me they were on the house.

It might have been the sugar high or simply getting away from the toxic atmosphere in the apartment, but I let my resentment melt away like the sticky chocolate on my fingers. As I walked around the Old Town, then ended up at the harbour watching fishermen doing stuff with slippery, silvery mounds of fish, I decided that I would try to talk to the girls in a really non-judgey way even though I was angry and hurt, more hurt than I'd felt last year when Ayesha had dumped me.

Although every fibre of my being wanted to stay exactly where it was, I got up from the crumbling wall I'd been perching on and hoped I could find my way through the bendy streets back to the apartment.

My knees were shaking slightly when I came to our front door but that was because I'd just climbed three flights of stairs and nothing to do with the fact that I could hear voices, which meant that they'd woken up and hadn't left for the beach yet.

I'd bought some fat, juicy peaches on the way back as a sweetener to accompany the speech that I'd been rehearsing in my head and I could feel sweat from my hand soaking the paper bag.

'You're not a pushover,' I muttered to myself, as I fished for the key in the pocket of my jeans. 'Firm but fair.' Then I took a deep breath and opened the door.

Chloe, Ayesha and Emma were huddled on the sofa each clutching big two-litre bottles of water while they watched Spanish cartoons. They all looked up as I walked through the door though Emma flushed before she turned her head away.

'You all right, Bea?' Ayesha asked with a smile that slid off her face in an instant as Ruby appeared in her bedroom doorway. 'I was wondering where you'd got to.'

'I went out for breakfast, then I walked around town until I found the harbour.' The words sounded funny coming out of my mouth as if I was reciting lines that I was going to get graded on. Ruby sauntered into the living room, wearing a bikini like she was as comfortable in that tiny red two-piece as she was in a pair of jeans, and ordered Emma to scooch over with a terse flick of her hand.

Which left me standing there, clutching my bag of peaches, and this was a good a time as any . . .

'About last night . . .' I began and I was sure I saw Chloe and Ruby share an eye roll. 'Not just last night, but yesterday as well, my feelings were really hurt.'

No one said anything, but they were looking interested. Or at least they were listening so I soldiered on.

'Maybe you've decided that you don't want to be friends,' I continued and in my head I'd planned to shrug casually when I said that, but I didn't feel as if I could pull it off when Ayesha was giving me an encouraging smile like she did still want to be my friend. 'I don't know why and I don't know what I've done, but if that's the way you feel then there's not much I can do about it. But not letting me have a bed to sleep in and ducking out on me last night was really not cool. And I'm sorry, Emma, but doing what you did on the sofa *while I was trying to sleep* was completely disrespectful and I think you should apologize.'

Getting the speech out had been scary but standing there waiting for Emma to say she was sorry was even scarier. I forced myself to stare at the top of her head until she had no choice but to meet my gaze.

'Well, like, I don't see why stuff I do when I'm drunk is my fault,' she blustered. 'You were asleep and we were being quiet.'

'You were humping my leg at one point,' I snapped and Chloe chortled in delight until she was silenced with one withering glare from Ruby. Which was good, because it meant that she wanted to hear what I had to say.

'Look, you were out of order, Emma,' I said quietly. 'And it was mean to sneak out while I was in the bathroom and not answer your phones and I just think that if we're going to—'

'Oh for fuck's sake, just shut up!' Ruby snarled, springing up from the couch so she could get so up in my face that I was able to count each one of her open pores. 'Are you too stupid to get it?'

'Get what?' I asked falteringly, taking a couple of steps

back and realizing that I hadn't really been scared before, because now that Ruby was following me and jabbing her finger into my chest, I was absolutely terrified.

'We're not your friends,' Ruby spat. 'We've never been your friends. You were just a parentally approved do-gooder that we had to suck up to so we could go on holiday on our own.' She spread her hands wide. 'Well, mission accomplished. We're on holiday without our parents and your services are no longer required!'

'But . . . but . . . you said . . . you spent weeks and weeks . . . I can't believe . . .' I was incapable of getting a whole sentence out because my brain was more interested in replaying the last couple of months. All those times when something seemed off and instead of going with my gut instinct, I'd given Ruby, and the others, the benefit of the doubt – God, I really needed to stop doing that. 'Well, I'm sorry that you're stuck with me for a fortnight. I guess that was the one part of your masterplan that didn't work out.'

Ruby gave a casual shrug like I'd wanted to ten minutes before. 'Oh, I don't know,' she drawled. 'Ayesha says you should always take someone you really hate on holiday, so everyone else can bond over how much they hate her. I think everything's worked out just fine.'

It was a relief to whip my head around in the direction of the sofa and not have to look at Ruby's smug, twisted, ugly little face a second longer. 'Is that true?' I demanded. 'Ayesha!'

Ayesha was resolutely staring at her feet. 'That's not what I said. Well, not exactly anyway. You have to admit that you don't really fit in with us. Like, we're friends and you're just not . . . you're like kind of a sub-friend. 'Cause you're not into the same stuff as us and you don't dress like us and you don't want to do—'

'You're the hanger-on,' Chloe supplied helpfully and she didn't seem to have any problem with looking me in the eye as she said it.

'No, not the hanger-on,' Ruby insisted. 'You're the whipping girl. And yeah, we're stuck with you for twelve days but, believe me, it's going to be much worse for you than it is for us.' She eyed me up and down as I stood there with my hands pressing down tight on my chest as I panted because all of a sudden I felt like I couldn't breathe. Maybe it was the effort of holding back the sobs, which really wanted to burst forth, but it was a point of principle that I wasn't going to start blubbering. 'What's the matter, Bea? Wishing you could go home and cry to your mummy who's also your bestest friend in the whole world?' She strode over to the front door and opened it. 'Hey, be my guest.'

But I wasn't even looking at Ruby but at Ayesha, because for the sake of years and years of being best friends, she'd stick up for me, tell Ruby to get off my case and to get out of the big bedroom because we were going to share it – but she didn't. She just sat there staring at her perfectly polished pink toenails.

'Are we going to the beach now?' Emma wanted to know, standing up and stretching. 'I don't want to waste the day stuck in here.'

'I'll just get my bag,' Ruby said, shutting the front door

and brushing past me like I was made of nothing.

'You can't treat people like this!' I heard myself say softly. 'It's not right.'

I didn't think anyone had heard me as they were hastily assembling their beach supplies, because either they couldn't wait to catch some rays or they couldn't stand to be in the same room with me any longer. But then Ruby stopped hurling tanning lotion and magazines into her bag and fixed me with a look that was almost sympathetic. 'We treat you like this because you let us,' she said slowly, hands on her skinny hips. 'Do you want to know what your problem is?'

People always ask you that when the answer's going to make you die inside just a little bit. Also, they never wait for you to say no, they just plough straight on.

'You've got no fucking backbone,' Ruby informed me. 'You just creep around with an inane smile on your face, because you think if you're super-super nice and never make a fuss, then people will like you. Well, they don't and you need to get a life before it's too late. God, even your mum knew how to have some fun when she was your age, though what kind of retard doesn't know how to put on a condom?'

'You leave my mum out of this,' I growled. 'You can say what you like about me, you already have, but don't start on her.'

'See? Wet!' Ruby summed up, putting her bag over her shoulder and snapping her fingers at the others. 'Just stay out of our way and we'll stay out of yours. Deal?'

I longed to snap out a jaunty 'whatever', but my throat was closing up and I knew tears weren't far off so I simply nodded and watched them line up by the front door. Emma still wasn't looking at me, Chloe was completely unconcerned as she checked her iPod and Ayesha waited until Ruby had turned to open the door, before she mouthed 'sorry' at me with a helpless, hand-wringing gesture thrown in for good measure.

Now it was my turn to stare at my feet as they trooped out of the door and, just before it slammed shut behind them, I heard Ayesha say, 'Jesus, Ruby, you were really harsh.'

'Yeah, well, she pisses me off and she des—'

The list of my other character flaws was cut short by the hollow thud of the door and I stood in the middle of the living room, the sun streaming in through the big patio windows, even though it felt as if there should be a dark grey storm raging outside, and waited for my body to fall to the floor so I could weep it all out.

Nothing happened. I shut my eyes extra tight so I could squeeze out the first few tears but my tear ducts were bone dry. I felt really odd; I had this urge to kick and punch and do something with my arms and legs because they didn't want to stay still and my mouth really wanted to open wide and unleash a God-holy racket.

Then I realized I wasn't going to cry because I wasn't sad; I was absolutely, fist-clenching, foot-stamping, limb-flailing mad. And when you were this mad, your only option was to get even.

I stormed into Ruby's bedroom and gathered up the mound of clothes that was heaped on the bed. She'd helpfully left the window open, which made it easier to fling out all her precious American Apparel, stretchy-tight clothes and the little black dress that she never tired of telling me was a genuine designer original even though I'd never heard of the name of the designer. Her Jimmy Choo sandals, which I knew she'd borrowed from her mum without asking, followed them down to land in the street below – but it wasn't enough.

I threw what I could find of Chloe and Emma's clothes out of their window too and I was going to start on Ayesha's because mouthing 'sorry' when Ruby couldn't see her didn't make things all right – but then I spied the neat row of bottles lined up on the floor. There was the duty-free vodka they'd bought at the airport, a bottle of Barcardi and several six-packs of beer from the little supermarket. It took three trips to move it all to the kitchen, then I methodically opened each bottle and tipped it down the sink, flushed all their cigarettes down the loo – and it still wasn't enough.

The black rage was ebbing slightly now. I was still furious but the fog clouding my mind was lifting slowly and I could begin to think. Trashing their clothes and getting rid of their booze and fags would only mildly inconvenience them, but I needed to wreak vengeance where it would really matter. Make them feel just as alone as I did right now; like they didn't have a friend in the world and wrong inside their own skins.

I jiggled from one foot to the other while I tried to

come up with something completely evil. After ten minutes, when Ruby would have devised and discarded at least a dozen completely evil somethings, I was still coming up empty so I started packing my case because there was no other option – and I really didn't want to be in the apartment when the four of them turned up and realized that most of their clothes were lying in the road and were currently being picked over by two women who were exclaiming excitedly in Spanish.

I debated whether to phone home. I knew Mum and James and the grandmas would be nothing but concerned and ready to buy the most expensive ticket EasyJet had to offer to get me on the next plane home. But sooner or later, probably sooner, Mum'd make herself a solemn vow that she'd never let me leave the house again. Not even to go to university, or else she'd let me study in London and see me to and from my lectures every day. But that was my uncertain future and right now in my even less uncertain present, I knew that the moment I heard Mum say, 'Oh, Bea,' in that throaty way she always did when I was upset, I'd lose it. I decided to call her on my way to the airport.

Once I was done with the packing, I wandered into the kitchen to grab a bottle of water for the journey and see if my fortnight's supply of peanut butter KitKats were still hidden away at the back of the fridge. They were – I'd stashed them under a bag of apples – but as I retrieved them, I caught sight of the whiteboard. Last night's message was still there, and this morning, it took on an even more hateful tone.

I could feel myself getting angry all over again. At this rate, I'd go home with dirty laundry, faint sunburn and the beginnings of a gargantuan peptic ulcer.

The exclamation marks, in particular, seemed to mock me and I dropped the KitKats on the table so I could skid across the floor and scrub the whiteboard clean with Ayesha's bikini bottoms, which were drying over the back of a chair.

'*See ya, wouldn't want to be ya!!!*' was quickly obliterated, like it had never existed, but those seven words represented months of premeditated hate stalking. They'd spent weeks getting me on side, pretending to like me, and all the time they'd been looking forward to the day when they could shoot me down in cold blood. And I'd been too bloody stupid to realize it. Instead I'd followed them around like a little dog; running their errands, listening to their sordid little secrets . . .

Sordid little secrets.

I groped for the marker pen, really calm now, as I knew exactly what to do to destroy them.

Though I say it myself, it was an absolute masterpiece. I was glad I'd paid attention in Maths when we did flowcharts and equations becuase it helped me to sketch out a clear, concise and annotated diagram of all the wrongs that Chloe, Emma, Ayesha and Ruby had done each other. Who'd shagged whose boyfriend or got off with them or had text sex with them. Then in a different-coloured marker I detailed who'd said what about whom, with particular reference to poor outfit choices and how Chloe, Emma and Ayesha had all said on separate occasions that Ruby was a skinny fat person with hooded eyes.

That was the thing about being dull and boring and having no backbone. People assumed it was safe to spill out all sorts of bitchery they should have kept to themselves, because they never imagined you'd have the stones to tell anyone. But it was all there. The absolute, incontrovertible truth spelt out in marker pens with colour coding, quote marks and an easy-to-follow timeline.

My work here is done, I thought, as I put down the marker pens. But there was a bare patch of whiteboard that was taunting me with its gleaming white splendour. It seemed a pity to leave it untouched.

I picked up the marker pen again and wrote:

Dear Ruby
If you knew just how zitty your arse was, you'd probably want to rethink the whole thong bikini thing.
No love
Bea

It was a cheap shot, the lowest of blows, but God, it felt so *good*.

After that, everything felt a little anticlimactic. Like, for once in my life I'd stuck my neck out, stood up for myself, got medieval on people's arses but there'd been no witnesses. It was typical really.

But my blood was still up, which meant I didn't have any thoughts about scrubbing the whiteboard clean or sticking around to see if I could sort things out with Ruby, her two evil cohorts and my ex-best friend. There was no point. Stuff was un-sort-out-able. So I hauled my case down the stairs and set off for the station, tutting loudly at anyone who dared to get in my way when it was obvious that I had a heavy case and a short fuse. I was being quite the badass, if I do say so myself.

So then I was at the station looking at the train indicator board and you can't get that riled up and expect that scribbling stuff on a whiteboard and chucking a few bikinis out of a window is going to satisfy the dangerous beast that had been slumbering in the pit of your stomach. That beast, it wanted adventure and excitement and it really, really, really wanted to go to Paris.

As I marched purposefully to the ticket office, I reasoned that going to Paris for, say, a week, wasn't such a bad idea. Or rather there was no way my mum could find out as long as I phoned her every day and made sure there were no onion sellers in earshot. Then I could retrace my steps back to Malaga, tell her that my fellow travelling companions were the spawn of several she-devils and I needed a new ticket home. What could possibly go wrong?

What went wrong was that when I got to the first available window, I got the woman who couldn't speak English. In fact, I wasn't even sure if she was speaking Spanish; it could have been Dolphin for all the sense she made.

'I want to go to Paris,' I said very slowly and very loudly, only to be met with a look of blank incomprehension.

'*Que?*'

'Paris.'

'*No entiendo.*'

I looked around helplessly, but apart from a foot-tapping, impatient line of people queuing for tickets, a handy translator didn't materialize.

'Paris in France,' I clarified. 'You know, France. *Français?*'

I let out a sigh of relief, as she nodded vigorously and began to press buttons on her little computer. '*Si! France! Paris!*'

'I need a week-long return,' I told her, even though she didn't understand, so I just handed over a huge amount of euros and, clasping my tickets in one sticky hand, I headed towards the trains.

I didn't even bother trying to ask what platform I should go to, I just found a man wearing a spiffy little uniform with epaulettes and a peaked cap and waved my tickets in his face until he pointed me in the right direction.

As I hurried towards Platform Five, I saw a man blowing a whistle and I ran like my life depended on it; only getting on to the train because a middle-aged man in a suit grabbed my hand and hauled me through the door just as the train began to move. With flushed cheeks and my hair sticking damply to my forehead, I dragged my cumbersome suitcase down the train until I found an empty table and collapsed on the seat.

I shoved my passport and ticket in the pocket of my jeans so I'd know where they were, gulped down half a bottle of lukewarm water because all that sweating and suitcase dragging had made me seriously dehydrated and then . . . and then . . . and then . . . I was on a train going to Paris, France. I was finally on my way to the land of my forefathers and my actual father. I was hours away from my destiny. And even the row I'd had with Ruby hadn't made my hands shake quite this hard.

The train was climbing uphill and the lurching made my stomach rollock and roil because really, this was the most stupid idea I'd ever had. I didn't even know my father's name or where he lived and, according to Monsieur Bradley, my French wasn't good enough to ask directions to the nearest loos, so how was I going to cope with *cherchez mon père?*

I was coming to my senses about an hour too late. I had no choice but to get off the train when we pulled in at the next station. Then no one would be any the wiser and I'd have learnt an important lesson about how dumb it was to act on impulse and that I was never to lose my temper again because it led to VERY BAD THINGS.

Except the train didn't seem to be slowing down and soon the lurching became a comforting, rhythmic noise that made me yawn because it had been *days* since I'd slept properly. I looked out of the window but all I could see were trees; pretty, green trees that made me think we were in the countryside and not about to pull in at a station any time soon so closing my eyes for a bit couldn't do any harm.

Chapter Ten

Oh God, I was asleep for *hours*, until I was shaken awake by an elderly woman who gesticulated and jabbered wildly to let me know that the train had stopped and wasn't planning on going anywhere else.

I squinted at the time on my phone. It was half past eight, which meant I'd been on the train and snoring my head off for nine hours. I felt really disorientated as I dragged my suitcase through the door and followed it on to the platform, which didn't look very French.

There were signs but they didn't seem to be in French either. In fact, they looked like they were still in Spanish and the station didn't have a French vibe. I wasn't expecting to see people in berets or maybe a man on a bicycle wearing a stripey, boatneck top but I'd seen pictures of the Gare du Nord when I was poring over the Eurostar website and this wasn't it. Maybe I was in a part of France that was really near Spain and they spoke some weird French/Spanish combo, I thought as I wheeled my case out of the station and looked around. There was a roundabout and lots of shops so at least I wasn't in a one-horse town. I stood there getting buffeted by the crowds coming in and out of the station until I saw a sign to '*La playa*' and I knew I definitely wasn't in Paris, because Paris didn't have a beach. I was ninety-nine per cent certain about that.

It felt like I walked for miles, my case becoming heavier and more unwieldy with each step. There was a complete lack of Tourist Information offices, but finally I came to a huge square and saw a branch of Zara. It was a bit like bumping into an old friend, but staring at clothes shops wasn't going to help me when I was totally lost and had no plan. No idea where I was going to spend the night either and I might just as well have had a sign pinned to my back, which said: '*I'm a stupid English girl who's completely and utterly lost. Why don't you mug me for my passport and euros?*'

I'd been trying to hold it together and tamp down all the scary feelings that I didn't want to feel but the panic was rising up in me so I thought I was either going to hurl or curl up on the cobble stones in the foetal position. I took a moment to take stock of the truly horrific dilemma I was in and decided to find the nearest café, have something to eat, then call my mum. Her wrath would be considerable and I wouldn't be allowed out on my own until I was thirty, but she'd know what to do. She *always* knew what to do.

It took ages to find a café that didn't look too scary to a girl who was miles from home and didn't speak the lingo. I came to a smaller, prettier garden square that was lined with cafés and chose one that still had an empty table outside. I'd never been more pleased to sit down and let go of my suitcase, which had given me a lovely welt in the palm of my hand, I noticed, as I grabbed the menu. It was a miracle but each dish came with a French and English translation and with the preference for tapas and fiddly bits of fish, I knew for certain that I was still in Spain. If I'd had the energy I'd have caught the first train back to Malaga and murdered the woman in the ticket office and the man who'd directed me to the 'right' platform.

A waitress came and rolled her eyes as I pointed at the words for a ham and tomato omelette and a Diet Coke. Once I had an icy-cold Diet Coke clutched in my head it fortified me to dig out my phone. There were two voicemail messages and two text messages, which I dealt with first. Both Emma and Chloe felt the need to inform me, minus any vowels that I was a FCKNG BTCH and a SKNKY WHR, respectively. I guessed that they'd made it back to the apartment and seen my masterful use of the whiteboard. I almost deleted the voicemail messages because I knew they weren't going to be anything I really wanted to hear . . .

Ayesha's message was a little ashamed, a lot reproachful. 'I feel terrible about what happened and I get that you're mad at me,' she said in a quiet voice like she'd had to lock herself in the bathroom so the others wouldn't hear her admitting that she might be somewhat to blame. 'But what you wrote on the wall . . . it was just mean, Bea. I told you that stuff in confidence.'

I waited for the guilt to kick in but either I couldn't feel it over the nagging pangs of hunger and the panic that was waxing and waning at regular intervals, or else I was devoid of guilt. Guilt-free, because all four of them had really, really deserved it. Ruby didn't think so though. She left me a message that was full of bile. 'You are so fucking dead,' she

111

shrieked. 'I hope your plane crashes on the way home because it will save me the bother. Seriously. I am going to make your life a living fucking hell come September if I ever have to see your plug fucking ugly face again. You vile, dykey virgin!'

Knowing I'd managed to incite homicidal rage in Ruby didn't make me feel vindicated. It made me fear for my life when I got home. Which led nicely to the part where I called my mum, but picking up my phone and pressing 1 on my speed dial wasn't something that my brain wanted my hands to do. Instead I nibbled at the omelette, which had just been placed in front of me, even though my appetite had completely disappeared. Death threats kind of had that effect.

The bruised, purplish dusky sky was darkening further and even though it was still too hot for even a slight breeze to ruffle the leaves on the trees, I couldn't help but shiver.

'Excuse me, is this chair spare?'

I gave a nervous start when my pity party was interrupted by a tanned, blonde girl standing over me. 'Huh?'

'Can I take this chair?' she repeated in a lazy American drawl, one hand already resting on the chair opposite me.

I nodded. 'Yeah, sure.'

She gave me a toothy white smile and dragged the chair over to the next table where five other people were sitting down; two more girls and three boys who were unloading maps and guidebooks from rucksacks. I glanced at them surreptitiously as I picked at my omelette, trying to work out which girl went with which boy and listening to them bicker goodnaturedly about which tapas they should order. One of the boys was poring over a map and when the girl who'd taken the chair caught my eye and smiled, I realized that I had no choice. They had maps and they spoke English. Or American.

I scraped my chair nearer to their table and cleared my throat. 'Um, I'm very sorry to bother you, and this is going to sound weird, but where am I?'

I had the undivided attention of six strangers all looking at me with the exact same blend of amusement and incredulity.

'For real?'

'For real,' I echoed glumly. 'I'm pretty sure I'm in Spain but which bit?'

The boy who had the map-reading privileges pointed at a speck that was within spitting distance of the French border, because I was *that* close. 'Bilbao. See?' He beckoned me closer and I stood up and leaned over to see where his long finger marked the spot.

Bilbao. Which didn't sound remotely like Paris even if someone rolled their R's a lot. A hell of a lot.

There was only one thing to say: 'Oh, *crap*!' They were definitely looking more amused than incredulous now. I could feel my cheeks burning like they'd been coated in petrol and set alight. I made signs that I was going to shuffle back to my table. 'Well, thanks anyway.'

It took every last ounce of willpower I had to sit down and pick up my fork again. But on the inside I was crying.

'Are you all right?' The blonde girl had come over again

and was looking down at me with concern. She probably thought I was on day release from a psychiatric institution and needed help finding my way back. 'Come and join us instead of sitting here all on your own.'

I bit my lip as I glanced over at the other table. The map boy smiled at me and one of the other girls – a pretty, mixed-race Glamazon, who looked as if she should be playing volleyball on the beach rather than eating grilled sardines scooched her chair over. 'There's plenty of room,' she said.

The blonde girl was already picking up my plate and my Diet Coke, so I didn't have a choice really. 'I'm Erin,' she said over her shoulder. 'This is Bridge – Bridget,' she added pointing at the Glamazon. 'Let me introduce you properly to everyone.'

Michael and Aaron were two blond brothers who looked like they played quarterback and ran track and other wholesome American activities I knew about from watching a lot of teen movies. They didn't make strapping, corn-fed boys like that in England or if they did, they didn't live in Crouch End. Toph ('rhymes with loaf, short for Christopher') didn't seem quite so daunting or like he played American football. He folded away his map and gravely shook my hand after I'd plonked my chair down next to his. Even sitting down, I could tell he was long-limbed with messy hair that was halfway between brown and blond, neither long nor short, which kept getting pushed back with an impatient hand. They all made welcoming noises except the other girl, Jess, who was

114

beautiful. Model beautiful with shiny, sleek caramel-coloured hair and features so perfectly moulded that it was hard to believe she hadn't been sculpted. Actually she'd have been more beautiful if she hadn't been looking so underwhelmed by my presence but after two days of Ruby's entire repertoire of glares, grimaces and scowls, I could deal.

I finished eating my omelette as Erin told me that they were all at university (though she called it college) in Phoenix, Arizona, and they were having one last blast backpacking round Europe before they went back to the States and started their final year. 'Then we work for minimum wage at the local drive-thru,' Toph finished for her with a smirky little grin. 'So, what's your story?'

'Well, I'm seventeen,' I said, and seventeen had never sounded so young and so far away from eighteen when I'd be a proper grown-up or at least could get married and vote and be able to buy fags and booze with a valid ID. 'And I'm not usually so scatty. But, see, I was in Malaga and I needed to get to Paris and I fell asleep on the train . . .'

It all spilt out – partly because I hadn't spoken to anyone properly since Mum had waved me off at the airport and partly because I needed to get it off my chest. But as I concluded my sorry little tale with the story of the infamous whiteboard, I couldn't help but cringe back on my chair because it hadn't been my finest moment. But unbelievably Jess snorted and gave me a grudging look of admiration, as I ploughed on. 'So I couldn't stay, and I thought I'd go to Paris to see my dad but I couldn't understand the woman in the ticket office and then I fell asleep on the train and when I woke up, I was here . . .'

'Maybe you were meant to change at Bilbao and not leave the station?' Aaron suggested.

'Well, I did think it was odd that no one woke me up to look at my passport,' I said slowly. 'But my ticket was in Spanish and—'

'Let me look at it,' Toph said. 'I speak Spanish.'

The ticket was dog-eared and crumpled from doing serious time in the back pocket of my jeans. Toph smoothed it out and studied it carefully. 'Yeah, you were actually meant to change at Madrid.'

I didn't even remember being in Madrid. 'Oh, bloody hell!'

Erin grinned. 'I didn't think English people actually said that.' She patted my hand. 'Look, Toph can take you to the station tomorrow and get it sorted out, though actually we're heading off to France ourselves in a couple of days if you wanted to wait till then.'

I blinked slowly. Toph was reading the back of my train ticket, Aaron and Michael were eating meatballs, Bridget was smiling encouragingly, only Jess didn't look like she was down with that. 'We're not going straight to Paris,' she said quickly. 'We were going to go to Marseilles first.'

'Oh, that's OK. Like, I could probably get to Paris under my own steam if I don't fall asleep again, or maybe I should just go back to London . . .'

'Well, I can help you with the ticket tomorrow,' Toph said and for some reason my heart sank. 'But if you don't mind a few detours, you should probably stick with us. My parents would have freaked out if I'd decided to cross even the state line on my own when I was seventeen.'

He smiled at me and my sinking heart perked up no end. I think it might even have done a little back-flip, because when Toph smiled, these deep grooves appeared at the side of his mouth and he looked like some Sixties popstar in a candid backstage photo. He also looked way out of my reach, but that had never stopped me crushing on a boy before. Actually, it was one of my prerequisites for crushing on a boy – less chance of speaking to him, going out with him, having my heart broken and incurring the wrath of Mum to boot.

Talking of my maternal signifier . . . 'I should probably go home,' I mumbled.

'But isn't your dad waiting for you in Paris?' Erin asked.

The question made me suddenly want to cry because I'd always thought about my father as this abstract concept. French. That was the only fact that I'd ever been able to latch on to but now this shadowy figure was emerging; this man a little bit older than my mum, with dark-brown hair like mine and a pointy chin that was like mine too and a big craggy nose, because in my head all French men over the age of thirty had big, craggy noses. And he'd be wearing jeans and a black jumper and standing at the door of an apartment that was on the fifth floor of a narrow apartment block in Montmartre with green shutters and window boxes, and when he saw me for the first time, he'd say, '*Cherie*, what took you so long?' Except he'd say it in

French and I'd totally understand without asking him to repeat it really slowly. He was just across the border, a train journey away.

'Yeah, I really, *really* want to go to Paris.' I couldn't keep the longing out of my voice.

'Well, that settles it then,' Aaron said, like it had been decided and everyone was OK with it, which they weren't because Jess was screwing up her face like she was chewing on tinfoil.

'But what if we want to go clubbing?' she demanded. 'Or go to a bar? Or other things that Bea can't do because she's underage.'

'Oh yeah, because we've been clubbing every night. Not!' Erin snapped. 'And anyway, she can go to clubs and bars if she's accompanied by an adult. We're adults!'

I was starting to feel as if I'd outstayed my welcome and I could see Jess's point. Sort of. They were meant to be having one last blow-out before they became proper grown-ups and having a seventeen-year-old tagging along was going to seriously cramp their style. Or as she'd probably say, 'I was one hell of a buzz kill.'

'I was only saying . . .'

'You always do this, Jess. You bitch about everthing.'

'I do not!'

'This morning you moaned because your eggs were too runny and the sand on the beach was more scratchy than the sand in Miami and . . .'

Toph nudged me with his arm, his tanned skin dusted with golden baby hairs brushing against my pink, freckled flesh. 'After five weeks, we're ready to kill each other,' he explained with another of those grins, which automatically made me want to grin back. 'We're bored stupid with each other, got nothing left to say that doesn't involve timetables and menus. Really you'd be doing us a favour.'

'I would?' I asked doubtfully, because I'd only just run away from four people who were equally high maintenance and they'd pretty much drained the life force out of me.

Jess looked at me contemplatively, like maybe there was more to me than a freckly-faced seventeen-year-old who was looking a little ragged around the edges. Then she suddenly smiled so she was beautiful again. Like, Angelina Jolie beautiful. 'What the hell,' she drawled. 'I'm game, if you are, kid.'

She'd almost had me until she used the K-word. 'I'll sleep on it,' I decided.

It was another hour before we headed back to their hostel. To be honest, I was a little anxious that they might drag me into a dark alley and either steal all my money or hand me over to their boss who trafficked young girls and I'd end up in a brothel, never to be heard of again.

Thankfully that never happened. Aaron carried my suitcase for me while Bridge and Erin shared their entire dating histories, which included both Aaron and Michael at different times.

'But not Toph?' I asked casually, as we walked over a bridge, a river gurgling below us.

Erin swiftly shook her head. 'He was dating his high school sweetheart all the way through college, then they suddenly split up just before mid-terms.' She angled a furtive glance at Toph, who was ambling almost within earshot, and lowered her voice. 'I think that's the only reason he came on the trip. Better than spending the summer moping in Austin.'

'Austin? Where's that?'

'The part of Texas that's not all cowboys and oil barons,' Bridge supplied. 'Their town motto is "Keep Austin weird". We went back home with Toph for Spring Break and I was in hipster boy and thrift shop heaven, plus I had the best *huevos rancheros* in the world.'

I didn't know what hue-huve-the ranchy thing was, but just 'hmmm'ed like I did. 'And what about Jess, is she seeing anyone?' I asked, though she was too pretty to be anyone's rebound romance.

'Jess has the worst luck with guys,' Erin exclaimed. 'It's like she gives off some weird chemical that only attracts complete losers. Her last boyfriend stole her car, sold it and disappeared off to Vegas.'

That made no sense to me. If girls like Jess couldn't find decent boyfriends, then what chance did the rest of us have?

'So, Bea, have you left some broken-hearted boy back in London?' Erin wanted to know.

'As if!' I snorted. 'Well, there's Harry; he's my pretend boyfriend.'

That took up the rest of the short walk to their hostel;

my non-romance with Harry and how having a pretend boyfriend had saved me from the all the boys that Ruby would have tried to make me snog, so she could spread rumours around school about what a slut I was.

'She really sounds like a total douchebag,' Erin mused, as she held open the door of a pretty redbrick building right on the riverfront.

'She really is,' I agreed enthusiastically. 'And I don't know why she acts like that.'

'It's high school,' Jess interrupted, as she caught up with us. 'It's the one time in your life, when you're going to meet a whole bunch of people who are mean for no other reason than they can be. God, I ate my lunch in the girls' bathroom every day for two semesters when I was in Tenth Grade.' She shuddered at the memory. 'Like, one morning I woke up with breasts and figured out how to do a hair flip and the entire cheerleading squad were out for my blood.'

Like I said, I'd seen a lot of American teen movies and every time I thanked God that I'd been born British and never had to be a Mathlete or worry about finding a date for the Prom, so I could empathize, or at least try to. 'But you got your revenge by being voted Homecoming Queen or something, right?'

Jess's mouth dropped open like I couldn't be more wrong but then she put an arm round my shoulders. 'You are freaking adorable,' she announced loudly. 'In fact, I'm thinking of adopting you. Now let's see if we can find you somewhere to sleep.'

Jess was right about mastering the hair flip. She used it to great effect on the manager of the hostel who personally found me an air mattress, lugged it up three flights of stairs and inflated it. Though there was hardly any floor space in a room that already had three beds crammed into it, each one covered with a really nasty bright-blue floral bedspread. But it was clean and super-cheap. Even cheaper after the smitten manager knocked five euros off the day rate and, when the boys peered into our room, he was fluffing up the two pillows he'd found for me, while Jess smiled and made encouraging noises.

Aaron dropped my suitcase on the floor with a thud and I began to root around for my wash bag, while the six of them sat on the beds and chatted about people I didn't know and places I'd never been. But I didn't feel left out; after all the dramas of Malaga, it was nice to be with six people who actually enjoyed each other's company. And as I sent my mother another text that was light on the truth and scant on the details: EVERYTHING IS FINE. WILL CALL YOU TOMORROW. LOVE TO JAMES AND THE TWINS AND THE GRANDMAS, they'd throw comments to me.

'We found this place that does the most amazing *chocolat con churros*, Bea. We'll go there for breakfast tomorrow.'

'Honestly, Bea, it was so funny. His puke was neon green. I just about peed my pants.'

I sat cross-legged on the floor and let the sound of their voices drift over me, until my eyelids began to droop and I had to stifle my yawns. Even though I'd had a monster sleep on the train, I was ready for even more sleep. I could feel another yawn coming on and the effort of trying to hold it back almost dislocated my jaw, I glanced up to see if my new, older, worldy, super-cool friends had noticed and Toph caught my eye and smiled, like we were the only two people in the room.

'I guess it's time to turn in,' he said, making a big show of stretching tiredly. 'Early start tomorrow, if we want to be in Marseilles by the afternoon. Especially if we're going to take Bea to the airport first.'

'Oh you don't have to do that,' I said quickly. 'I could just get a taxi.'

'So you're going back to London then?' Toph asked softly and there was absolutely nothing in his expression that gave me any clue how he felt about that.

'You're not, are you, Bea?' Erin wanted to know, and at least she looked slightly put out. 'Are we not, like, the very definition of fun?'

'You are. You've been great, all of you, but I probably should go home,' I said sadly. It was the sensible thing to do, after all. And though my new American friends seemed nice enough, I was beginning to realize that I was a terrible judge of character. There was nothing else for it – in the morning, I was going to have to bite the bullet, phone my mother and confess everything. She was going to *kill* me.

Chapter Eleven

'Bea! At last! I've been going out of my mind. Why haven't you been answering your phone when your favourite mother in all the world has been trying to call you?'

She sounded really pleased to hear my voice. Really, really, really pleased. Like just the sound of it was putting her in a good mood.

'I was charging it overnight and I put it on silent so it didn't wake me up. Hey, how are you?' I asked as I swung my legs against the wall I was sitting on and kept one eye on the others, who were finishing breakfast and poring over a train timetable.

'Never mind me, how are *you*? Bea, what's been going on?' Mum asked sharply. 'I've had four different mothers on the phone before seven this morning, informing me that I've been raising a devil child for seventeen years.'

I sent up a silent prayer to the heavens, before I remembered that I was actually in the right and Ruby and her minions were elbow deep in the wrong.

'Oh my God, they were so mean to me,' I began and it was just as well I'd charged up my phone because telling Mum exactly what had happened took a good fifteen minutes plus interruptions, which consisted of 'Just wait until I get my hands on them!' and 'I can't believe Ayesha

124

would stoop so low. I used to wipe her nose!'

'Aw, Bea, baby, I have taught you well,' Mum said proudly when I came to the end of the affair of the whiteboard. 'But where have you been? The girls said you'd disappeared and I get that you didn't want to spend another night in the apartment, but you didn't sleep rough, did you?'

'No, I stayed in a youth hostel,' I said truthfully.

'Good girl. Now I don't want you to worry, just go to the airport; James is going to get you a seat on the next plane out. Not a budget flight either. I don't want you bumping into those four little madams and—'

'Mum, you promise you won't get mad at me . . .' I said tentatively.

'Haven't we already established that I'm not mad at you? In fact, I'm glowing with maternal pride right now,' she giggled. 'You showed your arch nemeses a thing or two about revenge and you even found somewhere else to stay in Malaga without having to sleep rough—'

'But see, that's the thing – I'm not in Malaga. I'm in Bilbao.'

There was a weird little huffing sound and then silence, so I had no choice but to continue.

'I got to the station and I was going to go straight to the airport but then I had this really weird impulse to go to Paris but I got on the wrong train, or I was on the right train, but I had to change at Madrid and I fell asleep, then when I got to Bilbao I met these six American kids—'

'What do you mean by kids?' Mum demanded. 'Are they

on holiday with their parents?'

'Well, no. They're at university and they're very nice. Very responsible. They've taken me under their wing, like all of sudden I have six elder siblings all looking out for me. And it's this really funny coincidence because they're planning to go to Paris too.'

'Too? *Too?*' Mum's voice had got so shrill that it made my eardrum reverberate painfully. 'There's no "too", because you're not going to Paris. You're going to the airport, you're getting on the first plane to London and God help you when you get here, young lady.'

'Is that meant to be an incentive to come home?' I blurted out. 'That you're going to get all wrath of God on me?'

'Just don't even go there, Bea,' Mum growled. 'What has got into you? You don't know anything about these people. Are they boys? They're boys, aren't they? And you want to make googly eyes with them and next thing you know, it's all gone too far and you've been date raped, or worse! God, you're so naive!'

'I never actually said I was going to Paris. I said I was *planning* to go to Paris.'

'Well, you're not,' Mum said quietly. I hated her quiet voice. I was used to her ranting and raving but she only ever pulled out the quiet voice when I was in SERIOUS TROUBLE and it always sent icy ripples cascading down my spine. 'I'm warning you, Bea. Airport. Plane. Home. End of discussion.'

The injustice of it all made the anger of yesterday boil

up again, as if it had been on a slow simmer all this time. 'You haven't even asked me why I want to go to Paris! I want to go and meet my dad, because maybe he'll think there's more to me than a girl who's going to drop her knickers as soon as a boy looks at her.'

'Don't be so ridiculous. You don't even know where he lives . . .'

'Because you won't tell me! You won't tell me anything about him. Christ, you wouldn't even let me go to Paris for one measly weekend with Grandma Minor for my sixteenth birthday. You're the one who's ridiculous!' I couldn't believe what was pouring out of my mouth in this never-ending stream of viciousness that I was powerless to stop. All the stuff I'd silently seethed about but had never dared voice because Mum always got this pinched look if I ever asked about my dad. He must have really done a number on her and, just like that, my finely honed guilt reflex kicked in and I was opening my mouth to start blabbing apologies but Mum got there first.

'I don't want to talk about him. Not now. Not ever. And I'm certainly not telling you anything about him so you can go gallivanting off to Paris with a bunch of twenty-somethings who'll be pouring alcohol down your throat and taking advantage of you. I can hardly bear to think about it.'

'They're not like that at all! Why do you always have to think the worst of everyone?' I demanded.

She sniffed and Mum could pack several dictionaries into one of her sniffs. 'You're far too trusting for your own good. I mean, you thought Ruby was your best friend and look how that turned out.'

Sometimes arguing with Mum wasn't like arguing with a grown-up. It was like arguing with someone who really wasn't that much older than me in the grand scheme of things. She really didn't have the grown-up skills that the grandmas had, which meant that she fought dirty and right now it was really, royally pissing me off.

'I'm going to Paris and there's nothing you can do about it!' I squealed, which wasn't the best thing to say when I was trying to show how mature I was. 'I'm seventeen, I can do what I want!'

There was spluttering. I couldn't even make out actual words, until Mum shouted, 'Oh my God, you are *so* grounded.'

If we'd been in the same room, then the argument would have fizzled out when we both started laughing, but I was in Spain and she was in England and she couldn't exactly ground me when I was six hundred miles away.

'What*ever*,' I snarled and hung up. Then I turned off my phone so she couldn't call me and marched over to where the others were waiting.

'Everything all right?' Erin asked, probably because my face was redder than it had ever, ever been, which was saying something.

'Yup,' I said, trying to will my facial muscles to relax so I could dial down the furious grimace. 'In fact, everything's great. I've spoken to my Mum and I'm coming to Paris with you.'

'Really?' Jess arched an eyebrow, a move she'd probably mastered after she'd aced the hair flipping. ''Cause at one point it looked like you were about to throw your phone in the water.'

I was saved from having to reply by Toph looping his arm around my shoulders. I could smell the chocolate from the *churros* he'd had for breakfast; the sweetness offset by the sea-salt scent that hung in the air. Toph's body pressed against mine and I was sure I now had scorch marks on my cheeks as he squeezed me enthusiastically. 'Of course Bea is coming with us. Like, was there any doubt?'

I'd never got so physically close to any of my crushes before, and Toph was now officially a crush. In fact, he may have been the king of all my crushes, and my previous crushes had just been dry runs leading up to this point, where I was swoony from the nearness of Toph.

Or else it was the three cups of *espresso* I'd gulped down to fortify me before I called my mother.

Backpacking around Europe was not like being on holiday with my folks, where we'd always have to follow a detailed itinerary that took into account the twins' feeding and nap schedule. Or having to make numerous stops for the bathroom as Grandma Major couldn't even look at a stretch of water without needing a wee.

This had a much more laidback vibe. We ambled slowly to the station to catch the Marseilles train, pausing so we could look in shop windows. We even came to a complete halt when we saw a group of nuns stride through the market square. They looked like an army of penguins; their wimples snowy-white against the black of their habits, and Bridget wanted to take photos and Erin wanted to buy peaches and cherries to take with us on the journey and in the end, ambling turned into running at breakneck speed to get to the station.

It turned out that I really wasn't cut out for the laidback vibe. The others collapsed, laughing, in the first seats we came to when we got on the train, though I was pretty sure that we were in a first-class carriage. I stayed standing and tried not to have a stress-related heart attack.

'We are on the right train, aren't we?' I asked anxiously when I could speak again.

'Yeah, of course we are,' Michael said. Then he shrugged expansively. 'Well, we probably are and even if we aren't, then what's the damage?'

'But what time do you need to check in at the hostel in Marseilles? 'Cause you'll probably have to pay a cancellation charge if we don't turn up and—'

'Bea, sweetie, you need to learn to chill,' Erin laughed, pulling me down on the seat next to her. 'We haven't booked a hostel because we didn't know when we'd get to Marseilles. But everything will be cool. We always find somewhere to stay.'

'Yeah and most of the time they're cockroach-free,' Toph added in his easy-drawly way which made me think of how warm honey dripped slowly off the back of my spoon when I was making cakes. He frowned as he caught sight of the horrified expression on my face. 'It was a joke about the cockroaches. God, you're the most anxious teenager I've ever met.'

'I can't help being anxious,' I said, with just the teensiest amount of huff. 'It's hardwired into my DNA.'

That just made all of them laugh harder and I was flashbacking to Malaga and how I hadn't even realized that I was being laughed at, until Erin ruffled my hair and kissed my cheek and I realized they were laughing with me. OK, I wasn't actually laughing, I was pouting, until my mouth quirked into a half-hearted smile.

'Really, you have to be gentle with me,' I insisted, propping my feet up on my suitcase, which had been abandoned in the middle of the carriage. 'I've had experiences in the last forty-eight hours that are going to require therapy until I'm ninety.'

We whiled away the four-hour journey by putting our iPods on the table, then picking one at random to listen to. Unfortunately I chose Michael's, which was heavy on the dub and bass, very light on the melodies. I had a moment of sheer panic when I remembered there was a Jonas Brothers album lurking somewhere in my playlists, especially when Toph leaned across the table and tapped me on the knee.

'This is yours,' he stated, turning it over so I could see where James had had my name engraved.

'Yeah?' I said, all ready to deny all knowledge of any songs sung by God-loving, non-sex-having brothers.

'I'm digging the Sixties French pop – will you do me a mix CD when you get home?'

I nodded eagerly. The fact that I was never going home was but a mere technicality. 'You should listen to *Baby Pop* by Frances Gall; she gets a bit squeaky, but the songs are really good.'

'You know, it's obvious that you're half French. You have that way about you.' Toph tilted his head and looked at me intently while I inwardly squirmed and hoped that to the naked eye I looked inscrutable. 'It's hard to put it into words. I'd say it was *je ne sais quoi*, but that would be really lame and it's the only French I know.'

'Actually it's going to be great being in France with someone who speaks the language,' Aaron commented, smiling at me.

I looked at him blankly. 'Huh?'

'You speak French, right? You must be fluent, what with your dad and all.'

'I'm not fluent. Not at all and I'm very, very rusty,' I babbled because I couldn't speak French. Not as it is spoken by French people.

But they just thought it was bashful modesty and when we crossed the border and a French customs guard came into the carriage to check out passports, and I stammered, '*Monsieur, un moment, s'il vous plaît,*' when he started flaring his nostrils and tutting while I hunted for my passport, they all looked at me like I'd just recited *The Complete Works of William Shakespeare en Français*.

We arrived in Marseilles in the middle of the afternoon. It was blisteringly hot even inside the station and before I could get my bearings and take a moment to savour the feeling that I was finally in France (*France!*), Bridget gave an excited squeal.

'Bea! Look! It's the Tourist Information Centre,' she said, pointing at a blue-and-white hoarding. 'Ask them if there are any hostels with rooms available for less than twenty-five euros a night.'

'But—'

'Yes! You can ask them in French and then they won't think we're a bunch of ugly American tourists and try to rip us off,' Jess said, with a not-so-gentle hand at the small of my back to push me along. 'One room for the girls and one room for the boys and an en suite would be great. Shall I come with you?'

'No!' I yelped, hefting up my case and setting off at great speed. 'I'll meet you under that big clock.'

There was a long queue and after ten anxious minutes, I ambled along to the first available window, took a deep breath and blurted out: '*Je voudrais deux chambres avec en suite pour trois garçons et quatre filles.*'

The man behind the desk smiled sadly. 'Your accent is very good, *ma chère*, but shall we do this in English?'

That was my first practical lesson. A little effort went a long, long way and the French were so proud of their language that if you at least tried to speak French, rather than letting the funky music do the talking, they'd meet you halfway.

So I walked calmly back to the others with the details of a little hotel right by the marina for twenty-three euros a night. At the hotel, it was the same story. I spoke French

133

very badly and very rapidly and after beaming at me proudly for having a bash at it, the receptionist switched to English.

It happened again when we went out to dinner. Ordering pizza in French was, like, the easiest thing in the world. Because pizza quattro formaggio is the same in any language and so I just shoved in lots of *s'il vous plaîts* and *merci*s and *deux bouteilles de vin rouge*.

The weird thing was that the more I had to speak French, even really bad French, the more it made sense. Like, I was thinking about what I wanted to say and translating it in my head almost as a reflex action and I thought that if I stayed in France for another two weeks, I'd be jabbering in French fluently. I hadn't run away, I was having an educational experience and immersing myself in the French culture.

Chapter Twelve

By the end of our second day in Marseilles, I was loving my educational experience and immersion in the French culture. I'd drank a lot of coffee, ate tons of French bread and cheese, and spent every waking moment sight-seeing. I was starting to think that every city in Europe had a working harbour, an old town and at least one cathedral.

After spending the afternoon at Parc Borely to tour the art museum and hire rowing boats, I was starting to flag. I lay spreadeagled on the grass staring up at the sky, which seemed so much bluer than the English sky, and tried not to groan as Aaron and Michael announced that there was still time to visit the Musee des Rock Romains – 'It has shipwrecks!'

I gave a start as Toph and Jess collapsed on either side of me.

'Hey, Bea, what you doing?' Jess asked.

I closed my eyes. 'Every time I inhale and exhale, my feet throb in time with my breathing. That's weird, isn't it?'

'So, this museum . . .' Toph prompted. 'Might be good in a *Pirates of the Caribbean* way.'

'It won't be,' Jess said shortly. 'I read about in the guidebook where I saw the words "grain storage jars". I didn't travel across an ocean to look at grain storage jars. And we haven't been clubbing once since we got to France.'

'You mean *les discothèques*,' I remarked, because it was nice not to be mocked for inserting random French words into sentences. Besides any *parlez vous*ing *Français* I did earned me these looks of admiration from Toph, which were more addictive than peanut butter KitKats.

'I want to go to *le discothèque* then,' Jess said, snapping her fingers at Erin, who was taking pictures of the sailboats on the lake. 'Erin! We're *le discothèque*ing tonight. Shall we go back to the hotel and have a *discothèque* nap?'

'You don't want to go to the shipwreck museum?' Michael asked peevishly as we started packing up the debris from our picnic lunch.

'God, no,' Bridget snapped, giving Michael a mock punch on the arm when he pouted. 'We're heading back into town. Erin, do you still want me to do your highlights?'

'I didn't know Erin had highlights,' I said, squinting at her shiny blonde head as she eagerly nodded her agreement to Bridget's plan. 'I thought the sun had done that.'

'No, that's all me.' Bridget grinned. She came to sit down beside me and fingered the ends of my hair. 'This is lovely and thick but it could do with some shaping.'

Mum had warned me away from DIY haircare by telling me about the time she was fifteen and had persuaded her best friend, Claire, to bleach her hair and give her a spiky 'do, then showed me the photographic evidence of the neon orange fright-wig that had been the end result. 'Well, I'm not sure that—'

'Oh please, girlfriend,' Bridget sniffed and now it was my turn to get a mock punch on the arm. 'My mom has her own salon. Been styling hair since I was thirteen and unlike these sad-sack losers who have to pay their way through college by working in a call centre, I work part-time in one of Phoenix's finest hair salons.'

'Well, I've always wanted some oomph to my hair,' I confided, as Toph rolled his eyes and got to his feet, muttering something about 'girl talk'. 'It just sort of hangs there. I really like those exaggerated Sixties bobs where they're really short in the back and longer in the front . . .'

'And it would frame your face,' Bridget enthused, kneeling in front of me so she could place the side of her hands against my cheeks. 'Then maybe some very subtle highlights to give it some depth and texture. It'll look awesome.'

'So you're definitely bailing out on the shipwreck museum?' Aaron asked as we picked up our bags and set off purposefully; Bridget chattering away about finding a supermarket so she could buy tinfoil.

Bridget wielded her scissors like a pair of a gardening shears and said that she'd shape it after she'd done the highlights.

I sat in the bathroom on a hard wooden chair that we'd borrowed from Reception, with my back to the mirror because I wasn't allowed to see what horrors Bridget was performing until she was done.

'That face you're pulling is putting me off my T-section,'

Bridget muttered ominously as she sectioned off strands of my hairs, covered them in acrid-smelling gloop, then folded them up into strips of tinfoil.

'I'm sorry,' I mumbled and bared my teeth in what was meant to be a relaxed smile.

While I waited for the colour to develop, I watched Bridget trim Erin's hair, which calmed me down because she cut it properly between her fingers with lightning-quick clicks of the scissors, and by the time I was curled over the bath having the colour washed out, I was excited about having a foxy Sixties haircut and possibly getting into *le discothèque* without having to lie about my age.

Toph wandered in as Bridget was showing me how to blow-dry my hair with a big round brush and lots of volumizing mousse so I could get a slight bouffant without backcombing, which Bridget said would lead to split ends and nothing good.

'I brought provisions,' he said, holding aloft a bag from Burger King. 'You're taking so long we won't have time to eat before we go out.'

'It takes this long to look this good,' Jess informed him haughtily as she applied bronzer to her cheekbones. 'And you'd better have remembered extra ketchup.'

'You know that condiments aren't a food group in their own right?' Toph asked her as he leaned against the doorframe with a sly smile, like he loved nothing better than winding Jess up.

I tried to turn round so I could see if they really were joking because Bridget was blocking the mirror again but she rapped me on the shoulder with the hairbrush handle. 'Keep still,' she barked, as she tugged on the front ends of my hair to check that they were even. She carefully snipped at one of them, lined them up again and stepped back. 'My work here is done.'

Before I could even raise my head and look up, Toph gave a long, low whistle. The kind of whistle I'd always heard other girls get.

'Bea . . . You look . . . Wow!'

'You've made Toph go all non-verbal,' Erin giggled as she delved into the Burger King bag.

I stared at myself in the mirror in awe. I could see a shadow, a glimmer, of what I might look like when I was older. My hair curved against my cheeks, giving them definition and making my eyes look bigger. I turned my head experimentally to see the smooth cap of hair tapering down towards my neck and when I gave my shoulders a little wriggle, my hair fanned out and then came to rest exactly where it had been before. I shook my head again so it shimmered under the fluorescent light and I could see the subtle highlights Bridget had given me . . .

'Bea's non-verbal too,' Bridget said and she sounded pleased.

'I *love* it,' I breathed. 'I didn't know my hair could do this or that I could look like this . . . Even my freckles look glamorous. I can't wait to put on my liquid eyeliner!'

I was still looking in the mirror, preening really, when my gaze shifted to where Toph still stood in the bathroom doorway. Our eyes met and I started to smile until I saw the way he was looking at me; exactly the same way that Erin was looking at her fries as she delicately licked her fingers, then selected the biggest one. Considering I was wearing my oldest pair of jeans – hacked to just above the knee this morning – my *Herald Tribune* T-shirt (just like the one Jean Seberg wore in *Au Bout de Souffle*) and a hair-dye-stained towel, it was a minor miracle.

But later, when the four of us trooped down the stairs to the lobby where the boys were waiting for us, Toph barely glanced at me even though my liquid eyeliner had gone on perfectly for once and I was wearing a little black dress that Jess had lent me. She had loads more going on in the boob department than I did so I'd had to cinch it at the waist with a geometric-print silk scarf that I'd nicked from Grandma Major and I was wearing flip-flops because my feet were still throbbing, but I thought the overall effect was chic. In an *insouciant* way – which was French for laidback – and I'd added a slash of Bridget's bright-red lipstick. In fact, I looked as hot as I'd ever looked or would look again, but Toph's eyes swept me up and down, then he grunted once before he marched across the lobby and through the front door. Toph's dismissal did a really good job of piercing my euphoria and left me with a feeling of great foreboding – the last time I'd got such mixed-up messages from someone it had turned out very, very, very badly. I couldn't go through that again, so soon . . .

'Come on, there's no need to look so nervous, stick with me tonight,' Jess said, slipping her arm through mine. Jess was wearing tight jeans, a little cotton top and skyscraper-high heels but made it all look like *haute couture* and when we walked into a club called Le Beatnik, every head swivelled in her direction as she walked across the dancefloor, dragging me in her wake, as if it were a Paris runway.

'Um, shall we buy a drink?' I shouted in her ear, over the thump of some really bad techno.

'Bea, we don't buy drinks,' Jess told me sadly, stopping right in the very centre of the dancefloor.

'Oh, I can buy a round. It's OK,' I said, already fumbling for my purse, but Jess put her hand on my arm.

'No, we don't buy drinks. Not where there's a club full of men to buy them for us,' Jess said smartly. She pulled me towards her. 'Just do exactly what I do. I'm going to teach you Hair Flipping 101.'

In the end, I left the hair flipping to Jess because she was the expert and I looked as if I was head banging. She'd toss her head back and then run a hand through her hair 'like it's a silk sheet on my lover's bed,' she informed me. 'My aunt had this old book from the Seventies on how to get a man – it taught me everything I know.'

The hair flipping was definitely working. I warily eyed several man-shaped figures circling us on the dancefloor as Jess suddenly put an arm around my waist and started grinding against me. 'C'mon, work with me here,' she hissed in my ear. 'Two girls doing a bit of sexy dancing always seals the deal.'

Men were really lame, I decided, because when I started doing this half-hearted side step and shuffle in time to the music, two of them separated themselves from the herd and started dancing on either side of us. The one closest to me caught my eye, smiled, then sidled closer. I pointedly ignored him and wished that Jess would stop humping me when he leaned even closer and shouted something at me.

'What?' I bellowed back.

'What's he saying?' Jess wanted to know.

'No idea,' I said. 'I think he's German. And he's definitely not my type.'

I knew he wasn't my type because he was wearing a pair of shorts with socks and trainers (not even cool trainers) and was at least fifteen years older than me. Then he mimed holding a drink to his lips. Jess dug me in the ribs. 'Score,' she said.

We followed badly dressed, possibly German bloke to the bar. There was lots of smiling and pointing. 'Klaus,' he said proudly.

Jess giggled and pointed at me. 'Mary-Kate,' she said, and pointed at herself. 'Ashley.'

I started giggling too, which was Klaus's cue to take my hand and kiss it, which made me giggle even as I shuddered in revulsion. His moves were as outdated as his clothes. Then he gestured at the bar and said. 'Drink?'

Jess was already asking for a Cosmo and I figured that one drink wouldn't hurt. Then I could just stick to water. I looked at the collection of bottles behind the bar – there were so many to choose from.

'Vodka martini,' I said decisively because it was something women ordered in black-and-white films and it always came in a cone-shaped shallow glass with olives. I wasn't a big fan of olives but by the time I'd got round to eating my cheeseburger and fries they'd been cold and congealed, and I was really hungry. It turned out that I wasn't a big fan of vodka martinis either, especially when they came in a plastic glass with no ice. But Jess was looking at me approvingly and even though the first sip made my tongue shrink back in my mouth, I took an experimental sip.

'Down in one, girl,' Jess whispered, her fixed smile starting to look a little manic. 'Klaus doesn't smell too great when you're downwind and we have much better-looking fish to fry.'

Klaus seemed very put out when Jess and I slammed our empty glasses down on the bar, shrugged our shoulders and backed away slowly. We were swallowed up by the heaving, sweaty masses on the dancefloor before he could shout at us in German, and now that I had a drink in me, it was easier to shake my hips in time with the music.

The whole evening seemed to be a repeat cycle of suggestive dancing with Jess, catching the eye of some dodgily dressed older bloke who didn't speak a word of English or French, follow him to the bar, let him buy us a drink each, giggle a bit, then execute a sneaky cut and run when he wasn't looking. My plan to stick to water had got completely derailed by Jess, who said that we were on holiday and we deserved to have a bit of fun after looking round old churches all day. Besides, we were never going to see any of these men again and it totally served them right for perving on young girls when they should have been tucked up in bed with a good book.

She said all this while we were having a quick regroup and primp in the girls' loos and she also relented and let me drink a bottle of water because even though Jess was encouraging me to bump and grind suggestively against her arse to lure unsuspecting men to our sides, she was doing it in a responsible manner.

'Men are idiots,' she confided to me as we elbowed our way through a throng of tanned girls all jostling for mirror space. 'They just see tits and ass and nothing in between.'

'But Toph isn't like that . . .' I protested. 'Or Aaron and Michael.'

'That's because they're boys who are friends. Believe me, if they were trying to get into your pants, then they'd act like every other creep in here.'

I didn't exactly agree with Jess's pithy summing-up of the general crappiness of all boykind, but it was hard to think of a counter-argument when I was seeing the world in soft focus as if someone had smeared Vaseline over it. 'I think I'm quite drunk,' I told Jess, who peered at my face, wiped away a smudge of mascara with her thumb and told me that the next guy we pulled would buy me some peanuts.

The next guy didn't buy me peanuts, just another vodka martini, which was starting to taste better with each glass and when we got back to the dancefloor, I decided that I wanted to actually dance. By myself, with my eyes closed, so that if any skeevy men were trying to check me out then I wouldn't know about it.

'I'll let you dance for ten minutes,' Jess decided magnanimously. 'I could do with a bit of a breather.'

Jess wandered off and I had a moment of panic when I realized I was on my own, until I saw Toph standing at the edge of the dancefloor. I waved at him. He didn't wave back, but it was pretty dark inside.

I fought my way through the dancers to reach his side. Toph was leaning against the wall and raised his eyebrows as I approached, like he wasn't exactly overjoyed to see me, but he'd hear me out. I didn't know why he suddenly seemed so unapproachable and it made me tongue-tied before I'd even opened my mouth.

'You having a nice time?' I bellowed.

'No, not really,' Toph replied, barely raising his voice so the only way I could hear him was by standing on tiptoe and clutching hold of his arm to steady myself.

'I know the music is kind of crappy, but it's fun to dance to,' I insisted in the face of zero encouragement. 'Come and dance with me.'

Toph shook his head. 'I don't dance.'

'Well, have something to drink. Have a lot to drink, then you'll forget that you don't dance.' I smiled conspiratorially and expected Toph to smile back but he just stared me down with a completely stony face, so I took a faltering step back, the hurt welling up inside me because I was flashbacking to all the times I've overstepped the mark with Ruby and she'd also let me know that she was far from pleased.

145

'And just how much have you had to drink?' Toph suddenly asked, pushing himself away from the wall and looking at me intently as if he was about to produce a breathalyser.

'Um, not that much . . .'

'Bea! Are you dancing, 'cause I'm asking?' Two arms wrapped round my waist and Jess breathed heavily on my neck. 'Come on, beeyatch. Get your boogie shoes on.'

I was dragged away by Jess before I had time to think, and actually even getting perved on my older men was preferable to Toph treating me like I was a plague carrier.

Anyway, when Jess wasn't on the prowl for men to buy us drinks, she was a hilarious dancer. As yet another techno hit from yesteryear began, she started doing aerobic moves with her cheeks puffed out. Then she attempted a couple of star jumps and nearly fell over. I could see why she'd never tried out for the cheerleading squad.

'Come on, Bea,' she shouted. 'Work those quads!'

I took a hasty step away from Jess, only to tread on someone's foot. I looked up into the amused face of a boy who certainly wasn't a creepy older man, and stuttered an apology.

He said something to me in Spanish and I shrugged my shoulders and frowned in the universal language for 'Sorry, I haven't a clue what you're talking about'.

And it was the strangest thing, even though there was no Ruby to shove me in his direction and Jess was too busy with her star jumps to pay me any attention, within two more beats of the song, the Spanish boy and I were dancing together. When the song ended, we smiled at each other, paused long enough to realize that the next tune sucked and walked off the dancefloor together, Jess trailing behind us and asking, 'Hey, so are you going to buy us a drink or what?'

While we bought our own drinks, the Spanish boy and I discovered that we both spoke really bad French. His name was Iban and he had a friend, Santio, who was handsome enough in a ballroom-dancer way to keep Jess happy. Iban was really rather beautiful for a boy. He was quite small, not much taller than me, but he had close-cropped hair and dark, soulful eyes and a sweet smile. We shared a bowl of peanuts and a conversation that was basic First Year French.

'*Je m'appelle Bea. J'habite dans Londres et je suis sur mes vacances avec mes amies nouvelles.*'

'*Je m'appelle Iban et je travail dans la restaurant Espagnol dans Marseilles.*'

It was too noisy to talk near the dancefloor, so Iban took my hand in a very masterful way, which sent a little thrill through me, even though my palms were sweaty. We wandered up some stairs and into a room with sofas where we found Erin and Bridget. Across the way, Aaron and Michael were enthusiastically talking to two identical blonde girls with their hair in these tiny little braids, which looked very painful.

'Bea! Hey, Bea!' Erin shouted, grabbing my arm. 'Where you been, Bea?'

'Dancing, drinking, hair flipping,' I explained, leaning

against Iban because standing unaided was really hard work. Iban didn't seem to mind, he gave my shoulder a sympathetic little squeeze.

'You're drunk!' Erin gasped, clapping her hands in delight. 'I am too. Isn't it great?'

I considered the question for a long, long time. 'It is great,' I decided. 'But it's quite hard to stand up and talk to you, Erin, so I'm going to sit down with Iban. Also, when I talk, it sounds like my voice is coming from underwater.'

'Oh my God, so does mine!' Erin exclaimed, nudging Bridget who didn't seem that impressed.

In fact, she was eyeing Iban suspiciously as we perched on the end of Aaron and Michael's sofa, who both gave me the thumbs-up. 'Twins,' one of them said, though I couldn't remember which one was which. 'Swedish twins!'

There wasn't much room so Iban and I were smooshed together, thigh to thigh, as we talked. I had no idea what we were talking about and at one stage I think he was just talking Spanish with a French accent. I know I was just shoving 'la's and 'le's in front of all my English words to make them sound French. It didn't really matter, our mouths were saying one thing, but our hands were fluent in the language of love. I'd been rubbing Iban's cropped hair for so long that my fingertips had gone numb and he had one of his hands on my chin so he could angle my head, all the better to look deeply into my eyes, while his other hand stroked my left knee.

Our faces were getting closer and closer, so soon all I'd have to do was pout my lips and we'd totally be kissing.

Totally. As soon as I thought it, I moved my head back a couple of inches so I could ponder while burbling on to Iban about '*le Pilates etait moi très, très bendy!*' There were worst places to have my first kiss and worse boys to do the honour. I was in freaking France, my hair looked amazing and Iban was pretty, attentive and had very high standards of personal grooming. Part of me wanted to wait until I reached Paris but this might be as good as it got.

My mind was made up. I shifted on the sofa so Iban was in pouting distance again. '*Tu es muy bella,*' Iban husked in my ear and I prepared to pout . . .

'Bea! Your ten minutes is up. I need another drink,' I suddenly heard Jess whine and when I turned my head, she was crouched down in front of us. 'Come on, let's get back on the dancefloor.'

Iban's hand tightened on my knee because it was obvious that Jess wanted to wrest me away from the delights of his mouth.

'I'm kinda all right here,' I said. 'What happened to Santio?'

'He wouldn't buy me a drink and now he's all over some skank with a glow stick. How very two thousand and five,' Jess sneered, slapping Iban's hand off my knee. 'Keep your paws to yourself, Spanish boy!'

'Leave Iban alone,' I hissed because Iban's eyes were now flashing with irritation and he was muttering in Spanish under his breath.

'But Bea, I need you,' Jess implored me. 'You're so young and fresh-faced that the skeevy older men with lots of cash can't resist you. Come on, I'll—'

'Are you using Bea as beer bait?' said an angry voice and now Toph was looming over us, looking alarmingly like James the time he caught me looking at websites that I had absolutely no business to be looking at.

'I would never do anything like that,' Jess gasped indignantly, slowly standing up straight so she could put her hands on her hips and glare at Toph, who was looking at her sceptically. 'Would I, Bea?'

'Of course not,' I said quickly, because girls had to stick together and, as well as using me as beer bait, Jess had been given me loads of practical boy-getting tips, which had been really useful. I turned to Iban, who was still scowling and muttering, and stared at his mouth until he smiled at me and got that soulful look in his eyes again. Being drunk wasn't big or particularly clever but it really brought out this flirty, confident side of me that I hadn't known actually existed. 'Right, great, glad we cleared that up.' I didn't even bother to turn my head to look at Jess and Toph. 'Go away now, please.'

'I saw you from the balcony the whole time, Jess . . .' Toph began furiously, then paused. 'Bea's drunk and some guy who none of us know has his unknown hands all over her.'

'Um, say, *bonjour de mes amies*,' I told Iban, but he was already taking his unknown hands off me so he could get to his feet and get right in Toph's face and start spitting great globs of Spanish at him. Toph obviously didn't like what he was hearing because he pushed Iban away and then Iban pushed Toph and it was push, push, push until you could tell they were one push away from throwing down.

'They're fighting over you,' Jess told me gleefully, sitting down in the spot that Iban had just vacated. 'I've always wanted to have two boys fighting over me.'

Iban was squaring up to Toph now, mouth pursed so tight that it was a wonder he could still keep hissing Spanish words that made Toph ball his fists. It was just a lame display of macho posturing but it did make me feel, well, like the kind of girl that was so irresistible to guys that they had to fight over her. Like a girl from a French film.

'Oh, please, don't fight over me,' I said, more because it was the right thing to do than because I wanted them to stop. Then I saw Iban take a step back as he realized that Toph was almost a head taller than him, and Bridget sidled over to join our happy little crowd.

'Erin's been sick on the other sofa,' she said flatly. 'The manager is getting really snippy about it and have either of you realized that Bea is very, very drunk?'

'Right,' Toph said decisively, shouldering Iban out of the way, who made some aggressive gesture with the flat of his hand and his chin, then sidled away. 'Bridge, I'll meet you and Erin outside in five minutes. Jess, staying or going?'

Jess looked around the room, sizing up what was left of the available boy stock. 'Going, I guess.'

She prodded Aaron, or Michael, with her toe until he freed himself from the clutches of his braided, Swedish twin. 'We're going,' she said. 'Are you two staying here with the Barbie sisters or coming with us?'

He didn't even have to think about it. 'Staying,' he muttered and dived back in.

I waited to be asked if I had a preference, but Toph simply grabbed my hands and hauled me up. 'Yeah, like we're going to leave you here with Aaron and Michael to act as chaperones,' he snorted, keeping one hand locked round my wrist as he sped down the stairs.

'But I want to stay,' I whined, trying to dig my heels in, which was a tricky manoeuvre when you were wearing flip-flops. 'You've just ruined things with the first boy I've ever liked who actually liked me back.'

My words were swallowed up by the thud of the bass as Toph pulled me across the dancefloor and into the foyer. I could see Jess, Erin and Bridget standing outside. Well, Erin wasn't standing so much as slumping against them.

'Look, they're fine. We could go back in. For one more dance and one more drink because I've acquired this taste for vodka martinis, which just goes to show that I'm really mature for my age.' I tried to smile imploringly, but Toph opened the door and pushed me through it.

'There is no way you're drinking anything else but water on my watch,' he snapped.

'Why are you being so mean to me?'

'Yeah, who died and made you a fun Nazi?' Jess asked belligerently and for the second time in the space of fifteen minutes, someone was getting right up in Toph's face. 'Did you even, like, enjoy yourself for one second tonight?'

'Well, I tried to, in between watching you and Bea trawl

152

for old guys to get you drinks and trying to persuade Erin that it wasn't a good idea to pickle her liver.' Toph took a step back and gave us both such a disapproving look that I hung my head in shame.

Then Erin gave an unhappy moan. 'I need to lie down,' she said plaintively, sagging to the pavement.

Bridge wedged a hand under her arm. 'Wait till we get back to the hotel,' she said, her grim expression a perfect match for the one on Toph's face. She looked up the street. 'Cab. Stick your hand out, Toph.'

Erin managed to stay upright long enough to convince the taxi driver that she wouldn't throw up all over his back seat, Bridge slid in next to her and Jess suddenly yelled, 'Shotgun!' and was in the passenger seat faster than I could blink. Which left Toph and I standing outside the club watching the taxi driver take the corner too fast as he sped off.

Toph nodded his head tersely in the direction that the cab had just gone and started marching up the road, without waiting to see if I was coming too. I thought about going back into the club, but my feet and my head were both starting to ache so I followed Toph up the street.

We walked in silence for all of five minutes. I kept sneaking glances at Toph's face. It was like looking at a cement block with eyes, nose and a mouth. The next time I looked, Toph was looking right back at me and I could just *feel* that my mascara and eyeliner had smudged and my hair was less bouffant and more rats' nest. Why else would he be looking quite so disgusted?

'You're mad at me,' I stated for the record. 'Why are you mad at me?'

'I don't want to talk about it,' he rapped out, taking a sharp left, even though I was sure that we should be carrying straight on. 'I know Jess gets pretty wild when she's clubbing but you're not Jess and you shouldn't be doing stuff like that.'

'Like what?' I echoed incredulously. 'I was doing clubby stuff and OK, I wouldn't normally flirt with guys to get drinks off them, but Jess was with me the whole time. And sometimes it's cool to do stuff you wouldn't normally do. As a controlled experiment.'

'Oh, so I suppose letting that creepy Spanish guy feel you up was just a controlled experiment too?' Toph sneered, taking another left. He was so annoyed with me, that I didn't want to make him more annoyed by telling him we'd never walked past the harbour on our way to the club.

'Iban wasn't creepy and he wasn't feeling me up. He was just touching my knee and chin. That's not really feeling me up,' I said. There was a breeze coming off the water and a shiver coursed through me. Or it could have been the ice chips Toph was shooting out of his eyes. I'd obviously imagined those few seconds back in the hotel when Toph had looked at me like I was as beautiful as Jess, because now he was back to being the big brother I'd never had – and didn't want if they were as overbearing and judgemental as Toph. God, he was doing my mum proud.

I sunk down on the harbour wall and folded my arms.

Toph eyed me warily. 'What are you doing?

'I'm staging a sit-down protest against your completely unfair accusations,' I said, because I didn't want him to know that my feet were hurting and I couldn't take another step.

'You're not still drunk, are you? I thought the walk would have sobered you up by now.'

I was still a bit muzzy round the edges and when I spoke my voice didn't sound as soft as it usually did. 'You ruined my first kiss,' I said, stabbing my finger in Toph's general direction. 'Iban would have been a perfect first kiss. Originally I thought it should have been in Paris on the Pont Neuf with fireworks but then I remembered that Bastille Day has already gone and I don't think they have fireworks at any other time. So, Iban would have been the next best thing, but you came along and put your humungous feet in it.'

'Well, I'm glad I did ruin it,' Toph said, kicking a stray pebble with his toe. 'Because every time you turned your back Iban was making obscene hand gestures at his friend to imply that he was going to do more than kiss you. A lot more.'

I gasped as Toph smiled grimly, because he'd got the reaction he wanted. 'Iban wouldn't do that. He said I was beautiful.' He hadn't said much else because neither one of us had really understood a word that the other one said but . . . 'We had a connection. I felt it!'

'Bea, all you felt was the effect of the vodka you knocked back. Seriously, tomorrow when you're not completely slammed, you'll thank me for this,' Toph said, and I might have been a little bit slammed but I could still hear the self-righteousness coating every word. 'You might even apologize.'

'Like hell I will!' I snorted, jumping up from the wall. 'I came to France to get away from people telling me what I should and shouldn't do. I'm sick of it! My mum, Ruby and now you!' Toph was getting in the way of me storming off in a huff so I put my hands on his chest and gave him a good shove. 'I can take perfectly good care of myself.'

I was just in the middle of storming off with a head toss that made the world spin alarmingly, when Toph caught up with me. 'You're going the wrong way.'

'Actually, I'm going the right way,' I informed him sweetly, though my eyes were hurling daggers and all sorts of other pointy implements at him. 'You're the one who's been walking around in a gigantic circle.'

I could have added in a metaphor about how Toph obviously couldn't see what was right in front of him and was rubbish about reading the signs, but my brain was only firing on one cylinder so I saved my energy for a massive and contemptuous sniff and carried on walking.

Chapter Thirteen

I started throwing up at about six in the morning, just after Erin had finally stopped, and right before Jess began.

The smell in our tiny en suite bathroom was *foul* and Bridget swore that she was never going out after dark with any of us ever again.

'That's all right,' I said weakly as I lay on the bed with a damp flannel over my forehead. 'I'm never drinking alcohol again. I can still taste those olives at the back of my throat.' Just the thought of it had me dive-bombing off the bed again and racing to the bathroom so I could bring up a stream of bile that was so acidic I was amazed it didn't corrode the toilet bowl.

Jess was slumped on the bathroom floor, her pale face coated in sweat, but she tried to give me a wan smile. 'Once we're done puking, we'll go out for coffee and some carbs.'

When James had a hangover (except he always claimed it was a headache from sleeping too long) he said that the only cure was a fry-up and a pot of tea so strong that when you tried to stir it, the spoon stood up all by itself. But just the thought of bacon and eggs had my stomach roiling again and there wasn't a decent cup of tea in the whole of France.

'I'm dying,' I groaned, pressing the heels of my hands

157

to my aching temples.

'Well, do it quietly,' Bridget snapped, coming into the bathroom. But Jess and I must have looked so pathetic that it made the scowl slide right off her face. 'Look, I'll go out and get you full-fat Coke and some popsicles. Maybe croissants too for when you can handle solids again.'

'Thanks, Bridge,' Jess murmured, waving her hand feebly. 'Do you think you could help me up before you go?'

Jess, Erin and I curled up on one of the beds like a pile of newborn puppies whose eyes weren't accustomed to the light and dozed until Bridge came back. Even the scrape of her key in the lock made the three of us groan in unison.

'I'm back,' she announced unnecessarily and very loudly. 'And look who's come to see how you are.'

I opened one eye to see Toph standing behind her, looking disgustingly bright-eyed and chipper for someone who'd been out so late. I quickly shut my eye.

'Oh, I'm sorry,' he cooed. 'The three of you feeling a little peaky?'

Erin managed to lift her head. 'Did I throw up on your shoes last night?'

'No, that would have been our cab driver,' Bridget told her. 'But you gave him a hundred-euro note to make up for it.'

'Shit! Did I?'

Toph rested against the bureau, his hands shoved in his jeans pockets. 'Talking of money, Aaron had his wallet lifted last night by one of those Swedish girls. Bea, you up to coming to the police station with him? He had his passport in there as well.'

I really wasn't up to going to *le gendarmerie* and talking Grade C GCSE French to a uniformed official, but I was gingerly putting my feet on the floor and showing willing.

'I just need to have a shower,' I mumbled, because I couldn't look Toph in the eye. The hangover was starting to ease off and now I was remembering other things from last night that were another reason why I was never going to let another drop of alcohol pass my lips.

The fight with Toph last night had been horrible, though I'd been too drunk at the time to realize it, I mused as I showered in an icy trickle of water that was all I could coax out of the rusty plumbing. I really had begun to hope that my crush might become a light flirtation but Toph had made it pretty clear that he wasn't interested in me. It was probably why he'd been so off with me before we even got to the club – he didn't want to encourage me because I was too young and too unsophisticated, and I'd totally proved him right with my drunken antics.

It was a very chastened Bea who met up with Aaron and Toph in the lobby. Aaron looked even worse than I did. As he caught sight of me, he tugged at his T-shirt and ran a hand through his hair so it stood up in little tufts.

'Hey, sorry about your wallet and stuff,' I mumbled, staring at Aaron so intently he began to look nervous, but it was still better than looking at Toph. 'Listen, my French is OK to order pizza but I'm not sure it's up to sworn witness statements and I can't actually remember the French for wallet right now or passport.' I frowned. 'Maybe it's *le passport*.'

'But you'll try,' Aaron pleaded.

'Of course I will,' I assured him, giving him a sympathetic pat on the hand. 'It's a big tourist town, they're bound to have someone who speaks English,' I added hopefully.

Toph opened the door and ushered us through. 'I'm going to go back to the club and see if anyone handed in your wallet.'

Aaron sighed. 'It's worth a shot, I guess.' He turned to me with a sheepish smile. 'Can you lend me ten euros so I can get a coffee?'

After I'd given Aaron ten euros and asked him to get me one too, I forced myself to look at Toph, who unbelievably was smiling at me.

'I bet you feel like crap this morning,' he said sympathetically, tilting his head so he could get a good look at my puffy face. 'Do you want me to see if I can get you some Alka Seltzer?'

I'd had a polite but distant apology all ready to go after my pep talk in the shower but Toph's abrupt U-turn back to Friendsville left me all wrong-footed. 'I'm fine,' I said slowly. 'Thank you.'

'Oh, poor Bea,' Toph said with a teasing grin, while I looked back at him with the bulldog-chewing-on-a-wasp face I'd inherited from Grandma Minor, who often wielded it to great effect. 'Maybe you can have a nap this afternoon.'

I didn't like this – not knowing where I stood with Toph. It was giving me the worst case of deja ewww back to those weeks with Ruby, when she'd turn on me then turn on the charm. If only I'd gone with my gut instinct and extricated myself from her evil clutches then. But at least this time I was forewarned so I just continued to stand there with a face that would have registered minus figures on a thermometer.

'Jesus, Bea, you're really cranky the morning after,' Toph exclaimed in a hurt voice that left me even more confused. 'I'll see you when you get back from the Consulate and hopefully you'll be in a better mood.'

The next two days passed in an endless trudge between the police station and the American Consulate, broken up by lots of sitting around in cafés drinking coffee and Diet Coke and waiting for our next appointment to get papers stamped or statements taken.

On the plus side, my French was coming along a treat. On the minus side; Toph was still acting like we were best friends, which we weren't. I was polite, icily polite, but for the sake of my own sanity, I wouldn't return his warm smiles or engage him in conversation that was any more meaningful than, 'Do you want milk in your coffee?' The really annoying thing was that my head was telling me one thing but my heart was still smitten. Especially when Toph would get this deep, painful furrow between his eyebrows every time he got a bit of cold shoulder. Because Toph looked so pretty when he frowned, it just made my crush burn that bit brighter.

But I could handle the awkward situation with Toph, mostly, because after phoning home, I could handle anything; hostage situations, air missile strikes, swine flu.

I'd called Mum in between Gendarmerie and Consulate while I was not in a mood to be messed with, but she sounded delighted to get my call.

'Bea! Thank God, you're all right! You *are* all right, aren't you?'

'I'm fine,' I said truthfully. 'Is everything OK at home? How are the twins?'

'Missing you terribly just like the rest of us,' Mum replied. 'I thought Alfie was trying to say "Bea" yesterday but it was trapped wind.'

I could hear gurgling in the background and I wasn't prepared for the wave of twin-sickness that suddenly washed over me. I loved Ben and Alfie, I really did, but generally they were just there in the background demanding all my attention and putting sticky fingers on my stuff. But right then, I wanted to be lying on the living-room floor so they could climb all over me and plant wet kisses on my face.

'Aw, I miss the twins too.' It was the first sign of weakness and Mum pounced on it like a bear with a particularly yummy rabbit between its paws.

'Look, Bea, you've had a few days to get this out of your system and I understand the need to go wild sometimes, but come home. You *have* to come home. Where are you, anyway?'

'I'm in Marseilles,' I answered unwillingly, because I hadn't completely ruled out the scenario where Mum hired a private security firm to kidnap me and haul me back to north London.

'So you're not in Paris, then?'

'Not yet. By the end of the week, I think.' It was Tuesday and I knew the others were keen to stop off in Lyon before we got to Paris. 'So, like, I need you to give me . . . my dad's name and—'

'He's not your dad, Bea. He didn't stick around. He wasn't there to look after you when you were sick, or take you to school on your first day. You didn't get so much as a birthday card from him, so I don't know why you're calling him Dad, like you go to watch the football together every Saturday. It's simply not the case.'

I'd been thinking about that a lot – I had to when I was about to turn up on his doorstep. 'But he was only eighteen when you got pregnant. Maybe he couldn't handle the responsibility and he left it all on you, but he's not eighteen any more. He's older and like, if he has kids of his own now, he'd have been reminded that I was his first kid. Maybe . . .' I ended with this little hopeful note to my voice.

'And maybe he hasn't,' Mum said crushingly. 'There's no point in going to Paris when you don't know where he lives or if he even lives there any more. It's stupid and reckless and I want you to come home so we can figure this out together.'

'What is there to figure out?' I spluttered. 'If I came

home you'd just think of another million reasons not to talk about him. If he doesn't want anything to do with me, then he can tell me to my face . . .'

'God, Bea, how would you even deal with that?' Mum sounded appalled. Actually, not appalled. More like freaked out as if she'd never realized that I'd inherited her stubborn streak.

'Well, I won't know until I try. Grandma Major always says that women are like teabags and you don't know how strong they are until you put them in hot water.' Great, now I was missing the grandmas, even more than I was missing the twins.

'I don't want you go to Paris,' Mum said really firmly, like she could change my mind with the power of her resolve. 'I don't ask you for much . . .'

'Are you kidding me?' I took the phone away from my ear so I could gaze at it incredulously. 'You'd have me kitted out with a GPS tracking device and a chastity belt if it wasn't against child cruelty laws.'

'Honestly, Bea, I am begging you not to go to Paris.'

Suddenly I got a clue. 'Mum, this has nothing to do with you and me. If I meet him, I'm not going to love him more than I love you,' I said softly. 'But he's my dad and I have the right to at least meet him. Could you just please tell me what I need to know so I can find him?'

'I can't remember much about him,' Mum said tightly. 'It was a very long time ago.'

That rage, which had been a stranger up until a week ago, was tapping me on the shoulder again. 'Bullshit!' I howled down the phone, going from empathetic to enraged in five seconds. 'You just don't want to tell me! There are a million things you could do to track him down; you could Google him or look him up on Facebook or International Directory Enquiries, but you don't want to because you're selfish . . .'

'You don't bloody understand, Bea, and now is not the time when we're on the sodding telephone and you're behaving like an absolute brat because you can't get your own way.' As usual my hissy fits couldn't match Mum's. 'If you go to Paris, I will never, ever forgive you.'

'Right, fine,' I screamed in frustration, to the alarm of Aaron who'd just come to find me. 'I'm unforgiven. Great. I'll send you a fucking postcard from fucking Paris.'

It was really, really annoying that you couldn't slam down a mobile phone. I had to do with pressing the 'end call' button with great force and shoving my phone viciously into my bag, before I gave Aaron a smile that made him back away nervously.

'We're due at the police station in ten minutes,' he said nervously. 'You OK?'

'Never better,' I said in a voice that was about ten octaves higher than normal. 'And no, I absolutely don't want to talk about it.'

It was another two days of shuffling between Consulate and Gendarmerie to hand over Aaron's latest stamped forms, only to be told that he'd filled them in blue ink, instead of black ink. Or that Aaron had written outside of one of the boxes. Or, hey, here's another twenty-page form, which has to be taken up to the notary on the third floor and, what a shame, the notary only works every third Thursday of the month between 7.45 a.m. and 8 a.m.

On Thursday morning, we were sitting in yet another office at the US Consulate, awaiting our next instructions. 'OK, that's fine,' said the man behind the desk. We never saw the same person twice, but at least this one was smiley and hadn't told Aaron off for losing his passport. 'I just need to witness your signature here and there'll be a new passport waiting for you at our Embassy in Paris tomorrow.'

'What?' Aaron and I said in unison.

'They only issue new passports between nine and ten a.m., Monday to Friday by appointment,' the man said. 'You can make an appointment online.'

'You mean there's no more forms?' Aaron asked suspiciously.

The man shook his head. 'Would you like me to make an appointment for you to collect the passport?'

We nodded dumbly. 'Um, thank you,' I mumbled, when the man printed out our appointment details and handed them to me. He'd obviously decided that I was the designated adult. I even shook his hand just to do my part for Anglo-American relations, then we scurried out before he could call us back and make us fill in more forms.

'Is it true, Bea? Am I really going to get a new passport?' Aaron said, as we tripped down the stairs.

'It's official,' I said, waving the papers, all glowing with their stamped officialdom. 'You've got your driving licence and that temporary visitor's visa they gave you and we just turn up at the Embassy at . . . oh bloody, bloody hell! What's the time?'

Aaron punched me on the arm. 'Don't scare me like that?'

I punched him back, hard enough that we both squealed. 'What's the bloody time?' I asked him again after I'd finished rubbing my knuckles.

'It's ten after twelve, why?'

'Because we need to be in Paris in less than twenty-four hours, that's why.'

We ran all the way back to the hotel and couldn't find the others. When we tried to call them, we realized that we'd left our mobile phones at the Consulate's security desk and raced back to get them, only they were shut for lunch.

By the time we'd retrieved our phones and Aaron had called Michael, who refused to see the urgency of the situation, then called Bridget who did, because I could hear her screaming down the phone, it was almost two o'clock.

I was red-faced and dripping with sweat when we were eventually reunited with Erin and Jess. I couldn't even speak, just jumped up and down and made squeaking noises, which set them both off too.

'Toph says that there's a train in an hour,' Jess shrieked. 'And we have to pack . . .'

'. . . and check out and get to the station and I think I'm going to burst a blood vessel,' Erin finished for her.

Aaron had calmed down now he knew that he was still an American citizen. In fact if he got any more laidback, he'd fall over. 'Look guys, just chill,' he said lazily. 'I can go to Paris by myself and meet up with you after you've been to Lyon.'

'Nuh-huh,' Erin said emphatically. 'We're in this together. If you go to Paris, then we all go to Paris.'

'Besides, someone has to save you from skanky Swedish girls with stupid cornrows in their hair,' Jess added. 'We'd better pack before Toph and Bridge shout at us again. Honestly, her voice gets so high, she's only audible to dogs.'

Usually I was a very conscientious packer; carefully folding my clothes and making sure my bottles and pots were tightly screwed shut, before I checked them off on the list I had taped to the lid of my suitcase. But we were on a clock that was ticking faster than the laws of physics said it should, so anything that looked vaguely like it might belong to me got hurled into my case.

We hit the ground running as soon as we left the hotel and didn't stop. Or the others didn't stop, but I was coming to a halt every time I had to haul my suitcase over a kerb, or it decided to go in a completely different direction to the rest of me. I honestly felt like leaving it by the side of the road and buying clean knickers when I got to Paris.

'I'll swap you,' Toph said, after I'd stopped for the umpteenth time. He took off his backpack as I dropped my case and I let him thread my arms through the straps. Compared to my case, it felt like all he had in there was a couple of T-shirts and a shaving kit.

'Thank you,' I said stiffly, wishing that I could refuse his offer, but the throbbing welts on my palms said otherwise.

'I really wish you'd get over this snit,' Toph said, lifting my suitcase as if it was as light as feathers, which was infuriating. 'Don't you think you're being a little immature?'

I couldn't even glare at him because I had no pride and I really didn't want to have to carry my own case again. Instead, I set off at a really fast pace, but of course Toph's long-limbed stride matched me easily and we were forced to walk the rest of the way in a tense silence, made even tenser by Bridget insisting that we weren't going to make it.

We did make it – with three minutes to spare, but it wasn't the giddy adrenalin rush that getting on the train at Bilbao had been when we were all excited about going to France.

Paris was the last stop.

The end of the line. They were flying back to the States from Paris and I was . . . God, I didn't know what I was going to do. Because Paris had been this vague and foggy notion, and really the last week and palling up with my American posse had simply been a way of putting off Paris. Even Aaron losing his passport had been a welcome relief but now Paris was inevitable. Like when the end-of-year exams are looming but you're busy making revision schedules and running to the kitchen for snacks to increase your brain activity and sharpening all your pencils and not doing anything in the way of swotting.

Toph and Bridge had gone off to find the buffet car and the others were unpacking books, iPods, packs of cards and generally settling down to enjoy the five-hour journey, while I found myself hurtling into a full-blown existential crisis.

What if Mum hadn't been able to find out where my dad lived?

What if she had found out, but she was hell bent on withholding the information and was on her way to Paris to drag me home?

What if I found my dad but he'd gone on holiday? Or he'd never told his family about me?

And the worst what if – what if I turned up and he shut the door in my face?

'What' and 'if' had become my two least favourite words in the English language, totally surpassing 'gusset' and 'moist towelette'. I didn't know what Paris had in store for me, but I had this horrible feeling that it was nothing good.

'. . . we could stay with Bea and her dad.'

I looked up in horror as I caught the tail end of Erin's last sentence. 'Say what?'

Toph and Bridge were back from the buffet car with chocolate, pastries and coffee but my appetite deserted me when they all looked at me expectantly. 'I was saying that if we can't find a hotel, then maybe we could stay at your dad's,' Erin repeated. 'Honestly, we could just crash on the floor.'

'Well, see, yeah . . . actually I was going to stay in a hotel with you tonight,' I said hastily as I felt my cheeks begin to heat up. ' 'Cause like it will be late and he didn't know exactly when I was going to turn up . . . my dad, that is . . . and I need to speak to my mum first. It's like this whole thing. This whole family thing.'

I must have had a really weird expression on my face – abject terror perhaps? – because Jess actually raised her hand for permission to speak. 'But what if we can't find a hotel?' she ventured timidly.

'I will find us a hotel!' It was practically a scream. 'Seriously, I will get us hotel rooms,' I amended at a less screechy volume.

Jess opened her mouth again but Bridge elbowed her in the ribs and she subsided with a muffled grunt. I stared fixedly out of the window to show that I wasn't up for further discussion about Paris accommodation and everyone became very interested in their iPods.

When I was absolutely sure that I'd killed the conversation stone dead, I got out my own iPod and a book just to make sure that I was occupied. But I read the same page of *The Dud Avocado* ten times without a single word sinking in.

It was raining as the train pulled out of Lyon station; the fields green smears, as water cascaded down the windows. My funk had infected the others and we travelled in silence until I couldn't bear it any longer. But my funk was no match for my stomach, which was letting me know that it had missed lunch and wasn't very happy about it. I stood up.

'I'm going to the buffet car, does anyone want anything?'

It broke the spell. There were pleas for coffee and cake, change to be counted out and, by the time I left the carriage, they were all chattering happily and dealing cards for a game of Texas Hold 'Em.

When I got back, I even managed a smile that didn't droop too much and picked up my book and left them to their game of poker. Every now and then, I'd glance up because *The Dud Avocado* was still failing to thrill me and each time I did, like he had a sixth sense and knew exactly when I was about to raise my head, Toph was looking at me. And each time, he never looked away, but just gave me a tight smile and raised his eyebrows in a question that I didn't know the answer to.

Chapter Fourteen

It was still raining when the train pulled in at the Gare de Lyon. It was hardly an auspicious start to my Parisian odyssey.

At least this time I knew the drill. While the others were still fussing with their backpacks, I was heading towards the Tourist Information Centre.

It was almost six and the staff were trying to close the office, but I had such a look of utter desperation on my face, that the man locking up stepped aside so I could go over to the one booth that still had someone behind it and say, '*Excusez moi, parlez vous Anglais?*'

The problem was that most Parisians left Paris in August and headed south, leaving their city at the mercy of the tourist hordes. Long story short: there were no hotel rooms to be had in the whole of Paris. Or the rooms that were left weren't in the kind of establishments that a nice girl like me should be staying in.

'Please,' I begged. '*S'il vous plaît*. I don't care if the hotel is *très terrible*, it just has to have beds in it and be er, um, *moins cher*.'

There was a lot of head-scratching and my first really great demonstration of the Parisian shoulder shrug, which was everything it was rumoured to be and more. Then the girl who was helping me consulted with a colleague as they peered at her computer screen.

'*Bien, c'est propre*,' she muttered, before switching to English. 'How many rooms?'

The others were waiting for me as I emerged with the confirmation slip for our hotel booking clutched triumphantly in my hand.

'You got us hotel rooms then?' Erin asked. ''Cause we were just talking to these two guys we met from Tuscon and they said that—'

'I said I would and I did,' I snapped and cringed inwardly as Erin's face fell. 'I'm sorry. It's just been a really long day and I'm getting a headache.' It was the truth; there was a tell-tale throb pummelling at my temples as we walked towards the Metro.

I tried to get excited about going on the Paris Metro. But apart from the darling little map that lit up our route when I pressed the button for Pigalle, it was pretty much like the London Underground except the ads were in French. *Quelle* disappointing. And after their finesse at inter-railing, the six Americans seemed completely flummoxed about having to change lines and get on a different train after only two stops.

Eventually we got to Pigalle. The hotel was across the road from the station and my heart sank as I saw the dilapidated building, which looked like it hadn't quite recovered from being bombed during the Second World War; the masonry was crumbling, the paintwork was peeling and I had no idea why it was called Hotel du Lac, when there were no lakes anywhere to be seen.

'Cool!'

'It's just like that movie with Nicole Kidman, isn't it?'

'So there's, like, hookers with TB on every street corner?'

I turned to the others. 'Huh?' I asked and Bridge pointed up and to her left.

I'd been so busy looking at our hotel that I'd missed the gigantic red neon sign of a windmill right in front of me. I felt my heart skip a beat and a tear squeeze its way out of my right eye and trickle down my cheek, which I wiped away furiously. It was the Moulin Rouge. We were in Paris. *I was finally in Paris* and that should have been enough to jolly me out of my bad mood, or at least pause to soak it all in. But the only thing that was soaking were the soles of my ballet flats. I looked around again to give Paris another chance to work its magic on me, then I saw a handwritten sign pinned to the nearest doorway that read, '*jeunes filless sexy, deuxième étage*'. I decided not to share with the group that we were in the middle of the red light district.

Hotel du Lac was just as run-down inside as it was outside. The carpets were threadbare and the furniture was dark, heavy and very old. But there wasn't so much as a crumb on the carpet and all the scarred wooden surfaces gleamed dully.

The manageress was a huge woman with her hair pinned up in a complicated coil and a bosom that jutted out majestically. All my guidebooks had warned me that Parisians could cop some serious attitude but her face was wreathed in smiles as seven water-logged paying customers trooped through the door. And when I said hesitantly, '*Excusez moi, Madame, nous avons réservé deux suites au centre d'information touristique de la Gare de Lyon*,' she came out from behind her reception desk so she could enfold me in her arms and press my face into her breasts.

'*Êtes-vous Anglais, ma petite?*' she asked in a deep bass voice.

'*Er, oui, mais mes amis sont Américains*,' I squeaked.

She sniffed at that, then released me but only so she could pinch my cheeks. '*Jolie fillette Anglaise*.' Then there was some guff about how my accent was *très bien*, and how she would personally make sure that my friends and I would want for nothing while we stayed at Hotel du Lac, but she did require a fifteen per cent deposit up front.

We dutifully handed over our euros, were given two room keys in return and ushered to a sweeping suitcase.

'Where's the elevator?' Jess hissed in my ear, but when I asked Madame le Proprietress, she just shrugged expansively. I was beginning to realize that she shoulder shrug was French for, 'like, what*ever*'.

'Well, that's just great,' Erin grumbled as we climbed up the stairs. And climbed. And climbed. And climbed some more.

Our rooms, when we finally got to them just before our oxygen supply ran out, were ginormous. I glimpsed a huge canopied bed in the boys' room and our room had one too, plus two single beds and a motley collection of furniture, including wardrobes, chest of drawers, bureaus and some complicated device that might have been a trouser press or a ducking stool. There was also an en suite bathroom, complete with bidet, which sent Jess, Erin and Bridge into shrieks of laughter, and huge French windows, which led out onto a balcony. If the rain still hadn't been sluicing down, I'd have stepped out onto it to crane my neck and see the Eiffel Tower and pretend I was Carrie Bradshaw.

But I'd never felt less like Carrie Bradshaw or Amélie or any of my other Parisian heroines. I just felt queasy every time I thought about phoning home or knocking on a door and bleating, '*Mon nom est Bea et je suis votre fille,*' when it opened.

I flopped down on the nearest bed and stared up at the ceiling, which had large cracks running across it. I barely even raised my head when there was a knock at the door and the boys trooped in. 'Steak *frites*, anyone?' Aaron called out as the girls emerged from the bathroom.

'At a French restaurant?' Erin asked doubtfully.

I wasn't sure I had the mental capacity to speak any more French, but I tried to look as if I was up to the job of official translator.

'I don't want to sound like an ugly American completely dissing the culture of the country I'm in, but can't we just go to McDonald's?' Bridge asked plaintively. 'Then get some beer and camp out here, unless you think it's going to stop raining?'

We all turned to look at the rain pounding against the windows. 'Well, there's no point in everyone going out and getting wet all over again,' Jess said reasonably. 'So, who's getting the short straw?'

Toph shrugged – it wasn't a French shrug, not even close. 'I'll go but it will cost you the price of a cheeseburger and fries and four bottles of beer.' He lent down and tentatively tugged the toe of my sneaker. 'What's French for six cheeseburgers and fries?'

Anything had to be better than staring up at the cracks in the ceiling and pretending that I was fine and everything was fine and I was super excited to be in Paris. 'It's OK,' I said, as perkily as I could, which actually wasn't very much. 'I can go.'

'You can't go on your own,' Toph said. 'I don't need to understand French to know what a flashing neon sign with a naked girl on it means. Don't think we're in the best part of town. We'll go together.'

I hauled myself off the bed. 'OK, sounds like a plan.'

My perky act was obviously fooling nobody as there were raised eyebrows and grimaces, as Toph gathered a collection of crumpled euro notes.

I was actually glad that it was raining because it meant we couldn't talk or do anything but hunch our shoulders and inch down the street while we tried to see the friendly glow of McDonald's golden arches even though visibility was practically zero.

Eventually we found a KFC and joined the queue of sodden customers. My jeans were clinging damply to me and I winced as I took a step forward and my sneakers squelched.

'Shall we get two party buckets?' Toph asked as he scrutinized the menu board. 'How do I say it in French?'

'*Je voudrais deux party buckets, s'il vous plaît*,' I said automatically, which was just a tiny bit thrilling. Maybe I'd dream in French tonight. 'I've got it covered; why don't you go and get the beer?'

'Except there was that whole thing where I didn't want to leave you on your own in the middle of the red light district,' Toph reminded me. 'Look! They sell beer! That would never happen in the States.'

'Yeah, well, you're not in Kansas any more, Toto.'

'Wow, that was kinda bitchy . . .' Toph said in surprise and I had to agree with him. 'God, Bea, I'm sick of this. What is up with you?'

'Nothing,' I snapped immediately. 'Honestly, I'm f—'

'Yeah, you're fine. I heard that the first few times you said it, Bea, and it never sounds that convincing.'

I willed the queue to move faster so I could deal with the party buckets and stumbling over the correct change because I always got confused with French numbers once I was past ten. 'I don't know what you're talking about,' I said haughtily.

'You're either still sulking about the row we had in Marseilles, though I thought you'd have gotten over that by now, or it's something to do with your mom or your dad. Whenever that topic comes up, you get really twitchy,' Toph continued as I turned to stare at him in confusion, because I did not twitch. Not ever. Except my right eyelid would go into this icky muscle

179

spasm when I was really stressed out.

'Look, nothing is wrong and even if it was, which it isn't, then you'd be the last person I'd tell. You were off with me in Marseilles before we even had that row and I don't trust people who are nice to me one minute and then treating me like crap the next. I certainly don't tell them my deepest, darkest secrets.' I was being really, really bitchy but then I decided that calling Toph out for his appalling treatment of me wasn't being bitchy, it was just standing up for myself.

Besides, Toph didn't seem particularly perturbed at my outburst. He just eyeballed the people behind us, who were making no attempt to hide the fact that our argument was entertaining, then smirked. It was a really irritating smirk that made me want to stamp my foot, possibly on Toph's head. 'Aha!' he said smugly. 'So, you *have* got deepest, darkest secrets.'

'I don't! They're just, like, hypothetical deep, dark secrets,' I informed him. 'And you still haven't explained why you froze me out in the club, before you started yelling at me!'

Toph opened his mouth to explain or possibly to get on my very last nerve, when the huge crowd of people in front of us suddenly dispersed and I had to try to remember the French for 'Can we supersize our fries, please.'

'To be continued,' Toph whispered in my ear just as I started to order, and it might have been the thought that we weren't done with this horrible conversation or his warm breath against my neck, but I completely lost the perfectly conjugated and grammatically correct sentence I had in my head and blurted out, 'Er, two party buckets and twenty bottles of Kronenberg, please.'

Chapter Fifteen

When I woke up the next morning the first thing I heard was the frantic splatter of rain against the windows. I turned over with an unhappy little whimper and tried to go back to sleep but my cheek brushed against something stiff and papery. I groped for it, sat up and prised open my eyes to read the note that Erin had left.

> *Dear Bea*
> *You were dead to the world and we didn't have the heart to wake you. We decided to go to the Embassy with Aaron –*
> *we're all a bit homesick and wanted a little touch of the U S of A. It's an American thing.*
> *Be back soon-ish with ~~pan, du pain~~, those briochey things with chocolate inside them!*
> *Later, gator*
> *Erin x*

They weren't going to be back soon-ish. I'd had enough experience waiting at the Consulate in Marseilles to know they'd be gone *hours* and all the shops would be out of *pain au chocolat*, which were more of a breakfast pastry than say an *éclair*, which was a post-lunch cake.

After I'd got washed and dressed and breakfasted on my last peanut butter KitKat and some lukewarm Diet Coke, I knew what I had to do.

When I switched my phone back on, it beeped furiously into life. I had five voice messages from Mum; none of which had any useful biographical or geographical information on my dad, just dire threats about what would happen if I didn't come home. By the last call she was leaning towards phoning up the bank to get them to put a stop on my debit card and putting my framed *Amélie* poster in the garage. When I was at home and she was kicking off, her threats really worked, not that I gave her much reason to kick off. But sitting cross-legged on the bed of my Parisian hotel room she was nothing more than a voice squawking down the phone. I'd come this far and I couldn't go home; now now, not yet . . .

There were a couple of text messages from Ruby, along the lines of DIE, YOU STINKING WHORE, which I deleted without a single pang of fear, then I phoned Grandma Minor. I wasn't calling Mum, not when she was in squawk mode, and Grandma Major wasn't good over the phone, because it made her hearing aid buzz. Anyway, Grandma Minor could quell Mum with one look and she had the softest of soft spots for her oldest grandchild.

I knew I'd made the right decision, as soon as she answered the phone.

'Oh, Bea,' she said and there wasn't a single note of reproach, just concern and maybe a little wry amusement. 'Why couldn't you schedule your teenage rebellion for a more convenient time? Say, when you're actually at home. I think we could all cope with a little door slamming.'

'Yeah, well, I don't think you can schedule these things.

And is wanting to meet my dad really that rebellious? I just saw an opportunity and I ran with it and this is small potatoes compared to what Mum got up to when she was my age.'

Gran hmmed, which meant she wasn't going to get drawn into that discussion. 'Where are you anyway?'

'In Paris.'

'Is it living up to all your wildest dreams?'

I sighed. 'It's rained non-stop. So far I've seen the inside of two Metro stations and a KFC, but the sun has to come out eventually, right?'

'Of course, it's the law of averages and it's been pouring here too. Ravaged my roses.'

'So I take it from all the voicemail messages that she hasn't—'

'Bea, darling, I'm not sure this is the best way to have this conv—'

We were talking over each other, which always made me feel tongue-tied and awkward. 'It's all right, Gran. You go first.'

She took a deep breath, like she was nervous, which was ridiculous because Grandma Minor didn't ever get nervous. 'I really don't want to have this conversation with you on the phone. In fact, *I* shouldn't be having this conversation with you, your mother should,' She 'hmm'ed again until I was grinding my teeth in frustration. 'Why don't I get her to give you a call?'

'There's no point,' I gritted. 'It's all threats and counter-threats and shouting and hissing. So what's going on? I bet she's done absolutely nothing about tracing Dad's address in Paris.'

'Darling girl, he's not in Paris,' Grandma Minor said very gently. 'He never was. He's not even French.'

'You what?' I could feel my body lurching forward as if I was in freefall, even though I was still sitting cross-legged on the bed, not moving, apart from my mouth, which had gone slack-jawed and gapey. 'What are you talking about? He's French. *She* said he was French and he came from Paris and he went back there when she told him—'

'I told your mother she'd have to come up with a story and stick to it for when you were older, but by the time you were three you were already obsessed with the idea of fathers and why you didn't have one,' Grandma told me.

'Why did she need to come up with a story?' I demanded. 'Why couldn't she have told me the truth? Who's my father?'

It was kind of funny in a darkly horrible way that really wasn't. I felt like some girl in a straight-to-DVD movie called *Who's My Daddy?*

'Bea, you need to come home and have this talk with your mother,' she said. 'Please, don't be too hard on her. She was very young when she had you and she was also very young when she was making decisions like this . . .'

'But it wasn't a decision,' I burst out, tears starting to stream down my cheeks. 'It was a lie! Fifty per cent of my life has been a bloody lie. I hate her!'

'No, you don't,' Gran said sharply. 'You feel very hurt

185

and betrayed and you're angry with her, but you don't hate her.'

Right then, I did. I hated my mother more than I'd ever hated anyone, even Ruby. Every conversation we'd had about my father, and there'd been plenty, she'd looked me in the eye and lied to me. And when she hadn't been lying, she'd been skirting around the truth so much that it didn't even resemble the truth any more. Even stenciling the walls of my *Amélie* bedroom had been one more gigantic untruth on a road paved with untruths that had led me right to this moment in this very spot in a shabby hotel room in . . .

'Paris! She's ruined Paris for me!' I couldn't stop crying, but they were tears of sheer rage, which made the way I'd felt about Ruby and gang seem like a very minor snit now. I also couldn't bring myself to say the words 'mum' or 'mother', but I think Grandma Minor understood because she just made soothing noises. It was only when I was all sobbed out and hiccuping so hard it made my ribs ache, that she spoke.

'So who are these Americans you've palled up with?'

It was a relief to change the subject. I told her about falling asleep on the train and clubbing in Marseilles and Aaron having his passport stolen and being clutched to the bosom of Madame la Proprietress and by the time I was telling her how much spicier French KFC was compared to its bland English cousin, I was a lot calmer. Which had probably been Gran's intention; she was really good at damage limitation.

186

'So are you going to tell me I have to come home and face the music now?' I asked her, though it was pretty much a foregone conclusion.

'No, I'm not,' Gran said crisply, and my mouth gaped open again. 'I think you should stay in Paris for a little longer. Have some of those adventures that you're always claiming you want to have. What's your hotel like?'

I looked around at the mismatched furniture and the fraying curtains. 'It's a bit of a dive.'

'How much money have you got left?'

I rummaged in my bag. 'Well, enough for a week, not enough to get another room in some swanky-pants hotel and anyway, I want to stay with the others. We've made this promise to stick together.'

'How about I put some money in that online money thingy, what do you call it?'

'My PayPal account? Gran, you don't have to do that!' I protested.

'Nonsense. If you're going to have some adventures, then you need the proper funds, and I want you to promise me something, Bea . . .' Gran lowered her voice meaningfully and I knew the money was the carrot and I was just about to get the stick.

'What?' I asked suspiciously. 'I'm not calling *her*. I'm so mad right now it would be five minutes of non-stop swearing.'

'I'm sure it wouldn't – we've brought you up much better than that,' Gran laughed. 'And I think that you and your mother need a little time out. But I want you to promise me that you'll buy something utterly frivolous with some of the money so when you do come home, you'll look at it and think of Paris kindly.'

'I really am over Paris, Gran,' I sniffed.

'You'll feel better when it stops raining,' Gran insisted. 'You always get very peevish when it rains. Now, do you promise?'

'Yeah, I promise,' I said, though it was a silly promise and it would be months before I'd be in a frivolous mood. 'I love you.'

'And you know I love you too, darling. Now no more tears, all right?'

Of course, I said I wouldn't cry any more, though I was sure that when I hung up I'd burst into tears again. But the river had run dry. I got off the bed and walked over to the big, tarnished mirror and stared at my face, seeing the same echo of *her* in my familiar features but scrutinizing my widow's peak, and my long, long lashes, my freckles and my very pouty bottom lip – the bits of me that were unclaimed and that I'd always supposed I'd inherited from my French side of the family. Now I didn't know who they belonged to.

I was in the bathroom splashing cold water on my puffy, tear-soaked face when Erin and Jess burst through the door so hard that it crashed against the wall and I nearly skewered my left eye out with a finger.

'There you are!' Erin exclaimed, like they'd been searching Paris for hours in an effort to track me down.

'We're taking you out for lunch, our treat.'

'But I've only just had breakfast!' I angled a glance out of the window. 'And it's still raining.'

I might just as well have been talking to the hat stand for all the good it did. Jess and Erin were threading my arms through my mac, which the grandmas had insisted I pack 'just to be on the safe side'. They were both really hyper, like Alfie when we hadn't been monitoring his sugar intake. 'What happened at the Embassy?' I asked as I was pulled through the door and out into the corridor.

'It was fine,' Jess assured me breezily. 'We came, we saw, we waited and read *US Weekly* cover to cover, then Aaron got his new passport.'

'So that's good, right?'

'It's very good,' Erin agreed. 'So we're having steak *frites* to celebrate and to thank you for . . . er . . .'

'Why are you thanking me? You were the ones who went to the Embassy.'

'There wouldn't have been a passport at the Embassy if you hadn't kicked bureaucratic butt in Marseilles,' Jess said impatiently, pushing me towards the door. 'Jeez, Bea, it's a free lunch, what's your beef?'

There was no such thing as a free lunch, James always said, though I wasn't sure exactly what he meant. But as we got to the little wood-panelled bistro where we were meeting the others, I forgot my suspicions and for the first time since we arrived in Paris, I really felt like I was in Paris. The restaurant looked a lot like a Toulouse-Lautrec painting, complete with bowing waiter with handlebar moustache who ushered us to a cosy red velvet booth at the back of a room that smelt very pleasantly of fresh bread and garlic.

Aaron leapt to his feet so I could slide onto the bench (though actually this would be one of the rare occasions I could use the word *banquette* and not seem like a total poseur), then sat down again so I was snugly ensconced between him and Bridge, who nudged my arm and beamed at me while everyone else was saying hello and reaching over and around the table to pat and squeeze me. Kind of how I'd imagined my French family would react when I fetched up on their doorstep, before I was told that they didn't exist.

The only person who wasn't gushing over me like I'd just rescued a basket of puppies from a burning building was Toph. He sat on the opposite banquette, wedged between the wall and Michael, smiling thinly with arms folded as the general Bea worship carried on around him. I supposed that after the incident in the KFC we were officially back on no-speakers but really I had other things to worry about. Even being the bastard child of some unknown, not-at-all-French father couldn't compete with the paranoia that something was seriously wrong. Why else were they being so nice to me?

'Anything you want from the menu, Bea,' Aaron told me, as I opened the leather-bound volume that the waiter gave me. 'Appetizers, puddings, whatever.'

Jess enthused wildly about my hair, even though it was

frizzy from the rain, and Bridge kept squeezing my hand and seemed really upset when I asked her to let go so I could start eating my *frites*.

I couldn't finish my *frites*, which had to be a first, because there were a lot of little sidelong glances and nudging when they thought I wasn't looking, that ruined my appetite. But it wasn't until I was cracking the top of my *crème brûlée* that Aaron cleared his throat and everyone suddenly went silent.

'So, like, Bea, we went to the Embassy to get my passport and it was really cool . . . everyone talking American and telling us to have a nice day, but I had to pay a fortune to get a new passport so quickly.'

'That sucks,' I said. 'But on the bright side, at least you've got it now.'

'Yeah,' Aaron sighed. 'I guess what I'm trying to say is that I'm . . . we're ready to go home now.'

'But I thought you were going to stay in Paris for at least a week. That's what you all said.'

'Yeah, but I'm broke now I had to shell out for a new passport,' Aaron said heavily. 'And being at the Embassy made us realize that we're missing home.'

'And it's raining . . .' Jess chimed in.

'And I want ketchup on my fries, not mayonnaise.'

'And I'm so sick of being on trains. I miss driving.'

'It's just time to go home, you know?'

I didn't know because I was under strict orders from Grandma not to set foot on English soil until she gave me the nod. 'It's not going to keep raining,' was all I could say as I pushed away my uneaten *crème brûlée*.

'Sweetie, the only pro in the pro and con list we made is you, but you're going to stay with your dad and he doesn't want you turning up with six friends, does he?' Bridge said gently.

I should have told them that my dad wasn't expecting me – on so many different levels. Instead, I'd made it sound like he was getting the guest room ready and unrolling the welcome mat. 'When are you going?' I asked, because it was too late to go with the truth now. I could tell from the guilty looks that there was nothing I could say that would change their minds. It was a done deal. But at least we'd still have a couple more days together.

Erin winced. 'Promise you won't freak.'

Every muscle in my body stiffened. 'Why would I freak?' I asked slowly.

'We've managed to get a standby flight for late this afternoon through the Embassy's travel department. It was either that or wait until tomorrow when the airline wasn't sure that they'd have enough standby seats,' Aaron said in a garbled rush. 'Got to be at the airport for four.'

'But it's half past one now!' I pointed out, my voice shrill. 'That's not enough time to pack and check out and get the Metro.'

'Please don't freak out, Bea,' Jess begged me, nudging me with her foot under the table. 'You'll be fine. You'll be hanging with your dad – we'd never have bailed like this if we hadn't known you'd be OK. Can you be cool about this and not hate us too much?'

I was battling so many emotions but hate wasn't one of them. I was so consumed with hate for my mother that there wasn't enough left for anyone else. 'Yeah, sure. I'll even come and see you off at the airport,' I added, because that would kill a few hours of alone time. I knew one thing though; I was never going on holiday with anyone else ever again. From now on, I was going to kick it solo so there'd be no more nasty surprises like my so-called friends turning on me like a pack of attack dogs or my new friends suddenly bailing out.

'That would be cool,' Jess said, pulling a piece of paper out of her pocket. 'You can help the five of us if we run into any French speakers when we have to check in.'

'Five of you?' I queried, my heart lifting. 'Who's staying then?'

'I am. I'm not done with Europe just yet,' Toph said. It was the first time he'd opened his mouth. 'I want to go to Prague and maybe Berlin if there's time.'

James's young software designers were always going off for long weekends in Berlin and Prague and coming back with arty T-shirts and tales of all-night drinking in clubs that looked like coffee shops and drinking coffee in cafés that looked like nightclubs. If Toph was astounded that KFC sold beer, then Prague and Berlin would play his tiny Texan mind, I thought meanly. Because, God, he really brought out the mean in me. I didn't say anything, just turned back to Erin, who was still looking as if all her future happiness depended on me being happy that she was going back to the States. But not *too* happy.

'OK,' I said, resting my elbows on the table. 'I understand, even if I think it pretty much sucks.'

Chapter Sixteen

Everyone was very quiet as we walked to the Metro in the pouring rain a couple of hours later. 'Well, we'll always have Paris,' Aaron joked when Bridge stepped in a puddle, but that was all anyone said until we got on the train and had a heated debate about which station we needed to change at to get to Charles de Gaulle airport.

I waited while they checked in at the American Airlines desk, then we slowly made our way to Passport Control. Aaron and Michael gave me brisk, manly hugs and told me to steer clear of the vodka martinis. Bridge's hug was tighter and there was a bit of hair stroking as we both promised to keep in touch. Then Erin and Jess fell on me with pained little crics and we clung to each other in a group hug that got very soggy, very fast.

'Friend me on Facebook as soon as you're near a computer,' Erin reminded me when we finally came up for air. 'And I have a great calling plan. We can speak every week once I'm back at college.'

'Or we can do Skype for free,' Jess exclaimed. 'And we'll see you next summer. Road trip!'

'Road trip,' I dutifully repeated and I knew I should be crying and frantically promising to keep in touch but it felt as if everything that was good was ending and I was powerless to stop it. My eyes drifted over to the departure board. 'You should get a wiggle on. They've called your gate number.'

'I'm going to miss your weird British sayings,' Erin sniffed mournfully, gathering me in for another hug. 'Now, you're going to be all right, aren't you? You know how to get to your dad's place from here?' I'd checked out of Hotel du Lac so as not to give the game away but I'd tried to communicate through my eyes that I'd be back later on to check in again. I wasn't entirely sure that the receptionist had understood though.

'Erin, Bea's a whiz on the Metro – she'll be fine,' Aaron said as he started to corral the others towards Passport Control. 'Toph, Bea, shall we cut it short? I have to get some Toblerones in Duty Free.'

Toph grinned. 'Get gone,' he said. 'I'm sick to death of the sight of you five.'

They picked up their bags, checked boarding passes and slowly ambled over to join the long queue waiting to go through Passport Control. Eventually they got to the point where the line took an abrupt turn and then with some last shouted goodbyes, they disappeared from view.

I'd only known them for a few short days but it seemed like forever and I had a huge, immoveable lump in my throat as I turned round to face Toph. He wriggled his shoulders so his backpack was more comfortable, gave me a half-hearted wave and said, 'Right, well, see you. Have a nice life and all that.'

Then he walked off, leaving me standing there in the bustling throng of the airport. It felt as if everyone but me had an elsewhere to be, or people to greet or a plane to catch. They were all in the midst of life and I was stuck in one place, not able to go forwards or backwards.

I was alone.

I sank down on my suitcase and put my head in my hands and tried to think. I needed to get back to Paris and find somewhere to stay and something to do for the next week or so. Or else I could go home now and face my mother. But when I tried to picture her in my mind all I could see was an angry, swirly red cloud.

I gave a frustrated groan and curled in on myself because this was all too much to deal with and . . .

'Bea? Come on, it's going to be all right.'

I felt a hand on my shoulder. I raised my head to see Toph crouched down in front of me, looking concerned and caring and all the ways he'd used to look at me before we'd gone frosty.

'You've come back . . .' I mumbled because the lump was still lodged in my throat and it made talking difficult.

'Yeah, I came back,' Toph agreed with a rueful smile. 'See, I felt kinda guilty about saying goodbye like that. And when I looked over my shoulder, I thought you were crying.'

I shook my head, relieved that the tears hadn't started . . . yet. Also relieved that Toph had come back, even if it was just to say goodbye properly, before he went away again. 'I'm not crying,' I said. 'Honestly, I'm fine.'

Toph scrutinized my face for signs of crying, until I ducked my head because I had a feeling that my shaky hold

197

on being fine might start to crack under pressure. 'Your stiff upper lip is wobbling,' Toph remarked. 'And the bottom one too.'

He was right. My mouth was trembling like a washing line on a windy day and when I bit my lip to stop the tremors, the first tears began to fall. There weren't any sobs, which I was profoundly grateful about, as I scrubbed my cheeks with the backs of my hands. 'I wouldn't have started crying if you hadn't kept going on about it,' I grumbled.

Toph patted my shoulder again. 'Look, you'll see them again,' he said softly.

It wasn't really why the tears were still streaming, but Toph was being nice and I had this sudden urge to fling myself into his arms and cry and cry until I made his Los Campesinos T-shirt soggy. Instead I braced my legs and gripped the edge of my suitcase so I didn't give in to the impulse. 'Really, Toph, I'll be fine,' I croaked. 'You go and get your train. I thought you were going to Prague.'

Toph looked at his watch. 'I don't think that's going to happen today. It's a fifteen-hour journey.' He stood up and held out his hand. 'Look, even if I go to Berlin, I still have to go back to Paris first, so let's get the train together and get some dinner. I'm starving.'

I let Toph lever me up. 'Dinner sounds good,' I conceded, because I'd been in Paris two days now and I hadn't even had a *croque monsieur* and I'd barely been able to eat my lunch.

We both reached for my suitcase at the same time, but Toph batted my hand away and with an anticipatory grunt he lifted it up and we began to walk towards the station.

Toph asked me where I wanted to go for dinner and I decided on Montmartre because even in the rain Montmartre would be magical. It turned out that it wasn't; there's very little magic when you're negotiating a suitcase and an umbrella.

We stopped at the first café we came to even though it didn't have a striped awning, and it wasn't on a street corner with tables and little wicker chairs outside, which was how I'd imagined all French cafés to be. But it was warm and dry, even if the tables were made of Formica, the clientele of middle-aged men – mostly in overalls – were distinctly unchic, and the TV mounted to the wall was tuned to a football game.

Toph and I grabbed the last table and I ordered coffees and *croque monsieurs*. The lump in my throat was still there and it made swallowing a tricky manoeuvre as Toph and I tucked into probably the best toasted ham and cheese sandwiches in the world. Our coffees were so thick and creamy that it was like drinking hot coffee milkshake, but both of us still pushed coffee and *croque monsieurs* away half finished as Toph told me in a throaty voice about what he wanted to do in Prague, which included seeing this crooked building called the Dancing House and drinking absinthe. I liked watching Toph talk, as much as I liked listening to him. He would get so animated; everything he was feeling flickered across his face and his

199

long fingers would draw patterns in the air. But best of all, his eyes would keep catching mine, just to make sure I was paying attention, which I was. I was hanging off his every word because my crush still hadn't died; it had just been napping.

'And what are you going to do in Paris when it finally stops raining?' he asked.

I shrugged. 'I don't think it will ever stop raining.'

'Has to eventually. I bet your dad has all sorts of stuff planned.' Toph paused and looked at me and I knew he was staring at my right eyelid, which was pulsing away. 'What's going on with you, Bea?'

'Nothing!' I insisted. 'Why do you always ask me that?'

'Because I have three older sisters and they all look the exact same way you do when they're stressing about something and they all snap "Nothing!" in the exact same tone when you ask them what's wrong.' Toph grimaced. 'But it's always something.'

It was a whole lot of something but I didn't know where to start so I just hung my head and looked at the dregs in my coffee cup.

'Please, Bea . . .' Toph murmured and he reached across the Formica to gently touch my hand.

It was as if the brush of Toph's fingers was the secret combination that unlocked the box of secrets I'd buried away in the very heart of me. I opened my mouth and it was easy to form the first sentence. 'I'm not going to stay with my dad in Paris because I don't know who my father is.' And the second sentence was all cued up and ready to go too. 'I do know that he isn't French and he doesn't live in Paris but that information only came to light this morning.'

'But I don't understand.' I could see Toph trying to process what he'd just heard. 'You *said* you were going to stay with your dad who lived in Paris. You've been saying that for days.'

'And I believed it – but there was stuff I didn't say; like I'd never met him before because he'd hotfooted it back over the English Channel when my mum told him she was pregnant. Or at least that's what she always told me.' I wished Toph would stop looking at me in such an accusatory fashion. Only about, say, seventeen per cent of this was my fault. The other eighty-three per cent was entirely up to . . . 'None of this is going to make any sense unless I tell you about my mum.'

It took another hour, two more coffees and a shared piece of *tarte tatin* before Toph had the complete backstory. I had wondered if I was overreacting about the whole thing; but Toph gave a long, low whistle as I started and kept interrupting with 'No?' and 'She didn't?' and 'Un-fucking-believable,' so I knew I was reacting just the right amount.

'So, after you spoke to your gran, we come back from the Embassy to tell you we're leaving town,' Toph said when I got to the end of my unhappy tale. 'That was the worst timing in the world. You should have said something.'

'Nah. They were ready to go and I'd have felt awful, or

more awful, if they'd decided to stay when they didn't want to.'

We'd been prodding at the *tarte tatin* with our forks but not really eating it. I still had a lump in my throat, which seemed to have grown jagged edges. I'd seen Toph put away two cheeseburgers, two portions of fries, a side of beans and an apple pie in one sitting, but he was leaving the tart unfinished so he could steeple his fingers and look at me from over the top of them.

'So what's the plan?'

'I haven't got one,' I admitted. 'I guess I need to find another hotel and hole up there for a while.' I turned my head to get away from Toph's intense stare and looked at the raindrops trickling down the café's smeared glass windows. Then I admitted the most awful truth of all. 'God, I hate Paris!'

Toph chuckled, though it morphed into a cough halfway through, probably because I was glaring at him. 'No you don't,' he scoffed. 'You love Paris.'

I shook my head. 'I don't. And it has nothing to do with the rain and everything to do with the fact I don't belong here. I never, ever did!'

Toph picked up one of my many Parisian guidebooks that we'd been studying to figure out which station he needed to go to Berlin. He started to leaf through it. 'Well, I like Paris. What I've seen of it anyway. Shame we never got to go to Marais or the Île de la Cité . . .'

'That's where the Berthillon café is,' I blurted out. 'Apparently their chocolate ice cream is the single best foodstuff in the entire world and there's also this sweet shop – that would be a candy shop in American . . . I saw pictures of it on a blog and—'

'Maybe we can go there tomorrow,' Toph said casually. 'I think I've seen enough crumbling churches to last a lifetime.'

'But you're going to Prague by way of Berlin,' I reminded him, as I checked my watch. 'And you're going to miss your train.'

'Last time I checked, Berlin and Prague weren't going anywhere,' Toph said like it was no big deal. 'Sides, unlike you, I still have a soft spot for Paris.'

'That's really nice of you,' I said carefully. 'But you don't have to do that for me.'

'I know,' Toph said smartly, with that smirky grin which always made me want to clench my fists, crush or no crush. 'And that's a pretty high opinion you've got of yourself, but a) you're not staying on your own in a foreign place, b) having to spend some extra time in Paris isn't exactly a hardship, and c) I'm not feeling so great and I don't think I could stand to spend hours in a stuffy train carriage.'

I was all ready to bite out a passionate declaration of independence in answer to Toph's monkey crack idea that I couldn't look after myself, until he got to his last point. 'I've had this lump in my throat all day. I thought it was a sad lump but now it feels scratchy. Almost sore.' I swallowed experimentally. Yes, sore. Maybe even verging on swollen.

'The outside of my throat feels really itchy,' Toph said, rubbing his neck. 'And I have earache.'

I swallowed again. 'Oh my God! So have I!'

We took a moment to bond over feeling crap and decided that mooching around in rain of biblical proportions was the prime culprit.

'So we should probably find a hotel,' Toph suggested. 'It's nearly six now and we shouldn't leave it too late.'

'But let's stock up on munchies and drinks 'cause I really don't feel like doing much of anything for the rest of the day. Unless you do?' I really hoped Toph didn't and he was shaking his head and scratching his throat again.

'Right, let's make a move,' Toph said decisively, making no effort to move or do anything except huddle deeper into his hoodie.

I looked out of the window again and pulled a face. 'Maybe we should have one more coffee and wait for the rain to ease off.'

We left the café when the waiter started ostentatiously wiping down our table and muttering under his breath.

We started walking and decided that the first hotel we came to was where we'd hang our hats. The more we walked, the worse I felt. My nose was running and I didn't have a hand free to wipe it and after half an hour my back started aching, though that was probably due to humping my hateful, hideous bloody suitcase.

'I'm sure we've been down this street,' I whinged as we turned into yet another narrow cobbled street, because I was also getting very petulant. 'I saw that cake shop an hour ago.'

Toph came to an abrupt halt so I went smack bang into him, though I took the opportunity to wipe my nose on the back of his hoodie – the rain would soon wash my snot away. 'What's down there?' Toph asked, pointing at a narrow arch between a cake shop and a dowdy fashion store, which made Wilson's look like Chanel.

I tried to squint through the rain. 'Dunno.'

'Come on,' Toph called over his shoulder as he dived between the shops, even though the arch probably led to the place where they kept their dustbins.

But what it led to was a sweet little courtyard filled with flowers in pots and an elegant redbrick house with a sign above the door that said: '*Hôtel*.'

Toph and I both ran for the entrance, bumping each other to get through the door and out of the rain. I resorted to elbows and even a bit of foot stamping to enter a tiled foyer that smelt of beeswax and freesias from the huge vase of flowers sitting on the reception desk. The man behind the desk looked at me in alarm as I dripped water all over his floor and padded over with an imploring look. I knew it was imploring because I could feel my eyebrows knitting together.

'*Monsieur, avez-vous deux chambres*?' I bleated, abandoning my suitcase halfway across the lobby.

He shook his head and I felt my heart plummet all the way down to my sodden tennis shoes. '*Nous avons seulement une double*,' he told me sorrowfully. 'One twin room.'

'We'll take it,' Toph yelped from somewhere behind me. I opened my mouth to quibble but then I realized that I didn't care if it was a room with bunk beds, or a double bed that we had to share, or even one single bed that we had to fight each other over. As long as it was dry and there was a horizontal surface I could lie on, then I didn't care.

'Yeah, we'll take it,' I agreed.

The man, who was carved of cheekbone and had a very retro *Mad Men* vibe, which would have made me all tongue-tied and blushtastic in the normal circumstances, smiled. 'Welcome to the Hôtel Shangri-La,' he said. 'We'll check you in, then Henri will show you to your room.'

Henri, another *Mad Men* extra, did indeed show us to our room. As Toph shoved a handful to euros in Henri's hand, I collapsed face down on the nearest bed.

'Bea, if you're feeling as crap as I am, then you might want to take off your wet clothes before you lapse into a coma,' Toph groaned, sinking down on the other double bed.

It was the first time in my life that a boy was encouraging me to get undressed – a watershed moment in any girl's life – but I simply kicked off my shoes, pulled and tugged at my wet, unwieldy clothing and when I was down to bra and pants, I crawled into bed and sank down with a grateful sigh.

Not that Toph was driven mad at the sight of my goosepimpled girl flesh. He was too busy stripping off his own soaked clothes. When he was down to just his boxers, he dived under the covers. I got a fleeting glimpse of the knobs of his spine and that groove that boys have by their hipbones, but I was monumentally not interested. Not because Toph's spine knobs or hip grooves were hideous but because all I could think about was how swallowing didn't just hurt my throat but my ears, my head and even the backs of my eyelids.

Chapter Seventeen

For the next two days, our life shrank down to that one room and the en suite bathroom. It was a very nice room; painted the same zingy green as Ruby's Mac eyeshadow with a few Pop Art prints on the wall to break up the zingyness. The two double beds were heaped with cushions and pillows in every hue from baby pink to a deep, dark blood-red and the whole effect was colourful and chaotic.

Not that Toph and I appreciated it much. We stayed dozing in our beds, only rousing ourselves to compare symptoms and sit up when Henri or Michel, the night porter, appeared with bowls of soup from the kitchen, more tissues and the French equivalent of Sudafed. I didn't like being ill in a foreign country when I was miles from home without my ratty Emily Strange hoodie that I always wore when I was sick.

I'd been so busy being mad at Mum that I hadn't let myself miss her, but she really came into her own when I was poorly. She'd order sweet and sour chicken soup from my favourite Chinese takeaway and buy the really expensive Green & Black's organic chocolate ice cream. She also knew that the only thing I could bear to watch were old Hollywood musicals. And if it was a Thursday and I suddenly felt better, she always let me have the Friday off school too.

The grandmas had both rung me and I'd tried to sound perky but when I hacked up one of my lungs as I tried to say hello, Grandma Major was all for getting the first Eurostar to Paris and taking me home, but I realized that I wasn't ready to face Mum yet. So I told Grandma it was just a summer cold.

Toph also got phone calls from each one of his three sisters and his mum and his Aunt Dolores, who lived across the street. I tried not to eavesdrop but his side of each conversation was monosyllabic and consisted of, 'Yeah?' repeated frequently. Occasionally he'd mix it up by throwing in the odd 'You don't say?' and once there was even a 'Well, he never had a lick of sense.' It was very different to my conversations with the grandmas.

Every time I hung up the phone, Toph would roll his eyes and say, 'God, your family like to talk, don't they? I thought the British were reserved.'

'You've never met my grandmas,' I'd say and I'd launch into a long anecdote about how both of them loved to get all TMI at the bus stop or in the supermarket, and Toph would lift his head up off his pillows so he could smile at me and it was a smile that said that he knew my mum hadn't called and he wasn't going to make it worse by asking about it.

That was the one good thing about being ill in a hotel room in Paris – Toph and I hadn't just bonded, it was as if we shared one mind, as well as a bathroom. On the third day of our confinement, we both managed to rally when Henri bought up a plate of cream-filled pastries courtesy of the kitchen. We sat on his bed watching *The Simpsons* in French and licking *créme Anglaise* off our fingers.

'You know, we're always going to be friends now,' Toph said out of the blue. 'We've been through something together. This is how soldiers in Vietnam must have felt.'

I nodded, because OK we hadn't spent forty-eight hours in a foxhole hiding from enemy fire but Toph had seen me soaked in sweat and snot and I'd seen him blow his nose on his boxer shorts because I'd used the last of the tissues and Henri hadn't come back with fresh supplies.

'Friends forever,' I said solemnly and we shook on it with sticky fingers.

Toph looked at me from under his lashes and, even red-faced and with a chafed nose, he still made my stomach do a quickstep. 'Bea, if we're friends forever, can I have the last mini *éclair*?' he asked winsomely.

'All yours,' I said, pushing the plate nearer to him, but that was only because I was going to puke if I ate any more and had nothing to do with the permanence of our friendship.

The next day when I woke up, everything was different.

For a start, my tongue wasn't stuck to the roof of my Sahara-dry mouth, my hair wasn't soaked in sweat and I didn't have that sandpaper feeling in my throat any more.

Then I opened my eyes.

Within nanoseconds, I was leaping from my bed to Toph's bed, clearing the two-metre gap with an ease that would have amazed my games teacher, so I could bounce up and down.

'Wake up! Wake up! Wake up!' I chanted, my voice rising in pitch and my feet getting perilously close to Toph's legs as he opened one eye.

'What?' he asked in a rusty voice, but I couldn't tell if that was because he'd just woken up or because he wasn't a hundred per cent better like me.

'How do you feel?' I demanded, still jumping up and down, which made Toph moan pitifully in protest.

Toph stretched gingerly as if he was expecting a world of agony from his aching limbs. He looked surprised when he realized they were cooperating, then raised one hand to his throat as he swallowed. 'You know, I think I feel better,' he said with a note of wonder. He swallowed again. 'A lot better. Stop bouncing before you break the bed.'

'Look out of the window!' I yelped, sitting down on my next bounce. 'There's a big yellow disc in the sky and it's totally not raining!'

Toph scrambled out of bed and raced to the window, where the sun was high up in the sky and generally being all shiny and glowy. 'How can such a miracle be possible?' He wrestled with the window lock, hefted up the sash window and leant out. 'God, it's warm! It feels so good.'

With one eye on Toph's back, I inched off the bed and started stealthily padding towards the bathroom.

I was almost home and dry, when Toph said, 'Hey, you had the bathroom first yesterday. It's my turn.'

My fingers had already connected with the door handle and I opened it just in time to slam the door in Toph's face. 'You snooze, you lose, my friend,' I called out as he thumped on the door.

It felt so good to wear a dress and feel it float against my bare legs as I skipped down the stairs and waved at Henri, who looked at Toph and me in amazement. He must have begun to think that we were surgically attached to our beds.

The Shangri-La's courtyard looked much prettier when it wasn't under the onslaught of heavy showers. We took a moment to admire the flowers, but only a moment, because we were both starving and 'We need to find a proper Parisian café,' I told Toph excitedly as we set off on our travels. 'It has to be on a corner with tables outside and an awning and possibly a Perrier sign.'

'Like that café over there,' Toph said, grinning when I clapped my hands in joy, like he'd made it magically appear just to make me happy.

We grabbed a perfectly positioned table where we could see the action from the two streets that converged on the corner and ordered coffee and a proper *petit déjeuner*: a *tartine*, a small French stick still warm from the oven, which we slathered in salty butter, and sweet, sweet marmalade, orange juice and really strong coffee because it had been days since we'd had a caffeine fix.

When the *tartines* were just flaky crumbs on our plates, I got out my favourite Paris guidebook and started flicking through it. 'So where do you want to go today?' I asked Toph. 'We could go to Versailles or the Musee d'Orsay . . . Oh! And there's the Catacombs too or the Royal Opera and the Jardins de Luxembourg . . .' I could have rattled off Parisian things to see and do until sunset but Toph reached over and snatched the guidebook out of my hands.

'Please, Bea . . .' he protested. 'We've been ill and I've already done half of Europe with Bridge and Aaron, who are complete guidebook fascists. Can't we just soak up the vibe?'

'I don't understand this vibe that you want to soak up,' I said, because even though Paris would have to do some serious sucking up to make me like it again, I had a list of places I wanted to visit.

'Well, it involves picking one bit of Paris every day and exploring and meandering and lots of going to cafés to people-watch, and we should also find some old men who are playing *boules*,' Toph explained as if he'd given the matter some thought. 'No more cathedrals or museums, though the Catacombs sound pretty cool.'

I was feeling a little museum-fatigued and not completely recovered from my three-day bed-in, but I never kicked it free style – I just wasn't made that way. 'We can't wander around aimlessly for days, we'll miss stuff!' I folded my arms and gave Toph a stern look, which got me some eyebrow waggling in return. 'There has to be rules.'

Toph shrugged. 'OK, we'll have rules,' he said with a grin that I didn't trust one little bit, as he took my pen and began scribbling on a napkin.

I craned my neck to see what he was writing but Toph covered the napkin with his other hand. I passed the time by watching a twenty-something boy and girl a couple of tables along indulging in such an enthusiastic PDA that I got all red-faced just surreptitiously staring at them.

Blushing, I turned away to find that Toph had finished his list. 'Well, let me have a look at it then,' I mumbled, and Toph presented it with a very unnecessary flourish.

My eyes scanned the contents:

1. *We can only take the Metro twice a day. No taxis. No buses. We walk.*
2. *We have to talk to at least three strangers every day. Preferably in their native language.*
3. *If it doesn't fit in your shoulder bag, you don't take it with you.*
4. *We take an hour for lunch and at least one coffee break mid-morning and mid-afternoon.*
5. *Find some old men playing boules.*
6. *No map consulting, same goes for guidebooks, timetables and Tourist Information Centre employees.*
7. *We don't eat anywhere that has signage in any other language but French.*
8. *In our quest to find the real Paris, there will be no moaning about feet hurting, bags being too heavy or inclement weather conditions. We just hole up in the first café.*

It was a list designed solely so we could have adventures and stumble on cool little places and people that we'd never have found otherwise. Like, how we'd found the

Shangri-La, which was simply the best, most beautiful hotel in the world with the best and most beautiful staff.

'Am I allowed to add some stuff?' I ventured. 'In the spirit of the list?'

'Sure.' Toph handed me back my pen. 'Knock yourself out.'

I took a moment to think, then bent my head.

9. *We have to really sample the local cuisine; snails, frogs legs and* crêpes.
10. *We should always be sitting outside a café or bar for* l'heure bleu *(translation: the bit between dusk and sunset).*
11. *We take pictures of everything, preferably with us in them. And preferably in black and white.*
12. *We each have to buy a super-cool souvenir to remember our time in Paris, that costs less than ten euros. Bea is also allowed to buy something frivolous and expensive, courtesy of her grandmother.*
13. *We have to make the most of Paris at night, even if it's just walking along the Seine and admiring the lights.*
14. *I want to discover the secret of making really good choux pastry. (Toph, you're allowed to sit this one out.)*
15. *The first one of us to hear a genuine French person say, 'Ooh la la' should get a prize.*
16. *No more phone calls home as we immerse ourselves in* l'expérience Parisienne!

I looked at my half of the list, decided I was done, and handed it back to Toph.

I could tell from Toph's surprised look as he read that

he'd expected me to sneak in a few regulated, orderly points. It felt good not to be so predictable for once. 'We should shake on it,' I mused. 'Make our commitment to *l'expérience Parisienne* legally binding.'

Toph's fingers were cool against mine and, after we'd done the shaking, he gave my hand a little squeeze that felt as comforting as a cup of hot chocolate on a cold, wintry day.

'We'll go back to the hotel so you can dump the guidebooks,' Toph said, standing up. 'Even that little one that you've been trying to secretly stuff into the side pocket of your bag for the last five minutes.'

I'd been hoping that Toph wouldn't notice my stealth tactics but he was right. Stashing a guidebook in my bag went against the whole spirit of our pact. 'OK, OK,' I murmured with only a minimum of pouting. 'But if we're lost, super lost, I'm allowed to stop and ask for directions.'

'Agreed,' Toph said as we started to retrace our steps. 'But only if we've exhausted all other possibilities.'

'So what do we do once I've jettisoned the guidebooks?'

Toph sighed like he couldn't believe I had to ask such a dumb question. 'Well, we start walking, of course.'

So we walked. It was a glorious day; the sun so bright that sunglasses were essential but not so hot that we were footsore and sticky after ten minutes.

Montmartre was built on a hill and after an hour of wandering up and down steep streets we found ourselves staring up at the huge white dome of the Sacré Cœur, right at the top of the village. I realized that if Toph had banned guidebooks then he probably wouldn't appreciate a rundown on the history of Montmartre from its humble beginnings as the sight of the decapitation of Saint Denis to the eighteenth century, when a ton of Cossacks launched a smackdown right where we were standing.

There were thousands of tourists milling around the base of the basilica and watching the pavement artists on their little camp stools drawing lightning-quick sketches of anyone brave enough to hand over their euros. Toph's lips curled as we saw pencil sketch after pencil sketch that were high on the flatter factor, very low on artistic merit.

It wasn't the Montmartre I'd read about where artists lived in garrets, drinking cheap red wine by the carafe and having passionate affairs with their models. It wasn't even the Montmartre of my beloved Amélie, where even the mundane became magical when you least expected it.

'Shall we stop for a coffee?' Toph asked doubtfully. It was obvious that we wouldn't be able to find one that only had signage in French.

'Let's keep walking,' I said firmly and we circled the church and started descending down narrow streets. Without the aid of a guidebook, we found a sweet little museum stuffed full of wonders like a shadow theatre and a collection of posters celebrating the Montmartre that was fixed firmly in my head. Then there was the vineyard that we stumbled on, rubbing our eyes in disbelief as we stared at the lush green field that had suddenly materialized in front of us. It was a bit like finding an orchard just off of Piccadilly Circus. So when we saw two windmills as we continued on our wandering, we simply smiled and said, 'Ah, of course, windmills.'

Or Toph did. I stood there, eyes almost bulging out of my head, until I couldn't stand still any longer and had to start jumping up and down.

'Yeah, windmills,' Toph repeated. 'Don't they have windmills in the mother country?'

I pointed at the café in between the two windmills and squeaked wordlessly because the power of speech had deserted me.

Toph took two steps away from me. 'Bea, are you having some kind of psychotic break?'

'It's Café des Deux Moulins, the café from *Amélie*!' I yelped. 'She was a waitress here and Georgette worked in the cigarette kiosk and Hipolito came in every day to talk about literature . . .' I scrabbled in my bag, pulled out my camera and shoved it at Toph, who was looking at me in exasperated amusement. 'You have to take my picture outside and then we have to go in for coffee and you have to take more pictures of me but, like, really subtly so they don't think I'm completely mad.'

'You *are* completely mad,' Toph muttered, holding the camera up. 'Say *fromage*.'

I was devastated when I discovered the interior of des Deux Moulins wasn't exactly the same as it was in the film, but I rallied when I discovered *crème brûlée d'Amélie Poulain* on the menu and insisted that Toph took pictures of me breaking the crust, while the staff smiled indulgently.

After lunch, we carried on walking until we found Montmartre Cemetery, which was a beautiful tranquil space away from the hubbub of the streets outside, filled with sculptures and statues. I mean, there were graves, but the sun had chased the shadows away and Toph was a comforting presence at my side as we walked around and found the Pierrot statue on Nijinsky's grave, though Toph wasn't entirely sure who he was.

'Only, like, the most famous male dancer of all time,' I said aghast, nudging him with my arm. 'Did you never have a ballet phase?'

'That's a girl thing,' Toph snapped, but I knew his eyes were glinting mischievously from behind his shades. 'While you were pirouetting and . . . and . . . whatever else there is in ballet, I was playing in Little League and swimming in the creek.'

'You swam in a creek? Your childhood sounds a lot like *Huckleberry Finn*,' I told Toph, and he launched into a long monologue about being a kid in Texas where the summers seemed to last forever and he was vice-president of the local neighbourhood gang (The Texas Wreckers) whose main purpose in life was blowing stuff up and building rockets. Sometimes they'd build a rocket simply to blow it up as soon as it launched. And when Toph wasn't being Destructo Boy, his assorted sisters were always dragging him into money-making schemes like using him as tousle-haired bait to sell Girl Scout cookies or forcing him to man their lemonade stand.

I was bent in half from laughing as Toph recalled how he'd caught Brooke, his second oldest sister, kissing Billy Tyler, his oldest sister Julie's boyfriend, and blackmailed her for weeks until she discovered his secret stash of explosives and blackmailed him right back.

Just as Toph opened his mouth to ask me for some amusing anecdotes from my childhood, we came to François Truffaut's grave and I shrieked in surprised delight and launched into a lecture on French New Wave cinema that Toph probably could have done without.

We were hot and tired by the time we left the cemetery and though I was mapless, I was pretty sure that we'd walked the length of Montmartre and would have to rewalk it to get back to the Shangri-La. But as we came to the Place de Clichy Metro station, I got my bearings.

'Bea? Shall we use one of our Metro allowances for the day?' Toph begged. 'I might actually die if we have to walk much further.'

'We don't need to,' I told him, taking his arm and leading him around the next corner. 'See that road up there? I'm ninety per cent certain that's Rue des Dames.'

Toph looked at me blankly. 'And?'

'And that's where the Shangri-La is,' I said confidently, though I had my fingers crossed behind my back.

'Are you sure?' Toph was starting to whine, and I couldn't blame him. The balls of my feet felt like they were on fire.

'Pretty sure. I think we walked in a gigantic loop. You know, this would be so much easier if we just had a map.

Not a guidebook, but a map,' I persevered. 'Because I've lived in London all my life but I still take my *A–Z* with me if I'm going into town and—'

'Yeah, fine, map,' Toph muttered. 'Sorry, I need all my energy to put one foot in front of the other.'

We turned into the road that I thought might be Rue des Dames and yes, there was the fusty old ladies' clothes shop. And I was a . . .

'You're a genius, Bea! A freaking, goddamn, *bona fide* genius,' Toph yelped, taking my sweaty hand so he could lift it up to his face and press a kiss to my knuckles. I felt my legs shake a bit, but we had been walking for *hours*.

'It was nothing,' I said stoutly as Toph let my hand go, though the spot that he'd brushed against with his lips was still tingling. 'Do you think it would be OK to use the bidet in our bathroom as a foot spa?' That wasn't what I'd meant to say at all. But the bare-knuckle kiss had completely blindsided me and I blurted out the first thing that came to mind. I just wished it hadn't involved mention of stinky feet and the place where the French liked to wash their stinky bottoms.

But Toph just looped his arm round my shoulders as we padded slowly up the street. 'Why didn't I think of that?' he said enthusiastically. 'See, that's why you're the genius and I'm just your lowly sidekick.'

Obviously kissing my knuckles meant nothing. It was just Toph showing his extreme gratitude that we didn't have to walk the streets of Montmartre in endless circles. And I didn't know why it meant so much to me, because

Toph and I were just friends, who'd only just become friends after a week of not talking to each other. Travel buddies. Two foreign people in a foreign city. Move along, nothing to see here.

Chapter Eighteen

In the Paris of my dreams it was always that soft hour before dusk and the whole city basked in a mellow golden light as I wandered the cobbled, twisted streets of Montmartre wearing a black polo neck, black Capri pants, black ballet slippers, really big sunglasses and with my hair up in a chignon. Then I'd hole up in a café drinking *espressos* and watch the world go by until Jacques, my lover (because it's my fantasy and in my fantasy I don't have a boyfriend, I have a lover and his name is Jacques) arrived. He'd be a painter and we'd go off to a small bar and Jacques, who was dark and intense, would look at me darkly and intensely and tell me stories of how Simone de Beauvoir and Jean-Paul Sartre sat at the very same table. Then Jacques would start making eyes at some *petite fille* at the next table and we'd have a screaming row, which involved lots of broken china and Jacques stalking off, exclaiming, '*Mon Dieu!*' and '*Zut alors!*' under his breath. Then I'd sit in the bar on my own drinking cognac and crying because he'd broken my heart again.

That was what my Paris dream was like and I always thought it was completely ace.

But the Paris I was currently in wasn't too shabby. The days had quickly settled into a lovely, lazy pattern. Every morning I'd send Grandma Minor a text to let her know that I was still alive but then I'd shake off the demands of real life and let myself fall in love with Paris all over again.

Toph and I would always breakfast *al fresco* in the little walled garden of the Shangri-La while we planned where the day would take us. Then we'd head off to the Metro armed only with a map (I so stood my ground on that one), a camera and a ton of plasters.

We poked around flea markets and lingered over impossibly delicate vintage dresses (or I did; Toph was more interested in a stash of old TinTin comics that he found). We spent an afternoon in a branch of FNAC, France's version of HMV, where I went mad buying Françoise Hardy and Serge Gainsbourg CDs, DVDs of French films I'd had to borrow from Monsieur Bradley and the complete works of Jane Austen in French.

Then there was the food. We gorged on *croque monsieurs* and *croque madames*; we had steak so rare that Toph insisted it was still wriggling on the plate, and we ordered a bowl of snails, or *escargots*. They were kind of gross and slimy and we couldn't get the hang of prising them out of their shells with this implement that looked like a pair of eyelash curlers. Then there were the sweet things; little pots of chocolate mousse so dark and heavy it took a minute to eat each spoonful, and *tarte tatin* that was so far removed from the apple pie I knew that they weren't even third cousins. Each bite was sharp *and* sweet and I geeked out on the lightness of the pastry.

Toph reminded me then that I was meant to learn the secret of good choux pastry and though I pointed out that *tarte tatin* wasn't made from choux pastry, when we got back to the Shangri-La, I sweet-talked (pun intended) the pastry chef into giving me an impromptu lesson. I left the kitchen with a plate of profiteroles made by my own aching hands and an offer of a job as their kitchen bitch any time I wanted.

We stayed true to the spirit of the list and when we were feeling brave we'd try to talk to people. One day we even had lunch with Tom and Marlene, an Australian couple who were celebrating their silver wedding anniversary and had asked us to help them buy Metro tickets because they'd thought we were genuine French youths. And I did get to hear a French person say, '*Oh la la*', when I went into a chemist to buy a sticky bandage because my ankle was killing me from walking all day in flip-flops. The pharmacist was perturbed by my request for '*un pensement adhesif*' until I'd finally squeaked, '*Monsieur, regardez ma cheville!*' He'd sat me down on a chair, looked at my ankle, which was twice its normal size and muttered, '*Ooh la la!*' Toph owed me a prize, but he seemed to have conveniently forgotten about it.

Mostly we talked to people when we went out in the evening, after having a disco nap back at the Shangri-La. We'd stick to Montmartre or the neighbouring Pigalle, choose a restaurant and hole up there for hours. Then we'd find a bar, preferably with tables outside (though one night we listened to *le jazz* in *le jazz* club) so we could watch the world go strolling by and we'd always end up talking to the people at the next table. Eventually we'd push the two tables together, their surfaces sticky with condensation from our drinks, and talk until we were the only people left and the staff were sweeping the floor around us.

The words that came out of my mouth no longer sounded stupid, like I used to think they did. But maybe it was because I had stuff to talk about for once that wasn't just the usual humdrum routine of school and homework and locking myself in my room to dream about a life I wanted to live. I was living that life now and had a stream of funny anecdotes, from falling asleep on trains to learning to make choux pastry under the watchful eye of a tyrannical pastry chef. And all the time, Toph was there with encouraging smiles and a little brush of his hand on my knee when I said something particularly amusing.

I think I saved my best stories for Toph though, because I'd begun to notice that wherever we went for the day, no matter how many sights there were to see, we'd always manage to find a patch of long grass and lie on it talking and talking. I knew that whenever I thought about Toph when I was back in London (and I had a feeling that I'd be thinking about him a lot), I'd picture him with shafts of sunlight slanting across his face and making his eyelashes look as if they'd been painted gold. I told Toph stuff I'd never told anyone; about the worst two weeks of my life when Grandpa Minor and Grandpa Major died within a fortnight of each other, and all the silly fantasies I'd had about finding my dad and even how I used to pretend to be Holly Golightly or Amélie.

It worked both ways, the sharing of deepest, darkest

secrets. Toph told me that he'd been expected to follow his dad into the police force and that going to college to study anthropology had got him thrown out of the house for a week. He told me about the first time he kissed a girl (Nancy Mayhew when he was in Fifth Grade), and the last time he'd cried, which was when he split up with his girlfriend of six years because she said she wanted to experience life as a single person. Then she'd immediately started sleeping with other boys.

We were also holding hands. Not when we started out in the morning, but usually just after lunch, Toph would take my arm to stop me from getting jostled or so we wouldn't be separated by a crowd, then his hand would find mine and we'd stay that way for the rest of the day. It was about the one thing we didn't talk about though, because it would have been too awkward. As awkward as it was when we got back to our room at the Shangri La and Paris was no longer there to act as a chaperone. Even though we'd spent the whole day talking, suddenly there were stammered negotiations about who was going to have the bathroom first and I'd get really self-conscious about Toph seeing me in my pyjamas. And I couldn't even think about having a pee unless the cold tap was running. He knew in excruciating, mind-numbing detail about how Ayesha had dumped me, but God forbid Toph should find out that I had actual bodily functions.

I came out of the bathroom, after giving the cold tap some serious action on our seventh morning at the Shangri-La, to find Toph on the phone. On *my* phone to be precise.

He turned as he heard me leave the bathroom and made an anguished face. 'Yes, ma'am,' he said to the unknown caller. 'I can see that would be annoying. Bea's here now, I'll just pass the phone over. It was a pleasure to talk to you, ma'am.'

I raised an eyebrow at Toph's deferential tone, then I saw the serious expression on his face and all the things I'd been pushing to the furthest, dustiest recesses of my mind came flooding back.

'It's not your mom,' Toph mouthed as he handed me the phone, because we had that whole hive mind thing going on. 'Grandma Minor.'

'Hey, Grandma,' I said as Toph disappeared into the bathroom. 'How are things back in Blighty?'

'Everything's fine,' she said, and I knew from her wary tone what her next words would be. 'Darling girl, it's time you came home.'

'So stuff with *her*, with Mum, it's sorted out then?'

'Well, no, not exactly,' Grandma said in the same careful voice that made me dig my nails into the palm of my hand. 'But nothing's going to be achieved with you over there and your mother over here.'

'Who says I want to achieve anything?' I muttered. 'There's nothing to achieve, nothing to say, unless she's ready to apologize to me.'

'Honestly, Bea. How can you move forward if you're going to be so belligerent? I really don't know what's got into you.'

Two and a half weeks of freedom away from the maternal straitjacket had got into me and I wasn't in any mad hurry to return. 'Look, Gran, maybe I need another week . . .'

'I checked with Eurostar and there are plenty of seats on all the trains leaving Paris tomorrow,' Gran said, cutting right through what I was saying. 'Would you like me to book your ticket for you?'

'No, but I don't want to come . . .'

'I'm trusting you to be back in London by tomorrow evening,' Grandma said crisply. 'You've never let me down before, always kept your promises, I'd hate to think that had changed.'

Grandma Minor was good. She was like an evil genius when it came to manipulating her granddaughter into a corner with no way out.

'I'm not cool with it but OK, I *promise* I'll get the Eurostar tomorrow.'

'Of course you will,' she said, like there'd never been any doubt. I could already tell that after a few hours back in London I'd be safe, boring, predictable Bea again. 'It will be lovely to see you. We can't wait to hear about all your adventures.'

Yeah, I bet Mum couldn't wait. She'd probably already stocked up on pregnancy tests and the minute I got home, she'd frogmarch me to the bathroom and force me to pee on countless white plastic sticks.

I hung up with a deep sigh and turned to face Toph, who'd just emerged from the bathroom. 'You have to go home.' He didn't make it a question, because it wasn't one. It was an order.

'Yeah.' I sank down on my bed and stared blankly at the ceiling.

I felt the mattress depress as Toph sat down next to me. 'When?'

'Tomorrow.' I sniffed. 'Apparently there's a ton of spare seats on the Eurostar.'

'That sucks.' Toph tugged on the little strand of hair that would never stay neatly tucked behind my ear. 'But you knew that you'd have to go home eventually and you can't keep putting it off.'

I sniffed again and Toph tugged my hair harder to let me know that a sniff wasn't a suitable reply. 'What did Grandma say to you?'

'Oh, nothing much,' Toph said casually. 'Just wanted to know the highlights of my life so far, my prospects, my intentions towards her only granddaughter. You know? The usual.'

'Oh my God,' I groaned, because really? Embarrassed, table for one.

'She also wanted to know if you'd bought something totally frivolous and expensive yet?'

I'd bought lots of things but Françoise Hardy CDs were essential purchases. Then I sat up. 'I know! I could buy an apartment in Paris, like, today! Then I wouldn't have to go home. How does that sound?'

Toph put his arm round my shoulders and it was more touching than we'd ever done in the hotel room, but the circumstances were beyond extenuating so I allowed myself to rest my head on Toph's shoulder so I could inhale great whiffs of his clean scent – he'd been using my fig-scented shower gel again. Toph cleared his throat nervously, which made me start to panic. I really couldn't take much more bad news.

'I could come to London with you, if you wanted?' he said hesitantly.

I did want. I wanted a lot. For so many selfish reasons I wanted to say yes, but . . . 'No, it's OK. You don't have to do that,' I said, trying to sound firm and resolute. 'Really, I'll be fine.'

'Are you sure?'

It was just as well that I had my head on Toph's shoulder so he couldn't see the way my face was twitching.

'Yeah, quite sure. I mean, it's nice of you to offer but you'll want to be well away when World War Three breaks out.' It took an almost superhuman effort but I slid away from the comforting rock-solidness of Toph and stood up. 'Well, I guess I have a train ticket to buy.'

'Nuh-huh,' Toph said, standing up so he could take my hands in his even though it was well before lunch and we were in our hotel room, making it the wrong time and place for hand-holding. 'Jean on the front desk can sort that out for you.'

I shook my head. 'But he can't because—'

'No, I'll talk to him. Make sure you get a seat so you're not sitting with your back to the engine,' Toph insisted hotly and his ability to know *exactly* what I was thinking was really freaky. I was going to miss it so much. 'We have one day left in Paris.'

'I know and I have to pack and get presents and . . .' My voice tailed off as I was struck by the sheer enormity of all the things I had to do before I could go home for a major arse-kicking.

'It takes ten minutes to pack. It's one of those things where the thought of it takes much longer than actually doing it,' Toph argued, giving my hands a little shake. 'One day, Bea! Let's make it the most awesome day imaginable.'

I eyed my trusty suitcase and then pulled my gaze back to Toph, who was giving me his sad bunny face. The same face that I'd told him he should only use for the powers of good because it was *that* persuasive.

'I can't.' But my voice was wavering.

'But there are still a ton of things on the list that we haven't ticked off,' Toph said, playing his winning hand because a list geek like me couldn't let a to-do list go unchecked. 'C'mon, we'll go anywhere you want and do all those lame touristy things that we pretended to sneer about but I know you have them marked in your guidebooks. Just like I know that you've been taking your smallest guidebook out with us and sneaking peeks at it when you think I'm not looking . . . Ow!' Toph finished with a yelp when I trod heavily and deliberately on his foot.

'Well, I s'pose it wouldn't take me that long to pack,' I mused. 'And if we went to the Île de la Cité, I could go to that sweet shop and buy all my presents there. I mean, what kind of freak doesn't like chocolate?'

'That's the spirit,' Toph grinned, sitting down on his bed

so he could pull on his sneakers, as I began to get my things together. 'Better make sure you have everything you need for the next fourteen hours because we haven't got time to come back here for a disco nap.'

'I can't stay out for ages, I still have to pack,' I bleated, but Toph clamped his hands over his ears so he wouldn't have to listen to my protests.

Chapter Nineteen

We got the Metro to Notre Dame because the area was littered with stalls selling tourist tat and we could cover the souvenir part of our list. I bought two snowstorms to add to my collection: the Moulin Rouge and one of Paris at night. I had to stage an intervention when Toph insisted he was going to buy a jester's hat in the red, white and blue of the French flag (or Tricolour as the French called it) and he settled for an *I* ♥ *Paris* baseball cap, which should have been naff but he wore it well, like it was a trucker's cap advertising some retro brand of soft drink.

Then it was a quick trip across the road to Shakespeare & Co, the legendary English-language bookshop, which had been going for yonks and had been frequented over the years by literary types like Henry Miller and Anaïs Nin. Toph had me on a clock so I only had half an hour to select no more than five books and an adorable Shakespeare & Co tote bag to put them in.

Then we walked a little along the Seine, the great river that ran through the middle of Paris, until we came to the Pont de la Tournelle and walked over to Île St Louis, the tiny neighbouring island to the Île de la Cité where Notre Dame stood. It was like a little oasis of olde world calm right in the middle of Paris. No Metro, no backpackers, just a couple of narrow streets stuffed with tiny shops selling everything from pigeons to *foie gras* to cheese so stinky I almost reeled from the smell as we walked past. After a couple of wrong turns, we finally found the chocolate shop I'd read about on the interwebs.

It was an old-fashioned sweet shop, like something out of a Dickens' novel filled with slabs of chocolate, shiny foil wrappers in every hue imaginable, huge glass jars crammed with candy. I'd never seen so much yummy goodness packed into such a small space. Toph was already grabbing handfuls of chocolate as I slowly looked around.

I bought Alfie and Ben chocolate crocodiles and marshmallow twists, Grandma Minor got biscuits and caramels in beautiful Art Deco tins, that I was so having afterwards, James loved anything spicy so I bought chocolate infused with chilli, and Grandma Minor had a square of dark chocolate every day so I bought her two massive bars of plain chocolate studded with almonds. I also bought quite a lot of chocolate to stash in my secret hiding places when I got home. I finished by hurling bars of chocolate into my basket for Ruth, Lydia and Polly, before I went over to the till to pay.

'That's a hell of a lot of candy,' Toph remarked as the owner and I shovelled it into bags between us.

'That's for the twins,' I said as the chocolate animals were packed away, and continued to list all the people who'd receive my sweet treats so Toph wouldn't think I was planning to scoff all of it myself.

'What about your mom?' Toph asked with a faint hint of

reproach, which made me immediately bristle.

'What about her?'

'You *have* to get her something, Bea. You can't not,' Toph protested.

'Just watch me,' I muttered and I wasn't going to budge on this, but Toph was fixing me with a steely glare . . . Actually it wasn't steely so much as disappointed and he was really taking advantage of the fact that it was our last day together. 'OK, *fine*,' I hissed and a grabbed a box of crystallized fruits, because nobody likes crystallized fruits.

Though the sun was shining fiercely, as if the rain earlier in the week had never happened, I felt as if I had my own personal storm cloud hovering just above my head. It followed me all the way up the Rue Saint Louis, to the famous Berthillon ice cream shop.

We joined the end of a long snaking queue and I tried to school my features into something more anticipatory and a little less sulky.

Toph nudged my arm. 'What's up?'

'Nothing, I'm just trying to decide what flavours to get,' I lied, craning my neck to see the menu written up on a chalkboard, so I wouldn't have to look at Toph.

'Bullshit,' he snorted. 'You want to try that again?'

'Not particularly.' I looked around me at the tiny little shops with their whimsical window displays and, I kid you not, a man in a beret cycling past. 'It's just . . . this time tomorrow I'll be back in London and I know it's going to be awful. And when I think of the day after tomorrow and the day after that and all the days and all the weeks in the future, all I can see is extreme suckitude and rows with my mother and, God, Ruby is probably going to pay someone to push me down the really steep stairs outside the art block when I get back to school and . . . I just don't want to leave Paris.' And I didn't want to leave Toph, because for the first time in my life I'd met someone who really got me – even the parts that were pretty grim and disgusting or just plain lame.

Toph put his hand on my shoulder and squeezed a little. 'I know,' he said, and with those two words and the pressure of his fingers, I didn't feel quite so adrift. 'When I think about going home, back to Texas, it's like I'm leaving part of myself behind in Europe.'

'We could just not go back,' I suggested and it wasn't even a joke. 'I could get a job in the Shangri-La's kitchen and you could be a porter and I bet there's some small leaky room up in the eaves where we could live rent-free. It would be so cool.' Toph gave me the oddest look as we moved slowly towards the front of the queue. Like he was seriously considering it. 'You know I'm joking, right? Kind of.'

I allowed myself a ten-second fantasy of ten years from now when Toph and I were still in Paris and sharing a beautiful apartment in St-Germain-des-Pres with wooden floorboards and two Siamese cats. In my fantasy we wore a lot of black and would go out drinking with equally black-clad friends, who would tell new acquaintances, 'They came here for a week and ended up staying ten years.' By now Toph and I would have mastered the Gallic shrug so we'd just wiggle our shoulders like it was no big deal and order another *verre de vin rouge*.

'What?' I grunted, when I realized that Toph was saying something only because his lips were moving.

'I'd love to know where you go when you tune out like that,' he said, though really he was better off not knowing. 'I was saying, it's just as well we're queuing for ice cream. My sisters get through a metric assload of ice cream when they're going through some kind of trauma. I'm going to get the blood orange, the wild strawberry and the peach. What about you?'

I chose three scoops of dark chocolate, caramel and praline and we swapped our cones back and forth as we crossed the Pont Marie and walked towards Le Marais, which used to be the old Jewish Quarter before the Second World War. Toph's hand was firmly in mine now as we wandered the packed streets and looked in shop windows. Toph kept pointing out things that would make excellent frivolous purchases but I just shook my head to every one. I didn't want shoes or bags or even a gorgeous black lace dress. I didn't know what I wanted – but I'd know it when I saw it.

Eventually we came to Les Jardins du Marais because it was about the time that we liked to while away a couple of hours sitting on grass and talking. I gratefully collapsed on the first empty patch we came to, toed off my sneakers and starfished my limbs. Toph was folding his hoodie into a comfy little pillow and I stretched out my hand, the sunlight making my fingers look transparent, and stroked a line approximately two centimetres away from his spine. It was weird how you could be with someone and already feel like you were missing them. My mind started racing through questions that I wanted to ask Toph, of all the things I hadn't said yet, but when he lay down next to me, I just smiled and shut my eyes.

I was woken up from a mildly disturbing dream (Mark from *Ugly Betty* turned out to be my real dad and wasn't exactly ecstatic about the news) by the soft sensation of fingers stroking my face.

It was an effort to open my eyes and when I did, Toph was resting on one elbow as he traced the tip of my nose with his finger. This wasn't hand-holding; this was a whole 'nother kind of touching. But as I tried to decide what kind of touching it was, Toph stopped the stroking and picked up a tube of sunblock.

'Didn't want you to get burnt,' he explained, screwing the cap back on. 'Why do suncreams always smell of coconut?'

'I don't know,' I mumbled, though at any other time the question would have kept me engrossed for a good ten minutes. 'How long did I sleep?'

'About an hour.' Toph leaned back on his elbows. 'Kinda dozed off myself. So much for not having a disco nap.'

To the casual observer Toph might have looked relaxed, what with the lounging back and the lazy smile, but his right foot was jiggling uncontrollably, he had a muscle banging away in his cheek and he kept sneaking little glances at his watch.

'You got somewhere to be, Toph?'

Toph tried to check his guilty start. 'No! No . . . we should probably get going. Y'know . . . dinner.'

It was only five o'clock but if Toph didn't stuff his face every two hours on the dot, he could get very cranky. I staggered to my feet, relishing the feeling of the cool grass under my bare feet and tried to surreptitiously adjust the back of my dress, which was sticking to my thighs.

'Come on,' Toph called over his shoulder – he was already halfway across the grass. 'We've got loads of day left.'

I had to scamper to keep up with Toph as he hurried down the path that led back on to the street. This time, when he took my hand it was to drag me along at a much faster pace than I was used to.

'Hey, you're going too fast,' I complained as we practically speed-walked down the Rue de Rivoli. 'My legs aren't as long as yours.'

Toph glanced down at my legs, not in a lecherous way at all. More like he wanted to check they were in working order so I could carry on walking. 'Don't whine,' he warned me, but my attention had been distracted by something in the shop window in front of us.

'Shiny,' I said, letting go of Toph's hand so I could move in for a closer look. 'I'm just going to pop in here. Won't be long.'

'We haven't got time,' Toph insisted, but he was talking to my dust.

The woman in the shop couldn't have been more helpful. She explained very slowly and carefully that I could buy the silver charm bracelet I'd seen in the window or I could make my own from the trays of charms she started pulling out from under the counter.

It really was the most perfect, frivolous souvenir. I carefully sorted through the charms (trying to ignore Toph who was tutting and tapping his foot behind me) and picked out an Eiffel Tower, Arc de Triomphe and Moulin Rouge as well as a little sailboat, even though we'd only walked along the Seine. Then I chose a tiny bottle of wine to remind me of all the nights spent in bars, a snail because of the time we'd had the escargots, a poodle, a Tricolour and a little disc that said *I ♥ Paris*.

'Is there anything else I should choose?' I asked Toph, who gave this strangulated moan, but peered over my shoulder so he could root through the final tray with his long fingers.

'This one,' he said, holding up a tiny Converse sneaker. 'And this one.' He fished out a little heart and put it down on the counter. 'Jeez, Bea, how much longer?'

I shrugged, which was a little habit that I was secretly pleased to have acquired. 'I don't know.' The woman was attaching my charms with a pair of pliers. 'Do you think I should get one of those flat discs engraved with my name and the date?'

'No,' Toph said shortly, looking at his watch, then taking his phone out of his pocket. 'I'm going to wait outside. If you're more than five minutes, I'm leaving without you.'

I pulled a hurt face at Toph's departing back then turned to share an eye roll with the sales assistant, who muttered something about '*toutes hommes*' and how '*très impossible*' they were. I didn't know what Toph's beef was but I was starting to worry that he was bored with me. That, after a week, my true, dull colours were starting to show and he wanted this day to be over as soon as possible so he'd be done with me. Maybe that was why he'd been so funny with me in Marseilles that time.

The thought of it was enough to put a frown on my face when I finally left the shop, ten seconds before my five-minute deadline. I held up the little bag that contained my charm bracelet. 'All done.'

Toph peeled himself away from the wall he'd been leaning against. 'Right, good. Let's get a move on.'

I didn't budge but folded my arms and tried to appear calm. 'Look, Toph, if you're sick of hanging with me then I don't mind if you want to go off and do your own thing. Really I don't.'

Toph sighed in a long, heartfelt way. 'Is that your passive aggressive English way of saying you're bloody well cheesed off with me?'

'No, of course I'm not!' I protested. 'And do you know that when you talk like that you sound like Dick Van Dyke?'

Toph sighed again. 'Just so we're clear: I'm not sick of you, you're not sick of me.' He held out his hand. 'But I'm going to get really pissed at you if we're not on a Metro in the next ten minutes.'

Chapter Twenty

Toph wouldn't say why we had to get the Metro. He also wouldn't let me help him, even though he always had immense difficulty reading a very simple, colour-coded map. Sweat was beading beneath the brim of his *I ♥ Paris* baseball cap, and he fidgeted in his seat as we stopped at station after station. The train began to empty out, but Toph refused to tell me our destination even though my little observations that we were heading *out* of Paris got shriller and shriller.

'About goddamn time!' Toph announced when the train pulled in at Quai de la Gare and he was on his feet, tugging me with him, as he pushed past the other people who were trying to get off.

'OK, you're not even beginning to freak me out,' I huffed as Toph yanked me onto an escalator and started climbing to the top, though we could have simply stood still and let it do its job. 'You are officially freaking me out, you freak.'

Toph pursed his lips but didn't say anything until we were through the ticket barrier. He took a moment to get his bearings, before he tugged me towards the exit. By the end of the day, my left arm was going to be a good ten centimetres longer than my right one. 'I want you to run faster than you've ever run in your life,' he said.

I didn't have time to respond because Toph was pelting out of the station and I had no choice but to pelt with him as he ran straight into the road, traffic stopping in our wake with a furious honking of horns as we headed straight for the Seine, on the other side of the road.

It was an act of God that we managed to get to the riverbank without being mown down yet Toph wasn't slowing, but pulling me down slippery steps and across a jetty, while he shouted, '*Attendez! Attendez!*'

There was a big boat in front of us, one of the pretty river cruisers that I'd seen pootling up and down the Seine. A wizened old man with a peaked sailor's cap was just clipping a chain across the gangplank as we came skidding to a halt. He looked singularly unimpressed at our hot, sweaty selves.

'I booked it this morning! Tell him we're sorry we're late and he has to let us onboard,' Toph babbled. 'Tell him you only have twenty-four hours to live. Anything!'

I was halfway through an abject apology with a lot of pouting thrown in for good measure, when a woman with a clipboard came hurrying down the gangway to see what all the fuss was about. She then proceeded to give the man in the sailor's cap one hell of a tongue-lashing.

He unclipped the rope to let us onboard but otherwise seemed supremely unbothered. In fact, when I looked over my shoulder, he was spitting in the Seine to show his contempt for the whole situation.

'What's going on?' I whispered to Toph, as the woman led us along the deck. 'Why didn't you tell me?

How much do I owe you?'

'You don't owe me anything – it's your *ooh la la* prize,' Toph hissed back. 'This way we can see all the stuff we missed and we get to eat while we're doing it.'

'It's a dinner cruise!' I was about to insist that we went halves when the woman ushered us through a set of double doors with an impatient gesture and I clocked the other cruisers. 'Holy shit!'

'Holy shit is right,' Toph said quietly. 'Is that woman's dress made out of tinfoil?'

The other cruisers were all milling about a large room with tables and chairs arranged around a dancefloor and getting to know each other while waiters wafted about, holding trays aloft with glasses of champagne on them. The dress code was beyond formal; a lot of the men were wearing dinner jackets and the ladies had gone to town in taffeta, satin and the stuff we roasted the turkey in at Christmas, like the woman who Toph had pointed at.

At least I was wearing a dress (Jess had bequeathed me her LBD when she couldn't fit it in her backpack) but it was teamed with greying tennis shoes. Toph was wearing holey, faded jeans and a holey, faded T-shirt and that bloody *I ♥ Paris* baseball cap. We also had a gazillion carrier bags each and I could see eyebrows being raised and people talking out of the sides of their mouths – probably to wonder aloud exactly which sewer we'd just crawled from.

Toph took it all in his stride. Smiling grimly, he dropped his bags so he could take two champagne flutes from a passing waiter and handed one to me. 'Cheers,' he said, clinking the side of my glass.

'This must have cost a fortune,' I said, blushing as I caught the eye of the woman in the tinfoil dress, who was giving me serious evils. 'You have to let me chip in.'

'Nah, we're good,' Toph insisted as clipboard woman showed us to our table and a ragged cheer went up as the boat pulled away from the quayside.

'But when did you organize this?' I asked, because we'd been joined at the hip all week.

Toph took a sip of his champagne. Now that his plan had come to fruition, he'd stopped twitching and was leaning back in his chair like he went on dinner cruises all the time. 'Jean on the front desk sorted it out when I asked him to book our train tickets.'

'Train tickets in the plural? You're not staying in Paris, then?'

'Wouldn't be the same without you, Bea,' Toph said softly. 'And when you're back in London and I'm in Austin and we're Twittering and Facebooking, we can honestly say that we'll always have Paris.'

I mock-groaned, but secretly Toph's words sent a little thrill coursing through me. We would *always* have Paris. I leant across the table so I could give Toph's hand a quick squeeze. 'Thank you so much for doing this and for being the best travel buddy a girl ever had and just . . . God, you've been a legend. You really, really have.' There were other words I wanted to say but I didn't even know how to shape them.

'You haven't even finished your champagne and you're

getting all choked up,' Toph grinned. 'I bet you start crying before they've even served the main course.'

I had no intention of crying but then there was the tiniest squeal of feedback from the speakers dotted round the room and the tour commentary started, so I could stop looking at the teasing smile on Toph's face and stare resolutely out of the window at Le Jardin des Plantes.

I started enjoying myself as soon as a huge plate of scallops was placed in front of me. I had to stop myself from moaning in ecstasy as I dug in. Then there was lamb with this weird but delicious truffle and pumpkin flan and, although I could feel my distended belly straining against the fabric of my dress, I still found room for molten chocolate cake with violet ice cream.

Toph even managed the cheese course while I patted my tummy and tried not to fall into a food coma. We were passing the Pont Neuf and I craned my neck to get a better view of the bridge where I'd wanted my first kiss to happen. It was getting dark now and it was easy to see why Paris was called 'the City Of Lights'. Either side of the Seine was illuminated by floodlights, lasers and garlands of glowing bulbs strung between the lampposts.

'It's so beautiful,' I sighed.

'So you fell in love, then?' Toph asked, chasing a few stray crumbs of Brie from his plate with his fingertips.

My heart gave a warning thud. 'Fell in love?' I echoed, like I didn't have a clue what he was talking about.

'Yeah, you said not so long ago that you hated Paris and now you're sighing over how pretty is it,' Toph said. 'I think your love affair with Paris is back on.'

'Paris and I are just good friends,' I said primly, because I knew it would make Toph laugh, and he looked almost as luminscent at the sparkly banks of the Seine when he chuckled.

I wanted to ask him if he'd fallen in love too, because it would be the perfect excuse for him to tell me that it wasn't just Paris who had stolen his heart but there was another squeal of feedback and the lady with the clipboard (who'd now changed into a sparkly gold number) was walking across the dancefloor with a microphone.

'Oh God, this must be the after-dinner entertainment,' Toph said gleefully, sitting up straight. 'Do you think she's going to sing? I bet she's going to sing.'

'And I bet it will either be "La Vie En Rose" or "Je Ne Regrette Rien."' This warranted trying to sit upright. 'Oooh! Maybe there'll be karaoke.' If there was, then I had no intention of taking part but old people plus karaoke was made of total win.

Toph and I waited for the music to start but instead Clipboard Girl trotted over to the table nearest to her and stuck the microphone in some poor woman's face.

Turned out it wasn't karaoke. It was going to every single table (about twenty by my count) and asking the occupants why they'd come to Paris. There was a smattering of polite applause for each silver wedding anniversary or fiftieth birthday or person who'd saved up their loose change for twenty years because they'd always had a hankering to come to Paris. It was kinda boring, apart from the two fifty-something gay guys from Manchester who said they'd come to Paris to celebrate paying off their plasma TV.

Eventually the woman had done every table except for one. 'I'm going to say we came on the cruise because every restaurant we tried was full,' Toph said with an evil smirk.

'You can't,' I protested. 'Let's say it's your birthday.'

'Let's not.' As the woman moved towards us, Toph sat up and waved, as I slid so far down in my seat that my chin was almost touching the table.

'And last but by no means least, we have our late arrivals,' the woman said in perfect English. 'So, what are your names?'

Toph had already grabbed the microphone. 'I'm Bobby Jo Junior and this is Cindy-Lou,' he informed the room in the most outrageous Texan drawl. 'I can't tell you how awesome it is to be here with y'all. Say hello, Cindy-Lou,' he added, thrusting the mic at me.

I pushed it away but managed a feeble wave.

'Don't mind Cindy-Lou, folks,' Toph continued. 'She's just shy is all.'

The woman beamed at Toph because he was really down with the audience participation thing. 'And what brings you to Paris?' she asked.

Toph's smile got even wider. 'Well, ma'am, back in Texas we got a Paris too but I heard this was the City of Lovers and so we broke into Cindy-Lou's college fund and got ourselves on a plane . . .' Toph paused to amp up the dramatic tension. 'See, folks, we're here on our honeymoon. I married my little Cindy-Lou straight out of the school room.'

'Oh my God, stop talking,' I begged but I don't think Toph could hear me over the thunderous applause. I was momentarily blinded by a strobe storm of camera flashes as people started taking pictures of us.

'How romantic,' the woman cooed, tucking her clipboard under her arm so she could join in with the clapping. 'Now is time for the dancing. Would you and Cindy-Lou like to have the first dance?'

Toph had already leapt out of his chair. 'Ma'am we'd be delighted,' he said over yet another squeal of feedback as the PA kicked into life with the opening notes of "La Vie En Rose". Toph heaved me to my feet and led me to the dancefloor. All I could do was promise him a slow and painful death via the medium of my most withering glare.

'Now, now, Cindy-Lou. We don't want these good folks to think we're having a lovers' tiff,' Toph drawled, eyes twinkling, as he wrapped one arm round my waist and took my hand. 'Put your right hand on my shoulder. I hope you can waltz.'

Waltzing with Toph was very different to the times I'd used to climb on Grandpa Minor's feet and waltz round the living room. For one thing, Toph was playing to the cheap seats and kept swinging me around so people could take our picture. For another, he wasn't just waltzing but doing all sorts of fancy stuff like dipping and twirling me until I thought I was going to throw up from motion sickness.

'You said you didn't dance. You're such a liar,' I puffed as he seamlessly switched to a foxtrot.

'Youngest sister, Cassidy, used to ballroom dance professionally. I was forced to practise with her when she was between partners,' Toph recalled with a shudder, before he pressed his cheek against mine so Wilhelm and Marta from Austria could take yet another picture of us.

'No wonder you used to blow stuff up,' I giggled, and promptly trod on Toph's foot again. 'Sorry.'

After a particularly energetic tango, I persuaded Toph that we needed to sit down. Or I needed to sit down before I fell over. I poured us both another glass of champagne, even though after the vodka martini incident I'd vowed to only have one alcoholic drink per night, and as I licked a stray drop from my wrist, Toph gave me this quick glance that was so soft and warm that I decided to ask the question that had been niggling at me for days.

'Why were you so mean to me in Marseilles?' I blurted out before I could lose my nerve. 'Not just the fight we had after the club, but before that?'

Toph shook his head as if he were trying to dislodge the memory. 'It's in the past. Forgotten. We're friends again, Bea. Moving towards best friends if I get back to Phoenix and discover that my room-mate, Joe, has totalled my car.'

'Be serious,' I said quietly. I didn't want to go back to London tomorrow with any 'what if's' hanging over my head.

Toph didn't say anything for a moment. 'Those first few days that we hung out, I was so psyched that I'd met you. You were so different to the other girls I know.' Toph spread his hands. 'Come on, Bea, this isn't news. You're cool and smart and funny in this really dry way and you can speak French and sort out lost passports and lecture me about nineteen-sixties black-and-white French films without batting an eyelash.'

I stared at Toph, transfixed. The Bea that he was describing sounded quite a lot like me, but wasn't me. Like looking at my reflection in one of those distorted fairground mirrors. 'That's one hell of a character reference,' I mumbled.

'Well, you're one hell of a girl,' Toph said, and all traces of teasing were wiped from his voice. 'So I just wanted to keep on getting to know you because every day you seemed to get a little bit cooler, but that night when we went to the club . . . you looked so pretty and I didn't want to . . . I didn't want to get into *something* with you.'

'What kind of *something*?' I asked, hoping against hope.

Toph looked at me steadily. 'You know exactly what kind of something. I'd just come out of my first serious relationship and I didn't want to mess around with you when I knew we'd be parting ways soon. Wasn't fair on either of us and there was the age gap . . .'

'Three years is nothing!' I said, dismissing it with a wave of my hand to try and make light of the effect that Toph's words had just had on me. It seemed unbelievable that all the time that I'd been crushing on him, he might just have had a small crush on me too. Like I was actually crushworthy. 'So totally ignoring me was just your way of getting over me then?' I added a little waspishly.

'I was trying to get my head straight,' Toph snapped back. 'And to be honest, Bea, you weren't at your best when you started drinking. But I guess I put you on this pedestal and it was inevitable that you'd come crashing off it.'

'I didn't just fall, I *crashed*?' Yeah, I'd had a lot to drink that night, enough that I'd failed to see anything other than Iban's pretty dark eyes but surely . . .

'You were acting like a total asshole,' Toph said baldly, and I wished I'd never started this. 'I was doing the right thing by getting you out of there, but you just ripped into me about ruining your first kiss like I was the biggest buzzkill you'd ever met.'

'I'm sorry,' I said, resting my hands over my burning cheeks. It couldn't be good for me to blush this much. 'I'm really sorry. I just got caught up in Erin and Jess and all you guys thinking I was cool and letting me into your gang. And Iban was the first guy I'd ever met who seemed to think I was sexy.' It sounded so lame once the words were out of my mouth. 'I liked being that girl that he liked, even if that girl wasn't really me.'

Toph shook his head. 'You don't have to be anyone else. You can just be you.' He reached over to take my hand and entwine my fingers through his. 'I don't know why you're so down on yourself.'

'Because I don't know if I'm the Bea you think I am or the Bea I know, who's dull and boring and spends all her time in this stupid dream world because she can't figure out how to make her real life go the way she wants it to.'

'You think that a three-year age gap isn't a big deal but it's an important three years,' Toph said, tapping his champagne glass to make his point. 'I got to move away from home and start to figure out who I was without other people telling me who I should be. Bea, things are going to get really good for you if you can just hang in there.'

I think Toph could tell from my face, because all of my features, lips, eyes, chin were drooping downwards, that I didn't believe him. 'Honestly, Bea. I promise you.'

We'd been having such a great time and I'd ruined it by asking questions I shouldn't have asked, which had led to truths I didn't want to hear. 'You're probably the nicest person I've ever met,' I admitted, stumbling over the words so they all clumped together. 'And I'm sorry I froze you out after we had the fight but it was so much like what happened with Ruby. One moment she'd treat me like her best friend and then the next, she'd be really cold because I wasn't doing exactly what she wanted.'

'Maybe I didn't handle the situation that well,' Toph admitted, his thumb absent-mindedly brushing my wrist. 'But the next day when I saw you all grumpy and hungover in your PJs, I realized that even grumpy and hungover, I still wanted to be your friend, even if it couldn't be anything more than that.'

I knew then that if I was ever going to be the Bea I wanted to be rather than the pale imitation that I was now, I had to be brave, take risks. 'I'm glad we're friends because I like you . . .'

'Yeah, I like you too,' Toph said, finally disentangling our fingers so he could pick up his champagne glass.

'No, I mean, I *really* like you and part of not wanting to go home is because I don't want to leave you.' I was staring at Toph, who was staring right back at me, neither one of us able to look away. 'All the stuff at home – my mum, my total lack of a father – stops mattering when I'm with you.' I took the biggest, deepest breath I'd ever taken. 'You see, I didn't just fall in love with Paris, I—'

'Mind if I steal Cindy-Lou away for a dance?' said a voice behind us and I looked around to see Clive from Manchester standing behind my chair. I could have quite happily throttled him with his Eiffel Tower tie.

The moment was gone. When I got back to our table Toph was getting up to dance with a Swedish woman and I didn't get a chance to talk to him for the rest of the cruise as the ladies couldn't wait to get their middle-aged mitts on him.

Toph only came back as people started to disembark at the first dropping-off point and his dance partners started wearing thin. 'Guess it's time for us to think about heading back to dry land,' he remarked casually. 'Where do you want to get off?'

'I'm not bothered,' I said just as airily, to show that our conversation hadn't affected me in the least and that I wasn't bothered about anything I'd said or was about to say, before I'd been rudely interrupted.

'Well, make sure you don't leave anything behind,' Toph said, pulling out his chair so we could start gathering up all the bags we'd stashed under the table. It was the kind of thing you said to someone who was like a little sister, I thought glumly.

Toph turned his nose up at the next four drop-off points. 'Not central enough,' he complained when I said we should get off at Quai des Tuileries.

'The Seine runs through the centre of Paris so they're all central,' I said. 'It doesn't matter where we get off the boat, we still have to get the Metro back to Montmartre. As long as we're near a station then—'

'Yeah, yeah . . .' Toph sighed, holding his hand up in protest. 'We'll get off in a minute.'

We didn't get off in a minute because Toph didn't want to leave the boat at Quai Malaquais either. I should have been peering out of the window to get my last glimpses of floodlit Paris but I was too busy rolling my eyes.

I didn't stir when Pont Neuf was announced as the next disembarkation point, because Toph would have some reason why we should stay onboard until we'd sailed all the way back to Quai de la Gare, which was so far on the outskirts of the city that it would take us *hours* to get back to the Shangri-La.

I was so busy sighing and grinding down on my back teeth that I didn't even notice that Toph was on his feet, bags in his hands. 'Move, Bea!' he snapped. 'We need to get off. Don't just stand there!'

'All right, all right,' I grumbled, scooping up my belongings and following Toph, who was loping towards the exit at great speed. I didn't want to experience the Pont Neuf, my Holy of Holies, when I was feeling so uncertain and frazzled, but I obediently trooped down the gangplank.

'We're on the Left Bank,' Toph said when we were back on dry land. 'We need to be over there. Might as well cross over the old Pont Neuf.'

I thought about voicing an argument for crossing over via the Pont des Arts instead but it was stupid when we were standing at the foot of the Pont Neuf.

Roughly speaking, the Pont Neuf is at the very epicentre of Paris. I couldn't say for definite that it is the actual geographic centre but if Paris really is a City of Lovers, then the Pont Neuf is its romantic pulse. It's where people meet and greet each other with a kiss, it's where they hold each other in the bridge's shadowy alcoves and it's where they fall in love.

I reluctantly trudged across it, bags banging against my legs, as Toph strode on ahead of me, like he couldn't wait to find the nearest Metro, get back to the hotel and go to sleep so morning would come quicker and I'd be out of his tousled hair. Why did I have to open my big mouth and spoil everything that had been so perfect? The Pont Neuf was forever ruined for me now.

But as we got to the middle of the bridge, I happened to glance to my right. Then I glanced to my left, just to even things up. After that, I had to drop my bags to the ground and just be *still* enough to take it all in. Because on either side of me there was Paris laid out before me; glowing and twinkling and shining like a jewellery box. I think I gasped, but that was less to do with Paris's beauty and more that there was a gentle hand cupping the back of my head and turning me round.

The lights faded away into blackness because all I could see was Toph in front of me. He wouldn't look at me like that if he was annoyed with me or embarrassed by me or thought of me as an honorary little sister.

'Just so you know,' he said softly, leaning down so his breath tickled my ear. 'I didn't just fall in love with Paris either. I fell in love with . . .'

And then he kissed me.

Chapter Twenty-One

My first kiss was everything I'd imagined. There was actual swooning as Toph cradled me in his arms, his mouth moving gently on mine like a question.

The answer was yes. Yes. Yes! A thousand times yes! But I didn't want to use my mouth for talking when I was figuring out the whys and wherefores of being kissed and kissing someone back. So I wound my arms round Toph's neck so my fingers could tug at the little tuft of hair at his nape that would never lie flat. Then Toph tipped me backwards, without once taking his mouth off of mine, so we must have looked like some old black-and-white photo of a kiss – our world at a standstill while life carried on around us.

Toph pulled me upright and stopped kissing me, but only so he could take my face in his hands. I lifted my fingers to my lips, which were tingling – my entire mouth felt odd, as if I wasn't sure what it was for if it wasn't kissing Toph.

'That wasn't some cheesy way of giving you a perfect memento of Paris so you could always say that your first kiss was on the Pont Neuf,' he said softly. 'It was because I've been dying to kiss you for days now.'

It *was* the perfect Parisian memento, because no matter what else happened, my first kiss would *always* have been on the Pont Neuf with a beautiful American boy who could make me laugh until I coughed up Diet Coke all over my favourite T-shirt and made my knees buckle when he kissed me.

'It wasn't perfect,' I said, when I was sure that I had the power of speech again. 'There were no fireworks.'

Toph pursed his lips and I longed to be kissing them again. 'What do you mean, there were no fireworks?'

'Well, maybe there were a few.' I put my arms round Toph's neck again because it was all right to do that now. 'Maybe you'd better kiss me again to make sure.'

We kissed for so long that I couldn't tell where I ended and Toph began. Kissed until my lips were sore. Kissed until the evening breeze blowing across the Seine made us shiver and we had to take a crowded Metro train back to the Shangri-La. As soon as I walked through the door of our room and dropped my bags on the nearest bed, Toph came up behind me and planted a soft kiss on the back of my neck.

'What about that age gap you were so bothered about?' I asked, my voice was curious not angry, though I wasn't sure if Toph knew that. When I turned round and sat on the bed, I almost sighed in relief when Toph sat down next to me.

'I decided it wasn't that big a deal around the time I started obsessing about what it would feel like to kiss you,' Toph confessed, picking up my hand and tracing my heart line. 'Sides, I'm very immature for my age.'

Typically, predictably I was pinking up again and I

didn't know what to say. I mean, what is there to say when the boy you were convinced was out of bounds is suddenly in your arms? 'You know, up until about, oooh, two hours ago, I thought you just saw me as your substitute little sister.'

We both stared at each other and there was nothing remotely brotherly about the way Toph was looking at my mouth, like he was trying to figure out how long we had to talk about just what had happened before we could start kissing again.

But talking would involve a discussion about tomorrow, and after tomorrow there'd be no more Toph and no more kisses. I decided that I might as well make the most of both of them while it was still today.

I leant forward and upwards and, just like that, we were kissing again. We weren't on the Pont Neuf any more with people milling all around us, which meant that the kisses went from PG13 all the way up to 18. There were hands delving under T-shirts and up skirts and there was a lot of tongue. When I'd thought about French kissing in the abstract, it had seemed vaguely icky and unsanitary. But in reality, it was yet another French thing that I really, really liked.

The other crucial difference about kissing in a hotel room was the close proximity of the bed. When we lay on it, because kissing sitting down made our necks ache, the kisses became even more charged. Like kissing wasn't just kissing for kissing's sake but became *foreplay*.

Toph's T-shirt had been tossed on the floor and the

shoulder straps of my black dress were falling down as I straddled Toph and planted a row of kisses across his chest, when he gripped my hips and lifted me off him. I only managed not to land in a heap on the floor by grabbing Toph's leg, which made him gasp like he was in pain.

'I think we should go out,' he said in a strained voice. I didn't need to look down to see why Toph was red-faced and panting as if he had to fight for every breath. I'd felt *it* nudging against my thigh when we kissed. I wasn't entirely unaffected; my insides felt like they were liquefying and even the shift of air against my skin when I moved made me want to scream. I'd paid attention in biology and I knew *exactly* what was happening and what would probably happen if we stayed where we were for much longer.

That was something I needed to think about.

'You're right,' I whispered because I wasn't capable of speaking any louder.

After ten minutes to regroup and absolutely not kiss again, we trooped down the stairs hand in hand, just in time to wave goodbye to the evening shift. Jean from Reception gave a long, low whistle and the other members of staff all looked up and burst into a round of applause.

I didn't know why until Gaspard, the pastry chef, went into a long, fervent speech about how they'd all hoped Toph and I would give in to our grand passion.

'What's he saying?' Toph asked.

'You really don't want to know,' I told him as we reached the bottom of the stairs and Claudette, the sous chef, started going on about how a woman never forgets her first love. Considering how many French movies I'd seen, I'd forgotten how the French were really big on *l'amour*.

'How do you know he's my first or that I love him?' I hissed in French while Toph was having his hand pumped by Jean.

Claudette smiled knowingly. 'Jean says it's your last night,' she said, switching to English. 'We go to our favourite bar. We drink, we dance, we drink some more. OK?'

It was more than OK. With nine chaperones, Toph and I couldn't do anything more than kiss. We followed them through Montmartre's twisty, narrow streets, that seemed to get even more twisted and narrow the further up we climbed. Eventually Jean took a sharp left and tripped down a tiny flight of stairs and through an open door that seemed to glow red in the darkness.

'This is a good bar,' Gaspard told us, putting an arm round our shoulders, which made getting through the door very tricky. 'None of the tourists know it's here.'

It was dark inside and as we all hurried down a rickety wooden staircase, which led into a large room with a stage and a dancefloor that was surrounded by cosy little booths, the patrons greeted the Shangri-La staff with cat-calls and whistles. We were led to a large booth at the back of the room and introduced to Phillipe, the owner. He looked Toph and I up and down, then sighed. Apparently this was a good sign. If he hadn't liked what he saw, we'd have been back on the street.

I looked round the bar and everything brought joy to my soul; the red candles shoved into wax-splattered wine bottles, the girl in the tight leopardskin dress dancing by herself in the corner, even Phillipe with his craggy face and his nicotine-stained hands and his black turtle neck couldn't have been more perfect if I'd phoned Central Casting and asked them to find me a Parisian bar owner.

All I could do was clasp my hands to my heart and squeal.

'Oh my God, just sit down,' Toph said, pulling me on to the end of his banquette. 'You look like you're about to start speaking in tongues.'

'This place is just . . . it's too bloody perfect, isn't it?'

Toph looked around and I knew he couldn't see what I saw, but he turned back to me with a smile and kissed the top of my head. 'Yeah, it's pretty damn cool.'

Claudette had been right. There were drinks, jug after jug of a dark, smoky red wine, and dancing. And more drinking. And shouted conversations, but the best part was when a man wandered down the stairs as he played a mournful refrain on his trumpet.

Someone slid behind the piano, someone else produced a pair of bongos and there was an impromptu jazz concert, which culminated in everyone leaving the bar to do a conga line round the block to 'When The Saints Go Marching In'.

It was past three when Toph and I decided that we couldn't face another lukewarm carafe of red wine and anyway, I had to be at Gare du Nord in a few hours to catch the Eurostar.

A crowd of people followed us up the wooden staircase to wave goodbye. I could still hear their distant shouts as

Toph and I started down the hill. It was that weird, transient time when it wasn't night any more, but wasn't morning either. The sky was a smudgy, inky blue and it was cold, even though I was wearing Toph's hoodie and he had his arm around me. Neither of us spoke but it was a toasty silence that didn't need words. Besides, I needed to concentrate all my energies on following Claudette's directions back to the hotel.

We stopped at a *boulangerie* that had just thrown open its shutters to buy a baguette each, so hot they hurt our fingers and so fresh that the dough was moist and yeasty as soon as we shoved them in our mouths. We hadn't even finished our loaves when we came to the narrow little arch that led to the Shangri-La.

As I followed Toph up the sweeping staircase, there was a naughty little voice in my head that told me that missing the 9 a.m. train, and the one after that, and the one after that, wouldn't be so terrible in the grand scheme of all the terrible things my mother would accuse me of doing, but I tried to ignore it.

'Bagsy the bathroom,' I grunted, as Toph opened the door, elbowing him out of the way for the last time, then listening to him complain bitterly about it for the last time.

I showered sitting down on the floor of the cubicle because my legs were too tired to hold me up. Then, with my hair still dripping wet, I staggered to the bedroom.

Toph was already sprawled out on his bed, limbs at right angles, only the up and down of his chest told me he was still alive. My bed looked a very long way away and when

Toph reached out to touch my arm, it was all the incentive I needed to flop onto his bed and curl myself into the space he made for me.

'Your hair's soaking,' he grumbled when he got a mouthful as I wriggled to get comfortable. In the end, I rolled over so I was facing Toph, could look at him, and check that I'd correctly memorized every freckle and mole and millimetre of his face to keep me going until . . . well, forever.

'Hey,' I whispered sleepily, wondering if I had the energy to count every single one of Toph's girlishly long eyelashes.

'Hey,' he whispered back, leaning forward so we could rub noses, which made me giggle.

And of course, rubbing noses meant that our faces were touching and, inevitably, the face touching led to kissing.

Kissing Toph was so exciting that I didn't feel tired any more. I felt so energized that I was flexing my feet and clenching and unclenching my fists and maybe even writhing a little. And though Toph bit his lip every time I writhed a little bit too vigorously, he didn't seem to mind that much.

Maybe that was the reason our kisses became fiercer, like we were devouring each other in the same way that we'd torn into the baguettes. Toph's fingers skittered over my shower-damp skin and when he rolled on top of me so I could feel his cock pressing against my tummy, I knew I had to make a decision there and then. Well, one part of my brain knew that, but the other part of my brain that controlled my arms and my legs and my mouth wasn't listening.

'If we don't stop now, then it's going to be too late to stop,' Toph suddenly said through gritted teeth.

Part of me was tempted because if kissing and touching and writhing felt this amazing, then sex would blow the top right off my head. And we were both legal and we'd taken the time to get to know each other properly and I had a ton of condoms stashed in one of my socks but . . . If we had sex it would completely obliterate the week we'd had in Paris. When I'd think about Paris, inevitably I'd think about having sex. And it would be sex with a boy who lived half a world away and I wasn't even sure if I'd ever see Toph again after tomorrow.

Then Toph did something with his teeth and my left earlobe that made my entire body short circuit and destroyed all my good intentions about waiting. What was so bloody good about waiting? I'd been waiting my whole life to get to the good stuff and anyway, it would totally serve my mum right, especially when I pointed out how extremely easy it was to have sex and *not* get pregnant. I could just imagine her spluttering indignation and the way her face would squinch up and . . .

I rolled out from under Toph with a groan that was full of regret, because that last thought was like having a bucket of cold water thrown over me. If I was planning to have sex to get one over on my mother, then I was *so* not mature enough to have sex.

'We have to stop,' I said, flopping down next to Toph. 'Because, well, I don't think we should . . . I'm not ready to . . . this whole sex thing.'

Toph rolled over and propped himself up on one elbow so he could peer at me quizzically. 'Did you think I was going to put out on the first date?'

'No! Well, I don't know.' I was currently cornering the market in spluttering indignation myself. 'I just thought that you might have thought . . . Was that our first date? The boat cruise or the club?'

'Technically, you could say that our whole week in Paris was one super-long first date,' Toph mused, but then his face grew more serious. 'I've only had sex with one other girl and we'd been going out for, like, two years before we cashed in our V-chips.'

'Wow! Two years.'

'Well, we were only fifteen when we started dating and our high school was all about the abstinence and the True Love Waits rather than teaching us anything useful about sex – but I'm glad we waited. It made it special . . . well, until we both got totally wasted at Senior Prom.'

Teenage Toph sounded so different from the sweaty teenage boys I knew, who would never wait for True Love. The shadows in the room were receding and even though the curtains were drawn, I could tell that the sky was lightening. I closed my eyes but Toph laying just a whisper away from me was very distracting. Like his molecules were giving off a static hum.

'If it wasn't our first date, but, like our fifty-seventh date and we weren't going to have an ocean between us, would you want to have sex?' I asked, with my eyes still shut. My voice sounded so loud in the still of the room.

Embarrassingly, terrifying loud, but I needed to make sure that the kisses meant something, that *I* meant something to Toph and hadn't just been a holiday romance he'd tell his friends about when he got back to Texas.

'Do you think I'd be trying to remember the names of all the US Presidents in chronological order and seriously thinking about having a cold shower if I didn't want to have sex with you?' Toph sounded close to tears.

I knew there was other stuff we could do that wasn't full-on, proper, say-goodbye-to-your-maidenhood sex, but I didn't feel like I was ready for that either. I'd waited for my first kiss and that had turned out as special and romantic as I'd always imagined it. There was nothing special or romantic about groping and tugging at each other while we were on a clock.

I lifted my wrist and squinted at my watch. We had fifty-five minutes until we had to get up and it seemed a pity to waste them sleeping. I had the rest of my life to sleep.

'There's no point in sleeping,' I whispered, smoothing Toph's frown with my fingertips when he moaned in protest. 'We have to get up in less than an hour and I'd much rather spend that time kissing. Please.' Then I shaped my lips into a perfect kiss-shaped pout.

It worked. Toph moved the five inches across the bed that was all the space it took for him to be in my arms and we started kissing again, legs tangling clumsily against each other. I kept my eyes open the whole time, even though I knew that The Kissing Code Of Practice Manual would stipulate that they should be kept shut. But I didn't want to miss the swooping motion of Toph's lashes every time we ended a kiss, then started a new one, or the little line of three freckles across his right cheekbone and how, when we came up for oxygen, his lips were curved in a secret little smile that never dimmed so I could feel the shape of it when I kissed him.

I felt as if we were the only two people in the world and that world had shrunk down to a crumpled double bed in a zingy green room.

Chapter Twenty-Two

I didn't even realize we'd fallen asleep until we were woken up by the phone on the nightstand ringing and ringing. Burrowing deeper against Toph didn't make it stop.

'You're nearer,' Toph grunted, trying to lever himself into an upright position, then giving up in favour of staying horizontal.

I groped for the phone one-handed. ''*Allo?*'

'Mademoiselle Bea? It's Helene from the front desk. I remind you that you have to be at Gare du Nord in an hour. Shall I order you a taxi?'

'Bloody, bloody hell!' I shrieked. 'Yes, taxi! *Vite, vite!*'

I hurled myself off the bed at great speed, startling Toph out of his torpor as I ran around the room trying to dress and pack at the same time. 'Shit! Shit! Shit!'

'What?' he mouthed, watching me try to put on a pair of socks while stuffing dirty clothes into a carrier bag. I could see the lightbulb ping over his head. 'Oh? Shit. Shit! Shit!'

Toph jack-knifed off the bed and, now he was added to the mix, I kept falling over him as well as all the things I hadn't packed yet.

We were dressed, packed and racing down the stairs to check out of the Shangri-La in seven minutes. We had eleven carrier bags between us. I'd looped a vintage scarf round six of mine and was wearing them as a hastily improvised backpack. I now knew what 'Necessity is the mother of invention' really meant, apart from something Grandma Major said when she was cutting up old clothes to use as dusters.

Checking out took a teeth-grinding ten minutes, only slightly sweetened by the appearance of two cake boxes courtesy of the Shangri-La kitchen. There wasn't time for anything other than a hurried goodbye with Michel and Henri, who were changing shifts, and a promise that we'd return, before we were racing to the taxi.

Though it was the middle of August and most Parisians were meant to be at the coast, the ones who'd stayed behind had decided to get in their cars that morning and jam all roads leading to the Gare du Nord.

Our driver didn't seem that concerned, though occasionally he'd lean on his horn and shout a stream of abuse out of the window, while I fretted on the back seat. At 8.49 a.m. we pulled up outside the station and in one fluid motion I paid the driver, opened the door and threw myself out of the car. 'Eleven minutes before the train leaves!' I informed Toph, who was running full pelt alongside me, bless him.

Luckily there was no queue at Security. I could see the platform and the train looming in front of me when a man in a peaked cap suddenly appeared out of nowhere and tried to block my path as I heard a symphony of carriage doors shutting.

'*Vous êtes trop tard*,' he shouted at me, but I swerved past him and ran for the train. I ran like I'd never run before, my legs going like pistons, heart pounding in my chest though it wasn't like I was in a tearing hurry to go home. But catching a train on time was the Bea equivalent of the search for the Holy Grail.

I wrenched open the first door I came to just as the guard blew the whistle. I fell into the train. Toph threw in his bags, which landed on top of me as he hoisted himself up as the train began to move.

We sat on the floor for a second, panting and blinking at each other until a guard opened the door that led into the carriage. 'Can I see your tickets?'

It felt odd to hear English with an English accent. I got to my feet and dug out my ticket, only to be told that there were ten carriages between me and my designated seat. Sighing deeply, I gathered up my bags and we began the long walk through the train. I kept knocking people with my suitcase and my improvised backpack, but there was no need for them to get so snippy about it.

Finally I hefted my suitcase up on the luggage rack and sank into my seat.

'Well, that was bracing,' I said to Toph.

He was feeling his chest. 'Can't talk,' he said shortly. 'Waiting to see if I go into cardiac arrest.'

I gave him five seconds, then punched his arm. 'Toph! You need to get off the train! Actually . . . why did they even let you on the train?'

'I don't know. Maybe they thought I had an honest face.'

Toph waggled his eyebrows playfully.

'But you haven't got a ticket! You're meant to be going to Berlin or Prague . . . I guess when I started running, you started running and now you're on the wrong train.' I shook my head in disbelief. 'Should we pull the cord? God, you're going to have to get out at Lille and go all the way back to Paris.'

Toph was carefully unpeeling the tape from one of the Shangri-La's breakfast boxes. 'Guess I might as well check out old London town,' he said breezily, peering into the box. 'Jeesh, my *pain au chocolat* has staged a dirty protest.'

'You can't just decide *on a whim* to come to London,' I pointed out gently. It was sweet that Toph had bought into my hysteria about catching the train but he was currently about to cross an international border without a valid ticket and could be facing deportation or jail or being sent to one of those illegal alien places and, instead of being all freaked out about it, he was demolishing a battered *pain au chocolat* in three bites. 'Why didn't the guard say anything about your ticket?'

'Yeah, strange that. Might have had something to do with the fact that I got Jean to get me a ticket when he booked yours,' Toph said. It shouldn't have been possible to look as smug as he did. Or still look attractive when he looked that smug. 'Shall I get us some coffee?'

Toph was getting up like we were done with the conversation. I yanked him back down by his belt, which led to a strangled yelp and a reproachful look. 'What?'

'What?' I echoed incredulously. 'Why are you coming to London with me?'

'Because I want to see London during my grand tour of Europe. It's not my fault that London just happens to have a Bea in it.'

That put a gigantic Toph-shaped dent in my ego. 'Oh,' I said huffily, making a big show of shrinking back in my seat so Toph's arm wasn't touching mine any more. 'Oh. Right. Fine.'

'And even though we hadn't kissed yet, I knew that I didn't want to say goodbye just yet,' Toph told me, putting his arm around me. 'Figured you might need a friend when you got back to London.'

'You didn't have to do that,' I insisted weakly, even though I was terribly glad that he had. It meant that we still had some time together and I wouldn't have to spend it trying to find Toph a good immigration lawyer. 'But you might want to go for several very long walks while my mum and me are locked in this never-ending battle about her lying to me for seventeen years, which she'll try to deflect by yelling at me for bumming around Europe without her say-so.'

I could feel the motion of the train shunting me ever onward to London and already the memory of Paris was receding.

'If your mom is anything like my mom, she won't yell at you with a guest in the house. Think of me as a human shield,' Toph said, delving into his breakfast box again and pulling out an apricot Danish.

'I never thought of it like that,' I mused. The moment that Mum uttered the dreaded words, 'I want a word with you,' I could simply drag Toph into her line of fire.

'I have more female relatives that I know what to do with, so I'm way in touch with my feminine side.' Toph paused to lick apricot goo from his fingers. 'Honestly, your mom will love me. Moms always love me; it's their daughters who go off me.'

'I'm not about to go off you any time soon,' I said quickly.

'Really? You won't get me on British soil and decide that I look like a great big dork in your natural habitat?'

'As if!' I scoffed, giving Toph a dig in the ribs for good measure.

'Well, in that case, how about swapping your *pain au chocolat* for my almond croissant?'

I fell asleep halfway through detailing a huge list of dos and don'ts of what made acceptable conversation topics with my family. Like, they didn't need to know about vodka martinis and buying beer from KFC and Toph was adamant that his misspent youth as a firebomber wasn't to be brought up over Sunday lunch.

I was vaguely aware of someone coming to check our passports, but when the train came to its final resting place at St Pancras, I blearily opened my eyes to find that I was asleep on Toph's shoulder with a damp patch on his T-shirt where I'd dribbled on him. Toph had his head pressed against the window at a painful angle and was snoring gently.

He woke up when I levered myself off him and slowly began to gather my bags. Catching the train might have been a frantic scramble but I was in no mad rush to get *off* the train.

'Do we have to get the subway?' Toph asked as he helped me string my carrier bags on to my scarf. 'Except can we call it a tube?'

'It's *the* tube and we'll call it that because that's what we call it,' I mumbled. 'Have to get a bus too.'

'Cool! And everyone will talk British just like you,' Toph said happily as we stepped on to the platform and started walking towards the ticket barrier.

'Who was Saint Pancras?' Toph asked suddenly. 'What is he the patron saint of?'

'I have absolutely no idea,' I said, angling a glance at Toph, who was wide-eyed and staring around him in wonder. The new Eurostar terminal was pretty spiffy but I thought that Toph had seen enough railway stations in the last few weeks that one more wouldn't have impressed him this much.

'Right, we need to go this way,' I said, as we stepped on to the concourse and I spotted the London Underground sign. It gave me a little warm glow to see something so completely familiar and British, which surprised me because I'd been so in love with Paris. I was obviously a two-city kind of girl. 'It won't take long to get back to mine. Ten minutes on the tube, twenty minutes on the bus . . .'

'BEA! BEA! BEA! BEA! BEA! BEA! BEA! BEA! BEA!

BEA! BEA!' Two tow-headed creatures suddenly hurtled towards me and almost sent me flying on impact as they clung to a leg each: 'BEA! BEA! BEA! BEA! BEA!'

The warm glow upgraded to this raging torrent of love as I knelt down so I could hug Alfie and Ben, who obligingly smothered my face with kisses. Or licks in Ben's case.

'Twinnies! Hey, you said my name. Say it again!'

'Hello, trouble,' said a familiar voice and I looked up to see James walking towards me. My heart gave a jerk, but James was flying solo and looking fairly pleased to see me.

I stood up, which was hard when Alfie had me in a stranglehold and then James was giving me a quick, fierce hug, which he'd never done before, but I hugged him back for all I was worth.

'Your gran told me what time your train was coming in,' James said, trying to corral Alfie and Ben. 'How about you take the boys and I'll take your case?'

There was a polite cough behind me. I looked around to see Toph shuffling his feet and hanging his head. I grabbed his hand and pulled him forward. 'James, this is Toph. We've been hanging out. He's my friend. And my travel buddy and he's from Texas.' I couldn't find the right words to explain what Toph was and why he was by my side. 'I said that he could stay at ours until he has to go back to the States. In the spare room,' I added, as James's eyebrows shot up. 'Toph, this is James, my stepdad, and this is Alfie and this is Ben. Say hello.'

Alfie and Ben stared up at Toph with solemn, unblinking

blue eyes, then ducked behind James's legs like they were shy. Which, not even.

'Pleased to meet you, sir,' Toph said politely, holding out his hand. 'I promise I'm not a serial killer.'

It wasn't the most tactful thing to say but it made James grin and he shook Toph's hand with a slightly less wary expression than he'd had on his face ten seconds earlier.

'Good to know,' he said briskly. 'Come on, let's go. I'm on a meter.'

The twins had recovered from their uncharacteristic bout of shyness by the time they were strapped into their car seats and poor Toph, sitting in between them, was treated to every trick in their repertoire. Ben recited his colours, Alfie counted up to ten, then we were treated to an endless and tuneless rendition of the *Bob The Builder* theme.

Every time I tried to point out some interesting local feature to Toph there were indignant squawks from the cheap seats.

'See Dunn's on the right, Toph,' I said. 'It's this amazing bakery; they do this great cake covered in white chocolate icing and there's a really good vintage shop on the left and just up there is where I do Pilates.'

It took another five minutes to crawl up the hill, nose round the roundabout, then we were turning into the wide avenue of redbrick houses that was our street.

'Wow!' I heard Toph breathe. 'Everything is so old.'

'It's not that old,' I protested. 'It's only Edwardian. Early twentieth century.'

'Bea, in Texas, early nineteen-nineties is old,' Toph told me, eyes wide as James reversed onto our drive and the front door opened. I reached behind my seat and patted Toph's knee to let him know that everything was going to be fine. At least I hoped everything would be fine as the two grandmas came down the front steps, followed by Lilah from next door. Bringing up the rear was my mother.

I wondered if maybe I could just stay in the car but James had unbuckled his seatbelt and asked me to unstrap Alfie while he took Ben.

There was a chorus of 'hello's as I opened the back door and began to take Alfie out of his car seat. Toph was book-ended by the twins and looking nervous, especially when Alfie decided he'd rather stay in the car and started crying.

'You ready for this?' I asked over the top of Alfie's head. 'You could stay here and I could come out under cover of darkness and give you directions to the nearest youth hostel.'

Toph looked the tiniest bit tempted, but then I saw him visibly man up by putting his shoulders back and taking a few deep breaths. 'OK, let's do this,' he said decisively.

As I emerged, Grandma Minor hurried forward to give me and the furiously squirming Alfie a hug. 'I'm sure you've got taller,' she said, stroking my cheek. 'I can't wait to hear all about your adventures.'

'I'm sure Bea's dying for a cuppa,' Grandma Major added, but all I could see was the absolutely frozen expression on Mum's face. She opened her mouth to say something just as Toph got out of the car.

'Um, this is Toph,' I said, with a jerky hand gesture. 'He's a really, really, really nice person who's going to stay for a few days.'

The welcoming smiles all disappeared. I'd got used to what Toph looked like over the last few days. He was tall and lean and had a really goofy smile when he was eating something delicious. But now I saw him as my nearest and dearest were currently seeing him; a man in his early twenties. A man who was three years and seven months older than me – and when I thought about Toph in those terms, I almost couldn't believe that last night I'd been wrapped around him, kissing him, because now he seemed so scarily out of my league. It looked like Toph was rethinking things too. For a second I thought he was going to bolt but then he snatched off the baseball cap and stuffed it in the back pocket of his jeans, before advancing on Grandma Major with an outstretched hand.

'Pleased to meet you, ma'am. Bea's told me an awful lot about you.' Toph's accent was slower and drawlier, the way it always was when he was nervous, but props for correctly identifying the matriarch of our little clan. Then he was shaking hands with Grandma Minor and reminding her that they'd spoken on the phone before glancing awkwardly between Lilah from next door and Mum, who looked as if she'd downed an entire bottle of lemon juice. God help Toph if he mistook Lilah for Mum. Lilah had a good fifteen years on Mum and was currently sticking out her bosom and patting her bleached curls.

'I guess you're Bea's mom,' he said after a frighteningly

long pause and held out a hand to Mum, who shook it briefly, then dropped it like she suspected that Toph didn't wash his hands after he peed.

'I suppose I must be,' she agreed, ice encasing every word. 'You'd better come inside.'

Chapter Twenty-Three

The next couple of hours were a flurry of activity. Mum and James took the twins out to the park, because they were running around and getting into everything, everything being my open suitcase. There was laundry to be done and cups of tea to be drunk, while the grandmas interrogated Toph to within an inch of his tender young life. After hearing about the three sisters and the ballroom dancing, they both decided he was all right for an American and he was allowed up the stairs and into the little studio apartment in the attic that was for the au pair that we were supposed to be getting, but in reality was a graveyard for all of James's dead bits of computers.

'Are you OK?' I asked Toph as we made up the bed. 'The grandmas can be a bit full on.'

'They kept looking at me really weirdly,' Toph muttered as he struggled to get the fitted sheet tucked round all four corners of the bed.

'That's because you insisted that biscuits came with gravy and were served as part of a meal. Which is just crazy talk!'

'But what I just had weren't biscuits. They were cookies.' Toph shrugged. Now that we'd left Paris, our shrugs were getting less Gallic. 'Two nations separated by a common language and all that.'

I sat down on the bed and folded my arms. 'Why do you keep talking in a whisper?'

'I don't,' Toph hissed fiercely. 'I am! I don't know. This is all a bit strange.'

'Too strange?'

Toph sat down next to me and threaded his fingers through mine. 'I thought we'd spend a week in London doing all the stuff we did in Paris; the walking and the people-watching and hanging out. I kinda forgot that you had a family that includes two grandmothers and two little brothers. I need to make some mental adjustments.'

'Do you want to go?' I asked again, feeling Toph's pulse thudding steadily beneath my fingers.

'No! God, no!' Toph said throatily and then he took my lips in a kiss that was so sweet I could have had it for pudding. It was the first time we'd kissed on British soil and it was oddly comforting. He wasn't a scary older man. He was still Toph and I was still the Bea that he wanted to kiss. 'And I've got your back for when the screaming starts.'

'When the screaming starts, I advise you to take cover,' I sniffed. 'In fact, I'm surprised the screaming hasn't already started. So far, all that Mum has said to me was, "You've changed your hair," in a voice that was as flat as a week-old pancake. She hasn't looked too thrilled with her box of crystallized fruits either.'

'Hey, now that we're in Britain, are you going to talk fluent British all the time?' Toph teased. 'I'll have to buy a phrasebook, so I can understand what you're saying and not make another biscuit gaffe.'

'I have a feeling you're going to hear "bloody" said an awful lot over the next few days.'

Toph nudged me again, gently this time. 'We get BBC America at home. British people don't fight. They just say, "Will you get your father to pass the salt?" in a really passive–aggressive way.'

Obviously they didn't have *EastEnders* on BBC America. 'Nothing passive–aggressive about rows in this house. They tend to be aggressive–aggressive.' I sat up straight and stuck out my chin. 'She can shout all she likes, but I'm not going to take it. Not any more!'

'Just work out what you want to say in your head,' Toph advised me quietly. 'Otherwise you'll say a whole bunch of mean things in the heat of the moment and you'll regret them. You know you will. It took us a week to come back from that fight we had in Marseilles.'

'See, before I went away, I never had fights. I was meek and mild and I let people walk all over me and I don't want to be that girl again. I don't want to be *her* girl.'

'Then don't,' Toph said, like it was that simple. And maybe it was. But I didn't have time to ponder that bombshell any further because Grandma Minor was calling us down for dinner.

Toph had been right. There were a lot of passive–aggressive requests to pass the vinaigrette and the garlic bread, thank you very much.

It took a while for me to notice I had company in the doghouse, because Mum and Grandma Minor were on no-speakers too. Probably because Gran had actively encouraged me to stay in Paris doing unspeakably rude things with boys and drinking myself into a stupor – that's how Mum would see it. James and Grandma Major seemed thoroughly sick of the open hostilities and who could blame them? If there were an Olympics in being stubborn and wilfull, then there'd be a photo finish between Mum and Grandma Minor as to who'd take home the gold.

Paris was an incendiary topic of conversation but Grandma Major wanted to hear all about it. I told her about the cemetery in Montmartre and having lunch at Le Café des Deux Moulins from *Amélie*. 'It wasn't the actual café inside but they used the outside as an exterior shot.' I waxed lyrical about the Shangri-La and my cooking lessons and the chocolate shop on the Île de la Cité and no one else could get a word in edgeways. Toph did try but he was too distracted by Alfie, who isisted on throwing pieces of pesto-soaked pasta at him, no matter how many times he was told not to.

Mum didn't say a word. She kept opening her mouth like she was about to say something, then would think better of it and close it again with an almost audible snap. It was very unsettling – it meant that when the bollocking came it was going to be biblical.

'And I talked French all the time,' I rattled on, as James passed around bowls of strawberries. 'Monsieur Bradley was so right when he said you had to go and live in a country if you wanted to speak the language.' I looked around the table and realized that everyone's eyes were

286

glazing over. Only Ben was giving me his rapt attention, but he'd been an absolute cling-on ever since I got home. 'Anyway, James, have you got a spare laptop Toph can borrow so we can upload our photos and he can email home and stuff?'

James nodded eagerly. 'I've just upgraded . . .' he began and the grandmas both rolled their eyes (Mum didn't but I could tell by the way she stared fixedly at the water jug that she wanted to) because once James started on the subject of computers, he'd go on and on. Much like I'd been going on and on about what I did on my summer holidays.

'Um, Toph . . . is it Toph, or is it short for something else?' Mum asked and it was the first time she'd deigned to speak to Toph, which was either good or bad. It was too soon to tell really.

'Well, it's Christopher, ma'am, but no one calls me that unless I'm in righteous amounts of trouble,' Toph blurted out nervously.

Mum smiled and it was a proper Mum smile that was almost impossible not to return. 'Toph, then. Would you like to call home? You can use the phone in the living room.' Toph tugged at his T-shirt collar, but Mum rushed on. 'We have some complicated phone tariff that I don't understand but we get free international calls. Really, you must.'

It was the good side of Mum; thoughtful, considerate, with this unerring knack for knowing what you needed before you knew that you needed it. OK, she'd done a terrible, heinous thing but that didn't make her a terrible, heinous person.

'They must be worried about you,' Mum continued as Toph stood up. 'I know that when my child was in another country and refusing to phone me, it was very distressing. I didn't sleep for nights on end.'

Toph bolted for the door, while I glared at Mum. She wasn't thoughtful and considerate and big with the ESP; she was the Queen of the Guilt Trip, which was just left of Passive Aggressive Valley.

OK, we were going to throw down; everyone else seemed to think so. The grandmas disappeared in the direction of the kitchen, James took Alfie and said he was going to sort out the laptop, which left just Mum and me. Except she was calmly picking up the salad bowl and sailing out of the room, pausing only to give me this look that conveyed deep disappointment, like she didn't know where she'd gone wrong with me but she planned to find out and make sure it never happened again.

'Just you wait,' I told Ben as I lifted him out of his highchair and stroked the wispy bits of blonde fuzz, which hadn't grown into a full head of hair like Alfie's yet. 'She'll probably send you and Alfie to a seminary instead of kindergarten.'

'Yeah,' Ben solemnly agreed. 'TV, Bea. Want TV.'

Toph was saying goodbye as I walked into the living room. I placed Ben in the playpen as Toph crouched down and waggled his fingers through the bars. 'Hey, little man, what's up?'

'So, everything all right at home?' I asked.

'Yeah, though my mom said she's forgotten what I look

like so I shouldn't be surprised if she's standing there with a shotgun when I walk through the door,' Toph said with a grin. He picked up Ben's spit-stained blue rabbit and waved at him, then hastily put it down when Ben unleashed a volley of screams. 'God, should he be doing that?'

Now it was my turn to squat down. 'Ben, if you're a good boy, Bea's got chocolate crocodiles for you.'

Ben went from ear-splitting to mute in a nanosecond. Just a plaintive, 'Choccy,' leaked out of his mouth.

'Later,' I promised, as Ben decided that he would grab hold of Toph's fingers now. 'Come on,' I added, leaning heavily on Toph's shoulder as I stood up. 'I want to show you my room.'

We were just about to head up the stairs when Mum emerged from the kitchen. 'What was Ben crying about?' she demanded.

'Toph dared to pick up Mr Rabbit,' I replied coolly. Toph had paused on the third step, but I prodded him. 'We'll be upstairs.'

Toph took the stairs two at a time. Mum waited until he'd rounded the corner before she said, 'You know you're not allowed boys in your room, Bea.'

I didn't know because no boys old enough to pose a sexual threat to my person had ever come through the front door. I remembered Toph's advice not to say anything until I'd thought about exactly what I wanted to say, so I ignored her and actually had one leg on the first stair, when she stopped me in my tracks. 'I mean it, Bea.'

It was hard to flounce when you were between stairs but

I managed it. 'You have got to be bloody kidding me!'

'Do I look like I'm joking?'

She didn't; her face was tense and I kinda hated her then for trying to put me firmly back in my place. I felt like a dolphin who'd been gaily swimming the ocean with my dolphin buds for two and a half weeks only to get caught in a net and find myself in a tiny tank in an aquarium.

'Look, are you going to get on my case about going to Paris in the next five minutes?' I asked and boy, did it come out sounding all kinds of belligerent.

Maybe that was why Mum took a step back before she could check herself. 'Well, no. I don't really think that now's the time.'

'Fine, well let me know when you're going to schedule it in because there's plenty of things I'd like to get off my chest too.'

'I don't like your tone of voice, young lady,' Mum said.

But she hadn't made a move towards me and she wasn't issuing a stream of threats and warnings about what would happen if I went up to my room – though I knew all her worst-case scenarios would all reach the same conclusion; me plus bun in the oven.

'I'm going upstairs now,' I informed her and this time I managed a whole two steps . . .

'You are not!'

I whirled around and stabbed at her general direction with one finger. 'What do you think we're going to get up to in my room, with a house full of people downstairs, that we couldn't have got up to when we were sharing a hotel room in Paris? Huh?'

From the horrified look on her face and the way she was clutching the banister for support, Mum's mind had gone to a scary place where I had a tiny foetus growing inside me right at that moment. I could almost see the thought bubble: *This isn't Bea acting out, it's pregnancy hormones*, appear above her head.

So this time when I started stomping up the stairs she didn't try to stop me. Until I turned the corner, then she shouted, 'I want that bloody door kept open!'

But I was too busy slamming the bloody door to pay her any attention.

Toph looked up from the laptop in alarm. 'Everything all right?' he asked doubtfully.

I nodded my head. 'Never better.' After all, I'd just discovered an absolutely bulletproof way to deal with Mum – if standing up to her didn't work, I could simply walk away.

I sat down on my bed and glanced around the room. It was still the cosy inner sanctum it had always been and I felt like it suited me better now. Like, I'd grown into the rich, red walls and the motley collection of *objets d'art*. They weren't just props for a part I was playing. I could even look at my vintage French posters and understand every word printed on them (well, nearly every word) and even Grandma Major's frock on the dress form looked like the sort of thing I might wear, if I'd been brought up on wartime rations.

'I really, really love my room,' I announced to the back of Toph's head. 'This is the first time I've felt like I'm home since I got home.'

Toph looked up from the computer screen. 'I've never seen so much cool stuff per square foot – apart from the time I went to *Ripley's Believe It Or Not* in Grand Prairie and saw a huge picture of *The Last Supper* made out of postage stamps.'

'I thought about getting one of those but it didn't go with the general vibe of my room,' I sniffed in a mock-prissy voice, which made Toph laugh and grab my hand so he could tug me on to his lap, not that I needed much persuading.

The feel of Toph's mouth on mine was as much a homecoming as the faint smell of fig candles and singed hair because I always left my curling tongs on for too long. I was just sliding my hands up Toph's T-shirt as a prelude to taking it off when he pulled away.

'Not when your grandmas are on the premises,' he hissed in a scandalized whisper, soothing away my pout with another kiss. Which turned into another kiss and then Toph pulling away again. 'Stop trying to take advantage of me. Haven't you got emails to check?'

When I logged into Gmail, I nearly fell off the chair in surprise. I had over five hundred messages waiting for me. Usually I was lucky if I got five emails a day – and one of them was usually offering me free penis enlargement.

I scrolled through the new messages and realized that most of them were Facebook notifications. Again, weird because I only had twenty-one Facebook friends. Had I suddenly become popular overnight and no one had bothered to tell me?

The truth was even stranger than that. When I checked Facebook, I had sixty-seven new friend requests, thirty-five messages and another seventy-four notes written on my wall.

Next to me, Toph was Facebooking too. I accepted his friend request, then started on the other messages. Ruth, Lydia and Polly had all left messages, wanting to know what the hell was going on.

'I'm worried about you! Why is your phone always switched off?' Ruth had written a week ago. 'Heard something bad went down in Malaga. Please let me know you're OK and that Ruby hasn't lived up to her advertising and done something awful to you.'

'Bea-ster, please let me know you're AOK. Can't get through on your phone,' Lydia had messaged me via email, Facebook and MySpace. 'Called your mum but she just said you weren't there and sounded dead snippy about it.'

Even Polly, who was computer-phobic and didn't even have a mobile phone, had left me a beautifully punctuated and spelt email. 'Where are you? I saw Chloe hanging out at the stables and she said you were the skeeviest person to ever walk the earth and did I know you were a lesbian? Then she went on and on and on and on about Ruby and how she was also the skeeviest person to ever live. I think "skeeviest" is Chloe's word for the week. Please get in touch.'

I felt slightly ashamed when I'd finished reading their messages because I'd been so invested in moaning about how we weren't real friends but thrown together by default I hadn't even thought to text them while I away and had merrily switched off my phone after I'd spoken to Grandma each morning because I hadn't wanted my mum to call me. Maybe not all friendships had to be exciting and about shared passions; there could be other friendships that were gentler and less intense, but were still friendships in their own right.

There was also a ton of other people sending me friend requests, messages and wall posts to say, 'We don't know what happened between you and Ruby, but if she hates you then that automatically makes you cool.' I recognized a lot of the names from the parties Ruby had dragged me to and I recognized other names from school: girls that had never spoken to me. Or I'd never spoken to them.

Toph had finished his interwebbing and was hooking up his camera as I accepted friend requests from Aaron, Michael, Erin, Bridge and Jess, then decided to log out of Facebook before my brain exploded. We spent the next hour happily sorting through our photos, though I made a mental note to stop taking pictures of myself by holding a camera up to my face because all I ever got were nostril shots.

I sneaked downstairs to get supplies, then I stuck my *Amélie* DVD on. Toph knew that the whole future of our relationship depended on his reaction because he kept making me pause the disc so he could tell me off for staring at him, instead of watching the screen.

'It's too much pressure,' he complained. 'I feel like you're going to give me a pop test afterwards.'

'I wouldn't do that,' I protested, though I'd had plans to interrogate Toph very closely after the credits had rolled. 'It's just this is my favourite bit.'

'You've said that ten times already and we've only been watching it for thirty minutes.'

'Oh, shut up and have a KitKat,' I said, shoving one at him.

We carried on watching the film, though we had to pause it again when Toph made the happy discovery that British KitKats were a far superior product to their waxy American cousins, and we found a way to cuddle against each other without Toph's arm going numb. It was perfect; everything I'd always imagined having a boyfriend to be like, even if I did have the crinkly imprint of a KitKat wrapper embedded in my hand.

'Bea! Wake up! I think someone's coming up the stairs,' Toph hissed, pushing me to an upright position as I blinked my eyes and saw that Amélie and Nino were careering around Montmartre on his moped and I'd been asleep for most of the film.

By the time there was a gentle knock on the door and I heard James tentatively call my name, Toph was sitting on my desk chair and I was perched primly on the edge of the bed.

'Um, probably time to call it a night,' James said through the door, like he was scared he might be confronted with debauched scenes of wild teen sex if he came in. 'Did Toph get on all right with the laptop?'

Toph tousled my hair and gave me a grin as he loped towards the door because it was obvious that James was there to escort him to the spare room. Mum would never have been so discreet – she'd have just barged in and demanded to know what we were doing, and the fact that she hadn't meant that I'd won this round.

Chapter Twenty-Four

As soon as I got into bed with Jasper – the little velvet teddy I'd had since I was a baby – clutched to my chest, I was fast asleep and stayed that way until someone quietly opened the door and called my name. I forced my eyes open and looked at the clock; it was almost one.

I sat up to see Mum put a mug of tea and a plate of toast on the bedside table, before she pulled up a chair. 'We have to talk,' she said quietly.

We did but I didn't want to do it when I was befuddled with sleep with pillow creases etched into my face, besides . . . 'I need to pee,' I yelped, scrambling out of bed.

When I was finally composed enough to leave the bathroom, Mum was sitting on my desk chair with arms and legs folded and this look of steely determination on her face, which never worked out well for me. But she just said, 'Drink your tea before it gets cold,' as I arranged myself cross-legged on the bed.

Whatever Mum needed to say she waited until I'd finished my tea and nibbled on a piece of toast and didn't seem to be in any great hurry to get on with telling me I was grounded until I was ninety. I cleared my throat. 'What have you done with Toph?' I asked suspiciously.

'Well, I sprinkled rat poison on his cornflakes then the grandmas helped me dismember his still-twitching corpse and James took up the patio so we could bury him.'

'Mum!'

It was the first time I'd seen her smile at me since I got home. Still, it was without its usual mega wattage. 'I'm joking.'

'Well, thank God for that. Seriously, where is he?'

'He's fine. He's gone to Highgate Woods with James and the boys and yes, I made him breakfast and coffee and I couldn't stop apologizing for the tense atmosphere yesterday,' Mum finished with a wry smile. If her gameplan was to keep me completely off guard, then it was working.

'And what did Toph say?'

'That he had three sisters and at any one time two of them weren't speaking and he was treating his stay as an anthropological study.' Mum sighed. 'He's nice, Bea. Really, really nice, though I wish he'd stop calling me ma'am because it makes me feel like the queen.'

'He *is* nice.'

'And are you . . . are you and he . . . are you taking precaut—'

'No!' I cut right through her very predictable question. 'You don't get to ask me that kind of stuff any more! It's none of your business.'

'It *is* my business; you're my daughter,' Mum said hotly. I was almost relieved that neither of us could keep up the pretence of being cool, calm and collected any more, because we royally sucked at it. 'How many times have we had the sex talk? And then you just fall into bed with the first boy you meet without any thought to the consequences.'

'Oh, I know all about the consequences. When I have sex it won't be because I've made an informed decision about whether I feel ready or because I'm in a committed relationship.' I was ranting; words ricocheting out of my mouth like bullets and every single one of them made Mum squirm and twitch. 'It will be some horrific date rape scenario that I've brought on myself by wearing a dress that's, like, two centimetres above the knee and – oh my God! – sleeveless. And then I'll get pregnant. Because that's what happens when you're me and you have sex, you hit the baby jackpot first time! Did I cover everything?'

'That's not fair, Bea. I just don't want you making the same mistakes that I did,' Mum said earnestly.

'Sorry, I missed that part out,' I said, my voice curling round the words with disdain. 'I get it. I got it the first five thousand times you said it, your life would have been just fantastic if you hadn't had me. *I'm* the mistake you wish you hadn't made.'

I waited for Mum to come in on the chorus, but she was silent, her mouth hanging open as she gripped the sides of the chair like she was scared she might topple to the floor.

'I know it, you know it, so why don't you just say it?' I demanded. 'You screwed up when you had me.'

'I didn't screw up when I had you,' Mum croaked, wrapping her arms tight around her body. 'You're the best thing that ever happened to me.'

'Yeah, I'm such a good thing that at least once every day you remind me what a disaster it was that you got pregnant,' I reminded her bitterly and I was starting to think that this new Bea wasn't that much of an improvement on Bea version one. Bea version two was so angry.

Mum got up from the chair with a bitten-off exclamation and began to pace. She could never keep still when she was agitated. 'I don't regret having you, even when you're being an absolutely hateful little cow,' she gritted. 'But I regret having you when I was seventeen because you missed out on so much.'

'What did I miss out on?' I asked incredulously because when I thought about my life up until the time I'd started sprouting breasts and pubes and Mum had freaked out, things had been really blissful.

'Bea, you spent the first three years of your life sleeping in my bedroom at Mum's with my Nirvana posters still on the wall! I had no money and I was trying to do a degree and work part-time and you missed out on holidays and the latest it-toy and I'd have to trawl the charity shops to buy you clothes. That's not how it should have been. You deserved better than that,' Mum finished, scrubbing her eyes with the back of one hand.

I felt close to tears too because she'd got it so wrong. 'I didn't miss out on anything. I had the grandmas and the grandpas and we had picnics on the Heath and you used to make me the most amazing Halloween costumes, like the time I dressed up as a red Lego brick, and I loved sleeping in your old bedroom before they had the extension built. I used to try on all your make-up but Grandma would wash my face before you got home so you never knew.'

My voice was throaty and raw now, because when I thought back to those days, it was one Hallmark card cliché after another; love, laughter, grandparents and great-grandparents who spoiled me rotten and a mum who was young and silly enough to strip down to her underwear and run through the sprinklers in the back garden with me.

Mum swiped at the tears that were rolling down her face with her sleeve. 'You're just saying that to make me feel better,' she insisted.

'I'm furious with you, why would I say anything just to make you feel better?' I tried to growl but the lump in my throat made it sound more like a yelp. 'The only thing I missed out on was having a dad.'

'Please, just don't . . .' Mum held up one hand the way she did when she was singing "The Winner Takes It All" on Singstar. 'I'm begging you . . .'

'I shouldn't have gone to Paris, I know that, but I was hurting so much when I got to the station in Malaga and I saw all these exotic places on the destination board and I just got it into my head that I was so close to Paris, to my dad, that I might just as well go. But I wouldn't have even comtemplated doing that if you hadn't told me he was from Paris.' I balled my hands into fists. 'I had to hear from Grandma that you'd lied to me for years. So you are not going to pretend to be mad at me about running off when we both know it's because you want to avoid the real issue.'

'Really, Bea, you're better off not knowing,' Mum said,

sitting down next to me. She tried to take my hand but I pulled away from her because she felt like a stranger right then.

'It's not your decision to make any more. I have a right to know.' I swivelled round so I could look her right in her red-rimmed eyes. 'I want to know who my father is and if you don't tell me, I'm going to move in with whichever grandma will have me. I mean it, Mum!'

'If I tell you, you'll wish I hadn't.' Mum had one eye on the door, like she was about to bolt. 'I'm not sure if we'll ever come back from it. You'll hate me.'

There was a warning there, but instead of scaring me off Mum had piqued my curiosity and my mind was racing through half a dozen possible scenarios, each of them more awful than the last. Surely the truth couldn't be as bad as imagining that Mum had had an affair with a teacher, or she'd been date raped, or just plain raped.

'Oh my God, will you please tell me,' I begged, grabbing Mum's hands now so I could give them a little shake. 'Just tell me who he is.'

Mum shut her eyes really tight. 'I don't know who he is,' she said in a voice so tiny it was nothing more than a whisper. 'I got really drunk and had sex with a guy whose name I didn't know. By the next morning I could hardly even remember what he looked like.'

'*What?*' I dropped Mum's hands. 'You're making it up. You know who he is and you're trying to protect him because he was married or he was older than you, and I get that, but—'

'I'm not making it up,' Mum said, swallowing hard. 'I wish to God I was.'

'But you wouldn't have done something like that when you were a teenager. You were going to go to university; you were studying for A levels.'

'I was doing all that and I was also going out every night, even climbing out the window if I was grounded. I made Ruby Davies look like a Girl Guide. I'd get absolutely paralytic every time I went out, then I'd get off with my friends' boyfriends just to prove I was prettier than they were.' She shook her head. 'Mum and Dad were at their wits' end. That Saturday night my friends confronted me about what an evil bitch I was and I ended up storming off to a club in Camden and there was this guy . . .'

'Did you go back to his house? Where did he live?' It was a dumb question because if Mum was telling the truth and she really couldn't remember what he looked like, then it wasn't like she'd whipped out her diary and made a handy note of his postcode.

'I didn't go back to his house; there was a party and it happened there and that's all I can tell you.' Mum closed her eyes again and when she opened them her expression was determined. 'There are some parts of that night you don't need to know about, trust me.'

I felt as if I'd been encased in ice and when I glanced down at my hands, they were mottled and blue like it was deep winter and the sun wasn't high in the sky and making everything in the room glow golden. Everything except me and Mum, who was hunched over, elbows on her knees.

'Why didn't you tell me?' I winced as soon as the words had left my mouth. It was obvious why she hadn't told me. 'Why did you say he was French? God, you must have laughed at me every time I was tearing my hair out over my French homework.'

'Of course I wasn't!' Mum said. She was starting to sound a little exasperated. 'Look, I always knew I'd have to tell you about your dad—'

'Except you can't remember a bloody thing about him!'

'I knew you'd want to know something and I hoped that by the time you were seven or eight, I'd have some way of telling you . . . not the truth . . .' She paused. 'I didn't know what I was going to tell you. But you were three when you first asked me and you wouldn't let it go. You'd go up to men in the street and ask if they were your daddy. And one night I was bathing you, and it sounds so silly now, but Mum had bought me a bottle of Chanel No. 5 for my birthday and it was there on the window sill in the bathroom and so I said he was French, and you wouldn't let that go either. I know it's no excuse, Bea, but I was seventeen when I had you and I was twenty when I had to decide what to tell you about your father. I was really young and I screwed up. I'm sorry.'

I was sure that I wasn't going to cry, that I was too numb to feel anything, but the tears started coursing down my cheeks because my very reason for existing, why I was flesh and blood and skin and bones and had a brain and an imagination and an unhealthy passion for pickled onions was because of some drunken shag at a party. There had to be more to it than that. *I* had to be more than that.

'Are you all right, babes?' Mum asked carefully, not making a move to touch me, which was just as well because I'd have punched her.

'No, I'm not all right,' I choked. 'I'm all wrong and nothing is ever going to make it better. I wasn't planned, I wasn't wanted; I'm here because you drank too much cider.'

'You were . . . you *are* wanted. When I found out I was pregnant, I thought about having an abortion,' Mum said, her voice thick with tears again. 'I even had a couple of meetings with an adoption agency, but I'd lie in bed at night and I used to imagine I could feel you inside me, this tiny little person, and I wondered what you'd look like and what your favourite food would be and what you'd want to be when you grew up. And in the end I just couldn't wait to meet you.' She leaned over to take the box of tissues from my nightstand and passed them to me, careful to observe my not-touching rule. 'When you were born and they put you in my arms, you stopped crying and you grabbed hold of my finger and I've never felt anything like it. I was, like, overwhelmed with love. And you know what, Bea? I'm glad I had sex at a party with a random bloke because if I hadn't, I wouldn't have you.'

Mum was crying again. Weeping. The only time I'd ever seen her cry like that was when the grandpas died, and I was crying the exact same way, even my sobs sounded the

305

same. But we couldn't comfort each other because we were the cause of each other's heartache. It felt like my head might explode because I was grieving for the father I'd never, ever get to meet. And I was crying because my whole reason for being put on this earth was a flimsy series of events that had happened one Saturday night eighteen years ago. And, truthfully, I was also crying for my mum, for being the age I am now and being pregnant and scared but being the kind of girl that I would never be friends with because she really did sound like an early prototype of Ruby. And, more than that, I was crying because Mum had been right; we were never going to be the same after this. I couldn't see how we'd find a way to get back to being friends again.

I don't know how long we cried. Mum stopped before I did and when all I had left was a snotty nose and sobs that sounded more like ragged exhalations of breath, I was lying in a ball with Mum's hand warm around my ankle, like she was afraid to come any closer to stroke my hair or make me blow my nose into the sodden tissue that I was clutching.

'I don't regret having you, not for one second, but I don't want you to miss out on anything because of the choices you make now,' she said at last. 'I want you to be everything you can be.'

'But you don't,' I spluttered. 'You want me to have the life that you imagined having at seventeen. There's no room for what I want. I don't want to be a lawyer. I don't want to go to Oxford or Cambridge. I don't even know if I want to go to university at all.'

'Bea!' Mum gasped before she could stop herself. 'Of course you want to go to university.'

'Well, see, there you go again.' I sat up and swallowed. I had an ache in my throat from crying so much. 'I'm seventeen and I'm meant to make mistakes. I'm allowed to make mistakes. And I realize now I've been unhappy and pissed off with you for ages. You act like I'm running round London trying to shag anything in trousers, when I would never, ever want do something like that. As daughters go, I'm pretty stellar.'

'Apart from the whole running away to Paris thing,' Mum said dryly. 'OK, OK, I get it. The circumstances were extenuating.'

'For a teen mum, you kinda did an all right job in bringing me up, when you're not treating me like a little kid,' I admitted grudgingly. 'Like, when I was in Europe, things went wrong sometimes but I coped just fine. One of my friends had his passport stolen and I had to deal with the police and the US Embassy. And I found us hotel rooms and sorted out train tickets and spoke French all the time.' I hugged my knees. 'I'm not saying that university is out but maybe I'll do International A levels or the Baccalaureate and do my degree at a French university, or I might go to catering college.'

'You still have the whole French thing going on?'

'Yeah, just as well you haven't ruined that for me too or else we'd really be in trouble,' I sniffed. It was the tiniest olive branch. Maybe a broken-off twig from an olive branch, and when Mum gestured at the space next to me on the bed, I nodded and she came closer and put her arm round me. 'I loved Paris. I didn't want to, not after what Grandma told me, but the city just got under my skin.'

'The whole time you were in Paris, I wanted to call you. I kept telling myself that I was too angry but really I was scared because I knew we were going to have this conversation,' Mum said, winding a strand of my hair around her finger. 'And you're a hard person to argue with; usually you don't get mad or argue back. It can be really intimidating. I always shout first, think second.'

'I have a feeling that I might be arguing a bit more in the future,' I warned her. 'Ever since everything blew up in Malaga with Ruby, I've been like this different person. I argue and I stand up for myself. And I get really, really snippy.'

'It sounds like you're finally becoming a teenager. I was hoping you'd skipped that stage.' Mum sighed. 'It's my own fault. Sometimes I act like we're the same age and then sometimes I play the Mum card. I've been inconsistent in my parenting.'

It was a now or never moment. 'You can play the Mum card all you like but I'm not going to listen when you're telling me what I can and can't wear and who I can see and who I can date . . . Jesus, you wanted me to go on the pill! You decided to have a baby when you were seventeen and, quite frankly, it sounds like you were way more immature than me.'

It should have been Mum's cue for a hissy fit, except she

308

wasn't shouting, but cowering back slightly, which made me feel worse than if she was threatening to lock me up in a nunnery.

'You hate me, don't you?' she asked, flinching away from me with a haunted look in her eyes.

The whole time I'd been in Paris, I was sure that I did hate her. But now as she sat on my bed, backlit by the sun streaming in through the windows, it was different. I wasn't in Paris but sitting right next to her and she was my mum and my best friend and confidante and lender of clothes and provider of make-up tips and lifts to the tube and my favourite person to watch really cheesy movies with and, yeah, sometimes she was an absolute ginormous pain in the arse.

'I don't hate you,' I was able to say truthfully. 'Not one little bit. But I'm not OK with the true story of my conception. It makes me feel . . .' I shook my head. 'I don't know how I feel.'

'He held my hair back when I was being sick and rubbed my back,' Mum offered and she frowned as she looked up at the ceiling. 'And he was wearing a leather jacket and I'm pretty sure he let me borrow it when we were walking to the party. It's not much, but it's something, isn't it?'

'He sounds like he was nice. Like, he looked after you. He wouldn't have done that if all he wanted was to get into your pants.'

'And he had to have been good-looking,' Mum added firmly.

'You said you couldn't remember what he looked like!'

'Yeah, but I've always had very high standards. He definitely had to be a fox; and really, Bea, you lucked out. Because I'm pretty hot too, so you got a double dose of hot genes.'

It was in very poor taste to try and make a joke about my Bio Dad in light of the latest revelations but I had to press my lips together very tightly to stop myself from smiling. Because this was not a laughing matter, it was deadly serious.

I decided to sniff contemptuously, but it was more of a snort that turned into a definite laugh. 'I think it's a recessive gene,' I giggled, because I just couldn't help myself.

'Nah, you come from a long line of foxy ladies,' Mum said, nudging me with her elbow. And that was the thing. The line between mum and friend was always going to be blurred between us. Seventeen years seemed like an awfully long time when I tried to imagine what life would be like when I was thirty-four and I thought about electric cars that floated above the ground and Southend completely submerged under water because of global warming. But really, seventeen years wasn't so much. Kylie Minogue and Jennifer Aniston were both older than Mum and Madonna was much, much older. Old enough to be Mum's mum, in fact, if she'd got drunk at a party when she was seventeen.

So the age difference between Mum and me was always going to be a problem and also kinda wonderful, I thought, as Mum started giggling too, then we were both bumping each other with our elbows until my giggles suddenly morphed into sobs.

Mum transformed back into a mum again and wiped my tears away with her thumbs before taking another tissue from the box, holding it to my nose and telling me to blow.

'Oh, Bea,' she sighed, pressing her forehead against mine. 'I wish there was something I could say that would make all the hurt go away.'

We heard the front door open, and two pairs of tiny footsteps thundering across the parquet flooring in the hall, the murmur of male voices, then the door shutting again.

There were still a million questions that I wanted to ask her, more stuff we needed to get straight, but when I opened my mouth I couldn't think of a single thing to say. The spell had been broken.

'Why don't you take Toph out for a walk?' Mum suggested. 'It might help to clear your head.'

I could walk the entire length of the Great Wall Of China and my head would still be full of rocks. Besides, Toph would want to know how the chat with Mum had gone and I didn't want to talk about it. *Couldn't* talk about it because the moment I tried, I knew I'd start crying. As it was, I had to concentrate really hard on not crying, just sitting still on the bed.

'Mum, I can't be on my own with Toph right now,' I insisted. 'I can't tell him any of this because just saying it out loud makes it sound so trailer trashy and I don't want him to judge me, or you.'

'Why on earth would he judge you?'

'I'm judging me and I'm definitely judging you,' I confessed, ducking my head as I felt the familiar burn heating up my cheeks. 'I can't help it.'

'Well, Bea, the poor boy's here for a week,' Mum pointed out, standing up and smoothing down her top. 'You've got to be on your own with him sometimes.'

'You've changed your tune,' I pouted. 'If we hadn't had this talk, you'd be insisting we were chaperoned all the time . . . can't we pretend that we haven't had a talk? Yes! And you don't trust us to be alone together in case our rampant, youthful hormones get the better of us and—'

'James and I are going back to work tomorrow so you're going to have to deal with him sooner or later. Probably sooner.' Mum put her hands on her hips. 'C'mon, Bea, haven't you just learnt that it's best to have things out in the open?'

'I can't,' I wailed. Right on cue, my eyes started watering. *Again.*

'But you said you were all grown up now and, sorry to break it to you, kid, but when you're grown up you have to deal with all sorts of shit that you'd rather not.'

'Mum, please. I need time to get my head straight.' I clasped my hands together and I didn't even have to attempt to do anything puppy-dogish with my eyes, because they were brimming over with tears. 'At least, can't we all go out this afternoon? Please.'

'Well, OK,' Mum said without much enthusiasm. I reckoned I had a month to milk the maternal guilt for all it was worth. It was probably the perfect time to raise the subject of driving lessons. 'You'd better jump in the shower and I'll have a word with the boys. Maybe we can go to Whitstable for the afternoon, but tomorrow you're on your own.'

Chapter Twenty-Five

I cried a lot over the next few days. I'd get through an hour, maybe even two, as if everything was normal apart from this nagging, tugging feeling that I'd try to ignore. Then I'd forget that I was meant to ignore it and examine the feeling closely, then remember all over again. Each time I thought about never knowing who my dad was, it would lead to all these other thoughts. What if he was the carrier of some awful genetic disease and I had a timebomb tucked away inside my body? Or what if he'd died in some freak accident and I'd never, ever have even the faintest smidgeon of a chance of ever meeting him? Or what if it had been another lie and Mum didn't want to tell me the other truth that my dad was in prison because he was a serial killer or a paedophile. So each time I relaxed my guard and analysed why I felt so *wrong*, I'd have to excuse myself, find the nearest loo and have a quick weep.

'What is up with you?' Toph would say each time I reappeared. 'Since we got to London, your bladder has shrunk.'

I'd make some crack about how my bladder wasn't a suitable topic for conversation and insist that we go back to the people we were with, because Toph and I hadn't been on our own for longer than ten minutes over the last five days, even though I'd had to draft in a whole supporting cast to make it happen.

I volunteered to take the twins to London Zoo. The next day Grandma Minor accompanied us to the Tate, then along the South Bank to the Tate Modern, finishing up with a quick walk over the wobbly Millennium Bridge to St Paul's Cathedral. The day after that we met up with Harry to do the Highgate Cemetery tour. There were trips to the Gospel Oak Lido with Polly, who didn't stop talking about ponies. The cinema with Lydia. A stealth shopping spree to Oxford Street with Ruth, whose parents thought she was at a Bible study seminar. And the evenings all merged into one long, blur of barbecues, beer gardens and house parties. It was exhausting but at least it didn't leave me much time to let that awful tugging feeling pull me under.

I did feel guilty about shutting Toph out. But it wasn't like he knew he was being shut out. I was showing him a good time and as much of London as I could fit in to our packed schedule. Besides, he liked meeting new people – it was all part of the anthropology deal. I could sit him down at a table full of people he didn't know while I went to get drinks and by the time I got back Toph was discussing everything from the difference between American and English chocolate to the hidden meanings in Disney films. He even discovered things about my friends that I never knew; like Ruth had a secret Internet boyfriend she'd met on a *Doctor Who* discussion board, Lydia was saving up for a nose job and Harry was starting to think he wasn't gay but completely uninterested in sex with anyone whether they had boobs or a penis.

So I was sure that Toph was having a good time, but at least once every two hours he'd ask, 'Are you sure you're OK? You don't seem yourself.'

'But I am myself. This is my London self.'

Toph would nod and I'd convince myself that he'd bought it, but things weren't the same between us. That connection, the way we knew what the other one was thinking before they'd even thought it, felt like it was fizzling out. But that was only because there were always other people around – if I could trust myself to be alone with Toph without bursting into tears, we'd be back in the good place within seconds.

The relaxing of Mum's strict regime was about the only bright spot on my bleak horizon. The occasional 'Isn't that dress a bit too short?' or 'Will there be alcohol at this party you're going to?' popped out, but generally she was trying to be cool and go with the flow. Though sometimes it looked like the effort was slowly killing her, she really was trying to ease off on the teen pregnancy patrol. Or else she was in serious suck-up mode.

'Toph is going home on Sunday; do you want to have some people over tomorrow night?' she said when Toph and I got in on the Friday evening.

'You mean a party?' I clarified.

'Not a party. A gathering. A little soirée with a very select guest list. In the back garden. You can use the barbecue as long as you clean it properly afterwards and we'll provide the alcohol.' She paused to preen a little. 'See? I can do the cool mum thing.'

'And will Bea's cool mum be on the premises to ensure that her male and female guests observe a strict no-touching rule?' James asked as he finished making a cup of tea.

Mum swiped at him with a tea towel. 'I thought we'd drop the twins off at Mum's for the night then go out for dinner,' she said. Her evil plan was obvious. Get in my good books, have a date night with James *and* a lie-in on Sunday morning. Though I was still pretty pissed off with her, I could only be in awe of her awesomeness.

'You up for it?' I asked Toph. Throwing a party instead of attending one was full of all sorts of potential stress bombs from making sure no one puked on Mum's roses to knowing what to do when the barbecue started smoking. But all the preparing and policing and party-giving would be a distraction and, as an added bonus, it was something special to do on Toph's solitary Saturday night in London town that didn't involve candlelit dinners and being alone.

'Yeah, sure,' Toph muttered, as he took a sip of tea. I could tell he was trying not to pull a face, because he'd already confessed that he didn't get what the big deal was with tea. 'Sounds like fun.'

'Not more than twenty people, Bea. And I want everyone off the premises by midnight,' Mum insisted.

I invited Harry, Harry's emo little brother, Barney, and his weird little girlfriend, Jeane. Lydia, Polly and Ruth, if she could persuade her parents that there'd be no unChristian behaviour. Lydia asked me to invite this boy she'd been crushing on (which was news to me) who worked in the pet shop opposite Wilson's. I also invited two girls from my French class who I kept bumping into at various parties, along with their respective boyfriends. That took the guest list up to thirteen, including Toph and me. I was marvelling at my extreme lameness because I couldn't rustle up seven more people when Grandma Minor phoned to say she'd invited Toby, who lived next door to her. She'd been trying to set us up for years even though he was more interested in playing World Of Warcraft than breathing. And Toby would only come if he could bring another WOW freak, Bones.

I decided that fifteen people would do, even if it was an odd number, and was just adding more Tabasco sauce to one of my marinades when my mobile rang.

I glanced down to see Ayesha's name on the caller display and it was only curiousity that made me answer it.

'So I guess you pretty much hate my guts right now,' she said after my wary 'Hello'.

'Actually I hadn't really thought about it,' I said honestly. 'But now you come to mention it . . .'

'Well, I pretty much hate my guts too, if that makes you feel any better. Anyway, where have you been?'

I couldn't resist. 'Oh, well, after I left Malaga, I went to Bilbao, then Marseilles and ended up spending a week in Paris.'

'Shut up! Really, where have you been?' Ayesha gave a

bitten-off groan. 'No, that's not why I called you. I've been grounded for two weeks and I've had nothing to do but think, and after I got over wanting to kill you for what you wrote on that whiteboard, I thought a lot about you, all the stuff we used to do and I trashed all over that, didn't I?'

'Yeah, you did,' I said coolly. 'But that doesn't come close to the way you spent three months pretending to be my friend all over again so I could be an Access All Areas pass to Malaga.'

Ayesha gave a swift, nervous intake of breath. I guess she thought that she'd ring up and apologize and good old reliable Bea would forgive her. 'Look, Bea, I treated you like crap and I'm sorry.'

'Yeah? And I suppose Ruby's listening in on this call all ready to add it to the shit list she's got going in my name.'

'I haven't spoken to Ruby since I last saw her at Stansted airport over three weeks ago. Same goes for Chloe and Emma. I'm done with them; you'll see when we go back to school. So, like I said, where have you been?'

'Like I said, I've been in Paris.' It used to be that I could tell Ayesha anything – not that I ever had much to tell – and it was really hard to shut off the part of my brain that heard her voice and recognized her as friend rather than foe. 'So, was there anything else you wanted?'

'I get that you're mad at me but I've never heard you sound so *cold* before. Not even that summer when that freak Toby asked us if he could see down our pants every day.'

'I can't believe that my gran made me put him on the guest list for tonight,' It was out before I could haul it back in.

Ayesha didn't say anything but she made an encouraging 'Hmmm?' then lapsed into an expectant silence.

I looked up at the ceiling but failed to find any inspiration from the light fitting or the splodge where I'd made goulash and the baking dish had exploded. 'I'm having this thing tonight for Toph . . . he's a friend of mine I was travelling with. Anyway, he's going back to the States tomorrow and so I'm having a little Bon Voyage party. It's really not a big deal.'

I heard Ayesha gulp wildly. 'American boy? You've been travelling around Europe with an American boy? I need deets.'

I wished I'd never started this. 'Why are you acting like we're friends who tell each other stuff? We're not—'

'So you're never going to forgive me, is that it?' Ayesha asked and I didn't know why she sounded so gloomy about the prospect. 'Look, Bea, I know I screwed up but you've got to admit that when Ruby turns the charm all the way up to eleven, it's almost impossible to say no to her.'

Ayesha did have a point. There had been three months when Ruby's approval had meant the world to me, but I'd still managed to stand up to her. And in a really horrible way that I wasn't at all proud of, I still wanted Ruby and Ayesha to admit that there was some cool in me. 'I guess you could come tonight, if you're not doing anything,' I blurted out. As soon as the words left my mouth, I longed to pick up my paring knife and commit hara-kiri with it.

'You're inviting me to your party?' Ayesha yelped. 'So, we're cool, yeah? We're friends again?'

'Hardly, it means you're on probation,' I said firmly. 'And if you're going to turn up with Ruby and those two other dimwits plus a gang of rude boys, then what I did with that whiteboard is going to seem like jelly and ice cream. Got it?'

'Got it,' Ayesha yelped again. 'Again, I have to ask, what the hell has happened to you?'

I was beginning to yearn for those days, not so long ago, when nothing exciting happened unless it was going on in my own head.

Chapter Twenty-Six

I used to imagine throwing my own parties; I'd be wearing a little black dress and sailing through a glittering throng of witty people, with a martini glass in my hand, saying stuff like, 'Darling, meet darling.' This was when I was going through my *Breakfast at Tiffany's* phase.

But that evening there were no martinis, which I was grateful for, just bottles of lager in a bucket full of ice and a little group of people who all vaguely knew each other so I didn't have to do much work with the introductions. The only person who needed an introduction was Toph. I was starting to feel sorry for him when his eyes widened as Ruth and Polly turned up together. 'I can't remember which one is which,' he hissed out of the side of his mouth. And when Toby (who'd lost the postulating acne and had grown about six inches since I last saw him) arrived with a really tall, really skinny boy (who must have been Bones) Toph gave a deep sigh, which sounded like it started at the soles of his feet. 'Do I know them? Have I met them before?'

At least he remembered Harry and by the time Ayesha appeared half an hour after everyone else (obviously her deep remorse was no match for her inability to be anywhere on time) he was happily and expertly grilling steaks, sausages and king prawns on the barbecue. As Ayesha followed me through the French doors, every pair of eyes (except Toph's) swivelled in her direction. And stayed there. Not that Ayesha seemed that bothered. Her eyes were fixed on Toph, who'd looked up briefly in her direction but was now adroitly flipping steaks. 'Oh my God,' she breathed. 'He's delicious.'

Toph did look rather delicious. He was wearing a short-sleeved bowling shirt with his name embroidered on the breast pocket (he went bowling every Thursday night when he was at college – 'Cheap beer, chilli dogs and rented shoes, what's not to like?') jeans and an easy grin as he talked to Barney and Jeane. He didn't look like he belonged in a north London back garden with a bunch of teenagers but he fitted in just the same. 'He's taken,' I snapped, because Ayesha sounded like she'd forgotten I was the injured party and was planning to injure me all over again by making a play for Toph.

'Of course he is,' Ayesha assured me quickly. 'Can't blame a girl for admiring the view. By the way, like the hair. It really suits you.'

'Thanks,' I said, running a hand through it. Mum had managed to wangle me a quick appointment with her hairdresser that afternoon so my bob was practically shorn at the back and the ends were on a level with my chin. I was wearing Erin's borrowed LBD with flip-flops and generally feeling fifty per cent prettier and a hundred per cent more confident than last time I saw Ayesha. 'So you know everyone, right?'

'Yeah, but is that really Toby? He looks well fit, though

it might be the mood lighting,' Ayesha grinned conspiratorially and it took everything I had not to grin back.

'Oh my God, what is *she* doing here?' Ruth had been talking to Toby and Bones about *Doctor Who*, which seemed to be her MO for talking to boys. Lydia had been sitting with them, not saying a word as usual, but gazing adoringly at the boy from the pet shop; now she was racing towards us, her finger stabbing in Ayesha's direction. 'Don't tell me you invited her? Are you mad?'

'She's here on a trial basis,' I said, putting my arm around Lydia, so I could stop her if she tried to make any sudden movements. 'On her best behaviour, aren't you, Ash?'

Ayesha nodded. 'I would have worn a hair shirt, Lids, but it's really hot and TopShop didn't have any left in my size.'

Lydia exploded all over again. 'I can't believe you're cracking jokes! Not after what you did!'

'You don't even know what I did because you weren't in Malaga with us,' Ayesha said fiercely. 'Bea was, and if she can give me a second chance then why are you getting all up in my face? For Christ's sake, chill!'

'I'm getting up in your face because you're the biggest bitch I've ever met.' It was more than Lydia had ever said in mixed company.

'No, I think you'll find that Ruby is a bigger bitch than me,' Ayesha pointed out.

'OK, second-biggest bitch then.'

'Bea, the steaks are done,' said Toph behind me and then his hand was on my shoulder, centering me, calming me. I

324

leaned back against his chest for a second, because I really needed to, then straightened so I could sort out Ayesha and Lydia before they came to blows.

'Lids, can you help me to start getting stuff out of the fridge and, Ayesha, there's more drinks in the garage; will you bring some out?'

They went off, muttering, in separate directions and I turned to thank Toph but he was already back behind the barbecue.

I'd had this vague worrying idea that people would separate themselves off into the little pairs they'd arrived in and no one would mingle. But when I started to place platters of salad and French bread on the big table that was a permanent fixture on our patio, people simply dragged their chairs around it. Everyone praised my marinades and the sun-flamed tomatoes in the pasta salad and told me I should go on *Masterchef*, which led to a conversation about disasters in home baking, to talking about parents, to a quick round-up about what we were doing on our summer holidays. Every now and again I tried to catch Toph's eye but he never seemed to be looking at me at the same time that I was looking at him.

I thought he might get up to help me when I went to get pudding so we could have a quick debrief in the kitchen, but he didn't budge. He just kept on talking to Lucy and Sachiko from my French A-level class and their boyfriends, who were as cool as I'd expected of two girls who wore American Apparel and were into bands that I'd never ever heard of.

When I came back to the patio, no one was interested in my cupcakes. Instead they were hanging on to Ayesha's every word.

'And then Ruby called me a whore and I was all like, "Girl, why are you talking about yourself?" and then Emma said that Chloe was the biggest whore because she'd shagged every single guy that any of us had even looked at, and Chloe was like, "It's not my fault that boys want me," and Ruby said, "Yeah but it is your fault that you're a skeevy slag," and Chloe started to cry and . . .'

I set my cakes down on the table and coughed. I might just as well have climbed up on the rainwater barrel and done a striptease for all the notice anyone took. 'What are you talking about?' I asked, walking over to Ayesha so I could nudge her.

'Oh, just what went down with Ruby and the others,' Ayesha said casually. She gestured at the table. 'Now where was I? Oh yeah . . .'

'Actually what I want to know is what Bea did to make you all spin out,' Harry drawled.

'Nobody wants to know about that,' I said crisply, sitting down and shoving the cupcakes at Polly and Ruth so they'd take the hint and start passing them around.

There was a chorus of voices all clamouring to know what had happened. I opened my mouth to shut the conversation down before it went to the bad place, but Ayesha got there first. 'You mean Bea didn't tell you about the whiteboard?'

I sat there with my head in my hands as Ayesha

recounted the whole sorry tale. When Ayesha got to the part about me throwing their clothes out of the window, Ruth and Polly clapped their hands in delight and after she'd recounted the entire sorry saga of the whiteboard, Harry walked over to me and kissed the top of my head.

'I love you,' he said simply, then walked back to his seat.

I could have done without the audience but what I was dying to know was what had happened post-whiteboard, when I was snoring my head off on the train.

Ayesha was more than happy to fill in the blanks. They'd got back to the apartment after a heavy day's sunbathing and had been laughing at Emma because she'd fallen asleep without any sunblock on. Then they'd seen what remained of their possessions in a dusty heap on the side of the road, raced upstairs and found the empty duty-free bottles.

Ruby had wanted to hunt me down there and then. Seriously. She'd got as far as the front door when Chloe alerted her to my handiwork.

After that it was non-stop screaming. They screamed at each other. Then they took turns to scream at each other in turn, until Chloe, Emma and Ayesha had ganged up on Ruby and forcibly ejected her from the apartment. She came back with the caretaker, who let her in so they could carry on screaming. Ruby and Ayesha had even come to blows. 'She actually ripped out some of my hair extensions but I did split her lip,' Ayesha recalled. Then they'd decided to go back to London as they couldn't stand the sight of each other. They'd even been given a warning by the chief steward on the plane that if they didn't stop fighting, he'd have the police waiting for them at Stansted.

Once they got home and the parentals became involved, the shit really hit the fan. Ayesha had been grounded for three weeks, all allowances stopped, all electronic equipment confiscated. Chloe was sent to stay with her aunt in Basingstoke instead of going on holiday with her folks. Emma had also spectacularly failed all the GCSEs she'd retaken because she'd failed them spectacularly first time round, so her parents were talking about sending her to some really intensive crammer school out in the country. Only Ruby got off scot-free as Michelle refused to believe her darling girl had done anything wrong.

Ayesha folded her arms. 'So that just about covers it.'

'And now you thought you'd come crawling back to us?' Ruth said flatly.

Ayesha shrugged. 'Sort of. But also seeing that whiteboard . . . it was all there in black and white, y'know? A whole year of my life wasted. I should never have become Ruby's bitch – I'm way better than her.'

'Can we stop talking about this?' I begged, because it was just picking at scabs and making them hurt all over again. 'I made cupcakes!'

'Yeah, but why didn't you come home straight away, Bea?' Natasha asked. 'Didn't you go to France or something?'

'She struggled on in Spain for a while,' Toph said. It was the first time he'd spoken in an hour. He must have been bored rigid from all the teenage drama. 'Bea was going to Paris but she fell asleep on the train and got out at Bilbao instead.'

'Which is where I met Toph and his friends, who were backpacking around Europe.' I hoped Toph would take the hint and launch into some funny anecdotes about the trip. His story about the world's worst ravioli made with half-frozen tuna chunks he'd had in Sorrento was so funny that I'd snorted Diet Coke out of my nostrils when he told me.

'Wow!' Ayesha exclaimed. 'Did you meet your dad? What was he like? I've been rambling on for ages and you were sitting on that info. Spill!'

'There's nothing to spill.' It came out as croaky little whisper and the only thing I was going to be spilling were tears. 'Just . . . I found out . . . I didn't . . .'

'. . . didn't call ahead,' Toph said smoothly, picking up my ragged thread. 'And he was actually out of town for a couple of months.'

Toph still wasn't looking at me.

'But Paris was really cool. We had a great time, didn't we?'

'Yeah, great,' Toph echoed. 'So is anyone going to have a cupcake? Bea's been slaving in a hot kitchen all afternoon. Thought she was going to pass out from heatstroke at one point.'

That wasn't quite true – though I'd had to have a sit down at one stage – but it was enough to change the subject and get people eating my cupcakes. After we cleared away the dinner things, I put my iPod in its dock, so we could listen to Fleet Foxes as Harry and Bones started a game of charades.

After I'd finished loading the dishwasher I sat down next

to Toph, who was perched on the little wall that separated the patio from the rest of the garden, his long legs stretched out in front of him.

'Hey,' I said, tentatively prodding his arm, because he looked so distant sitting there; not touchable, not mine. 'You all right?'

'I'm fine,' he said evenly and with barely trace amounts of fine.

'Is it really boring with everyone talking about going back to school and filling in their UCAS forms?' I tightened my hold on Toph's arm. Not in a painful way, but a significant way.

Toph looked down at my hand in surprise, like he hadn't even realized it was there. 'No, 'course not. All your friends are really nice.'

'They kinda are, aren't they?' I looked around the patio where the game of charades was getting louder and Ruth and Lydia were chatting with Sachiko and Lucy, which would never have happened at school. 'I didn't even know I had this many friends. I think hanging out with you guys in Europe improved my socialization skills. They were really lame before.'

I waited for Toph to say something, because that's how you had a conversation. I'd say something. Toph would reply and say something else for me to respond to and away we went. Except he wasn't giving me anything to work with.

'Well, thanks for coming to my rescue on the whole thing with . . . when it got sticky and they wanted to know about my . . . when we were in Paris.' It was weird but no matter how hard I tried, I couldn't even think the D-word in my head, let alone say it out loud

I finally had Toph's undivided attention. 'You mean your dad?' he said, and he seemed to draw out the word, which meant he had plenty of time to see me wince.

'Yeah, I s'pose,' I muttered.

'So did you get to the bottom of all that with your mom?' Toph asked.

I removed my hand from his arm. 'I should see if everyone has a drink.'

'Y'know, I'm beginning to wonder why you start panicking if we have to spend longer than five minutes together without someone else present,' Toph remarked, putting his hand on my arm this time.

'I don't panic,' I insisted shrilly. 'Like, am I panicking now?'

'Well, now you come to mention it, yeah, you are totally freaking out.'

I was trying to settle my features into something calm and totally not freaked out when Lydia came trotting in from the kitchen. 'Someone's at the door,' she informed me. 'They're, like, leaning on the bell.'

I got to my feet so quickly I nearly fell over. 'I'd better see who it is,' I yelped.

As I stepped into the kitchen, I could hear the insistent peal and hoped that it wasn't Lilah from next door. She seemed to think that being head of the Neighbourhood Watch Scheme gave her the same powers as the fricking

Special Branch. It wasn't even that late, only ten-thirty, and I hadn't been playing Fleet Foxes at full volume. Besides, they were very melodic.

I opened the door and felt my heart skip a beat.

'Hey there, Bea,' Ruby said. 'Did you miss me?'

Chapter Twenty-Seven

In my head Ruby had assumed almost Medusa-like properties, so seeing a small, skinny girl with stringy hair on the doorstep was a bit of a let-down. I looked past her and saw a gaggle of girls from the year below us – it looked like Ruby had had to downgrade on the friend front.

'What do you want?' I asked, folding my arms. Inwardly I was quaking in my flip-flops as Ruby's posse gathered behind her like they were going to rush me and get into the house.

'Well, you don't write, you don't call, you don't invite me to your dumb party,' Ruby said coolly. 'So I thought I'd pop round, catch up on all your news and get the money you owe me.'

Ruby tapped her foot while I searched my brains for any outstanding debts I might have racked up while she was pretending to be my friend. There weren't any. In fact, quite the opposite. 'And what about the money *you* owe *me* for booze, taxi fares, groceries – and hello, what about the time we all went to Pizza Express and you all happened to forget your purses. Let's call it evens, shall we?'

'Let's not,' Ruby snapped, taking a step forward. I didn't budge from the doorstep. I was pretty sure I could take Ruby if I really had to. Her nails were bitten down so she couldn't really scratch; hair pulling was another matter but, as she'd always been so eager to point out, I had a good thirty pounds on her. 'My Dior sunglasses were shattered and my Marc Jacobs dress, my Rock & Republic jeans and all my Miss Sixty tops were stolen when you threw them over the balcony. And by the way, overreaction much!'

'You were wearing your bloody Dior sunglasses when you walked out the door, just like you're wearing your Rock & Republic jeans right now—'

'No, they're new ones—'

'Whatever! I'm not giving you any money. I'm glad I threw your stuff off the balcony. Think of it as payback for treating me like crap.' I was shouting now, because Ruby had given me the gift of anger and it was the gift that kept on giving. Her eyebrows had shot up when I'd first raised my voice, but she stood her ground with a self-satisfied little smirk that I wanted to rip off her face with my bare hands.

'Get you! You think that just because you're having a lame party for some lame social rejects and you get your hair cut, it makes you cool. But you'll always be a pathetic loser.'

I heard the inner porch door open behind me but I didn't dare look round because I was intent on staring Ruby down. It was surprisingly easy not to blink, bite my lip or look away.

'Ruby's here!' someone whispered and then Ayesha's anguished, 'Don't look at me! I haven't spoken to her in three weeks.'

I felt a hand squeeze my waist and hoped it was Toph but

it was Lucy. 'I Tweeted before I came out. I think Ruby follows my Tweets,' she murmured apologetically.

Sometimes I wished the internet had never been invented.

At least Lucy, Sachiko and Harry were flanking me and the others were peering through the open door, so I wasn't on my own. I had a vision of everyone spilling onto the driveway and throwing down in a *West Side Story* battle of the gangs, but without the song and dance numbers.

'Just go away,' I snapped at Ruby. 'No one wants you here.'

'Give me my money!' Ruby stepped right up to me and jabbed her hand in my face. It didn't make contact but it was a declaration that she was spoiling for a fight. I would have loved nothing more than to slap her really hard, but I wasn't going there because I wasn't, like, five.

'Jesus, Ruby, just grow up,' I said in a voice that throbbed with scathe. 'Go and have your little temper tantrum somewhere else.'

Now that I had back-up, Ruby's posse of mean-looking sixteen-year-olds had moved in closer. Their faces up close weren't quite so mean, more curious as to where this was going.

It was going really badly, was where it was going. Ruby snapped her fingers right in my face, just missing my left eye. She was trying her best to make me lose me temper and, my God, it was working.

'What a sad-sack dork you are,' she taunted me, stepping back so she could survey her handiwork, while everything in me roared with the urge to seize her round her scrawny throat.

'Easy, tiger,' said a voice in my ear and Lucy was stepping back so Toph could take her place. My body sagged in relief. Toph was here and he'd make everything all right. It was what he did . . . when I let him.

'This your new boyfriend?' Ruby asked, her eyes running over Toph as he stood there. 'What's wrong with him? I mean, there has to be something wrong with him if he's hanging with you. Or is he another gay you're bearding for, like Harry? You given it up yet, Bea?'

'Come back inside,' Toph said softly.

Ruby didn't like being ignored. Especially by good-looking boys. And Toph was just as good-looking as those floppy-haired boys who used to fawn over her on those endless Saturday nights. Better-looking, in my opinion.

'Nah, you're still a virgin,' Ruby decided. 'Too scared of getting knocked up like your mum. God, I bet she wishes she'd had an abortion.'

There was an excited little murmur stirring both sets of supporters, now Ruby had gone and played the Your Momma card.

'You really have a problem . . .' Toph began angrily, but I moved forward so I could jump off the doorstep and advance towards Ruby. I guess Ayesha would have said that I got up in her grill and, once I was in her grill, I stayed there.

'What is wrong with you, Ruby? Are you totally

incapable of engaging your brain cells before you open your mouth?'

'Oh, you finally got some backbone, did you, Bea?' Ruby asked tauntingly, but it lacked bite and when I took another step forward, she took a step back, like we were dancing. Because I didn't just have thirty pounds on her – right there and then, I was a hell of a lot meaner.

'I'm pathetic? A loser? And I'm having a lame party with my lame friends, am I?' I growled each question at Ruby, whose eyes were darting from side to side. 'Well, what does that make you, huh? You've got nothing else to do on a Saturday night but come round here with your little underaged gang because nobody else likes you or wants to hang with you. I'd say that was the dictionary definition of pathetic.'

'Oh, you would, would you?' Ruby bristled and I should have been about to pee my pants because now I was surrounded by her friends, but all I could think about was how small and scared Ruby looked. When you took away the designer labels and the attitude, there wasn't much left.

'Yeah, I would. Unlike you, I've got better things to do with my Saturday night than come down to your level because you're incapable of coming up to mine.' I pointed at the garden gate, in the same imperious way that Audrey Hepburn directed George Peppard to the door of her tiny apartment in *Breakfast at Tiffany's*. 'Go!'

'We're not done,' Ruby hissed, but she was going. 'You're haven't heard the last of this.'

'What*ever*.' I turned on my heel and glared at her

hangers-on, who had lost the girl-gang vibe and were standing in my front garden looking rather aimless. 'Come on, show's over. Time to leave.'

They started trooping down the path, apart from the smallest one, who was a Ruby Next Generation if ever I saw one. She was standing right in the middle of the path, looking at the living-room windows and then down at the empty Barcardi Breezer bottle in her hand.

'Don't even think about it,' I gritted, marching over to her so I could grab the collar of her jacket. 'Seriously. I do Pilates with your grandmother!'

I watched them trail down the road. When they got to the corner, Ruby turned and shouted something, but her words were carried away by the breeze.

'That was impressive,' Harry said as I strolled up the drive to where the others were congregated. 'You didn't even resort to swears.'

'I am so over that girl,' I growled and it was true. I was done letting anyone make me feel that I wasn't worthy because they thought I wasn't pretty enough, or cool, or clever. I was better than that.

Ayesha fought her way through the throng. 'I'm so proud of you,' she said, flinging her arms around me, although hugging was a violation of our fragile truce. 'Lucy and Sachiko have been live Twittering the whole thing. You're like a micro celebrity.'

'Don't be ridiculous,' I said and I could feel all the fight draining out of me. It would have been nice if they'd all gone, and it was just me and Toph so we could curl up on the canopied swing seat in the back garden. Not talking, just rocking. But everyone was trooping back into the house and talking about me and Ruby and what this would mean when we got back to school and how the little red-headed girl had totally been rolling her eyes every time Ruby opened her mouth.

'You OK, Bea? That was some scene.'

I shut the front door and leant against it so I was facing Toph. 'I was all right when the adrenalin was pumping but now I feel like someone's knocked all the stuffing out of me.'

'You rocked it,' he scoffed and I realized it had been a while, a week in fact, since I'd seen that lazy smile on his face. 'And "I do Pilates with your grandmother" – best last line ever.'

I peeled myself away from the door, which wasn't such a great idea because my feet didn't really want to hold me up. 'I wish you weren't going home tomorrow,' I said, wrapping my arms round him. Despite the copious quantities of chocolate he'd been eating all week, Toph was still as reassuringly lanky as ever.

'Yeah?' I looked up to see Toph giving me the old eyebrow arch.

'Of course, yeah!' I said, squeezing him tighter, until I realized I was the only one doing the squeezing and that Toph wasn't doing much of anything but letting me squeeze him. Then I remembered that we'd been about to get into something when Ruby had rung the bell. I let go of Toph because one-sided hugging wasn't much fun. 'I never meant to act so weird with you this week.'

'It's not your fault,' Toph said, cupping my cheek, and the spark between us felt stronger than it had done for days. 'It's my fault. I should never have come to London with you. It was, like, the daddy of bad ideas.'

'No, it wasn't,' I protested, reaching up to remove Toph's hand from my face so I could twine my fingers round his, the way I had when we were in Paris. 'Nothing's changed.'

'Yeah, everything's changed,' Toph said, pulling me down so we could both sit on the foot of the stairs. 'You come home, real life happens. I get that. When we were in Paris we were both taking a raincheck from reality. But now, I feel like we've forgotten how to talk to each other, really talk. Something's missing.'

'OK, things were different when we were in Paris but the way I feel about you is the same.' I tried to put all my passion into what I was saying, and even push it out through my fingertips as I clutched Toph's knee in a convulsive grip, but he was shaking his head.

'No, it isn't,' he said sadly. 'You organized this mad week of doing stuff because you wanted to show me London, but by Tuesday it was beginning to feel like some elaborate plan you cooked up so we'd never be alone together, never get to talk about anything important.'

I should have known that Toph would have been able to see right through me as if my clothes and skin were completely transparent so he had a clear view of my battered, aching heart. But his X-ray vision only went so far – he could see the cover up but not the reason why.

'That's not true,' I insisted doggedly. 'I just wanted you to see my favourite bits of London and meet all my friends.'

'Don't lie to me, Bea. Just don't,' Toph said, resting his hand on top of mine to take the sting out of his words. 'Look, we had a holiday romance, that's all. An intense, wonderful holiday romance and we should have left it in Paris.'

'Was that all it was to you, then?' I asked in a broken voice, slipping my hand out from under his so I could wrap my arms around myself. All of a sudden I felt cold. The kind of cold that made your bones hurt.

'Not at the time, no,' Toph admitted. 'But it's all it can be. You're here in London and I'm going back to Texas. And I've got my finals this year and you've got those exams that are like SATs but aren't . . .'

'A levels,' I supplied.

'Yeah those.' Toph cupped my chin and turned my head so I had no choice but to look at him, and it was so very wrong that he could stare at me like that, as if I was his reason for waking up every morning, and tell me that it was over. 'Look, I was with someone for five years and she meant everything to me, but it was nothing compared to the way I felt about you in Paris. We packed *lifetimes* into those days, Bea.'

'You can't say something like that as part of your break-up speech!' I wrenched myself from Toph's hand. 'If you knew what I've been going through this week, you'd understand why I've been acting like this. It's nothing to do

341

with you. It's because of . . . my mum . . . I can't even . . .'
I hadn't even managed to spit out the words but already I
was crying. Not pretty, girly crying either, but snotty, open-
mouthed sobbing.

'I knew your mum had said something,' Toph sniffed.
And I wished he'd get angry, tell me I was being stupid,
show some sign that he wanted to fight for what we had,
but he was being so reasonable, so resigned. I always loved
how open Toph was, his expression always so unguarded,
but now everything about him was closed off from the
shadowed look in his eyes to his pursed lips. 'See, that
three-year age gap feels like three decades sometimes.'

'No, it doesn't,' I spluttered. 'I won't let you leave like
this. You've got everything so very mixed up.'

'Then unmix it for me,' Toph said. 'You can't, because
you know what I'm saying is right.'

'It's not over,' I insisted. 'What we had in Paris; you can't
just turn that off.'

'It's not over, but it's not the same as it was. It can't be,'
Toph said hurriedly before I got the wrong idea. 'Look, we
have the internet and we can talk on the phone. And you'd
better be making plans to save up for the road trip next
summer but, right now, that's all we've got.'

I didn't say anything because I was crying and the only
thing that could make me feel even a little bit better was to
throw my arms around Toph and bury my head in the
toasty little crook between his shoulder and neck so I
could get snot and tears on his T-shirt and let him hold me.
It sucked that he could make me hurt so badly but when

his arms were around me, he was the only one who could take the hurt away.

'Shhhh, shhhh,' he whispered soothingly. 'We'll always have this special bond and there isn't an ocean wide enough that can break it.'

'You think?' I lifted my head so I could scrub at my face with the back of one hand.

'I know,' Toph said gravely and now that I could see his eyes were glassy with unshed tears, it made me feel slightly better. 'Maybe ten years from now we'll bump into each other somewhere completely random and fall in love all over again.'

'You might be married then,' I pointed out but my lips were curving in a watery, weak smile because I could just see us knocking into each other on a New York street or on a railway platform in Budapest or even in a lift in an office building in Tokyo.

'I'll leave her,' Toph assured me. 'Promise.'

'Now you're just being stupid,' I said, but then I was leaning forward so I could wind my arms round Toph's neck and kiss him for maybe the last time. It was a chaste, closed-mouth kiss that felt like a full stop.

Chapter Twenty-Eight

It took ten minutes for Toph to take what was left of my heart and break it so utterly that it could never be put back together again. Then we went back into the garden and acted like nothing had ever happened.

I saw everyone off the premises, cleaned up and loaded the dishwasher and brushed my teeth and put on my pyjamas, and it seemed so odd that I could just get on with all the mundane stuff that made up my life when I felt that my life was over. But as soon as I turned out the light and snuggled down under my summerweight duvet, I started to cry.

After ten minutes it was obvious that I wasn't going to stop crying and I certainly wasn't going to go to sleep. Making Toph a mix CD of French singers seemed like a good way to pass the time but it just made me cry even more – there's nothing like a song about lost love sung by a throaty-voiced *jeune fille* to really amp up the angst. I was leafing through my Françoise Hardy CDs when there was a soft knock, and Mum stuck her head around the door.

'I'll turn the music down,' I said, my voice thick with tears. I didn't have a curfew during the holidays but making mix CDs at two in the morning was pushing it. Instead of getting on my case, Mum just came into the room and sat down next to me on the floor.

'I knew something up with you the moment we got home,' she said softly. 'Is it because of your dad?'

'No.' I wasn't capable of saying anything else so I just shook my head.

'Is it Ruby?'

This time the headshake was more vehement.

Mum sighed. 'OK, I'm guessing it must be Toph then. I know you're going to miss him but America isn't so far away. Well, not with the internet and ... Oh, Bea!' she exclaimed, when a fresh wave of tears spurted out. 'Baby!'

We'd been warily circling each other all week. What with Mum trying to be all relaxed with the mothering and me trying not to take advantage of it and neither of us mentioning the chat we'd had, it had ended up being rather strained, but all that melted away as I lay my head in her lap and bawled. There was also a lot of 'And I said ... So then he said ... but I said ...' as I tried to explain what had happened.

Mum stroked my hair and made sympathetic noises but didn't say anything until I was finished spluttering and sobbing.

'You have to tell Toph how much he means to you before he leaves,' she said as she helped me to sit up. 'And I don't want him thinking that I warned you off. Makes me look bad too, Bea.'

I gave a choked laugh. 'I can't spend the last few hours before he gets on a plane crying all over him! I don't want him to remember me like that.'

Mum hugged her knees. 'It's like that bit in *Amélie*, isn't it? Right at the end, when she can't tell Nino how she really feels and she's trying to make a cake and she's crying . . .'

'And then he knocks at her door and when he comes in he kisses her forehead . . .'

'And her cheeks.'

'And her eyelids and then he kisses her, and he knows and she knows that he knows,' I sighed. 'What would Amélie do?'

'Well, you haven't got time to organize a scavenger hunt with photographic clues given out by helpful passers-by,' Mum said dryly. 'You could send him an email.'

'But he won't get it until he's back in Texas,' I wailed. 'He has to know before he gets on the plane.'

Mum gave me a pitying look. 'Then write him a letter,' she said, rolling her eyes a little. 'That's what we did before they invented Apple Macs.'

'You think that would do it?' I asked doubtfully. 'I could give it to him along with the We'll Always Have Paris box I've been assembling.'

'Yeah, and the fifty quid's worth of chocolate you made me buy in Tesco's,' Mum reminded me, as she struggled to her feet. She tapped my head. 'Put what's going on in there down on paper and we'll stay out of your way tomorrow morning so you can make Toph brunch and give him the letter. OK?'

'OK.' I flexed my fingers to limber them up. 'It's worth a try.'

Mum bent down and kissed me. 'And James and I still get to have a lie-in, so it's all worked out rather well.'

I couldn't remember the last time I actually wrote something properly. My handwriting was so rusty and I was so unsure of what I wanted to say that the first five attempts ended up in the bin.

In the end I made a slideshow of our holiday pictures so I could conjure up that Paris feeling all over again, that was as much about Toph as it was about Paris, then before I could overthink it, I picked up my pen again.

Dear Toph

You got it all wrong, you know. It wasn't just a holiday romance. It was so much more than that.

I've been scared to be around you, because of that connection we have and the way you always seem to know what I'm thinking. The thing is I've been terrified of the thoughts in my head ever since we got back to London.

I know you think my mum warned me off falling in love with boys from Texas but it's simply not true. What happened was that she told me who my father really was. Or she didn't, because she can't remember him.

She got really, really drunk at a party when she was seventeen and ended up having sex with some guy whose name she didn't know and whose face she can't recall and that's my dad. I say that's my dad, but he isn't really. He's just a phantom dad.

I've been trying really hard not to think about it, and

dragging you around London and forcing you to spend time with a whole bunch of strangers was a great way of not having to deal with it.

I want to lie and say I was sparing you and that you've already had too much drama from me these past few weeks, but the truth is that I can't think about him *and the night I was conceived because it makes me feel horrible. It's like I've always had this empty gap where my dad should have been, which I filled with these elaborate fantasies, and now I know I'll never have a father to fill that gap. I'll always be a little bit empty and hollow inside because I have to put those fantasies away now.*

But that's kinda OK because before this summer, the stories and fantasies in my head were so much better than my boring real life – until I fell asleep on the train and when I woke up, there you were. It was like I'd woken up from this deep sleep and I saw the world in a new way. That I didn't need to dream any more because the life I was living was better than anything I could make up. And that life had you in it, Toph.

I know that a year from now, ten years from now, I'll still feel the same way about you. That just seeing you look like a big dork in your I ♥ Paris baseball cap makes me need to catch my breath. That laying on long grass next to you, not even talking, makes me feel like I've come home. That your kisses break me into tiny pieces then put me together again. That the touch of your hands and the way you smile and the soft look in your eyes as I'm talking to you are things I need in my life.

And I get all the good sense you made about the age gap and how holiday romances always have an expiration date and long-distance relationships never work. Yeah, I get it. But sometimes the way you feel about someone doesn't make sense, it just is.

I've been so unsure of so many things, but I'm sure about us. It's like my very existence is so random; at any time that night my mum could have stopped drinking, or her friends could have turned up to take her home, or she'd have remembered to ask him to use a condom. But she didn't. Like, it was preordained that there was going to be a Bea in the world.

And the way we met was so random too. If I hadn't fallen asleep on the train. If I hadn't turned right instead of left and found that café. If you hadn't pulled the maps out of your bag when you did so I had a reason to come and talk to you. It was like the universe wanted us to meet – and who are we to turn our backs on fate?

We can comment on each other's Facebook status updates and Tweet to our heart's content. We can even talk on the phone. Fine. Great. But I'm not waiting ten years for our paths to maybe cross again. It feels sometimes like my whole life has been nothing but waiting. I waited for my dad and that didn't turn out so well. And I waited to fall in love and be the girl I always wanted to be, and that girl doesn't wait for life to happen to her, she makes it happen. So, on the seventeenth of August next year at ten o'clock (night, not day,) I'm going to be standing on the Pont Neuf. And if you still feel the same way about me, you'll come and meet me.

Love

Bea xxx

When I woke up the next morning, I was still sitting in my chair, slumped over my desk, with my cheek resting on my computer keyboard.

I put my hand to my face and could feel the imprint of the keys pitting my skin, which was not a good look when I wanted to be all bright-eyed for Toph. I'd cook him brunch and while he was munching on the buttermilk waffles he'd specially requested yesterday afternoon, I'd give him the letter. And I wouldn't cry at all. Repeat, not going to cry.

It wasn't until I came out of the bathroom that I saw the piece of paper pushed under my door. I thought it was Mum reminding me yet again that she was having the first lie-in she'd had since the twins were born as they were sleeping at Grandma Minor's, but then I saw my name written in a crabby, left-handed scrawl that wasn't hers.

Seemed like I wasn't the only one who'd spent half the night working on their penmanship.

Toph had written:

Dear Bea

I'm sorry. I suck at goodbyes. I know that if I see you this morning, then all that crap about holiday romances and the age gap won't matter any more and I'll make you all these promises that I have no business to make.

I know you'll cry and when you cry, it cuts me up inside

because I hate to see you hurting. What's worse is when you try to smile even though you're sad, that's one of the sweetest things about you. So I'm heading off for the airport, even though everything inside of me wants to stay. Not just for a goodbye kiss or to make plans to stay in touch, but because part of me just wants to stay here with you forever.

See, I have these mushy, unmanly feelings for you and no matter how hard I try to think of a way to make this work, it can't be anything more than that magical week in Paris.

Don't be mad at me for bailing out on you. It's better this way. You can tell me how much you hate me via the medium of the internet but please don't hate me too much.

Because I kinda love you.

Toph x

I burst into Mum and James's room without pausing to wonder if 'lie-in' was actually Mum-speak for having sex. Thankfully it wasn't. James was snoring and Mum was face down on her pillow.

'Mum!' I screeched. 'Get up! Get up! Get up! You have to take me to the airport now!'

'What the fu . . .?' James rolled over as Mum gave a little grunt and pulled the duvet over her head.

'Get up!' I shouted again, climbing onto the bed and shaking each of them by the shoulder. 'Toph has gone and I haven't given him my letter! Or my We'll Always Have Paris box or the chocolate.'

'Can't you shove it in the post?' James mumbled, sitting up and glaring at me. 'We're having a lie-in.'

'It's ten o'clock, you've had a lie-in,' I said, shaking Mum harder. 'Wake up!'

'Who's gone?' Mum asked.

'Toph!'

'Did you give him the letter?' Mum levered herself into an upright position.

'No – and he left this for me,' I said, thrusting Toph's note at her.

Mum swore she didn't need reading glasses but she had to hold it pretty close to her face. I could see her eyes flickering from right to left so rapidly I thought she was going to have an aneurysm.

'I'll make some tea then, shall I?' James grumbled, pulling back the covers. 'God, the drama in this house never ends.'

'No tea,' Mum said sharply, handing the letter back to me. 'We're going to Heathrow now!'

Chapter Twenty-Nine

We didn't go to Heathrow right then. Not after James helpfully pointed out it was only ten and Toph's flight didn't leave until four.

'It's going to take him hours to get to the airport on the tube, then he's going to have to wait ages before his flight gets called,' he said, as he poured his second cup of tea and opened the *Observer*'s sport section. 'So both of you can stop giving me filthy looks.'

Mum lasted ten minutes before she snatched the cup out of James's hand. 'What if he goes through Security as soon as he's checked in?' she demanded, hands on her hips. 'We are, going *now*, or I swear you're going to be sleeping on the sofa from now until Christmas.'

I wish I could say that it was like something out of a movie. That the traffic was terrible and I was crying and wringing my hands as I kept looking at the clock on the dashboard, but it only took us ninety minutes to get to Heathrow. We even knew what terminal and flight because Toph had printed out all the details earlier in the week. As soon as James stopped the car, moaning all the while about the exorbitant parking fees, I was racing through the crowds of people and nearly breaking my neck on their suitcases in the process.

Mum and James caught up with me at the check-in desk

trying to explain to some uniformed Nazi that I didn't have a ticket but I needed to ask the people with the computers a really important question. 'I have my passport,' I insisted, waving it around. Mum and James didn't know that I'd brought it with me in case Toph had already gone through Security and I needed a ticket to go through too. A ticket they were going to have to buy because I was totally skint.

'I'm sorry, but if you haven't got a ticket, you can't join the queue,' Mr Peaked Cap said firmly.

'But I just need to see if someone's checked in,' I begged. 'It's a matter of life and death.'

He looked at me sceptically. 'Somehow I doubt it.'

Mum fixed him with her patented 'Don't fuck with me or my daughter' look. I think it was a personal best. 'Have you ever been in love?'

'Someone asks me that at least once a day and yes, I'm happily married and no, your daughter can't join the queue without a ticket.'

'James . . .' Mum said imploringly and I knew she'd be totally onboard with buying me a ticket, even if she still wasn't one hundred per cent convinced that Toph had left me with my hymen intact.

James, however, was not onboard. 'Are you sure she can't talk to one of your colleagues without a ticket?' he asked hopefully.

There was nothing for it but plan C. I burst into really loud tears. All the crying I'd done over the last week had really paid off because I'd never been able to weep on cue before.

'Bea, baby, it's OK,' Mum cooed, rubbing my back. She was laying it on a bit thick, but the man gave this deep sigh, held up his hand and then went to talk to someone behind one of the desks.

I was still crying a little bit when he beckoned me over. Then it was the same rigmarole as before, like I was some kind of terrorist who was going to breach all sorts of security regulations if they told me whether Toph had checked in or not.

'But I have a letter for him,' I told the woman. 'And British chocolate because he said American chocolate sucked and a whole bunch of French things I know he'll love and I *have* to see him. Please.'

It was never like this in the movies. They raced through Passport Control, caught up with their one true love just before they boarded the plane, and lived happily ever after.

'I'm very sorry but I can't divulge information about whether an individual passenger has checked in or not,' the lady behind the desk told me.

'He probably hasn't because the flight's not for ages but I need to know . . . Look, couldn't you just tell me if anyone's checked in for the flight to Dallas . . .'

The woman was wavering I could tell. 'Well, you are early. That flight doesn't leave for another four hours.'

'I don't need names, but if a very tall guy about yay high with mid-brown, mid-blond hair that flops into his eyes, which are also brown – golden brown, the same brown as condensed milk when you're turning it into caramel – and he might be wearing an *I ♥ Paris* baseball cap and—'

'Miss . . .'

'And he might look really tired because I don't think he got much sleep last night and—'

'Miss!'

I stopped talking so abruptly that I bit my tongue. 'Sorry. You were saying?'

'The only people that have checked in for that flight are a family of six. Can't say any more than that, I'm afraid,' she said with a grin.

'And he definitely has to check in here before anything else?'

'Well, he could use one of our automatic check-in points but if you wait by that fire extinguisher over there you can see them and the check-in desk and the escalator that he'll come down if he took the tube.'

After ten minutes Mum and James reached their boredom threshold and went off to have coffee and work their way through the papers and left me to it.

The waiting wasn't so bad at first. The check-in area started to fill up and I could people watch; ogling the Louis Vuitton luggage of the first-class passengers, and smiling at the huge family in traditional African dress with tons of adorable kids in tow. But after half an hour I was bored. Bored and panicking because there were so many people milling about and what if I missed Toph? Every time I saw a long, lean guy (every single long, lean guy in Britain seemed to have congregated in Terminal 3) my stomach would lurch. But none of them were Toph.

After an hour of waiting, I had a cramp in my right foot and I desperately needed to pee. I couldn't even look at anyone carrying a can of Coke. Mum and James came back to see what was going on, which was precisely nothing, and I posted them at two separate lookout spots while I raced for the loo.

When I came back, James suggested I try Toph's mobile, like I hadn't done that a hundred times and each time it had rolled straight over to voicemail, because he had to be on the tube. He had to be.

I waved James and Mum off so they could do another circuit of the airport shops and resumed waiting for Toph, who was still a no-show, even though other people were now arriving to check in for the Dallas flight. Every time I heard a man speak with a slow Texan drawl, my body would jerk in his direction and I knew that another hour and I'd be nothing more than a gibbering, dribbling wreck.

Just over an hour before Toph's flight took off, I suddenly saw a long, lean guy in a baseball cap coming down the escalator. Then a crowd of people all surged through the doors at once and I lost sight of him.

I hopped from foot to foot, not knowing whether to head towards the escalator. But what if it wasn't Toph and I wasn't there at the precise moment that Toph came in another way and decided to use the automatic check-in?

My head moved this way and that, like a demented nodding dog, then the crowds parted and it *was* Toph stepping off the escalator. I started to raise my hand and in that split second he saw me.

357

That had to be a good sign that in a crowded airport he could find me in a sea of people and just the sight of me made his face crease into a brilliant smile. Then the smile was gone and he was striding towards me as I took the first tentative step that would take me to his side.

'What are you doing here?'

'I couldn't leave it like that!'

We were both talking over each other.

Then there was an even more awkward silence.

'Why did it take you so long to get here?' I asked finally and wished it hadn't come out sounding so sulky and reproachful.

Toph rubbed the back of his neck. 'Well, I left your house too early so I got out the tube at Piccadilly and had a walk around. Got this.' He tugged at his head and I noticed that he was wearing an *I* ♥ *London* baseball cap. At any other time, I'd have started laughing and told him that he looked ridiculous. But it was now and . . .

'You had to check in, like, half an hour ago,' I burst out. 'And there's no time.'

'Look, I'm sorry I ducked out on you but I didn't want to go through a big tearful scene at the airport,' Toph said heavily and I hadn't imagined my long wait would end like this – with us standing a metre apart from each other.

'I'm not going to cry,' I said fervently. It was true. I think I'd used up my tear quota for the next two years.

Toph looked at his feet. 'Not talking about you,' he said.

'You *have* to go and check in,' I said, like the only reason I'd come was to make sure that Toph actually got on the plane. 'But listen, I wanted to say goodbye and . . . Bloody hell! I've been waiting for hours and now I don't even know what I want to say.'

'Didn't we say everything last night?' Toph asked and he closed the gap between us so he could tuck a strand of hair behind my ear.

I couldn't help myself from nuzzling against his hand. 'You said a lot of stuff last night, but I didn't really have a chance to tell you anything.'

'What do you want to tell me, Bea?' Toph asked softly.

'I have presents for you,' I said quickly. 'Like, a ton of Cadbury's chocolate. Seriously, a whole ton and I wanted to give you the We'll Always Have Paris box I put together.' I handed over the Laduree cake box that contained a copy of *The Dud Avocado*, a Serge Gainsbourg CD, a DVD of *Amélie* and the mix tape I'd made the night before, as well as an *Au Bout de Souffle* postcard and a Deux Moulins snowstorm.

'Um, thanks,' Toph said, cradling the box to his chest. He looked a little disappointed. Maybe I hadn't been the only one imagining an airport goodbye scene like they had in the movies. 'That's really sweet of you.'

'I want to say goodbye properly but I don't know how to,' I said helplessly. 'I have this horrible feeling that you'll get on the plane and I'll never see you again and I'll wear out the memories of us so they won't even feel real any more.'

Then I did what I should have done when I first saw Toph come down the escalator and I wrapped my arms tight around him, crushing my We'll Always Have Paris box, but I didn't care because Toph was hugging me back and kissing my forehead and my eyelids and the tip of my nose and I didn't even think he'd been paying that much attention when we watched *Amélie*.

'It will always feel real,' Toph said fiercely. 'And some day we will make new memories, just not now because—'

'No!' It would probably have been more romantic if I'd just placed a finger on Toph's lips instead of clamping my whole hand over his mouth. 'I don't want to hear the second part of last night's speech. I wrote you a letter, everything's in the letter.' I rooted through my bag and pulled out the envelope, which was looking decidedly dog-eared, and handed it to Toph, who started tearing it open. 'Not here! Wait until you're on the plane, which you're so going to miss.'

Toph looked around and blinked slowly as he suddenly remembered where he was and why he was there. 'Shit! I need to check in!' He stroked my hand, my arm, my face, until I took his hand, gave it a quick, fervent squeeze, then let go.

'You've got a plane to catch,' I reminded him, stepping back.

'Please stay here till I'm checked in,' Toph pleaded. 'Even if I only have two minutes, I want to spend them with you.'

I nodded and watched Toph lope over to the check-in desk. There were no other passengers now – they'd probably started boarding already and he'd have fifteen minutes, twenty tops, to get to the gate before it closed.

It looked like the woman behind the desk was telling Toph the exact same thing with a bollocking on the side because he hung his head and smiled sheepishly. I was glad I'd waited, glad that I had these last few minutes to drink in the sight of him, because that would be all I had to live on for nearly a year. Or maybe longer than that if he read the letter but didn't believe me. Wasn't waiting for me on the Pont Neuf. Then I'd have to wait maybe decades, maybe never, to bump into him and make him fall in love with me all over again.

I saw Toph put his backpack on the luggage belt, take his boarding card, then he was turning and walking over to me. Which was sweet, but . . .

'Go!' I yelled, pointing at the escalator that led up to the main terminus. 'Go! You're going to miss the flight.'

'I don't care,' Toph said as he got nearer and then he was sweeping me into his arms and bending me backwards as he took my lips in a kiss that really was the appropriate Hollywood ending to any airport goodbye scene.

I tried to memorize everything about the kiss: Toph's arms tight around me, the flutter of his eyelashes against my skin and his mouth moving on mine so gently, so slowly that it was a little bit devastating.

Then there were a hundred little kisses, each one getting smaller and smaller until we were just standing there locked together but lips barely touching.

'I have to go,' Toph said in a voice tinged with regret. 'Don't want to but I have to.'

'Read the letter,' I said, finding the strength to take a step

361

away. 'But will you please go and catch your plane?'

'After all this, you're not even going to say goodbye?' Toph grinned, but it was a shadow of his usual grin.

'I've decided that I don't believe in goodbyes,' I said. Then I reached up and kissed Toph quickly on each cheek, in the French style. '*A bientôt!*'

Toph frowned as he took five seconds to work it out. 'I'll see you soon,' he said and I didn't know if he was translating what I'd just said or making me a promise. 'Well, guess I'd better get gone.'

'You do that,' I said as he started backing slowly towards the escalator, only turning round to get on it.

I stood there watching him, waving when he kept turning back to make sure I was still there. And even when he disappeared from view, I stayed there watching, watching, watching and waiting.

Epilogue

eleven months, two weeks and six days later

It's a beautiful Parisian evening. A light summer breeze ripples off the Seine as I stand in the centre of the Pont Neuf and watch the cruise boats gaily strung with lights, chug along the river. If I listen closely over the roar of the traffic and the hum of conversation from the people around me, I can even hear "La Vie En Rose" tinkling up from the boat that's just emerged from under the bridge.

Nothing could be as special as the first time I'd stood on the Pont Neuf, but the second time is almost as good. For one thing, I'm an honorary Parisian now; back at the Shangri-La – not as a paying guest but as kitchen bitch/chambermaid/junior receptionist in exchange for two hundred euros a week, room and board. Officially it's just for my gap year until I go to Sussex University to study French because, yeah, I totally aced my French A level, but I'm taking my Baccalaureate in January with the vague idea that I might do a degree at a French university instead.

Mum isn't happy about it, which isn't a new development, but it's less to do with getting impregnated and more to do with leaving home. Things have really changed between Mum and me over the last year. I still love her to pieces but we're not close like we used to be. It makes me sad but I still can't quite forgive her for the dad stuff. I still feel weird and prickly about not having a father too, but I'm getting used to it. Even turned it into a killer personal essay for my UCAS form, so in a funny sort of way my dad helped me to get into university just as much as Mum did when she stuck up Post-it notes all over the house with quotes on them from *The Great Gatsby* and *Wuthering Heights*. This year I learned that life doesn't have these neat, tidy endings that you can wrap up with a bow. It's messier than that.

Like, the stuff with Ruby never really got sorted out. When we got back to school there was a month of her spreading Facebook rumours and shoulder-bumping me when we passed in the corridor but I ignored her, just like everyone else did. During the last few months of Year 13, all the little cliques banded together as we went into deep cramming mode and on Saturday nights everyone was too busy trying to make the most of their few hours of freedom to worry about Ruby.

I come to with a start when I'm buffeted by a crowd of German teenagers and their day-glo backpacks. I check the time on my watch: 9.53 p.m. I shudder because I'm so excited, seriously excited at the thought of seeing Toph again; hearing that treacle-voice drawl out my name, watching his face come to life when he looks at me, and the kisses — I've almost forgotten what his kisses feel like. Almost.

But there are other not-so-fun emotions. Panic, and fear and a dull, dirty resignation because really, logistically, I'm asking Toph to buy a massively expensive plane ticket at the height of summer to cross a humungous ocean to meet a girl he'd spent three weeks with a year ago. When I think about it like that, I don't even know why I'm anxiously scanning the knots of people ambling across the bridge. And I really don't know why I thought it would be a good idea to pluck a red rose from the Shangri-La garden when I left the hotel because I'm getting these amused, indulgent looks from people. I know that in ten minutes when my shoulders are slumping and the first tears are trickling down my cheeks, the looks will be more sympathetic. God, I can never do anything simply, I have to get stood up on the Pont Neuf, the bridge of lovers.

9.56. As hard as I try I can't picture Toph coming towards me in four minutes. Obviously the revelations in my letter didn't repulse Toph too much because we've stayed in touch. In fact, there is hardly a day without checking in with each other, even during my A levels and his finals. Toph's signed every IM, every email, every Tweet with three Xs, which I treat as kisses, just like the bag of Hershey Kisses that arrived for my birthday. (Toph was right: American chocolate sucks.) I also stayed in touch with Jess and Erin, and the road trip didn't happen. Erin's interning for some fancy-shmancy photographer in New York and Jess is working in Gap to try and make a dent in her student loans. Maybe last-minute, Aaron, Michael and Bridge are road-tripping and have taken Toph with them I don't know because Toph hasn't told me . . . My heart gives another furious slam-dunk against my breastbone because

I *know* Toph isn't coming.

9.59. I peer through the traffic so I can see the other side of the bridge. But we'd been standing on this side that night, I was sure of it. Unless I'd got all turned around because I approached the bridge from the Left Bank tonight. I do a full three hundred and sixty degrees as I dither about crossing the road or staying put.

10.01. I get stuck giving directions to a pair of Swedes, my eyes flickering from side to side as I talk just in case I miss Toph.

10.05. Of course, he's always late. Hadn't I spent a large part of last summer running to railway stations to catch trains with only seconds to spare? And it's only five minutes and Toph had never been on the Metro unsupervised. Just because he's five minutes late doesn't mean he's not coming.

10.10. Toph isn't coming. Boys who are as foxy and clever and funny as Toph, wouldn't spend a year pining for a girl who was still figuring out what she wanted to be when she grew up. Some other girl would have snapped him up by now. A girl from Austin who maybe even lives on his block and doesn't have unresolved daddy issues.

I contemplate throwing my rose into the water and letting the Seine carry it away. I'll give Toph five more minutes, then I'll go back to the Shangri-La to catch Claudette and the others on their way to Phillipe's so they can help me drown my sorrows.

10.15. There's no point in standing on the Pont Neuf in my stupid LBD with my stupid rose and a stupid hopeful expression on my face.

I'm done waiting. I take a decisive step forward, then another, and another and I'm definitely heading towards the Metro and off the bridge, not looking left or right at the lovers entwined on every single one of the Pont Neuf's benches. It's a complete lie when people say that the world loves lovers. I bloody hate them.

As I get to the end of the bridge, I can't stop myself from one last futile look over my shoulder. I needn't have bothered. There's just people and none of them are Toph. Then I look again because I'm sure I can see something bobbing along the heads of the crowd; something white with a red blob on it. The crowd part to let it through and as it gets closer I see it's a baseball cap with a heart on it – and it's on Toph's head.

I hate the crowds even more now as I fight my way through them to get to Toph, snapping out, '*Excusez moi!*' in all directions.

As I emerge from between two burly men, Toph catches sight of me, a massive ear-to-ear grin on his face as he half raises his hand, and it only takes seconds to close the gap between us but they last as long as hours until I fling my arms round his neck and my feet lift off the ground as he picks me up and swings me round.

Even though my arms are full of Toph and no one has ever looked *that* pleased to see me, all of a sudden I feel so shy that I don't know what to say and bury my head in Toph's neck.

He's babbling enough for both of us. 'I'm sorry I'm late,' he says, as he puts me back on my own two feet, eyes fixed on a spot over my shoulder like he's scared to look at me, just in case I turn out to be a dream, because that's how I feel right now and why I'm staring at one of the lamp-posts instead of Toph. 'I came straight from the airport and we had to fly around for ages until we had a spot to land and then I got all confused on the Metro and I didn't even know if you'd be here and I had to stop and get you this . . .'

Toph holds out a red rose that's a perfect match for the one I plucked from the Shangri-La garden. 'Snap,' I say, and then I can't say any more because I just want to look at Toph. He's red-faced, sweaty and when I had my nose in his collarbone he didn't smell too fresh, but everything else is the same: the soft caramel look in his eyes, the smile that always feels as if it's just for me. I still love him. In fact I think I love him more than I did, as if the year apart has made that love deeper and more profound.

I don't know if Toph feels the same as he looks at me, eyes travelling up from my flip-flops to my shaking knees to my 34Bs straining against my LBD, until he gets to my face. Surely he couldn't look at me like that if it was all a terrible mistake?

'Hey,' I say tentatively.

'Hey,' he says.

And then he kisses me.

Glossary for Le Cool French Stuff

Your guide to all things groovy and Français . . .

Books
The Dud Avocado by Elaine Dundy
Sally Jay Gorce is an eccentric American girl living in Paris in 1958. Her days and nights are a chaotic whirl of unsuitable lovers, squalid apartments, dark bars and going to breakfast in a ballgown.

Bonjour Tristesse by Françoise Sagan
It's OK, it's in English! Seventeen-year-old Cecile is everything you'd hope for in the heroine of a French novel; she's hopelessly romantic, a terrible flirt and impossibly jaded.

Films
Amélie
Surely one of the greatest, most enchanting, magical and romantic movies ever made. Amélie, a shy waitress with the most perfect bob ever, lives in Montmartre and performs acts of quirky kindness on the people around her.

Au Bout de Souffle
It's one of those French New Wave films that our heroine

Bea is always banging on about. It's also kinda thin on plot but Jean-Paul Belmondo is one louche, lean hunk of boy flesh and Jean-Seberg will make you want to go out and get a pixie crop.

Funny Face
Not so much a French film as a film set in France, Audrey Hepburn is a bookish young woman lured to Paris by Fred Astaire to model gowns by Givenchy and break into big song and dance numbers.

Music
Baby Pop by France Gall
Recorded in 1966, *Baby Pop* is a stomper of an album stuffed full of three-minute songs of pop perfection that you'll want to put on loud and dance round your bedroom to, even if you can't understand a word she's singing about.

Les Chansons d'Amour by Françoise Hardy
Smoky-voiced Françoise was a huge style and fashion icon in France in the Sixties and even recorded a song with Blur during her comeback a few years ago. *Les Chansons d'Amour* is a greatest hits of her most feel-good, summery songs.

Swinging Mademoiselles: Groovy French Sounds from the Sixties
Does exactly what it says on the tin!

Also by Sarra Manning

guitar girl

Seventeen-year-old Molly's band was always just about being a girl, singing Hello Kitty Speedboat and pretending to play instruments with her best mates Jane and Tara. But then the arrogant Dean and his sidekick T hijack the band and suddenly the fluffy girl band becomes *The Hormones* - a real band with a record deal - and they're heading for the big time. Molly slips further and further away from her old life and straight into a tangled love-hate relationship with Dean. Then there are the constant parties, the drugs and the phonies who pretend to like you when they don't ... Molly is living her dream, and she's never felt lonelier in her life. But has she got the strength to walk away from the band, and start again?

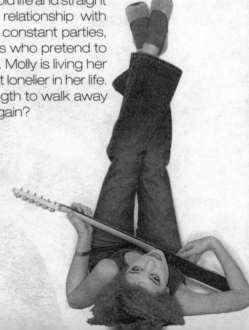

978 0 340 860717

Also by Sarra Manning

Pretty Things

Set against a backdrop of North London and drama group, four unforgettable teens' struggle for identity, self-esteem and some kind of significance in life in this wittily, wickedly observed comedy of teen manners!

978 0 340 88372 3

Brie is in love with Lancome Juicy Tubes, Louis Vuitton accessories and Charlie, her gay best friend. But Charlie is in love with 1960's pop art, 1980's teen movies ... and serial heartbreaker, Walker. Walker has only ever been in love with his VW Bug, until he meets Daisy. And Daisy is far too busy hating everyone to know what love is ... This is a story about kissing people you shouldn't, falling in love and off your heels, and breaking hearts because there's nothing to watch on telly.

Also by Sarra Manning

Diary of a Crush

978 0 340 95590 1

When Edie first spots moody, dark, delicious Dylan at college, she just know that this is the start of a roller-coaster, big-big time love story.

978 0 340 95591 8

Edie says she is so over Dylan, and when vile Veronique muscles in on him, Edie starts dating creepy Carter. Deep down she knows she still wants Dylan, but does he feel the same way?

978 0 340 95592 5

Together again at last, Edie and Dylan are set for the road trip of a lifetime. They're travelling across America for nine whole weeks. It's going to be a huge test for their relationship. Is being crazy in love enough to see them through?

Also by Sarra Manning

let's get lost

Some girls are born to be bad ... Isabel is one of them. Her friends are terrified of her, her teachers can't get through to her... her family doesn't understand her. And that's just the way she likes it. See, when no one can get near you, no one will know what keeps you awake at night, what you're afraid of, what has broken your heart ... But then Isabel meets the enigmatic Smith, who can see right through her act. Bit by bit he chips away at her armour, and though she fights hard to keep hold of her cool, and her secrets, Isabel's falling for him, and coming apart at the seams when she does

978 0 340 87701 2

Don't be a Nobody, go and check out Sarra's amazing website
www.hodderchildrens.co.uk/sarramanning

Follow Sarra on Twitter
http://twitter.com/sarramanning